Lucy Pinney's jou. magazines and newspapers, including *The Observer, The Sunday Times, Cosmopolitan* and *She*. As an unpublished manuscript, her first novel, *The Pink Stallion*, was awarded a runner-up prize in the 1987 Betty Trask Awards. She lives with her husband, children and Ardennes horses near Honiton, Devon.

Also by Lucy Pinney

The Pink Stallion

Tender Moth

Lucy Pinney

CORONET BOOKS
Hodder and Stoughton

British Library Cataloguing in Publication Data

Pinney, Lucy
Tender Moth
I.Title
823.914 [F]

ISBN 0 340 50891 4

Typeset by Avon Dataset Ltd, Bidford-on-Avon

Printed and bound in Great Britain by
Cox & Wyman, Reading, Berks

Hodder and Stoughton
A division of Hodder Headline PLC
338 Euston Road
London NW1 3BH

For my mother, who *is* a real lady.

Grateful acknowledgement is made for permission to reprint excerpts from the following works:

The poem by Christopher Dilke was first published in *Cosmopolitan* magazine in November 1988.

Lines from *The Blue Fairy Book* by Andrew Lang are reprinted with permission of Constable Publishers.

The rhyme from *A Dictionary of Slang and Colloquial English* by Farmer and Henley is reprinted with permission of Routledge and Kegan Paul.

Lines from *Eve Was Framed: Women and British Justice* by Helena Kennedy are reprinted with permission of Chatto & Windus.

Acknowledgments

This book owes a great debt to other people's memories of the past. It arose from conversations with Devon villagers Bill and Margaret Broom, the late Reg Crudge, Douglas Daymond, Philip Elford, Cyril, Doris and John Ellis, Henry Harris, Margaret Husbands, Wendy Lane, Kathleen and Fred Lee, Basil Pike, William Tavender and Don White.

Stories about life in a country house in the 1930s came from my mother, Alice Dilke; the Hon. Mrs Mackinnon and my aunt, Helen Best, were also very helpful.

Roger and Cheryl Clark gave me advice about working horses, Arthur Lyall helped me with legal details, Gina Cox with medical descriptions, Lesley Elford with pig obstetrics, Geoff Harris with information about vintage cars, Coinneach I Moireasdan of 'Canan' supplied the Gaelic; and if there are any errors in farming detail they are entirely the fault of my husband Charlie, who sternly checked the manuscript – and supplied all the best jokes.

Time erases and defaces
Names of loved ones long ago
Few are now the certain traces
Of their mortal joy and woe.

All are bidden to remember
Robert (Nothing) Loving Fath
Who died (illegible) December
And lies beside the churchyard path.

Safe in Paradise reposes
She who joined Departed Broth
And dozes in a bed of roses
Faithful Frien and Tender Moth.

Christopher Dilke

PART ONE

1929

'They will not waken and turn to us, our lost loves, our lost chances, not for all our service, all our singing, not for all our waiting seven or twice seven long years. But in the fairy tale, he heard, and he turned to her.'

Andrew Lang, *The Blue Fairy Book*, 1889

One

Florrie felt her way through the darkness, set down the bucket and clicked her tongue. Somewhere up ahead the straw rustled. It was the kind of movement a creature makes when it is terribly afraid. She had to strain to hear it, because there was plenty of other noise around. Above her head, on the low tile roofs, cats were making soft, plaintive cries. It was nearly time for their breakfast, and it drove them wild to smell Florrie's full bucket of milk.

A little further away than the cats – just the other side of the shed wall – hammers tapped, rising steam warbled, and three men talked. These sounds all came from the traction engine, which, together with the threshing machine, had thundered down the lane into the farm yesterday evening, tearing a branch off the chestnut tree as it came. The owner, and his two helpers, had lit the furnace and begun heating water for steam at half past four that morning.

Earlier, while Florrie had been milking, the noises from the machine had been scarcely more than a low murmur, but out here, at the far edge of the farm buildings and next to the rickyard, she could catch every word.

'Has he bags?' someone shrilled. This was Jesse Coffin, the owner of the thresher. He had one of those queer, high-pitched Devon voices, always so surprising when they come from a normal-sized man.

'He's some of they all right. Samuel fetched they in from

the tallet. Didn't he, Samuel?' This voice was deeper and more sympathetic, and belonged to Ellis Rawes, who helped Mr Coffin all winter. The rest of the year he and his nephew, Samuel, survived on odd jobs in the parish: shearing, haymaking, hedging or rabbiting.

Florrie lifted her long skirt and climbed over the woven hurdle into the pen. The straw, and the stray bits of bark sticking out of the hurdle, caught at her legs, and she disentangled herself carefully. She didn't like getting holes in her stockings: holes had to be mended, and there was nothing she loathed more than sitting indoors with a darning mushroom. The straw rustled again. Florrie heard a hasty, indrawn breath.

'Not to fret,' she whispered. She felt for the bucket of milk and pulled it in after her.

'I hope this bugger can pay,' Mr Coffin squalled from the other side of the wall. 'You know Jack Lemon out at Kittenhole? He says to me, "Oh, Mr Coffin, I can't pay you sooner than a twelvemonth." How's I to manage if I ain't paid? That's what I want to know.'

'Cuh,' Ellis answered. Florrie liked Ellis. He had thick hair growing round his head in a glossy ruff, like the fur of a tomcat in prime condition. Like a cat, too, he seemed always to have a slight smile on his face. His favourite remark was a word he'd invented for himself, a compound of 'Cor!' and 'Huh!' As he was saying it he'd tip his head back and raise his upper lip, a resigned, contented look on his broad face. Florrie had often thought that Ellis's 'Cuh' was like the 'Amen' at the end of a prayer: it expressed his personal philosophy, which was that times were bad, and people difficult, but what could a decent man do but make the best of it?

Setting the bucket firmly in the deep straw by the hurdle, Florrie crept towards the back of the shed. She didn't want to scare the animal crouching there any more than necessary, so she moved quickly. Her hand seized a warm ear, and the calf it belonged to flinched, wriggled, and tried to fling itself backwards. One of its hooves struck her leg, caught in the stocking, and stamped uselessly on the side of her leather boot. The calf couldn't escape her arms, though, and realizing that it was trapped, it gave a loud blare of misery.

'Do I hear a calf?' Mr Coffin asked. 'Has he calves?'

'Oh, he'd be lost without his calves. Cuh! Thinks the world of his cows, Cecil Tavender do. Talks to them, don't he, Samuel?'

Ellis's nephew didn't reply immediately. He must, Florrie thought, be somewhere under the machine, because when he spoke his voice was muffled, and had a note of strain in it, as if he were at an uncomfortable angle.

'Talks to them like they was maids,' he said. Florrie had to admit this was true. As she pushed her calf towards the waiting bucket – it resisted, stiff-legged, for as long as possible, taking minuscule, reluctant steps – she couldn't help smiling to herself at the thought of her father, and the way he spoke so tenderly to his cattle.

'Why, only last evening he was at it,' Samuel went on. 'He says to this big red heifer out by the yard gate, "Ain't your hindquarters filled out nice, my dear? And ain't your dugs good and fat?" He did, true.'

'So that's how a man talks to a maid, is it, Samuel?' Ellis enquired, breaking into a cackle of laughter.

Florrie had got her calf to the bucket now, and while she kept a tight grip on its neck she dipped her other hand into the milk and pressed a few drops to its mouth. It twisted away and sneezed. She pushed its nose right into the milk and its body tensed with distaste. She was careful not to push too deep – she didn't want to choke it – and she put her fingers in the milk and tried to ease open the calf's clenched teeth and teach it, by manipulating its jaws, how to drink. Fear gave it strength, and it threw its head back so suddenly that it caught her a hard blow on the jaw. She didn't let go, even though her eyes watered with pain; instead she made the animal try the milk again. This time it bit her, its teeth like sharpened clam shells. They fought silently in the darkness, but Florrie wasn't worried: she knew she'd win. You always did, if you were persistent enough.

She thought she heard the calf swallow, and she leaned in, so that the inside of her elbow was resting against its throat. Yes, there it was again: a tiny ripple.

'See, it ain't so bad to sup, is it?' she whispered. 'It's quite nice, really, once you get the measure of it.' The calf moved its mouth against her fingers, puzzled as it tried to adjust to this strange and uncomfortable method of absorbing food.

The other side of the wall Florrie could hear Samuel explaining exactly how he'd set up the canvas screens that winnowed the grain. Ellis and Mr Coffin were quizzing him to ensure that he'd done the job correctly, and Florrie didn't bother to listen to the words – just let them flow over her. It was cosy here in the straw, now that the calf had stopped struggling, and she knelt down and listened sleepily to the men's voices. There was a special interest for her, somehow, in listening to Samuel's. She liked its huskiness, its masculinity – but equally, she was just a little annoyed by it, too.

She felt the same when she saw him in the flesh. He was as tall as his uncle, and had similar thick black hair, except that Samuel's was straighter, with a lock that flopped across one eye, but what she noticed most about him was his air of vulnerability. His large brown eyes and generous, sensitive mouth seemed to give far too clear an indication of his feelings. When they'd both been younger she'd enjoyed the way he laughed so easily, listened with such intensity, even cried when told tales of misfortune; but now she'd begun to wish he was more reserved. In the last year he'd started gazing at her in such an imploring, hopeless fashion. It unsettled her; she didn't like it.

The calf decided it had drunk enough, and gave a sudden skip sideways, dodging out of Florrie's grasp. She felt the milk with her fingers: it had only had a cupful, but that was enough for the first time. As she climbed back over the hurdle she heard the traction engine start up, and a steady chugging filled the shed, together with a warm oily smell.

She gave the rest of the milk to an older calf in the next pen, which drank it all in one rude slurp. After that she felt for the cats' bucket, which she'd covered with a piece of sacking, and began to climb the steep wooden ladder to the tallet – the loft. The air was indefinably greyer and paler now: the rungs of the ladder visible, the air around them grainy. She could just about make out the lumps of stale bread that she'd put in the cats' milk too.

'Did you hear as how the hall was sold?' she heard Mr Coffin ask, the other side of the wall. He had to shout now, to be heard above the engine.

'Would that be the hall over Earlshay?' Ellis called back.

Florrie paused halfway up the ladder, eager to catch the next words – much to the irritation of the cats, who nudged at the bucket and glided up and down the ladder beside her. One of them pressed its furry face into hers, leaving a small wet mark on her cheek. If the hall at Earlshay had been sold, she was interested. She'd been there a few times with her brothers, exploring.

'Five shillings the acre, that land made,' Mr Coffin declared. 'And I'll swear it was five *pound* the acre back along, after the war.'

'Cuh.'

One of the cats bit Florrie on the nose. It wasn't a painful bite, just a nip, to remind her about the milk. She climbed the last few rungs of the ladder and reached – through a woolly forest of cats' legs – for the dented tin dish they ate out of. It rattled as she pulled it towards her. There was something in it – a stone, perhaps.

7

'Who've bought the hall, then?' Samuel asked.

'Some sour old bundle from the town,' Mr Coffin answered. 'So much paint on her face it drips out on her teeth. Still, if she've plans to open the place up she'll be wanting labour. Butlers and footmen. Gamekeepers too, I shouldn't be surprised.'

'It'd suit this blossom here,' Ellis said. 'Nice little parlour-maid she'd make.'

It didn't feel like a stone: it had a hole in the middle. Florrie slipped it into her pocket and emptied her bucket into the dish.

'She've plimmed up proper, recent, ain't she, Samuel?' Ellis continued, and Florrie realized, with a shock, that the men were talking about her.

'She've a good fat front on her, too,' Mr Coffin added, his voice so close to Florrie the other side of the tallet wall that she looked up, startled, thinking he might be beside her. 'Lord, how I hates these scraggy, winnicky maids. What I always says is . . .' Whatever other remarks Mr Coffin intended to make about Florrie's figure were lost as the belts connecting the engine to the thresher tightened. There were two loud slaps as they connected; then the thresher roared into life.

The sound startled a distant duck. Florrie heard it quack irritably and interminably, as if reciting a long list of grievances. She paused on the ladder, gazing out at the grey landscape which had at last become visible. The hills, trees and fields seemed rounder and fuller than usual, almost menacing, set in a low mat of mist.

It was a sober opening to her sixteenth birthday. She sat down on a rung and looked sleepily down at herself. Ellis was right: she had plumped up recently. Her old jersey – a black one stiff with darns – was almost too tight now. It would be a long time, though, before she could say the same of the skirt, a cast-off from her stout Aunt Louisa. All that held it in place was a belt Florrie had cut herself out of an old piece of harness.

The skirt stopped halfway down her calves, and her thin legs poked out at the bottom, tipped with a clumsy pair of boots passed on from her elder brother Joe. She'd never possessed a pair of ladies' boots in her life: always the low-cut men's kind, because she either had to wear Joe's cast-offs, or else new boots which could be passed on to her younger brother Albie.

She put a hand up to her hair. This was the one part of herself she was proud of: her long, light brown curls. In sunlight they could look red, or even gold, and she wore them loose at the back – where they came down to her waist – and cut in a fringe at the front. The fringe wasn't wonderfully even, but it was the best Mother could do with the sheep-shears. (Florrie felt sorry for her brothers: it was shameful the mess shears made of a short head of hair. Both Joe and Albie always looked surprised, even when they weren't, on account of the tufts sticking out at odd angles from their scalps.)

As for her face, the two best features were the dimples in her cheeks – which strangers always commented on – and her greeny-blue eyes. She'd been lucky, too, to inherit her mother's neat nose, rather than the huge lumpy one that ran in the Tavender family. Albie, Joe and Father all had it, and it made them look like cockerels. She had the wiry frame of her father's family though, and the physical strength. Ellis had once told her, in an awed voice, that her father was the strongest man he'd ever met. He was the only one in the village who could lift Aunt Louisa at arm's length in a shovel. Florrie privately hoped to be just the same herself, when she finished growing. She often practised, but hadn't managed to lift Albie on the end of a shovel yet.

Two

When the threshing began in earnest Florrie noticed that Samuel had chosen an odd place to work. In the past he'd always preferred to be with Joe; yet today he was dismantling the corn-stack on his own.

His job was to pull the tightly packed bundles out and hurl them across a wide gap to Florrie. She stood on the trembling, scarlet-painted bulk of the thresher and acted as go-between, passing each sheaf on to her mother, who cut each string carefully and tucked it into her apron pocket before feeding the stalks into the mouth of the hopper. From there, the machine winnowed it into grain, which poured out of the back into sacks, sternly watched over by Father; chaff, which flowed smokily out of the side on top of twelve-year-old Albie, who was supposed to sweep it into a neat pile; and straw. The straw dropped in bundles on to an elevator and was carried up to Ellis and Joe, who were building a straw-stack together, amid much teasing and horseplay.

'It ain't the *straw* on the front edge needs sorting out,' Joe shouted cheekily. 'It's the beggar that's standing there.' Florrie didn't catch Ellis's reply; she was distracted by an eddy of wind, which threw chaff into the air around her. The autumn sunlight made it glitter. She glanced down and saw the top of Father's head, covered by a dusty trilby hat, as he fitted a new sack in place. Behind him, Mr Coffin stood at the controls of the brass-bound traction engine, constantly adjusting levers

11

and shovelling coal. Both of them were shouting the odd remark at each other, and Albie, too, would occasionally call to Florrie; some statement that was supposed to make her smile – about the amount of chaff he'd swept, or how hot he was getting. His face furry with dust, he'd bawl up at her from the dark chasm between the corn-stack and the threshing drum. She'd always nod and smile – even though she couldn't, mostly, catch what he'd said. There was too much noise from the constant shaking and rattling of the machine.

But she, her mother, and Samuel weren't speaking at all. This was entirely due to Mother, who liked to work with intense, silent concentration. She was two inches shorter than Florrie, and much fuller in shape, wearing a dignified black dress that buttoned high in the neck and came down so close to the soles of her boots that the hem was always dusty. Her hair was cut in a strange little puff in front, and the main body of it wound in a coil round the top of her head. She always wore a cotton bonnet, too, to keep the sun off her face, and it was quite startling, the difference between her and Father when they stood side by side: his face so brown, and hers so pale. They had the same forearms, though: slender and muscular, with large veins that stood out on the surface.

Ever since Florrie could remember she'd been aware of her mother's clever hands, and deftness at making butter – a skill learned on the island of Islay, where Mother's family came from. Florrie had often woken in the early hours of the morning to hear the thudding of the churn. Downstairs, in the back kitchen, she'd find Mother weighing her butter into quarter-pound lumps, her skin smelling fresh and soapy, like a wet sheet hanging on a line.

She'd step to one side when Florrie entered, and move her head in a swift bob of acknowledgment, and Florrie would take over the weighing while Mother set about the more skilful part of the work. Mother would pat each yellow mound into a square with the paddles, then take a bit of muslin, dip it in a cup of cold water, wring it out, and bend forward. Sucking in a breath of air, the veins on her arms standing out, she would be still with concentration, her pale eyes opened wide. And before her, on the face of the butter, she would carve – using only the scrap of wet muslin – a flower. There were three designs: a rose, a daisy, and a lily of the valley. The carvings stood out in deep relief, like sculpture, and they were so exact, so perfect, that you would swear they had been made that way with a wooden mould. The first time Mother entered her hand-decorated butter in the Furzey Moor Spring Show it was disqualified because the judges thought she'd cheated. Furious, she'd tracked them down, called for a cup of water and a clean hanky, and before their eyes wiped out her designs and effortlessly recreated them. Father often told the story; he loved it when Mother was angry – because she was so much smaller than him.

'You should have seen her that day,' he'd say, his eyes misting with sentiment. 'She were so wonderful fierce – like a angry little hen.'

Personally, Florrie didn't find Mother's anger quite so seductive. She'd learned to hide whenever Mother began speaking in Gaelic – always a sign that a critical point of irritation had been reached. '*Spideagan beaga!*' (Little brats!) Mother would hiss, like a spitting kettle, and Florrie and her brothers would dive for cover.

The work on the thresher was difficult, a strain. Florrie was used to hard labour; from her mother, she'd learned how to establish a steady rhythm, which she could keep up until everyone around her collapsed with fatigue.

'Men may have the strength,' Mother would often say, a note of disapproval in her voice when she used the word 'strength', as if it were something flighty and fundamentally unsound, 'but it's women as has the *endurance.*'

13

Samuel was working at a killing pace: his shirt had great damp patches across it; his face, too, whenever he turned to hand Florrie a sheaf, looked more vulnerable than ever, the eyes wetter and darker, perhaps because the lashes and the skin around them were damp with sweat. Florrie struggled to keep up with him, throwing the sheaves quickly on to her mother – and she was puzzled when Mother stopped work and stumped across the thresher towards Samuel.

She stopped just across the chasm from him. 'We ain't taking your sheaves so fast, Samuel Rawes,' she shouted crossly, 'and there's an end of it. So you can just quiet down and behave decent.'

Samuel blushed deeply. The blush even made his neck go pink. He turned away from Mother without answering, but Florrie noticed that when he lifted his pitchfork again he was careful to work at a steady, regular pace that no one, however cranky, could possibly object to.

This time all three of them moved smoothly in unison, and it was possible to allow stray thoughts to slip into your head without disturbing the flow of the work. Florrie found herself wondering why her mother disliked Samuel so much – it was obvious that she did, if only because she always addressed him formally, by his full name.

He often called at the farm, because he was a close friend of Joe's. He'd walk over in the evenings and help Joe clean harness; the two of them sitting side by side in companionable silence. Once they'd gone to a dance together at Kittenhole village hall. Florrie remembered looking out of the kitchen window and watching them walk off arm in arm up the lane, their best coats too tight across the back.

She'd been mending at the time, and she'd heard Mother say behind her, 'I don't trust that Samuel Rawes. Never have, neither.'

'Why, whatever's wrong with him?'

'I don't know where he comes from.'

Florrie didn't think this was enough of a reason to dislike someone, although it was true. No one knew where Samuel came from – he'd just arrived in the village on the back of the coal-cart one morning, when he was ten, and stayed to be raised by his aunt and uncle. Some disaster (which he would never discuss, not even with Joe) had befallen his family. Florrie remembered how thin he'd looked that first day, and how old and shabby his clothes had been.

Mind you, they were shabby now. His aunt had died a couple of years ago, and ever since he and Ellis had looked grimy, their clothes smelling of soot and bacon fat. Shabby, shabby, shabby, Florrie thought to herself, and the thought slipped into the constant shaking and rubbing and rattling of the thresher. Whenever Samuel lifted his pitchfork a split widened under his right arm, and the side-seam of his waistcoat was coming unravelled. She gazed at these flaws scornfully, and he turned round and caught her at it.

Before she had a chance to look away, the thresher slowed down and stopped. You could still hear the steady throb of the engine, but even so the quiet was a relief. A blackbird in the walnut tree beside the rickyard burst into song, and a young cockerel ventured a crow. He'd only been born at the end of the summer, and hadn't yet mastered the end-flourish of his call.

'Cock-a-doodle-urgh,' he cried, and then fell silent, as if embarrassed.

'It's a blockage!' Albie shouted. 'The drum's jammed!'

Mother went over to the extreme edge of the thresher to see what the men were up to. She had a look of disapproval ready on her face; soon she'd begin shouting suggestions.

Samuel was still gazing at Florrie. He hadn't taken his eyes away since the thresher stopped. Florrie wondered what he was thinking. Was he annoyed at her? She didn't care if he was; if he didn't want folk to stare at the holes in his clothes he should mend them. That was her opinion, and she didn't mind giving it to him. But his question, when it came, was entirely unexpected.

He spoke shyly, searching her face, as if looking there for an important sign.

'Did you . . . ?' he faltered. 'Has you fed your cats?'

'I always feeds them.'

'Has you fed them this morning?'

'They ain't crying, so I must have.' Bored of this conversation, Florrie turned to look over the side of the thresher. Ellis had undone an inspection panel and was leaning inside while Mr Coffin and Father watched sagely from a small distance away.

'Tell Ellis to take care the thresher don't do him an injury,' Mother shouted.

'You hear that, Ellis?' Mr Coffin called.

'I heard it,' Ellis boomed from inside the machine.

'It's a petticoat government on this farm, I can see,' Mr Coffin remarked. Father pretended not to hear.

'Only I wondered,' Samuel said softly, 'I wondered if there were aught *in* the dish.'

This was such an odd remark that Florrie turned back to him. 'Yes,' she said. 'There was a hard round flibbert in there. I reckon it was a pebble or something the cats had from a rabbit. It's here in my pocket.' She pulled it out into the sunshine and saw, for the first time, that it was brightly coloured: scarlet and blue, her favourites. It was a carved ring, clumsily whittled from a piece of wood, and painted with flowers. She examined it, astonished.

'Do it please you?'

'It's quaint,' Florrie said slowly. She'd just noticed that the letters of her name were painted in, one beside each flower. 'Did you make it?'

16

Samuel nodded and blushed.

'There's a bit of cloth in here,' Ellis called, his voice echoey. 'It's all woven in and out.'

'It's for you, for your birthday,' Samuel whispered. The words almost seemed to choke him; he breathed easier once they were out.

'I like it. Thank you.' Florrie slipped the ring on her finger and smiled at him.

'It's a bit of your washing, Mrs Tavender,' Mr Coffin shouted from the ground, holding up an oily, ragged strip of cloth. 'I won't say which bit, it would be indelicate.'

Mother shook a finger at him in mock disapproval, but Florrie could tell she was secretly pleased. She took Mr Coffin's cheeky remarks as a compliment, a tribute to her femininity.

'He's a caution,' she said to Florrie, a laugh in her voice, and noticed the ring at once. 'Why, whatever's that on your finger?'

'It's a ring Samuel's give me for my birthday. Wasn't that good of him?'

'You can put it in your pocket,' Mother said crossly. 'It ain't safe to wear rings on a farm.' She frowned at Samuel. 'And as for you, Samuel Rawes, if you want to pay court to my daughter, you can come talk to *me* first.' She jabbed her finger into her breast as she said 'me', and it didn't make a dent. Mother might look substantial, but she wasn't made of anything nearly so soft as fat. If you cuddled her, her body felt as hard-packed as a sack of corn.

Florrie was secretly pleased by her mother's hostility. If Samuel was feeling soppy and romantic, Mother would soon put him off. Florrie knew that soon she'd have to sort the problem out for herself, but just for today it was pleasant to hide behind Mother's fierce, dumpy figure, and see Samuel rebuffed by proxy. He looked at both of them, puzzled. Then he nodded. 'I will at that,' he said with quiet dignity, before turning back to his work.

Three

Threshing was almost over when they heard the hunt. The horn sang out in the distance, and the yelping of the dogs sounded like a rusty wheel being turned over and over. Father beckoned to Florrie.

'Go up to the lee field,' he said, 'and cast a quick eye over the ewes for me, hey?'

Florrie knew what he wanted her to do. It wasn't just a matter of making sure the sheep hadn't escaped or hurt themselves; she was to prevent them coming to any harm if the hounds passed through their field. It wouldn't be easy; it was quite likely that Father's landlord – or an agent of his – would be riding in that hunt, and she knew she had to avoid annoying anyone so powerful.

'And I'd go by the top coppice, if I was you,' Father called after her, as she scrambled over the stackyard fence. This meant he had some snares out. He often set wire gins there to catch the rabbits, and though he was careful to put a knot in the loop, so that pheasants might poke their inquisitive heads through and survive, where stouter-necked rabbits couldn't – it was always worth making sure. Knots could slip, and Florrie knew there was a clause in Father's tenancy allowing him to be evicted, on a month's notice, if he killed a fox, a hare, or a pheasant on the farm.

It was heavy work getting up to where the sheep were grazing. The farm was set into the side of a hill, and this meant that while half the fields were tolerably flat, the rest were as steep as a pitched roof. When Florrie was a child even the steepest had been ploughed, but nowadays Father abandoned most of them to pasture. They were gradually going wild: the hedges becoming little woods of their own, the fields seeding themselves with docks and thistles – and the livestock roamed this steep land as if it was a prairie, the sheep preferring, out of some woolly-headed whim, to spend their nights in the field Father rented on the lee side of the hill.

Halfway to the skyline Florrie glanced back at the buildings below. The dipping sun cast long shadows across the yard, and all the colours of walls and roofs – even the skins of the cows as they gathered for evening milking – looked richer and rosier. Smoke poured from the farmhouse chimney; it went almost straight upwards, because there was so little wind. Florrie could hear rooks calling above her; they swept out of the top coppice and circled off towards the west.

She rubbed her arms. It was cold enough for a frost tonight. She should have stopped to put on her coat, because now she wasn't pitching sheaves she was aware of the chill. But she didn't like her coat. It was old, with a ripped hem and a piece of string for a belt, and though it was fine for working in, she felt like a tramp-woman when she wore it, and was ashamed.

The coppice on the brow of the hill was still when she entered, the atmosphere in there as hushed as a church. She could see the trees meeting high above her head in the gloom, and a squirrel bounded up a trunk in front of her. This coppice was loosely connected to a much larger wood that spread down the other side of the hill. There were plenty of foxes up here: Florrie had often seen them.

Once, when she was only six, she'd found a fox cub sniffing at the leaves under these very trees. It had been half-grown, and to her surprise had allowed her to walk right up to it and pick it up. She'd carried it back to the farm, and though, every so often, and not meaning to, she'd stumbled and tripped on its tail, it hadn't minded. It had been miraculously tame. She remembered how she'd taken it into the back kitchen and scooped out some of the milk Mother had set there to skim for cream. It had lapped this from a pie-dish quite frantically. She'd filled the dish ten times before her pleasure at the cub's thirst had changed to fear. She'd run to fetch Joe, then, and by the time she'd got back the cub had been dead. It had twisted back on itself, its mouth open in a snarl. Joe hadn't been particularly surprised. He'd buried the cub under the dung-pile, and it had been maybe five years before Florrie fully understood the mystery, and connected the cub's death with the small bottle of strychnine that stood on the top shelf of Father's medicine cupboard, and sparkled there in the midst of other, dustier containers, its glass as clean as new ice.

The snares were all empty. For safety's sake Florrie gathered them up and hid them under a pile of leaves to take home. She could see Father's sheep through the tree trunks. They were spread out across the pasture, because there was so little grass for them to nibble, but as she watched they seemed to sense danger, because they lifted their heads uneasily, and one or two ran together for comfort. She doubted that the hunt would come this way now: the yelping of the dogs sounded much more distant than when she'd been standing on the thresher. To be honest, she was disappointed.

Father hated it when the hunt crossed his land – they damaged his fences, and often his crops, and every now and then the hounds got out of control and attacked his sheep, and whatever happened he had to endure it without complaint. To him, the gentry were like bad weather – an unpleasant but necessary part of life that you had to learn to tolerate – but Florrie loved the colour and excitement that rich people carried about with them. She was always spellbound whenever she saw the hunt pass by. It was so different from the world she knew: the clothes, the horses, the voices – even the huntsmen's skins seemed finer and more transparent than ordinary people's.

She sprang on to the gate leading from the coppice into the sheep field and balanced there, counting the ewes. Father didn't allow his children to sit on gates, but luckily he was a safe distance away: she could hear him calling the cows.

'Ho! Ho! Ho!' he shouted, far down the hill, and it seemed to her, for one puzzling moment, that she could hear the same call coming from the opposite direction too – but that must have been an echo.

A partridge whirred up from the hedge below the sheep, and there was a distant drumming of hooves. Perhaps there were bullocks beyond the wood, and they were racing each other in play – the field wasn't one of Father's. She listened more carefully, it was a good day for sound, since the air was so still and cold and dry. No, it was just one animal galloping, probably a horse. As she thought this, the sheep suddenly took fright, and careered off down the hill, their backsides bouncing up and down. She didn't think they were really panicked; when she stood up on the gate she could see them far below, in the most distant corner of the field, bending their heads to graze again.

The noise of the hooves grew louder. Florrie could see odd flashes of colour through the trees now: tan, black, yellow, and reddish-brown. A horse was approaching, with a rider on top. He was sprawled across the saddle, his hands gripping the pommel, his feet out of the stirrups. He had no hat on either, and from the glimpses Florrie caught of him, he seemed perilously close to falling off. The horse must have bolted, but it was tiring now. The wood beside the sheep field was thick with undergrowth and young saplings – it hadn't been properly copsed for years – and in taking this route for its escape the animal had set itself a hard task. It was not only going steeply uphill, but having to dodge numerous disagreeable, spiky obstructions at the same time.

As the horse crashed through the trees and brambles below her, Florrie jumped off the gate and ran to the centre of the little clearing beside it. She remembered all those times when, as a small girl, she'd opened gates for riders in the hunt, and been given a sixpence. Perhaps, if she could catch this horse just before it came to a standstill, the rider on its back would want to reward her, too.

Just as she thought this, horse and rider burst from the trees with a crackle of foliage. The horse, eyes staring, saliva dripping from its mouth, was just aware enough of Florrie to try and dodge her – but it was too late, she already had its reins in her hand. She pulled hard, intent on deflecting the animal towards the gate, and the next she knew leather was burning into the palms of her hands. She dug her boots into the woodland floor and tugged back as determinedly as she could. Something smashed into her right arm, and she felt a mat of brambles rip her stockings; she was beginning to regret her impulse when the horse stopped dead.

She opened her eyes. It was standing with the top bar of the gate pressing into its chest, just staring into the sheep field. There was a blank, crazy look on its face and its sides heaved with effort. They were so wet that sweat dripped continually off them on to the fallen leaves scattered across the ground. It would have sounded like the start of a summer shower – if the horse hadn't, at the same time, been taking great agonized gasps of air.

Florrie hobbled the short space to the gate and wrapped the reins round the top bar, wincing at the pain in her hands. Luckily the flesh wasn't torn: life became so vexing when she damaged the skin of her hands, because twice a day – whenever she scoured the milk-pans – she had to put them in soda and hot water. She noticed that her jersey was torn where her shoulder had banged into a tree, and worse, that her stockings had entirely disintegrated. Where they'd once been the skin was deeply scratched and starting to well with blood.

'Blooming heck!' she said, thinking of all the mending she was going to have to do.

There was a crackle from behind her.

She turned round. The rider had slipped off his horse and was standing beside it, one hand still holding the saddle, as if he didn't quite trust his legs to support him. He was a big man, both wider in the shoulders and taller than Florrie's father, but much younger. His face, which had been screwed up in a grimace while he was riding, had smoothed out now. Someone had daubed it roughly with blood: there was a long streak along the forehead, and two stripes on each cheek. This didn't surprise Florrie much, she knew it was some quaint ritual the hunting gentry went in for, but even without the blood the stranger's appearance would have been arresting.

He had an oval face, the skin unnaturally white. His hair was pale too, the colour of old, faded straw, and arranged in loose curls over his head. These curls were remarkably even in size: Florrie found herself wondering whether they grew like that, or had to be rolled on rags each night, like a lady's ringlets.

She wasn't entirely sure she liked the stranger's features. He had a long, straight nose with a slight downward curve at the tip, as if an invisible finger were pressing it down, and two deep lines that ran from his nostrils to the edge of his large, wide-lipped mouth. Florrie couldn't help being reminded of the face on a Roman coin Father had once ploughed up in the ten-acre field. It had had the same curls, lips and nose, and borne a similar expression: cold, disappointed, weary.

As she thought this, she realized that the stranger was staring at her as if he thought her strange, too. His eyes were an odd colour: deep blue, almost purple.

'Where am I?' he asked.

Florrie pointed through the trees towards the farmhouse. 'Down there's Fightingcocks Farm, sir, and you ain't above three hundred yards from the old sheep-dip.'

'Why the devil would I want to know where a sheep-dip was?' The stranger smiled. It wasn't altogether a pleasant smile. You couldn't see his teeth, and also, Florrie distrusted the way he was looking at her. It was a little like the smile the schoolteacher used to put on when one of her pupils fluffed an answer: sarcastic. And yet there was an extra quality to it, too, that Florrie hadn't encountered before. It made her uneasy.

'Do you live in this wood?' the stranger asked. He must have sensed her unease, because his voice became gentler. It was a wonderful voice – deep and smoky-sounding, full of life. It was as if all the warmth that should have been in his face had hidden itself there.

'Of course not!' Florrie was stung by the rudeness of the question. 'I lives in a proper house like all decent Christian folk.' Glancing down at her clothes, she added quickly, 'And most days I ain't covered in tree bark, neither. Nor is my stockings torn. It was your gelding did that.'

'You're right. It was good of you to stop my horse.'

'I didn't rightly *stop* him,' Florrie said. 'You *can't* stop a runaway, not if he's really going. Gallop straight through you, he would, and never even know you was there. No, your horse was well and truly out of puff when I caught him hold.'

It was a disconcerting experience, delivering this speech. Florrie began by talking animatedly and gesturing with her hands, just as she would if she was with one of her brothers, yet ended by folding her arms and tailing off self-consciously. The stranger seemed to size her up, as if she were a cow in the market. There was a long pause, which she eventually filled by adding: 'Of course, you'll have to walk the gelding back careful, and rug him up well. He's terrible hot and no mistake.' She patted the horse as she said this, noticing how slender and delicate it was. It hadn't been too badly marked by its journey through the wood, either, all the scratches were superficial.

'I'm not going anywhere near that animal,' the stranger answered disdainfully. 'I don't care if I never see it again.' He turned his head, and picked a bit of moss off the shoulder of his black coat.

Florrie stared at him open-mouthed. 'Well, what's you reckoning to do with the poor creature, then?'

'What do you suggest?' When Florrie didn't answer, the stranger tipped his head a little on one side, as if it was easier to assess her mood from that position, and gave a brief laugh. 'I know what,' he said. 'You take the beastly thing. You take it back to whatever decent Christian hovel you live in, and look after it for me.'

Florrie felt herself go pink with anger. 'I told you,' she said, 'I don't live in a hovel or a wood or a pile of fuzz, neither. I lives in a proper house like you does.'

'I very much doubt that,' the stranger replied. He looked at her coolly, no real expression on his face, and she found herself wishing, not for the first time, that she was as tall and brawny as her Aunt Louisa, and could look at him straight on, instead of from a lower, more humble position. Florrie tried to stare the stranger down – she was good at that with her brothers – but he didn't flinch, and his blue eyes kept steady. If it hadn't been for their odd colour she would have said they were like a rat's: intelligent, but devoid of all feeling.

In the end, she was the first to look away, more out of caution than anything else. Father wouldn't like her to be insolent to one of the gentry. That kind of behaviour caused trouble and cost money. So she frowned at her boots instead.

'Tell me,' the stranger asked, 'if I walk back through those woods, will I come to Kittenhole church?'

'I'd say so.' She didn't look at him. She didn't intend looking at him again, if she could help it.

'And how far would that be?' The stranger's voice sounded amused, he seemed to be enjoying her petty defiance.

'Near on six mile.' Florrie thought about making some comment about the stranger maybe not being quite up to walking such a vast distance of six miles in his fancy riding-boots. She was mentally constructing it, when he suddenly said, 'Here,' and caught hold of her hand.

The shock was immense. No one touched Florrie nowadays. She'd given up cuddling Mother years before, and they weren't a demonstrative family. She'd grown used to thinking of herself as enclosed in an invisible fortress which no one could breach without her permission – and yet this stranger, whom she disliked, just reached through and grabbed her, as if there was nothing to prevent him. She tried to snatch her hand away, but he held it firmly, his fingers so white that they made hers look brown and clumsy, like an animal's.

It was the strangest thing, but her whole body seemed to quake when he took her hand. She didn't look at him, and he opened her fingers gently, put a piece of folded paper in her palm, and closed her hand over it again. Then he let go. When she finally looked up he was disappearing through the trees, his movements surprisingly graceful and assured.

Four

'Why, it's a five-pound note!' Mother said, in astonishment.

Florrie had had a difficult journey back down the hill with the horse. Not wanting to move from the gate, it had snapped at her hands when she tried to untie it, and then stubbornly refused to budge. She'd had to use her most coaxing tone of voice and, when that failed, hurl pine cones and lumps of earth at its backside to get it to move.

Once she'd rubbed it down in the stable she'd run to the kitchen, to tell Father, and it had given her an odd feeling, looking in through the window and seeing everyone gathered round the table, eating their evening tea. The traction engine was waiting by the gate, its furnace purring to itself, and because she knew it would be leaving soon the scene had an edge of sadness: it would be lonely at the farm, once Mr Coffin and his helpers had gone.

While she'd watched, Father had turned to Mr Coffin and made some remark – from his smile, a friendly, good-natured one – and Mr Coffin hadn't responded, just frowned at his plate. Mother was following the encounter, her face concerned, and Florrie guessed that the scene was about money; that Father had promised the impossible – to pay Mr Coffin at once – and was trying to smooth over an awkward situation.

She'd often heard it said that people married their opposites, and it seemed true in Father and Mother's case: he was always willing to take calculated risks, always certain his luck would

29

hold, whereas Mother was a desperate worrier. She hoarded each penny she made from selling her butter to hotels on the coast, and spent the barest minimum on housekeeping, constantly trying to lay up defences against the disaster she was sure was about to happen. The shelf in the cupboard under the stairs was filled with bottled fruit and vegetables they weren't allowed to touch; the wooden box by the fire brimmed with never-to-be-used emergency supplies of underpants and knitted socks.

Each time a large amount of money was due to be spent on the farm – as when corn had to be threshed, so it could be fed to animals or used for seed – there'd be a heaviness in the atmosphere. Florrie's parents didn't argue: Father made the decisions and that was that; but Mother's silent anxiety, hanging round her solid, black-clothed figure as she cooked and cleaned and mended, ate away at his confidence, so that he became edgy and bad-tempered.

'You sit yourself down, Florrie,' Mother said kindly. 'You must be wore out.' She placed a dish of rabbit stew in front of Florrie, and added two boiled potatoes with a caressing touch of her spoon. Then she readjusted the angle of the plate, and moved Florrie's knife and fork so they would be easier for her to reach. As she straightened, she smoothed Florrie's hair with a gesture that was too light to be a stroke. Florrie could tell, from these gentle attentions, that Mother *had* been quite desperate over money.

Albie was sitting beside Florrie, his face level with her shoulder. He'd washed it since she last saw him: it was shiny and pink now, the hair sticking up round the edges in wet spikes.

'Who give you the five pound?' he asked.

'A gentleman up in the top coppice.'

Her account of this person didn't satisfy the company round the kitchen table in the slightest. All the most crucial pieces of information were missing from it. She'd neglected to ask the stranger his name, his address, the village he'd been born in, or any details of his family history. In fact, the whole conversation she'd had with him appeared mysteriously witless once it was related to an audience.

'So you didn't think to ask – and he didn't trouble to say – when he fancied having his gelding back?' Father said doubtfully.

'Well, no.'

'He were rude enough,' Samuel said. 'What did he look like?'

'Big,' she replied, 'and dressed handsome, with hair like a dandelion clock. He were gentry, all right.'

'Do you reckon he'd be one of the Marshalls, from down Poffit way?' Mr Coffin asked Father, and Florrie quickly interrupted.

'Oh no, I never seen him before. He weren't like anyone round here, didn't talk like them, neither.'

Florrie found herself wishing the others would stop asking questions, and discussing the subject. She'd never be able to explain the encounter: she couldn't possibly have described the stranger accurately, not without sounding foolish. She'd thought him horrible, and yet . . . She couldn't seem to concentrate properly, either. She kept remembering stray details she'd hardly been aware of at the time, like the way the strange gentleman had smelt of flowers and fruit – sharp and lemony – when he'd leaned forward to take her by the hand. Her heart beat painfully when she thought of this, and she found herself touching her own bruised hand, as he'd done, and folding the fingers shut. Some sixth sense made her glance in Samuel's direction as she did so, and she thought she saw, although she must have been mistaken, a shadow of pain cross his face, as if he'd eavesdropped on her thoughts.

* * *

31

Suddenly wide awake, Florrie lay in her bed and listened, eyes open in the darkness. Above her, in the low attic that ran under the thatch, she heard a mouse trundle a heavy object across the beams. She wondered who'd coined the expression 'quiet as a mouse'. They couldn't have spent much time with rodents to think *that* one up.

She'd had a bad dream, and it troubled her. She rarely had nightmares, and couldn't remember much of this one, just a feeling of dread, of impending disaster. It was impossible, now, for her to go back to sleep without first checking the livestock and making sure nothing had gone wrong on the farm. She couldn't help being superstitious about warnings, even if they did come from the inside of her own head.

She got quietly out of bed and pulled her skirt and jersey on over her nightgown. She was almost certain her nightmare had been set on the stairs of Earlshay. Perhaps the talk she'd heard yesterday, about it being sold, had set her mind running on the place. She'd been there a few times as a child – it was set in a wide sweep of land, with a lake her brothers liked to swim in. The house itself was almost deserted; no one had lived there properly since 1915, when the heir had died.

She fumbled under the bed for her boots, careful not to knock over the chamberpot. Then, pulling aside the curtains that acted as entrance to her tiny room, she crept down the stairs. Something about the cold on the back of her neck, where her hair was pulled back in a plait, and the feel of the wooden risers under her bare feet, reminded her of that day years and years ago, when she'd been eight, and gone exploring at Earlshay.

Albie had been not much more than an infant, then, and Samuel newly arrived at the school. Samuel had had no friends, and spent his days hunched miserably on one of the front baby benches, right under the teacher's eye, copying out letters of the alphabet. The teacher had been horrified to discover, on his arrival, that he couldn't read or write. A ten-year-old who couldn't spell his own name! Even Florrie had been appalled: she'd gazed, with prissy disapproval, at Samuel's slate, where he'd scratched, with agonizing effort, the 's' back to front, the letters all wobbly and misshapen, the word 'Samel'. But Joe, who was kinder, had felt sorry for him, and invited him to come on an adventure.

When they'd reached the outskirts of the village, and were out of sight of any grown-ups, they'd taken off their smart outer clothes and stuffed them in the hedge. They always did this before exploring; it stopped Mother getting angry about rips and mud. Joe had only pulled off his jersey, but Florrie, who went to school in a starched dress and pinafore, had removed both, leaving herself quite decently, if oddly, dressed in a wool liberty bodice and red flannel petticoat – not to mention numerous underpinnings. She remembered how annoyed she'd been by Samuel's round-eyed astonishment; she'd hated anyone assuming that just because she was a girl, she couldn't behave exactly like her brother.

That afternoon had been hot; it was the scorching summer of 1921, and they'd passed through fields and fields of ripening corn, most reaching only to the tops of their arms, on account of the drought. The pastures had been silver-yellow, the hedges pale brown, and the whole landscape had smelled dry and burnt, like toast.

The lake at Earlshay when they'd reached it, had shrunk in on itself. The water had been dark and opaque, clumps of bubbles breaking suddenly from its depths, great areas misted over with tiny green discs of weed. The boys had stripped naked at once and dived in, but Florrie, made uncomfortable by Samuel's interest in her, hadn't cared to remove any more clothes while he was around. She'd heard him chant a rude rhyme, over on the little island where the moorhens nested, and felt he was doing it to annoy her.

'Gimlet Eye!
Sausage Nose
Hip Awry
Bandy Toes!'

She'd turned her back on him and gazed across the lake instead, at the house that shimmered on the horizon, its windows black in the sunlight.

There were odd rumours about the caretaker. According to Joe he was a single gentleman whose wife had run away, escaping so hurriedly that she'd forgotten to collect her clothes. Out of economy, or maybe just plain craziness, the caretaker had begun wearing her dresses, and for this reason was known as the 'Skirty Man'. Joe said he ate small children; Joe also claimed that once, when he'd been exploring the ruined gardens at Earlshay on his own, he'd turned a corner and seen the Skirty Man drinking from a water butt, and only just escaped in time. But Joe liked making stories up; he'd once told Florrie he'd seen a pack of tigers under his bedroom window, and that certainly hadn't been true.

Anyway, on this stifling hot day, the vest under her bodice sticking to her back, and her whole body prickly and slippery with sweat, Florrie had crouched down beside the lake, pulled off her boots and dangled her toes in the water to cool them.

'Do your Florrie take her clothes off?' she'd heard Samuel ask from the island. 'Or do she swim in her knickers?' The word 'knickers' had sounded especially rude in his mouth, since his voice had a darker, furrier accent than Joe's.

'She don't do neither if there's ignorant little boys about,' Florrie had yelled back furiously, almost suffocating, and longing more than ever to dive into the cool green water. To take her mind off the heat, she'd got up and walked round the edge of the lake. Behind her she'd heard the boys shriek and splash, and the unhappy conviction that they'd ganged up on her had made her walk on, up the sloping parkland, dotted here and there with huge oak and elm trees. The grass had been short, not cropped by animals – there'd been no droppings – it had been mown. In fact the whole place, the nearer she'd got to the house, had revealed a queer mixture of carelessness and close attention. The gate leading to the gardens had rotted into a pile of sticks, yet inside there'd been occasional flower-beds, meticulously weeded. One, that Florrie always remembered most sharply in her dreams, had been crammed with yellow pansies, each with a peevish expression on its face.

The walled vegetable garden had been heaped with dead nettles – all except a piece perhaps three yards square, which had been sown with potatoes, carrots and peas, their leaves still damp from a watering. Florrie'd become more careful after seeing these vegetables – she'd wanted to avoid meeting any caretaker, fearsome or not. She'd slipped along the edges of the walls like a spy, coming at last to a spread of gravel, starred with dead clumps of weed. There, looming above her, had been the house.

It had looked occupied: a door had stood ajar, a full bucket of water waiting on its threshold. Next to it, a small, square window had been left open a few inches; Florrie had hesitated before deciding, on impulse, to push it up and look in. It'd rolled upwards smoothly, and when she'd poked her head through all she'd seen was a storeroom, its shelves coated in reddish dust. She'd felt a surge of excitement, of daring. Why shouldn't she find out what lay beyond? Then she'd definitely be braver than Joe. In the past, if Joe did anything crazy – balanced on the top roof beam of the cowshed, or rode a sow with piglets – Florrie always had to follow suit, but so far she'd never done anything he hadn't. This was her chance; she'd scrambled through the window.

The instant she was inside she'd noticed how still and cold the house was. Entering it had been like falling into a deep hole, after the heat and activity outdoors. Even the singing of crickets had become inaudible. She'd crept to the storeroom door, opened it, and found herself in a corridor. Just beside her a narrow staircase had twisted upwards – without pausing for thought she'd run up it.

She hadn't thought much of the corridor she'd reached when she'd got to the top. She'd assumed that people who possessed a huge, grand house would decorate it inside like a fairytale, with gold and silver hangings and crystal chandeliers. Instead, this had been painted a drab green colour up to the height of Florrie's head, and above that a dirty cream. Each of the doors she'd opened had revealed a sad, pinched little room containing a rusty iron bedstead, and sometimes a lopsided chair.

Florrie's hot little chest had swelled with indignation. She'd felt as if a shabby trick had been played on her. Why, the furniture they had at home was finer than this! The bed her mother and father slept in was made of brass that shone pink-white when polished, and every chair at Fightingcocks was at least kept nailed decently together! Perplexed by this odd glimpse of the private life of the rich, Florrie had been about to retreat back down the stairs when she'd noticed, at the far end of the corridor, a completely different type of door. Instead of being painted, it had been covered in a curious green, fluffy material. Florrie had searched for a doorknob but, finding none, had shoved at the door with both hands, and it had given way with a smooth, oiled motion.

Beyond had been a vast hallway full of motes of dust. A wide flight of stairs had led down one side and up another; she'd found herself standing on a broad landing suspended between the two. Ahead of her had been a huge window hung with tattered cream-coloured curtains, through which she'd seen the park, and a little piece of the lake. The floor beneath her feet had been carpeted in pale yellow, and she'd realized at once that this was the grandeur she'd been seeking, even if it was dusty and ragged. The ceiling had seemed to soar right up to the sky; the banisters had been white and very thin, and curved as delicately as a hare's ribcage.

Holding her breath, Florrie had tiptoed forward, her toes sinking into the carpet. She'd jumped when the green door had closed behind her with a stealthy click. Something close at hand had been making a sweeping noise; Florrie had conjured up a vision of a lady in a long dress moving slowly and stealthily across the carpet – she'd spun round to make sure she wasn't being crept up on. Then, annoyed by her own nervousness, she'd made herself seek out the source of the sound. It had come from a little extra landing on her left, where two steps led up to a door that stood open.

Inside, there'd been a broken window, and a long piece of curtain, frayed and rotted into twisted ropes of silk, had rustled against the floor. Florrie'd thought it the strangest room she'd ever been in. The wall facing her had been filled with the life-sized photograph of a man. He'd been standing in a murky brown garden – the shape of one of the trees in the background had made Florrie suspect it was the garden at Earlshay – and there'd been an awkwardness, a self-consciousness, about his pose, as if he'd been told to stand arms akimbo, one foot in front of the other, but wouldn't naturally have chosen such a proud, confident way of holding himself. Also he'd been wearing a uniform that was clearly too big for him: the cuffs had covered his hands, even the cap on his head had seemed to eclipse his face. He'd had a sympathetic face, too: a timid, fearful one. Although the photograph was all browns and whites, you could guess that his skin was delicate and often broke out into rashes. Florrie hadn't been able to stop herself thinking that he also looked the kind of person who might wet the bed.

37

Pushed up against the walls of this room had been a dozen tables, piles of seemingly unrelated jumble laid out on their tops: assorted books, a worn gunmetal case that had sprung open to reveal the inscription 'To RH from VB', the cap from the photograph, three pairs of boots, some muddy kid gloves, two crumpled cigarettes; and among it all Florrie had noticed a yellowed envelope. Someone had written across this in wavery, trembly handwriting: 'The handkerchief the dear lad had in his pocket when he fell.'

Florrie had glanced back at the photograph with sudden, fearful understanding. So this was the dead heir, the boy who would have been living here now, if he hadn't died in the Great War? Somehow, once she'd realized this, Florrie hadn't wished to stay in the house a moment longer. She'd been filled with dread; it was said in the village that there was a curse on Earlshay: no male heir had come into his inheritance there since the place had been built. The photograph had seemed to stare at her accusingly; the curtain had moved as if it was alive. She'd backed out of the room on to the landing.

She'd had a shock, almost at once. On the higher landing above her she'd seen what at first looked like the figure in the photograph: a timid-looking man dressed in clothes too big for him. Then she'd blinked, and realized that it wasn't an illusion, but a real person. He'd been half-hidden by shadow; as she'd continued to stare she'd noticed that he wasn't wearing riding-breeches and puttees, like the lost heir, but a stiff brown skirt, under which a pair of large hobnailed boots could clearly be seen. All at once she'd become horribly conscious of her smallness and of the fact that Joe didn't know where she was. She'd frozen with apprehension – and then bolted.

She'd raced back across the landing to the green door and pushed it open. 'Flap' it had gone, and clicked shut, then flapped and clicked again. She'd reached the winding stairs and been about to plunge down them when a hand had caught hold of her arm and she'd found herself gazing, terrified, into the inflamed, desperate-looking eyes of the Skirty Man. At that moment she'd known exactly how the rabbits on the farm felt, when they were seized by the cats. She'd nearly screamed herself; her mouth had opened, but no noise had come out.

'I knows just what you's thinking,' the Skirty Man had said, breathing heavily after his run. His hand had trembled on her arm. It had been a strong, muscular hand, like her father's; the fingers had entirely encircled her, she hadn't had a chance of breaking free. 'You was wondering, wasn't you,' he'd continued, 'if I couldn't jump these here steps in one go?'

Florrie hadn't answered. The man had smelt peculiar: musty and sour, like a sick animal; it hadn't astonished her that what he said was weird, too.

'Well, I've a surprise for you!' he'd said, and before she'd realized what was happening he'd let go of her arm and heaved himself on to the banisters. He'd rocked there, the wooden rail cutting into his stomach, for one dizzying instant, then plummeted down the stairwell, turning in mid-air. He'd landed at the bottom with a painful thump, and grinned up at her, and she hadn't been able to avoid noticing that he wore no underclothes at all.

Ever afterwards, Florrie couldn't remember the exact details of her flight, but she must have raced back through the green door and down the main staircase, because she did recall, with nightmarish accuracy, struggling in vain with the rusty bolt on the front door. She'd dodged down a flight of steps into a cellar then, out of some primeval need to hide in a dark place, and found herself scrabbling hopelessly at the wrong side of a wooden hatch sealing off a coal chute. Above her there'd been almost inaudible, stealthy sounds and, as she'd crouched in a corner, finally paralysed by terror, the coal hatch had opened, and Samuel's face had peered in, accompanied by a flood of sunlight and the shrilling of crickets. He'd never really been able to explain why he'd run up to the house and opened that wooden hatch at that particular time; he'd just said that he'd had a feeling about it. He'd been unbearably cocky, too, about his rescue of Florrie, and had kept turning round and smiling at her all the way home, as if he owned her.

Still, the relief of being out of that house! She felt an echo of the same sentiment now, as she shut the door of the kitchen, where the air was close and greasy, and let herself into the velvet coolness of the night. It had just rained, and a light glowed in the stable window. She followed it across the wet black puddles in the yard.

Just before she reached the stable she passed the sty where Albie's two pigs were kept, and one of them woke with a snort. The straw rustled as it came out to see who the intruder was, and Florrie touched the wet tip of its nose with her hand.

Father was in the stable, his coat off, his shirt-sleeves rolled up, grooming the new horse and whistling to himself. He didn't look tired, but then he didn't have the kind of face that ever showed fatigue, it was so brown and deeply creased. He seemed different tonight. The blue and white striped shirt he always wore looked dazzlingly clean in the lamplight and, together with the trilby shading his face, gave him a dandified air. It was odd, really, because most of the time Florrie was only aware of him as a harsh, uncompromising character who had to be pandered to, and rarely showed appreciation. Then, she just noticed his big, beak-like nose and the deep frown-lines on his forehead, and she thought of him as brown: brown wrinkly waistcoat, brown breeches, and dull brown boots and gaiters. It was a surprise to see him another way, to catch him in a relaxed, colourful mood.

She slipped into the stall beside him.

'I couldn't sleep,' he said in a quiet, reflective voice, as if talking to himself. 'I got to thinking about this horse, and how badly it would go for us if he was to get sick.'

Florrie nodded. The two cart-horses, Smart and Violet, were also in the stable, having been brought in ready for the next day's work, and Smart, a big black Shire cross, leaned over the stall divider behind Florrie and mumbled at her sleeping-plait. He seemed to specially enjoy the taste of the binder twine at the end. After a bit, Florrie pushed him away with the flat of her hand, and he blew moist air into her ear instead.

'Look at his feet,' Father said softly, 'and tell me what you see.'

As Florrie obediently bent to pick up one of the newcomer's slim back legs he added, 'Careful, he's a kicker, he is.'

Florrie gripped the hoof between her knees, as if she was shoeing, and examined it with care. The light in the stable wasn't bright, but fuzzy and imprecise. Even so, she could tell there was an oddness about the texture of the animal's hoof. It was creamy-grey, and should have been uniformly smooth, but instead here and there faint lines of a slightly different colour were visible, like gussets fitted into the curves.

'Yes,' Father said, smiling at her. 'You know what that is?'

'No.'

'That's the neatest bit of plasterwork I ever did see. He's a poem, this horse is, a real dealer's masterpiece.'

Father continued brushing. Under his care the gelding had dried completely and its coat now shone. It was calmer, too. It wasn't eating its hay, just standing, eyes half-closed, in a trance. Father had a real gift with animals: he knew just where to stroke or scratch them, in order to induce a state of dreamy pleasure. When he tickled the pigs their legs would even buckle, collapsing them into a quivering heap of ecstasy. This horse looked pretty close to doing the same.

'His teeth's been filed back, too, to make him look younger,' Father went on, his tone affectionate, as if he were describing something clever the animal had done. 'Bishoping, they calls

41

it. I never seen it done before, just heared about it in market.' Father shook his head. 'Cor, ain't the world a wicked place; ain't it ever?' The thought of this wickedness didn't make him sad, though. It seemed, rather, to amuse and excite him. He pulled on his coat and unhooked the lantern and, as he ushered Florrie out through the stable door, she almost expected him to put his arm around her shoulders; which was odd, because Father had never been affectionate.

A stray drop of rain hissed on the hot metal of the lantern. Father chuckled to himself. 'Whoever this fellow is,' he said, 'what you met out in the wood, he knows sod all about horses.'

Coins jingled in his pocket and he gave her a sixpence, whispering so softly into her ear that it was hard to catch the words. His breath smelt of cider, too. 'That's for your birthday,' he said. 'You're a good girl, you are.'

Five

Sybil glanced round her new drawing-room. It was half-complete. The ceiling had been done, and the windows mended and painted, but there was no paper or carpet yet. Already, though, it had started to have a special feeling, perhaps because it had been scrubbed very clean, a fire had been lit, and two of the newly upholstered chairs were in place before it. The room was going to be pure white, the only touch of colour two Chinese vases with a curious milky-blue glaze.

Outside, it was raining, a hopeless, cold November day. Water streamed down the outside of the windows, and a dead, grey light drifted into the room. Sybil had switched on the electricity some time ago, but it hadn't really made her surroundings any brighter; the glow was too feeble, and flickered intermittently. Electricity might be new and fashionable, but to see clearly enough to read, you still had to send for an oil lamp.

She walked across the bare boards just for the pleasure of it, her dress rustling against her legs. It was a pretty frock, a simple crêpe Vionnet, cut on the bias; it showed off her slender, youthful figure. Everyone said she looked young enough to be Vallie's sister, not his mother, and when she looked in the mirror she saw hardly any wrinkles. Her skin was pale and unblemished, her eyes clear, her teeth good. The two places a woman aged first, in her opinion, were the teeth and the neck, especially that strip of delicate, tissue-thin skin above the breast, and she'd always taken enormous care of hers. She never went out in the sun without a hat or an old-fashioned parasol, and she scrubbed her teeth with salt and bicarbonate of soda twice a day.

The mirror was rococo, all gilt ribbons and bows; she smiled at herself and frowned. She did wish that flecks of lipstick wouldn't keep getting on her teeth. It was so annoying. She rubbed them away with a lace handkerchief, and at that moment the doorbell rang.

Sybil went back to the fireplace and composed herself, listening for the click of the green baize door and the flat-footed tread of Ruby, the parlourmaid. Ruby wasn't at all satisfactory, but she was the best Sybil had been able to find: a lumpy country girl who smelled strongly of perspiration. She ate too much, too. All the servants smelt bad, and all of them ate too much. Sybil was astonished by the vast quantities of beef and potatoes that vanished into the servants' hall. They must be stealing; smuggling the stuff out to their filthy families.

'Don't bother, I'll show myself in,' a female voice murmured outside the door. It was Veronica, dressed in a jersey suit. It looked like Chanel, but you couldn't be sure. Veronica had the blade-thin figure, and the gall, to pass a cheap copy off as couture.

'Darling!' Sybil rose and held out her arms.

Veronica spun round, crying out, 'How marvellous it all looks! How clever you are!' before giving Sybil two light kisses that didn't touch her cheeks and perching in front of her, on a little carved armchair upholstered in silky white stripes. 'I can't get over it,' she went on. 'It's such a transformation. And it's all happened so quickly, too!'

Sybil gave an embarrassed laugh. 'It's hardly begun, really, but I felt we had to come and see what the decorators were doing.'

'We? Is Vallie here?' Veronica raised her thin eyebrows.

She was interested in Vallie, Sybil knew. She always became
far more animated in his presence. Sybil didn't mind; in fact,
she got a curious, wicked pleasure from watching Veronica
throw herself at Vallie. She didn't have a chance. Vallie's tastes
were altogether different.

'He's out walking. I don't know how he can bear to do it in
this weather. It's all he does, you know, when we're alone
down here. He doesn't hunt, and he won't take a dog with
him. He says he loathes animals.'

'What an idiot Vallie is!' Veronica said, her tone
affectionate.

'It makes it awfully difficult,' Sybil sighed. 'You know what
people in the country are like. I'm afraid Vallie just won't fit
in.'

'Nonsense,' Veronica replied, leaning forward, so that the
firelight shone on her cropped black hair. It was just a fraction
too dark to be natural. 'They'll all love Vallie, you'll see.'

Sybil smiled at her friend. She liked the way Veronica
pronounced things, she had the most delicious voice. When
Veronica said 'nonsense', you couldn't help enjoying it, she
put such humorous, sensual warmth into the word. It was almost
as if she was eating it. Sybil noticed voices. She knew she had
a pleasant one herself, but it was nothing compared to
Veronica's. However hard you tried, you couldn't get quite
that quality into a voice, just by imitation and practice. Vallie
said it was money you could hear when Veronica spoke, but
that wasn't strictly accurate: it was breeding, education, a
lifetime spent among the very best people. Besides, Veronica
wasn't wealthy. She had a pretty house a few miles away, at
Cullerton, lent her by an uncle; she went abroad twice a year,
as a guest of rich cousins; and when she gave parties her friends
always brought their own champagne and food, as if going on
a picnic. She was supported by a fine net of family and grand
friends; her life looked like a conjuring trick, but in reality,

Sybil knew, it was much more solidly based than that.

Veronica crossed her legs. 'So,' she said brightly, 'when are you going to give a party?'

'I don't know if I shall.'

'But you must!'

'I don't know anyone round here. I don't feel secure. And Vallie's bound to make a fuss. You know how difficult he is about my soirées.'

'Don't tell him, then. Spring it on him. Oh come on, Sybil, do. It'd be such fun.'

'Well.' Sybil leaned forward and traced the outline of a letter on her knee. It was a habit of hers, whenever she concentrated; she wasn't even aware of doing it. Veronica noticed, because the letter Sybil drew was a V: V for Veronica, V for Vallie. Veronica liked Sybil, she couldn't help herself – she was pretty, she was generous, and she was always so anxious to please – but the real reason for their friendship was Vallie.

All the time Veronica sat on the edge of the little silky armchair she quaked, her ears were pricked, she listened for Vallie's step. It was getting greyer outside, even Vallie wouldn't want to walk in the rain and the dark. She'd spent over an hour this afternoon deciding what to wear in case he appeared: she both hated and adored seeing him. She hated it because she felt so aware of her own physical imperfection when he was near – she found herself worrying whether she looked too old, or her breath was sweet enough. Once, after spending an evening playing piquet with him, she'd discovered, to her horror, a long, unplucked, corkscrew hair growing out of the side of her jaw. Had he seen it, had he been revolted? He was the kind of man who would be repelled by a tiny flaw like that.

At twenty-two he was eight years younger than her, and the age gap made her uneasy, stripped away her confidence. And yet, whenever she was with him she became mesmerized. She couldn't stop watching him; she couldn't sleep afterwards, either, for thinking of what he'd said and how he'd looked. She didn't really know what she wanted from him. Often she'd imagined him as a lover, and drawn back from the thought with some fear. He wouldn't be kind. And yet, she couldn't help wishing that just once, in all the hours they'd spent together, he had touched her hand or tried to kiss her. As it was, she was always in a state of uncertainty and torment. Did he care anything for her? Could he? She'd made enquiries, and no one in her vast circle of friends had ever heard a whisper of Vallie having a mistress or a male lover. 'He's a tame cat,' Veronica's brother had said, implying that Vallie had no sexuality at all, but Veronica wasn't convinced.

'What do you think about a costume ball?' Sybil asked suddenly. 'Would that be too boresome for words?'

'Heavens, no.' Veronica caught Sybil's hand, pressing it warmly. 'It'd be absolutely perfect.'

A door slammed somewhere in the recesses of the house. It was a masculine slam. Veronica could imagine a wet coat being flung carelessly on the floor; Vallie sitting on a bench in the gunroom pulling off his boots with a weary gesture. At the same moment the green baize door beyond the hall opened and Veronica heard a trolley rattle towards the drawing-room. The house was full of painters' ladders, rubble and sacks of plaster, but somehow the old noises remained. Veronica remembered when it had belonged to the Holdens: the green baize door had clicked and flapped in just the same way then, the tea trolley rumbled slowly across the acres of hall with a similar note of gossipy complaint. If she shut her eyes she could imagine herself back at the Holdens' before the war, at one of their interminable children's parties.

'What do you think? A baby party like the one Mrs Sanders gave last year? Vicars and tarts? Or a Mozart party?'

'A Mozart party, of course!' Veronica laughed. 'Think of Vallie in a wig and knee-breeches!'

'He would look too adorable, wouldn't he?' The women chuckled together: talking about Vallie as if he was still a little boy cut him pleasantly down to size.

'Who'd look adorable?' Vallie asked. The clatter of the tea trolley, as Ruby jerked it sullenly across the hall, had masked his arrival. He was dressed in dark reds, a white shirt glimmering at his neck. Veronica loved his clothes. They were always subtle colours, but slightly wrong: the cut unfashionable, or the material too rich to be properly unobtrusive. He never looked exactly a gentleman, but maybe he would, in time, once he got used to handling his new inheritance.

'*You*, of course,' Veronica said at once, her tone arch. 'Who else do we ever talk about?'

'Mama,' he said tenderly, and kissed his mother.

'Dearest boy,' she answered, in a low, passionate tone. Ruby goggled at both of them, startled but interested. 'That will be all, Ruby,' Sybil snapped, and the parlourmaid stumped out of the room, her heavy tread rocking the mirror by the door. 'Did you have a nice walk, darling?' Vallie didn't answer, he walked over to the window instead. There wasn't much beyond it, only a croquet lawn, enclosed by low stone walls. From where she was sitting, Veronica could see both halves of him: the neat blond back of his head, still wet from the rain, his wide shoulders and long legs, and his face, reflected in the dark glass of the window. The skin looked polished, his expression unhappy. It was a strong face. He'd been to a minor public school, what her brother rudely called a 'Trouser Lodge' – one of those places that ape Eton or Harrow at a fraction of the cost. She could imagine him being a ruthless school prefect, not at all kind to the poor little boys in his power, and the thought was strangely exciting. His eyes were fringed with thick, pale brown lashes that gave him a disconcertingly pretty look, and the wide mouth could sometimes smile with great sweetness. Often, when she'd called at Sybil's London house, she'd seen him sitting at a window writing or sketching on a great mass of paper, and she gathered that since he'd left school he'd dabbled in art. Even though they'd scarcely had a penny to their name back then, Sybil had been insistent that he shouldn't work. 'I always swore to myself that at least Vallie would be a gentleman,' she'd once said to Veronica, her voice vibrating with emotion.

'It was that bad, was it?' Veronica laughed.

'What?' Vallie turned from the window. He looked confused, as if he'd momentarily forgotten where he was.

'She means the walk, darling, you do look frightfully grim,' Sybil teased.

'Has Vallie a secret sorrow, do you think?' Veronica asked, and Sybil smiled back at her, her eyes sparkling.

'Sorrow?' Vallie turned from the window. As always, when she saw him after being with Sybil, Veronica was surprised by how big he was, and how alarming his physical presence. 'Why should I be unhappy?' he continued, his voice angry. 'Haven't I everything I could possibly want?'

'Of course you have, darling,' Sybil answered. 'And wouldn't you like a cup of tea as well?'

Six

The sky was dirty white, the trees and bushes black and dripping with moisture. Every now and then there'd be a sudden flurry of rain, thin and penetrating, which seeped down Florrie's neck and in at the wrists of her sleeves. She was pulling up mangolds, trimming off their roots and leaves with a big knife, and dropping them in a basket which she hauled along through the mud beside her, and emptied, at frequent intervals, on to a great pile in the corner of the field.

In the evening, when the horses were free, one of them would be driven up here to collect all the plants she'd cut, but at the moment they were both too busy, ploughing in the next field. Each time she straightened to rub the ache out of her back she could see through the thin beech and hazel – Father kept the hedges on this flat part of his land relatively well-trimmed – to where Albie was stumbling along behind Smart and Violet, trying, and usually failing, to keep the ploughshare in the ground and his furrows straight.

Earlier, Florrie had helped him measure out a plot with marker sticks. She wasn't meant to do this – Father had intended Albie to work on his own – but when she was pretty sure Father was out of sight she'd run into the next field and tried to sort her little brother out. He was quite hopeless at ploughing, but that was only to be expected, because it was his first time. She remembered how she'd first done this work when she was twelve, too, and how difficult it had seemed. At that age she'd

51

been far too small to control the big, adult-sized plough, and the handles had kept slipping out of her fingers and catching her a blow under the chin. They were doing that now, to Albie; every so often she'd hear a sharp yelp from the other side of the hedge.

He wasn't being as philosophical about the job as she'd hoped, either. Last time she'd run over to help he'd come to a standstill and been staring at the ground, his head in his hands. If it hadn't been raining she might have thought there were tears on his face – which was odd, because Albie never cried. Perhaps he wasn't feeling well. He'd been complaining on and off for the last few days, saying that his bones ached, and that his throat was sore, but since he'd still kept walking about and eating heartily no one had taken much notice. And then yesterday he'd come back pale and sleepy from school and climbed on to the old settle by the fire, and just lain there silently until evening tea.

Florrie had done his milking for him, and Mother had given him some elderflower wine, and even Father had been concerned. But this morning, a Saturday, Albie had seemed his usual self again. He'd crept downstairs before anyone else, eaten half a loaf of bread, spilt a jug of buttermilk, and been curled on the hearth, teasing the dog, when the others got up. So Father had lost his temper, and sent him out to try his hand at ploughing.

Florrie didn't think it was a good day for any kind of work, let alone mastering a complicated skill. It was what Aunt Louisa called 'boil-growing weather': damp, cold, and thoroughly dispiriting. Wrapping her piece of sacking more tightly round her head, Florrie bent down again over the rows of mangolds, and tried to make the job more bearable by daydreaming. Up until a week ago she'd passed times like this pleasantly enough by thinking about the stranger in the wood. She'd puzzled over that encounter so often that her memory of it had changed altogether. The stranger's face had grown softer and more handsome, and the rude remarks he'd made had become far less important than two details she constantly relived: the feel of his hand, warm, dry – with that strange accompanying tremor which had shaken her body – and the wonder of finding herself in possession of such a large amount of money.

And then he'd visited the farm. It had happened a week ago, before the rains began. Back then, October was just merging with November, and you could almost swear it was still the end of summer, or at least autumn. There'd been plenty of deep yellow sunlight, and although the air was cold it had had no damp in it: washing had flapped dry quickly on the line, and the hens had still been laying.

She'd been chopping wood outside the house when she'd seen a movement at the top of the lane. Two men had been coming down, one small and leathery-looking and on foot, the other blond, riding a bay horse. Florrie had run to the cowshed to call Father, then washed at the pump, dodging into the back kitchen to glance at herself in the jagged scrap of mirror that hung there for the men to shave in. Her face had gazed back at her with a shy smile, looking, to her eyes, ridiculously plump and pink, her hair hanging round it in a thick golden-brown haze. She'd wiped her hands dry on her skirt, swallowed, and walked back round the side of the house. The small jockey-like man had disappeared with Father by then; she'd heard their voices coming from the stable.

The stranger had been sitting on his horse by the gate, his back to her. She'd seen his breath, and his horse's, floating up through the cold air like wisps of cloud. His horse had stamped, and shifted position, and his hand, dressed in a black leather glove, had pulled at the reins to restrain the animal, but with not enough authority. It had been obvious the animal was thinking about nibbling at the long grass by the bank, and if Florrie'd been on its back, she'd have reined it in so tightly

that the idea of eating would have skipped its mind altogether.
But the stranger had done nothing, and after a minute or two
the horse had shaken its head, leaned forward, and begun
pulling greedily at the grass. Florrie had crept a little closer.
The stranger still hadn't noticed her. He'd been wearing a suit
made of a black fabric that glittered faintly in the sun; against
it his hair had looked more golden than before.

Reaching her pile of logs, Florrie had climbed on the
chopping-block for a better view, quite amazed that the stranger
had no sense of being watched. She could never have gazed at
either of her two brothers for this long without them turning
round and catching her at it; but maybe, she'd thought, the
gentry's instincts that way were more blunted. At that instant
the stranger had turned round, not with a sudden reflex, but in
a lazily controlled manner, as if he'd been aware of her presence
all along but not chosen, until then, to acknowledge it.

As their eyes met he'd raised his eyebrows slightly. His
face had looked the way it had in her daydreams – this time
she hadn't noticed any harsh lines from the nose to the edges
of the mouth; she'd been struck, far more, by its physical
perfection. It was so finely proportioned – it was like a statue's
face, or a doll's: the wide, steady eyes, the straight nose, the
white skin. He'd smiled at her, too, a proper smile that held a
mixture of sweetness and wickedness.

'So this is where you live?' he'd asked, his tone amused, as
if he thought there was something comical about the farm.

For an instant, Florrie'd wondered whether she ought to
curtsy. Father would have liked her to, she knew. But she'd
sensed, in some odd way, that the stranger wouldn't think much
of her if she did. Instead, she'd straightened her back and
answered boldly, 'Yes, I lives here all right. Have done ever
since I were six month old. It's a wonderful place.'

'I can see it is. Especially the roof.' The stranger'd pointed
with his whip at the thatch; the left-hand side, where it was

black with mould and sagged like a badly risen cake.

'Oh, that's not our fault,' Florrie had countered quickly. 'It's the landlord's. He won't patch it. Besides, it don't let in the rain too bad.'

The sun, coming through the bare trees, had struck the stranger's head, making his hair blaze like a halo. He'd seemed in a different mood from the last time she'd met him: merrier and more relaxed.

'Is he a good landlord?' he'd asked.

It was an odd question, Florrie'd thought. What was it to him? Still, she'd answered as truthfully as she could. 'Is any of them good? At least he leaves us be, and last Michaelmas only made Father pay a half-rent. Mind you, even that was hard enough to find.' As she'd become absorbed in speaking, Florrie had begun to illustrate her words the way she always did, with vigorous movements of her arms and body. This time, the stranger had made her feel not uncomfortably self-conscious, but enjoyably so. It was as if she was on a stage, in a spotlight. She was suddenly aware, as never before in her life, of her own delicacy and prettiness: the slimness of her waist, the curve of her skirt, the roundness of her arms.

'Our landlord, he come round here, and he looks at they fowls over there, and he says: "Can't you sell the eggs from that lot to make up the difference?" And Father, he says: "If I could it'd be a flaming miracle, 'cos most of they's cockerels!"' Florrie had laughed heartily at the finish of this anecdote. She'd heard it related many times to friends and neighbours, and at each telling the company had convulsed with merriment. It improved on the original, too. In reality Father had stood stiff-faced when the landlord made his remark, and only thought up his rejoinder hours later, when the interview was safely over.

It was odd, but the stranger hadn't been as amused by the tale as she'd expected. He'd tapped his whip on the palm of one glove with a thoughtful expression, and his horse had looked up, startled by the odd noise, its lips dripping with grassy saliva.

'So your father's short of money, is he?' the stranger had said. It hadn't really been a question. There'd been a disturbing note of pleasure in his voice.

Wishing she'd never brought up the story about the cockerels, Florrie had said hastily, 'Money's always tight on a farm. It don't mean nothing.'

'That's not true. Money can mean a great deal,' he'd answered. His voice had taken on that smoky, caressing quality she remembered so well from the wood, and he'd added slowly: 'For instance, I bet you'd like a pretty dress, wouldn't you?' He'd leaned forward to say this, his head dipping out of the beam of sunlight so that the colour of his hair had changed, becoming whiter and colder.

Florrie had stared back at him, almost hypnotized. She would, indeed, have liked a pretty dress; she liked the stranger, too; but the hairs on the back of her neck had prickled up with apprehension. She'd sensed that he was dangerous – she'd even enjoyed that feeling of imminent peril – but she'd known, too, that she had to draw back. So she'd doubled her hands into fists and planted them firmly on her hips, the way Mother did when she was seeing off a cheap-jack.

'No, I wouldn't,' she'd answered. 'I got plenty of fine clothes already. Of course,' she'd added, trying to make the lie more convincing, 'I never wears them for work. Just when I goes to church.'

The stranger had looked at her with a mixture of surprise and amusement, and it was at that moment that his groom had reappeared, trotting round the corner of the stable on the gelding. The two of them had clattered up the lane towards the road, the stranger giving her a last glance before he disappeared.

* * *

Thinking about this as she pulled mangolds, Florrie kept shaking her head at her own behaviour, which was a mistake, as the piece of sacking unwound, and rain got in her ears. Father had told her the stranger's Christian name. He was called Valentine. It was the right kind of name for him, she thought; too pretty, too girlish altogether. Just saying it made her tingle with a feeling close to embarrassment.

Father had managed to winkle all sorts of other odd bits of information out of the groom, too. The stranger was a baronet; he and his mother had bought Earlshay – and staffed the place with the ugliest women in all Devonshire. He had a lot of money too, all made by his father, who'd supplied tinned meat to the soldiers in the war. 'And they do say,' Florrie'd heard Father whisper to Mother later in a scandalized tone, 'that the beef in those there tins weren't altogether what it should have been.'

The sky had grown dark, and a stronger gust of rain hissed into the ground beside Florrie. She stood on tiptoe and tried to catch a glimpse of Albie in the next field. She couldn't see him, only the two horses, Smart and Violet. They were standing with their heads down, either lost in thought or asleep. It didn't look as if they'd moved for hours.

She scrambled through the hedge, hearing, all around her, a continuous rippling, trickling noise as water streamed off the wet land into drains and ditches.

'Albie!' she shouted, but there was no answer. When she reached the horses she saw that the plough had fallen over and embedded itself deeply in the earth. It made her smile to see the mess her brother had made of his work: the ground looked as if a dog had been growling and biting at it, leaving jagged rolls of turf spread about. She glanced round, puzzled. Surely she'd have seen Albie if he'd left to go home? It was growing darker all the time; behind her she heard the horses shake their harness. Albie could be anywhere in the field. It was the biggest Father had, ten acres, and in this light the hedges around it looked vast and smudgy.

She began walking slowly along, peering into each ditch and bush she passed, and after about five minutes the rain stopped. Somewhere in the dripping damp that followed Florrie heard a cough. It could have been made by a sheep, but she didn't think it had. Its tone was soft and bubbly, and it ended with a faint whooping noise. She waited for another, and followed the sound, and almost at once found Albie. He'd wrapped himself up tightly in his coat and lain down beside the hedge. He was muddy and wet, but what bothered Florrie most was his lassitude. He didn't move when she bent down to look at him, and his eyes stayed shut. She picked him up with difficulty, and he was so heavy he nearly slipped out of her grasp. She shifted him upwards so that his head was lying against her neck, and began stumbling back home, his face hot against her skin. She could tell his eyes were opening by their flutter, and a few steps further on his arms began to move, and he wrapped them tightly round her neck, the way he used to years ago, when he was a baby and she'd carried him around for the fun of it.

Seven

Florrie touched Albie's hand. His skin felt cooler now he was asleep, but his breathing was odd. He kept taking in sudden harsh gasps of air and letting them out with an almost imperceptible sigh. She was lying in bed beside him; Joe was away at the moment, looking for labouring work, and she hadn't liked the idea of Albie sleeping alone, not after finding him in the hedge that afternoon.

She'd brought him back and put him straight to bed, and Mother had bustled round with bowls of stew and cups of hot milk, none of which he'd touched. He'd said they hurt his throat, and that all he wanted to do was rest. At six o'clock Florrie had come upstairs and slipped in beside him. He'd looked better then: his skin had been pinker, and his breathing normal, and she'd almost believed what Father had said, that Albie was only suffering from a bit of a cold.

She'd lain here ever since, dreamily looking round at the familiar room. She'd slept here with Albie and Joe until she was ten, and Mother had decided she was too old to sleep with boys, and she'd forgotten, until this moment, how the old feather bed smelt – it reminded her of a full hen-house when you walk past it in the dark – a warm, comforting aroma of companionable bodies pressed tight together, plumage, and the faintest drop of pee. (The pee was left over from when Albie was four, and used to wet the bed.) The ceiling sagged, and was blotched with mysterious stains, and when all three of them used to lie here together, Joe would claim that a huge bear had fallen asleep above them, and it was his hairy body which was pressing the plaster down.

Joe had liked the idea of being surrounded by menacing, alien bodies. There was an old fireplace in the room, too, its flue stuffed up with newspaper to prevent soot and jackdaws from falling down, and in windy weather it used to make a rustling noise, and Joe would say that there was a man hiding in the chimney upside-down, and that at any moment he'd push his head through the paper and grin at them. Florrie had been scared of that fireplace for years.

There was a rattle downstairs, as the fire was riddled with a poker, and she heard Mother say quietly in the kitchen below, 'He's not well, Albion isn't. Not well at all.'

'I'll see to it,' Father's voice replied. 'Don't fuss yourself.'

Listening carefully, Florrie thought that Father sounded annoyed. He'd said the words too heavily for real good nature. She could imagine the scene down there: Mother would be sitting beside the fire, mending, and Father would be at the table, clutching the remains of the loaf of bread to his waistcoat and cutting small triangles off its crust with a clasp knife, his fat thumb guiding the blade. He liked to pass his time in the evenings absent-mindedly eating bread. Mother disapproved of this dreamy consumption of valuable resources – her head would keep twitching as she darned, and occasionally she'd frown at the loaf, but she never said a word about it to Father. It always surprised Florrie that Mother, who was so fearlessly tough where her children, neighbours, or any stray tramps were concerned, should be so tentative when it came to getting Father to do what she wanted. It wasn't exactly that Mother was frightened of Father. It was more as if she didn't feel able to challenge him straight on, but had to go a circuitous route.

The fire crackled to itself, and the dog gave a long, sad sigh, and for a while all Florrie could hear was Father masticating his bread, bits of crust getting caught behind his false teeth and having to be worked out again with a wet kissing noise. It was odd, somehow, lying down and listening to these intimate sounds, and not seeing the creatures that made them. It was as if, Florrie thought, she was ill, too, like Albie: the noises had the unreal quality of snatches of conversation heard through a troubled dream, or the darkness of a headache.

'Will the doctor be in now?' Mother asked suddenly. 'I can't never seem to recall his hours proper.'

'You don't want to bother he, night-times.' Father's voice went blurry from a fresh piece of crust. 'No. I'll saddle up Violet come the morning, if the lad's not better. But he will be. It's only a passing fever, and he've always been pusky.'

'It's his breath I don't like.' Mother's voice seemed to dart and flicker like the candle that stood beside the bed, its flame attacked by gusts of air from the cracked windowpane. 'I hate the way it pains him. I won't rest easy till he's seen the doctor. I *can't* rest easy.'

There was a clatter from below, and the spindles of Father's chair groaned in protest. Florrie guessed that he'd dropped his knife and leaned back to look at Mother. Often, when he was trying to defeat her in the gentle disagreements they had – they were hardly arguments, since Mother never fought head-on, but skirmished from the sides – he'd clinch the matter by tipping back his chair and smiling at her in a particular way: boyish and exaggeratedly charming. Florrie and her brothers couldn't bear to watch him when he did it, but it nearly always worked with Mother.

It didn't this time, though. There was the sound of a chair slamming back on all four legs, and Father said angrily, 'Damn it all, Sheena! You'm always the one says we can't afford this and we can't afford that. I'll saddle up and go now if that's what you want. Is that what you want?'

Florrie raised herself up in the bed expectantly. Any minute she expected to hear the front door open, footsteps in the yard, and the jingle of harness being thrown over Violet. She glanced sideways at Albie and was almost disappointed that he didn't look worse. But the noises she was anticipating didn't happen. There was a low murmur from Mother, more a cooing noise than distinguishable words, matched by an equally soft reply from Father, and the next thing Florrie knew she was opening her eyes sleepily to see Mother, a faint smile on her face and her hair in two slender plaits, kiss Albie on the forehead and blow out the candle.

The wind rose in the night. It whistled against the side of the house and blew open the bedroom window with a bang. Florrie sat up and fought to close it again, feeling frozen. It wasn't surprising she was cold: Albie had taken all the blankets and covers and rolled himself up in a ball. He was right the other side of the bed, tossing about and making the wooden frame creak. He was giving odd, jerky snores, too. Florrie pushed at him crossly to make him stop, but he wouldn't. She tried tugging at the blankets, but they were so tightly cocooned around his body that she couldn't work them free in the dark.

So she got out of bed, lit the candle, and climbed wearily on top of the great mound of bedclothes that hid her brother. Inside, she could hear him whiffling and snorting like one of his pigs. She started to unwrap him, and the more frenzied he grew, the more covers she pulled off. The last sheet to come away was as moist and hot as a pudding-cloth, and the sight that met her eyes terrified her. For a moment she scarcely recognized her brother. His face seemed to have gone grey, his eyes were half-open and glittered silver in the light, and he was throwing himself violently from side to side in a kind of agony, his whole body stretched taut, his head tipped right back as far as it could go. From his mouth came a hoarse snoring sound, which no longer sounded comical, but appalling.

Without thinking she seized him round the waist and pulled him into a sitting position, dragging pillows and blankets behind his back to keep him upright. She worked by instinct alone, but it did seem to do him good: the terrifying noise stopped, he relaxed, and when she held the candle closer she noticed that his skin had gone a more natural colour. He opened his mouth and coughed with that whooping noise she'd noticed out in the field. She watched anxiously, remembering how, when he was smaller, he'd sometimes seem as if he was having a fit, trying to breathe. He'd get it specially badly in the summers, when they were out in the hayfields, but she'd thought he'd grown out of that by now.

'My throat hurts,' he whispered. She pulled the remains of the bedclothes round him to keep him warm and, finding a cup of water on the chair beside the bed, offered it to him. He was eager to drink, but winced at the first mouthful and pushed the cup away. A tear rolled down one of his cheeks, and she rubbed his back through the nightshirt, making small, soothing circles.

'Can you get your breath?' she asked. He nodded, and she ran to fetch her parents.

It was Mother's opinion that Albie had the croup, so while Father hurriedly dressed and saddled up the horse, Florrie and Mother carried Albie down to the kitchen, where they put him on the settle in a huddle of blankets. Every pot and kettle was set on the fire to boil water and fill the room with steam, and Mother found her precious bottle of ipecacuanha. She dropped tiny amounts down Albie's throat to make him cough and keep his air passages open.

As the night wore on they took it in turns: one would hold Albie while the other went outside to fetch more firewood and water, and watch for Father's return. The steam and the medicine did make Albie more comfortable. He still breathed harshly, but he didn't brace himself so much before he took each mouthful, and when he coughed it was with a loose, wet ripple. The ipecac ran out while Mother had gone, and Florrie sat beside her brother, trying to hold him in the path of the fresh steam that rolled out from the fire.

'I's scared for my pigs,' he said suddenly, his voice faint and hoarse.

'What about them?'

'Who's going to mind them if I's took bad?'

Florrie sighed. 'I'll do it.'

Minding Albie's pigs was no easy task. It was a major one, involving at least two hours' labour a day. He'd got them back in the summer, when he and Florrie and Mother had gone on a Sunday visit to Aunt Louisa at Poffit. She was housekeeper at the vicarage there and, while the two women talked in the kitchen, Albie and Florrie had wandered round the gardens and into a farmyard so small and clean that it had looked more like a toy than a real workplace. A sow had recently farrowed, and they'd peered over the top of the sty and watched the ten little piglets playing. Florrie had enjoyed the fights: the way the piglets had pushed head-on against each other's shoulders, getting so inflamed by the contest that they broke into a miniature frenzy of aggression, and began biting and snapping at each other's tiny pink ears. When she'd turned round she'd discovered that Albie had removed a loose brick from the side of the sty, and was squatting down, trying to lure the two runts of the litter – what they called the 'nissletripes' – out through the gap. He'd sprinkled bits of the sweet biscuit Aunt Louisa had given him on the ground, just out of range of an inquisitive snout, and waited until the two nissletripes came questing through. They were dreamier than the other piglets. Where the plump, tough ones fought each other for entertainment, stopping the instant the sow lay down, in order to be first at a teat, the nissletripes tended to wander off on their own, lost in thought. This made them easy to catch. The vicar had found Albie with the nissletripes up his jumper, and offered to sell them to him for five shillings the pair.

The kettle had boiled dry. Florrie stretched out and shifted it off the heat, looking round anxiously at the kitchen door. Mother was taking a long time. She must have walked up to the main road. Albie inhaled another agonized breath and his face contorted. Florrie clasped him more tightly in her arms, hearing the green metal clock on the mantelpiece click as its hands reached three o'clock; she couldn't see the thin hand, because the glass dial was too misted over with steam, but the fat one was just visible.

As she sat there she remembered how Albie's two nissletripes had thrived in an old lean-to beside the stable. At first they'd been fed on ground barley and buttermilk, but as times became harder and the pigs larger, these supplies had dwindled in importance. Instead, Albie had got into the habit of cutting bagfuls of fresh green food from the hillsides each morning and evening, and supplementing this with swill he begged from the few big houses on the outskirts of the village. It was strange how the pigs had transformed Albie's attitude to farming. He'd always been an absent-minded, careless boy, who tried to weasel out of the chores he was given each day, but the pigs had changed that; they'd sharpened his interest, made him suddenly see the value of hard work.

Another pan boiled dry, and the air in the kitchen was starting to clear. Albie was aware of the difference: his whole body tensed this time, as he sucked in a breath, and Florrie could feel him bend back like a bow in her arms. He began a series of coughs, each more violent than the last – it was as if he was trying to expel a great wet cloth that half came up with each convulsion, only to settle back against his throat. Eventually he stopped, but more from fatigue than because the obstruction had cleared. Florrie's back and arms were numb from holding him, but she didn't dare put him down to fetch more water; she thought he might convulse and fall off the settle if she did. She wished, above all, that Mother would return. She didn't think she'd ever spent so much time alone with Albie, in such close quarters. She was beginning to be aware, too, of an odd, disagreeable smell whenever his mouth came near her face. His breath stank the way the dog's did, after a dinner of lamb's testicles. But it seemed wicked to even think such a thing, when her brother was so ill.

The door flew open, and Mother came in, a bucket of water in one hand and a bundle of sticks in the other.

'I don't know where your father's to,' she said cheerfully, stirring up the fire and pouring water into pans and kettles. 'I been right up the village and beyond, and there ain't a whisker of him.'

'What did the doctor say?'

'He weren't there, neither.'

Mother poked the sticks into a blaze, and shifted the kettle above the hottest part. As she stooped, the back of her coat swept near the settle, and Florrie could feel the coolness of the night air. It still clung somewhere on the fabric.

'His windows is all lit up,' Mother went on, 'but there's no one home. It's queer.' She rubbed her fingers and smiled at Florrie. 'Cheer up, my bird,' she said. 'Father'll be back in no time, and Albie's had trouble with his breath before now and come to no harm.'

Florrie gave her the empty bottle of ipecac – it was hard to lift her hand that high, because Albie had fallen asleep across her lap and was snoring with his mouth open. 'It's all gone,' she said. 'And I reckon he's worse.'

Mother pushed on to the settle beside her and opened her

66

arms. 'Give him here,' she answered. 'You deserve a rest.'
Florrie leaned her head against Mother's capable bulk and shut
her eyes. It was good not to be in charge any more. Sometimes,
when work was hard, or circumstances especially difficult,
she did long to be a little girl again. She felt Mother pull Albie
out of her grasp, and heard her say in a sad voice, 'Cor, ain't
you ever bad? Poor little soul.' When she looked up sleepily
she saw a look of anguish and disbelief on her mother's face.
Mother turned to her and whispered, quite horrified, 'There's
fur in his throat.'

'Can't be.'

Albie was so pale against the blackness of Mother's dress –
white nightshirt, white arms, white legs, and bluish-white face
– and there was so much steam coiling around him from the
fire, that the scene was like a Victorian print. Florrie got to her
feet and leaned over her brother. 'Where?' she asked.

Mother held the top of Albie's head steady with one large
hand, and pulled down his jaw with the other. It was true. For
a moment Florrie could have sworn she saw a thick greyness
moving in his throat. Then he swallowed and twisted away.

'You'd best go,' Mother said. 'See if you can't hurry them
along.'

Running up the lane, Florrie felt a terrible uncertainty about
what to do. Should she try and fetch Aunt Louisa, or maybe
Joe, or should she just run to the village? The trees either side
of her creaked and groaned in the wind, and a thin moon had
come out; by its light she could make out the two grassy lines
that ran up the middle of the lane, showing up black against
the paler stone. Father had once seen a ghost here, when he
was checking ewes in the middle of the night. It had been the
ghost of a working man, a thin, stooped fellow with a cap on
his head, and it had leaned on the stile and watched him in a
friendly way. Father claimed he hadn't been at all frightened,

but just *thinking* about the story now gave Florrie the shivers. She ran faster. She could hear the wind wail out here; it was doing it in a queerly regular, musical fashion.

As she reached the crossroads leading to the village the wind swooped on her skirts and blew them out in front of her like a sail. She could see a figure approaching. It wasn't Father, it was walking too bouncily for him, and it had a cap on its head. For a wild moment she thought it might be the ghost, but it was whistling a hymn tune and slashing at the hedges with a stick, and she didn't think ghosts ever did either of those things.

'Why, it's Florrie!' the figure said in a pleased voice, and she realized, with a sinking of the heart, that it was Samuel.

Eight

Returning to the farm, Florrie dreaded opening the front door. She couldn't see through the kitchen window, it was so steamed up, and the light from the fire glowed only faintly behind it. Samuel was standing beside her, far too close for comfort. When she'd met him on the road she'd tried to have only the swiftest of conversations with him, meaning to hurry on and find the doctor, but he'd obstructed and delayed her. He'd wanted to know why she was on the road at such a peculiar hour, and then every detail of Albie's illness.

It had annoyed her intensely, the sight of him standing in the way, his arms dangling like an ape's – his stick forgotten in the fingers of his right hand – a lock of hair falling into his eyes. She'd wished that he could just let her pass by; why did he have to be so slow and intense, and ask so many questions? When she'd protested, he'd said that he'd just walked past the doctor's house himself, and the place was deserted, so there was no point in going there.

Hearing this, Florrie had rolled her eyes with vexation, and begun to describe Albie's symptoms more thoroughly, showing her irritation by using a monotonous, singsong voice. Samuel had listened with total, silent attention. He'd hardly blinked. It had made a sharp contrast with the restlessness of his clothes, which had fluttered constantly in the wind, dancing a wild polka with Florrie's skirt and coat. When she'd got to the bit about Albie's disagreeable breath, and the grey furry stuff

69

Mother'd seen, Samuel had suddenly pushed her aside and begun running to the farm, and she'd had to sprint her fastest to get there first.

'I don't know what Mother'll say,' she warned, as she opened the door.

The heat and damp inside was intense. The very air in the room had become as intrusive as another human being. It pushed against Florrie's skin, touching her hair with clammy fingers, and forced itself down her throat when she drew breath. It carried a sweet, decayed smell, too, a distant cousin of what she'd noticed when Albie had been in her arms.

Her mother didn't turn round as they entered. Through the rolling mist of vapour that came out from the fire Florrie could just see the back of the settle, Mother's bolster-like body sitting in the nearest corner. One damp plait stuck out at an angle from her head, giving her a childish look.

It had always amused Florrie to observe the remnants of youth that hung about the older women in her life. It wasn't just plaits, ringlets and ribbons, and queer, leftover cravings for cheap fairings and sweets – it was their names, too. It seemed bizarre to her that a stout person like her aunt, who resembled nothing so much as an elderly monk, should still retain a pretty, girlish name like Louisa. And Sheena, even the word 'Mother', seemed, at this moment, equally inappropriate for the grim, bulky figure facing the fire.

Mother was sitting so straight because she was holding Albie. He was half-sitting, half-lying, in her lap, and though her arms were around him he appeared unaware of her, lost in a private storm of agony. He was throwing himself from side to side, his head back, his eyes half-closed, his mouth wide open. His upper half looked more swollen than before, especially the neck, which had grown solid and bull-like. His face was dark with effort, the lips – even parts of the skin – a leaden, bluish colour, the eyes watery and inflamed.

Mother sensed Florrie beside her and moved her head. 'Is it the doctor?' she asked eagerly.

'No. It's Samuel.'

'What use is he?'

Her tone was sorrowful, and as she spoke Albie launched into a series of retching coughs, seizing at the black cloth of her blouse, and hauling himself up with a desperate ferocity, as if he thought the air would be easier to breathe if he could only get himself a little higher. His coughs were growing more stifled when Florrie heard a noise behind her in the kitchen. It sounded like someone opening the drawer in the side of the table and rummaging among the rolling pins and old metal spoons that were kept there – only it couldn't be. Then Samuel shoved past her and dropped two things into the nearest cooking-pot with a splash. She recoiled from the scalding water, and he crouched down in front of Mother and Albie, pushing the fringe out of his eyes with the back of one hand. His hair had already gone wet from the steam. He looked at Albie with a grave expression, his large, doe eyes wide open. He felt her brother's wrist for a few seconds, then moved his hands up to the neck, spreading his fingers to feel the swellings there. Finally he opened Albie's mouth and peered inside.

It was odd, Samuel's movements were so dignified and formal. He reminded Florrie of a child playing doctor: his actions didn't fit with his awkward, adolescent face, where his nose looked out of shape and too large, and there was downy hair on the upper lip. His hands were wrong, too: they were big and red, with ingrained dirt round the nails.

Albie didn't like the examination. He flinched from Samuel's touch, struggling even further upright, and drew in a breath that had a dreadful hoarse, cobwebby sound. His face grew darker, and his eyes bulged.

Samuel kicked the cooking-pot on the fire, so it tipped

almost completely over, but not quite, and the water it contained spilled on to the burning logs with a sharp hiss. There was a damp, mossy smell, and a huge gush of steam and smoke, and through it all Florrie, who was now leaning forward with her hand on Mother's shoulder, saw Samuel snatch a knife from the bottom of the freshly emptied pot. It was a little fat clasp knife, the same kind that Father used for trimming sheep's feet or cutting bread. Wincing at the heat of it in his right hand, and joggling it up and down, Samuel felt her little brother's neck with his left, putting one of his fingers on the Adam's apple, which was now vibrating, as Albie sucked in a rattling breath. Then he drove the point of the knife into Albie's throat, just below the lump of the voice-box.

There was a sudden mist of blood. It speckled the front of Samuel's coat and shirt in a vee and spattered in a faint band across Mother. Florrie was so shocked she couldn't speak or move, and besides, all this was happening too fast for her to be able to. Samuel felt in the pan behind him for the other thing he'd thrown in there – this time too absorbed in what he was doing to be aware of the heat – and when he came out with it Florrie almost laughed at its utter incongruity. It was Mother's old, bent pair of kitchen scissors with the blue-painted handles. He stuck the blades into the shallow hole he'd made in Albie's throat and opened them slightly, withdrawing the knife.

While this was happening Mother cast him a look of pure horror, and began to call out, 'What's you . . . ?' But she stopped, because Samuel didn't look guilty or frightened, or worried, or show any of the other feelings one might have expected. He looked pleased, instead. He rocked back on his heels and smiled up at Florrie, and the corners of his eyes sparkled. He looked as delighted as if he'd just successfully delivered a calf.

'I did it!' he said, an edge of disbelief in his voice. A small, thick stream of blood pulsed from the hole where the scissors were. The hole itself gaped black, the blood on the very edges of the wound trembling in a tiny draught. Florrie's puzzled, fascinated glance, moved from that strange sight up to Albie's face, which was now entirely, and astonishingly, transformed. The blueness had gone from his lips, his skin was becoming paler and pinker as she watched, and bit by bit all the tension was draining from the muscles of his body. His eyes closed and he turned towards Mother's breast, as if snuggling in there for a sleep. Samuel readjusted the scissors before they could fall out.

'What've you done?' Mother asked, her voice husky.

Samuel's face was bright with enthusiasm. 'I cut into his windpipe,' he said. 'See, he has this moundery stuff in his throat, and it stops him breathing? So I opened him up lower down. Proper job.'

Much later, as Florrie scrubbed at the walls of Albie's bedroom, the whitewash falling off in handfuls on the floor, she thought about Samuel's actions. It was the first time she'd ever seen him be skilful. And yet it wasn't so unusual, what he'd done. Farm people had to perform that kind of rapid, perilous surgery all the time. Father did it whenever he cured a sheep of bloat.

The sound of church bells floated in through the window as she scrubbed: first the changes, then a mournful tolling to hurry stragglers. It was wicked to be doing housework on the Sabbath, and missing a service, too, but she was only following doctor's orders. Albie's room had to be scoured, and all his bedding boiled, and the family were to isolate themselves until the doctor was certain they were free from infection. He hadn't been surprised by the appearance of the disease; apparently there had been a rash of similar cases round Poffit (one of which had called him out the night before).

Mother was downstairs rocking Albie on her knee by the

fire. He had a proper glass tube in his throat now, and the doctor had wanted to take him to hospital, but Mother hadn't allowed it. She was scared of the hospital: she was convinced children died of neglect there. However difficult it was going to be, she'd rather nurse Albie herself. The doctor had frowned over her decision. He hadn't been too impressed with Samuel's work, either; he'd delivered a stern lecture on how dangerous it was, planting knives in anyone's neck: another quarter-inch and Albie could have died.

When he'd left, Florrie had wandered outside, to where Samuel had been leaning against the gatepost. He'd got his coat and cap on, ready to go, and the dawn had been coming up grey around him, but he'd lingered, as if reluctant to leave. She'd walked over and nudged his arm, and looked up at his face, which had appeared then, in profile and in the dim light, and viewed with the knowledge that he'd almost certainly saved her brother's life, to have a certain nobility about it.

'How did you know what to do?' she'd asked.

He'd given a slight shake of the head, and swallowed; she'd seen his throat move. Other people's windpipes had had a grisly fascination after the scene in the kitchen.

'I knew it were diphtheria,' he'd said. 'I knew it when you told me his trouble up the road.'

'But cutting him? Where d'you learn that?'

There'd been a long pause before he'd replied. 'I saw a doctor do it once.'

His voice had sounded as childish as Albie's. Florrie'd had a sudden intuition about how lonely he was. 'Who did he do it to?' she'd asked gently, feeling, as she spoke, that the conversation was like stepping on an iced-up river you weren't certain of. You took a pace forward and listened for that swift rustle that meant a crack, and if it didn't come you took another.

'My sister.'

'I didn't know you had family.'

'I haven't, not now.' His voice had sounded uneven, and not knowing what to say, but moved by sympathy, she'd patted his elbow with her fingers. His hand had come up then, scratchy with calluses, and caught hold of hers. She hadn't liked to pull away at once. It would have been unkind. Besides, she'd been so tired from the sleepless night, and the drama, that she'd felt as if they were both very old, worn-out working people, friends, just watching the dawn come up together.

'The whole village catched it,' he'd said quietly. 'Nigh on all the children, that is.' He'd turned to look at Florrie, eyes bright. 'I knew the signs of it so well, you see.' He'd smiled, weakly. 'You couldn't have found yourself a greater expert if you'd walked a hundred mile.'

Ahead of them was the ten-acre field, its hedges swathed in mist, and from such a distance it wasn't difficult for Florrie to imagine that the clumps and bushes were low cottages, and that she was looking down on a whole village; a ghost village, where the children had died. She'd shivered at this vision of Samuel's past. Then a window had banged open behind her, and she'd snatched her hand away, suddenly anxious that no one should see her and Samuel together and misinterpret the situation.

'You want to watch your brother careful,' he'd said, his voice low. 'There's still a long way to go, he's not safe yet. But I'll be here if you want me. Always.'

Nine

Florrie was sitting beside her little brother, watching him, as instructed. A kettle boiled in the freshly opened fireplace, giving the air in the room a soft, moist feel. It wasn't hot, or oppressive, because the window was wide open, and Florrie could hear birds talking comfortably to each other as they settled for the night. Evening was just beginning, and it was shadowy in the bedroom. It all looked slightly unfamiliar, too, because the bed had been moved round, so it was closer to the fire, and stripped of all its usual plump, feathery eiderdowns.

Under a neater, more austere pile of blankets, Albie was lying motionless, on his back, his head turned so he could look at Florrie. He was still desperately ill: he wasn't allowed to sit upright, or even move, until the doctor was certain that his heart wasn't affected by the diphtheria. The fifteenth day after the onset of the disease was supposed to be the most dangerous, but Florrie thought he looked bad enough now, and this was barely the second day.

The tube had gone from his throat. In its place were three stitches in coarse black thread, but it hurt him to talk, so Florrie occasionally filled the silence with a random remark. She'd already mentioned how, with the window open and the fresh air in the room, she could almost imagine herself out of doors. It was like, she'd claimed, being in the leafy camp they'd once made together in a big clump of bracken on the top of the hill. (It wasn't really. The bracken camp had been filled with green

77

light, and far more interesting: there'd been all sorts of odd-shaped beetles and slugs living in it.)

Albie's eyes were half-open. They held a cloudy expression, close to self-pity. Wishing to distract him, Florrie said, 'Now, the pigs . . .' And he brightened at once.

'Well, now,' she continued, 'they was making a bit of a snortle, back along, rooting about and that, like they was wanting their victuals. I expect you heard them from up here.'

Albie made an eager movement and his mouth opened. Despite all the sleep he'd had in the last thirty-six hours there were still deep papery-grey rings under his eyes.

'So I fetches them some gorse tips, and a stack of grass from Cowbelly Lane, and a handful of cresses from old Arthur Boucher's water meadow – when he weren't looking, of course – and two of Father's best swedes, and they was quite pleased, considering.'

Albie's eyes blinked, and he gazed at her almost pleadingly, willing her to continue. Florrie searched her memory for anything else, anything at all, to say about the pigs. She wished they *had* performed an amazing and unusual stunt: vaulted their pen and tap-danced across the yard, maybe.

'One of they swedes I give them was a bit snooky. And they pushes it with their noses, and the smaller of the two – the gilt with the fair eyelashes? – her says to me, "Where's that Albie to, then? A right silly he be, not coming to visit." ' Florrie pinched her nose, to give the pig a convincingly different voice, and Albie giggled weakly.

There was a whistle from outside and, thinking it might be Joe come home at last, Florrie looked out of the window. It wasn't him; it was the postman.

Downstairs, he unpacked a great parcel from the back of his bicycle, and handed it to her with a wink.

'I thought your birthday was October,' he said.

'It is,' she answered, turning the package over. It was

wrapped in white paper, and there was no return address.

'I wonder what it could be?' the postman enquired, and Florrie, annoyed by his curiosity, and feeling another sensation – uneasy, almost afraid – said in a sharp voice, 'I'd keep my distance if I was you. There's sickness in the house. Diphtheria.'

She was gratified by his horror. When he'd gone, some instinct made her hide the parcel behind a stack of wood in the linney, and not open it at once.

Later, after tea, when Father was sitting before the fire, relaxing with a largish chunk of bread, Florrie offered to bed down the horses for the night. She picked up the parcel on her way to the stable.

Fixing the lantern to the wall, feeling apprehensive, she examined it. It was fastened with white string, the ends sealed together at the back with blobs of scarlet wax, and the address on the front was written in jet-black ink, the lettering so contrived and elegant that it resembled a series of tiny drawings. Florrie especially noticed the 'g's in 'Fightingcocks Farm', which had square heads, each with a sharp spur as decoration, and rectangular tails. Facing sternly left, they reminded her of insects – wasps, perhaps.

She guessed at once that the parcel had come from Valentine, if only because no other person of her acquaintance had access to such astonishingly clean paper. It even reminded her of him, being so white and perfect. She couldn't help being flattered, either, when she saw he'd gone to the trouble of finding out her full name: Florence Cherry May Tavender. His careful lettering made those words look uniquely feminine and flowery, and she studied them a long time, searching for an unevenness in the script, a clue to the motives of the writer, but there wasn't one.

Smart and Violet turned their heads and gazed at her sorrowfully, wondering why she didn't bed them down, so she climbed into the tallet above, and shook a quantity of hay through the open hatches above the stalls. Afterwards she brushed herself off before picking the package up again and gnawing sideways at the string. It tasted fresh and gluey – like a postage stamp.

Inside the stiff wrapping was a dove-grey box. She lifted the lid and saw there was no card or letter inside, just layers and layers of grey tissue paper, through which a paleness glowed, like a dim light. Her heart beating fast, she tore the paper away, and pulled out a dress. It was cream, trimmed with the darkest navy, the blue so deep as to be almost black. Holding it up against herself, she felt the most powerful sensation, far stronger than greed. She literally shook with longing to possess such a beautiful thing. It had a delicious perfume, too, one she'd never encountered before, but recognized at once: the scent of newness.

The style was very fashionable. (Florrie rather prided herself on her knowledge of couture. She'd spent many hours studying the fashion plates that cropped up, from time to time, on squares of newsprint in the privy.) It didn't have a waist in the expected place, but dropped to a point about a third of the way down her thighs before flaring into neat pressed pleats, each one a miracle of precision. She couldn't quite visualize how it would fit, so she pulled off her own skirt and jersey, and slipped it over her head.

She could see at once that when she wore it properly – out into the world for a smart occasion – she'd have to take off her liberty bodice, because it was visible in the V-neck of the dress, disagreeably coarse, yellowed and felty. And, of course, she'd need different trimmings: her farm boots and old wool stockings looked slightly wrong.

She twirled round, admiring the way the skirt belled out into a flower-shape. She liked the deep blue neck best. It was a sailor dress, she realized, the type of garment a wealthy child might wear; except that the cut was a little too slender, too adult.

She danced about the stable for a while, striking attitudes and piling up her hair with one hand, while the two workhorses watched her with blank astonishment. Then, longing to see what she looked like, she scrambled up on to the old metal water tank, and balanced on the rim, squinting down at her reflection. She could see only a ghostly silhouette, but even that made her seem transformed: slimmer and more delicate. When the stable door opened and her elder brother Joe came in she was delighted. An audience was almost as good as a mirror. She did a perilous curtsy.

'Do you like it?' she called.

'No.' Joe was tired and dirty, a heavy bag slung across his shoulder. He couldn't have shaved for a week. He leaned against a stall divider and lowered his bag to the floor.

'Why ever not?'

'Who give it you?' Joe pulled out a tin of tobacco, rolling himself a thin, wrinkly cigarette.

'I were sent it, by that gentleman I met in the wood.'

Joe licked his cigarette paper. He had fair, sandy eyebrows that met above his nose. He frowned at her from underneath them, his expression unfriendly; which was odd, because he was usually so sympathetic.

'What did you do for it?'

'Nothing.' Florrie was annoyed. She jumped off the tank. 'Only talked to him, polite-like, when he come to fetch his gelding.'

Joe struck a match. He didn't look at her. 'If it's all so open, and innocent and good-hearted, like you says, why ain't you trying that dress on in the house, in front of Mother?'

Florrie shrugged.

'When's you planning to wear it, hey? And what's you going to say when them nosy old pussies up the church ask you where it come from?'

Florrie folded her arms, so that she was clasping her elbows. She could feel the soft, creamy fabric under her fingers, and the sensation was almost painful. 'I love it,' she said sadly. 'It's the prettiest thing I ever had give me. And I didn't do nothing bad to get it.'

Joe nodded. He had an ugly face. It was thin, with a huge nose and crowded-up teeth, but the eyes were wonderful: green, like hers, with gold flecks floating on the surface. 'You can't keep it,' he said. 'It's like a promise, if you do.'

'A promise to see him again? I don't mind that. I like him.'

'You know what I mean.' The harshness had gone from his voice; instead he sounded weary. 'A maid can't take a present like that from a man, not if she means to keep her good name.'

'I'll make my own rules, then.'

'Not about this.' Joe pinched out the stub of his cigarette and bent down to open his bag. Inside was a dead roe deer. He stroked it with his fingers, smoothing the fur round the eye, then tightened the string and hid it again, hanging the bag behind an old coat on the wall.

'*You* don't show Mother the game you've poached,' Florrie said. 'Or the money you gets from it. Why can't I be like you, and have a secret of my own?'

''Cos,' Joe answered, catching hold of her by the shoulders and giving her a small, fierce shake, more like a strict father than a brother, ''cos you'm a maid, and it's different.'

'You always said it weren't. You swore you'd treat me the same as if I was a boy.'

'You'm older now,' he said. 'And if you don't give that dress back, I will.'

'If anything's to be done, I'll be the one to do it.' Florrie was incensed. 'You can't tell me how to behave. You ain't even here half the time. Look what happened to Albie – and who had to sort it out? Me and Samuel.'

Florrie described Albie's illness then, and Mother and

Father's behaviour, and Joe watched with a faint smile as she acted out the different parts. They leaned against the wall together, and their conversation gradually relaxed into its usual form: intimate and detailed. Joe described the odd people he'd met on the road: the sour, bewhiskered farmer's wife, who'd paid him with a Cornish pasty so tough and inedible he'd nailed it to her front door as a reproach; the team of workmen hauling raw, fresh lime from the quarry, and cooking a piglet in the middle of the pile.

As she listened to these stories, Florrie thought about Joe's attitude to the dress, mentally nibbled away at the edges of it, until his opinion didn't wound any more, but appeared reasonable. If she was honest with herself, receiving that parcel had made her feel awkward. It would be more honourable to give it back. She wouldn't send it by post, though; the postman was such a gossip that everyone in the village would get to hear of it if she did. No, she'd return it personally, leave it at Earlshay. Planning this, she enjoyed the picture it conjured up: herself as a heroine of stainless virtue. And somewhere deep in her mind an unworthy thought did surface: mightn't such behaviour make her even more attractive to Valentine?

Ten

The entrance to Earlshay was bleak and forbidding. Two great pillars stood either side of a tall, wrought-iron gate, and on top of them were set a pair of stone deer with haughty expressions. Beyond, a wide drive, edged by woods, curved into the distance.

It was a cold winter afternoon, only three weeks from Christmas. Earlier there'd been a hard frost, but since then the sun had come out. You could still see traces of ice, though, in the depths of the undergrowth. As Florrie began walking down the drive she could hear the odd twig snap, or dead leaf rustle in the trees beside her. It made her feel exposed and vulnerable, as if the wild creatures hiding there were spying on her.

When she'd set out from home over two hours ago she'd felt delighted with her appearance: she'd kept casting happy, sideways glances at the clean hair bouncing on her shoulders; and her best black blouse – softened by countless washings – had felt like silk against her skin. But now, oppressed by the trees soaring up either side of her, and the newness of the gravel on the path, it slipped into her mind that maybe, even in her Sunday best, she looked shabby and poor. She considered taking off her worn coat and hiding it under a stone, but it was too cold to do without it. Then, noticing the shadow that fluttered along beside her, she felt oddly comforted. She liked the look of her long skirt with the boots underneath; it might not be fashionable, but the shape was pretty.

The pigs had come into season this morning, perhaps

affected by the crisp weather. She'd noticed they were a bit
puffy under the tail as she'd approached with the feed bucket,
so she'd scrambled into the sty to confirm the matter, and when
she'd laid her hand on the nearest gilt, just rested her fingers
lightly on the bristly hairs above its spine, the animal had
immediately stiffened, its ears pricked with excitement. The
other one had given a strange, high bark. Albie would be
pleased, because Joe was now on his way to Aunt Louisa's, to
find out if she knew of an unrelated boar. That was Florrie's
alibi – she was supposedly accompanying Joe – but really, it
hadn't been necessary to concoct one. It being Sunday
afternoon, both her parents were dozing: Father in the kitchen,
and Mother in the chair beside Albie's bed.

A dead branch fell beside the drive with a hollow rattle,
and Florrie almost jumped. Ahead, above the tops of the trees,
she could see the grey roofs of the house. She had planned to
go up to the front door, ring the bell, and leave the dress with
whatever butler or footman answered, along with a dignified,
regretful message, but now that the moment was approaching
she wasn't sure whether she wanted to do it like that. Maybe it
would be better to go round the back, to the kitchens, and give
her package to a friendly maid.

She couldn't imagine herself talking to a butler, but it was
easy to visualize a kind country girl, who'd give her a cup of
tea and promise to pass on a few words. So she glanced round,
and seeing a faint path on her left, skipped off the drive and
began exploring the mixture of copse and shrubbery that edged
it. She enjoyed running along the low, leaf-filled alleys, almost
like ditches, and scrambling up banks where tree roots stuck
out in hoops, the earth around them eroded by rain.

As she got further from the drive she could smell the smoke
of a bonfire and, climbing a low slope, she saw ahead of her a
semicircle of dark green bushes, and in the middle a curious
statue. It was a large duck. A badly carved one, made by a

sculptor who obviously had only the vaguest idea of what a duck should look like, and it seemed to be constructed out of dark wood with a faint stripe. Curious, slightly scornful, Florrie strolled up to it, and just before she came within touching distance it turned its head, hissed angrily at her, then squatted down and crept under one of the bushes.

The dress box in one hand, Florrie got on her knees to look for the bird. It was definitely still under the bush: she could see its big webbed feet in the shadows under the leaves. Enjoyable though the woods were, this example of Earlshay livestock was far more fascinating. Wriggling on her stomach, she edged her way towards it, and though one of its feet trembled, she thought it would probably be stupid enough to keep still. Birds tended to think that if their heads were well concealed, the rest of them was invisible, too.

Slowly, Florrie inched her right hand towards the bird's feet. Then she grabbed. The creature made a tremendous honking noise, and flailed about, but it was no use, she'd got a firm grip on it. Thinking it would be easier to go forward than back, Florrie squeezed under the bush and came out quite easily the other side, with only a few twigs and feathers in her hair. Still, that didn't matter, because she had the duck, and could examine it more closely and see what kind it was.

The bird had stopped beating its wings and was emitting a series of throaty, despairing groans – much like the sound a chicken makes when you seize its legs in the dark – and Florrie was pulling the rest of her body free, when she had a strange, exposed, self-conscious feeling, and looked up, startled. Valentine was leaning against a tree a few yards away, watching her.

'Oh!' she said, releasing the bird, which immediately ran off with an ungainly, splay-footed tread, and hid itself in the undergrowth. She got to her feet and brushed her clothes down. The dress box had got a bit squashed, but was still intact.

'I were just looking at your duck,' she explained, quite unnecessarily.

'What were you planning to do to it? Wring its neck?' He said this in a sarcastic tone, but immediately smiled, so she knew he wasn't annoyed. She was so pleased to see him that she felt the skin on her face grow hot. She wanted to put her hands up, to cool it, but didn't, thinking that might call attention to her confusion.

'Oh, no,' she answered. 'I were interested. I never seen a fancy one like that before. He's shocking big. What kind is he?'

'I haven't the faintest idea.' Valentine's hands were in the pockets of an overcoat, and his hair looked longer than she remembered it, the curls looser.

'Has you many fowls?'

He shook his head, still smiling, as if he hadn't a sensible answer to that question, either.

'Well, you want to find out how many ducks you has, and keep a close eye on them, 'cos otherwise they inbreeds, and you don't want any of that. They gets this extra leg on their backs when they inbreeds, a real one, with proper webs on.' She demonstrated on herself, using her arm.

'I can't think of anything more revolting.'

'It *is* bad. But it don't seem to vex them much.'

As she was speaking he walked towards her. He moved slowly, as if restrained by shyness, and this pleased her. It made her feel curiously powerful. If he hadn't had that air of diffidence she might have been alarmed by his approach – he was so much bigger than her – and the woods were as quiet as a churchyard.

'It's no use talking to me about ducks,' he said. 'I know nothing about them, and I don't want to. But I like trees. Would you like to see mine?'

He was standing right beside her, and she nodded, unable,

for an instant, to speak. She thought he might put his arm
through hers, or touch her hand, and the thought both terrified
and excited her; but he did neither. He just began walking at a
slow, easy pace, and she fell in beside him. She tried to hide
the box in the folds of her coat. She didn't want to mention the
dress, not immediately. Besides, he'd probably seen it already
– he hadn't asked her why she was here, he must have guessed
the reason.

He began talking about the trees and bushes they were
passing, and occasionally he'd stop to touch a leaf, and she
tried to listen carefully, and study what he showed her with an
expression of interest. She *was* interested, she wasn't
pretending, but strangely, she couldn't seem to grasp the sense
of anything he said. It was almost as if he was speaking a
foreign language, or his voice was coming to her across a great
distance, because all she really noticed – and these things were
so intensely powerful that she could register nothing else, there
was no space left in her mind for other thoughts – were physical
details. The deep blue of his eyes, his intoxicating perfume,
the shape of his fingers as he turned a leaf in his hands.

Once, as they were walking down a narrow path filled with
fallen leaves that had gone soft and black, he moved
awkwardly, and for an instant his hand touched hers, and at
the feel of his skin a jolt seemed to go through her whole body.
But after that he walked further apart from her, so she thought
it couldn't have been intentional.

The smell of the bonfire grew stronger, and it seemed to
her that they were walking a wide circle, rather than gradually
approaching the house, as she had expected, but she couldn't
be sure, because she hadn't really been paying any attention
to the details of their journey.

'I like this,' he said, touching a sapling, half Florrie's height,
that had been carefully planted and staked in a clearing.
'Willow. There were willows in the garden where I grew up.

89

Mama disliked them and had them pollarded. You know what that means? They chop all the branches off and just leave the trunk. It's a kind of castration. Horrible. I'd never do it to a tree of mine.'

He paused, and looked at her with a smile on his face, an open, childish one, without a trace of sarcasm or wickedness in it. With his head at that angle all his features looked different: something about the line of the jaw and the curve of the eye reminded her oddly of a picture of the Virgin Mary she'd seen at the vicarage where Aunt Louisa worked, a painting that had come from Italy.

He caught hold of her hand in his – his fingers warm and eager – and before she'd even registered the shock he'd leaned forward and begun to kiss her. He kissed her gently on the lips, and then began to rain numerous tiny kisses on her cheeks, moving down to her throat. He opened the front of her coat, and gently undid first one button of her blouse, and then another, nibbling the skin as it was revealed. She shut her eyes, not daring to move, her arms open. She loved his kisses. Her body shook, overwhelmed by hot waves of feeling. She wanted this to go on for ever.

Then, unannounced, an image dropped into her mind: of the pigs that morning, their skins flushed, their backs stiff. She pushed her hands against Valentine's shoulders. 'No,' she said.

He kissed her on the mouth again, wetter, more deeply, and she didn't like it so much this time. She could feel the roughness of her skin where he'd shaved, and he didn't seem childish any more, or even an equal, but too strong, too powerful, a threat.

She wrenched herself away from him, breathless. Her lips felt odd, smeared out of shape. His face looked wilder, too.

'You like it,' he said. 'I can tell you do.'

She didn't deny it. She looked up at him, tormented by

opposing feelings. 'I has to go now,' she said. 'I really has. I'm sorry.'

The box had fallen to the ground. She picked it up and brushed off the worst of the mud. 'And I can't keep this dress, neither. That's why I come here today, to give it back.' It seemed to her now that everything she'd done this afternoon had been fearfully ill-advised, foolish. 'I didn't ought to have come,' she added, her voice almost tearful.

'You certainly shouldn't.' He didn't take the box, and it fell to the ground again. He looked at her coldly, his eyes narrowed, the skin of his face still pink from kissing. Watching him, she thought she saw a particular expression gather in his eyes; it was like the look that Father's old dog used to get, just before it bit you. She took a step back.

'But since you did . . .' he said, seizing her left hand. He was holding so tightly his fingers dug into her skin. She knew she only had one chance to get away, and she acted without thinking, quite on impulse. She raised her right hand and punched him on the nose. His grip slackened and she pulled free and bolted. In doing this she was only following what Joe had told her. Giving her lessons in fisticuffs, he'd instructed her always to catch any adversary off guard, and then, if possible, make a run for it.

'In a real fight,' he'd once said, his voice mocking, 'no one follows these here Marquess of Queensberry Rules. Not if they wants to keep breathing, they don't.'

She didn't look back. She just ran, quick as she could, which was fast: when they used to have races she always beat Samuel and Joe. When she'd gone a good long way into the wood she paused and listened, and crept carefully through bushes and trees, until she came to a high fence, and heard, beyond it, the rattle of a spring-wagon on the road.

She didn't feel proud of herself. She hadn't behaved decently. If Joe had seen what she'd done he'd have said she'd

91

led Valentine on, teased him. She was aware that, without intending to, she'd broken one of the rules she wanted to live by. She climbed over the fence and buttoned up her coat. Still, it didn't really matter. She'd never see Valentine again. And after all, surely no one learned anything in this life without making mistakes?

They were playing chess at a small table placed in front of the drawing-room window. Veronica was concentrating hard, determined to win, but Vallie, even though he kept glancing out at the garden, and seemed entirely distracted, had the advantage.

Sybil was near the fire, throwing lengths of silk across a sofa and examining them with her gold spectacles on, giving brief cries of exasperation and impatience.

'What's that girl doing?' Vallie asked suddenly.

'Which girl?' Veronica looked up from the chessboard, and one of the purple beads round her neck nearly knocked over a castle.

'Ruby.'

The parlourmaid was running, doubled up, across the croquet lawn. When she reached the low wall, barely knee-high, which bordered it, she ducked down and disappeared, although they could still see the top of her cap bobbing along behind the brick.

'She looks as if she's retreating across enemy territory.'

Sybil laughed from the sofa. 'I told the servants I didn't want to see them when I looked out of the windows. They rather spoil the view, don't you think?'

'It must make gardening frightfully difficult,' Veronica remarked. She made a face at Vallie; she thought Sybil was being a bit feudal. Vallie didn't look as beautiful as usual. He'd had an accident with a horse, and his nose was swollen. It gave him a dissipated expression.

'I've been meaning to ask you,' he said. 'Do you know anything about a village called Furzey Moor?'

'I should think I do! My brother's a JP and he has no end of trouble with the beastly place. It's quite unlike the other villages in the area. I mean, Kittenhole and Poffit are part of the Flay Estate, but nobody's ever owned Furzey Moor. It all belongs to small farmers and their tenants. It's fiercely independent, and full of rogues.'

'Why do you want to know about it, darling? It sounds perfectly foul.' Sybil held a piece of grey silk against the window ledge and frowned.

'Because I'm thinking of buying it,' Vallie answered.

Eleven

Whenever Florrie felt especially confused or unhappy, she'd go to the stable in the evening and climb on Smart's back. It was a wide, safe place to be, rather like lying on a small rick of hay, and it listed a little to one side, because the old workhorse, dismayed by this intrusion on his leisure hours, would shift uneasily, and stand with one back leg half-cocked. He'd go on eating, though, and Florrie would press her ear against his neck and listen to the muffled sound of his jaws as they champed at a mouthful of hay. She'd let her arms and legs dangle limply either side of his body, and try to empty her mind of everything – except, perhaps, for vague thoughts about Smart himself.

He was a steady, dignified animal, yet there was a lighter side to his character, too. One Sunday a few years ago, when Father was up the top of the lane, talking to his neighbour, Arthur Boucher, Florrie had taken one of the newspapers which Father hoarded so carefully, piling them in a corner of the feed shed, ready to be snipped into squares for the privy – and, just out of devilment, thrown it into the orchard where Smart and Violet were grazing.

Smart had looked up immediately, his ears pricked, his eyes bright with intelligence. He'd walked over to the paper and sniffed it, his investigation becoming more and more enthusiastic, until he was snuffling it wetly with his mouth. After much licking and snapping he'd managed to grip it in his teeth, and had trotted lightly round the orchard, tail held high, bapping the newspaper against the trees in his path. Excited by this noise, he'd snorted, and flailed the paper harder against the trees, shaking his head vigorously from side to side. Bap bap bap, he'd gone, in a positive frenzy of pleasure, until he was surrounded by a flurry of torn newsprint. Then he'd thrown back his head, given a high whinny of triumph, and, sinking to his knees, begun to roll from side to side on the remains of the paper, his giant hooves waving in the air, his whole stout body undulating with sinuous grace.

Florrie had watched, spellbound, until Father had come pounding down the lane, calling out, 'What ails that horse? Have he colic?'

She smiled at the memory; he was a silly horse. Mind you, she could be just as foolish herself. Lying on Smart's back, her fingers buried in his warm coat, she shuddered as she remembered her recent visit to Earlshay. She'd told no one about it. Even now, attempting to think clearly about the incident was like trying to make herself peer into the writhing innards of a wasp nest. It was hard to recall any of the pleasure and excitement; all she kept seeing, over and over again, was the cruel look on Valentine's face, and his fingertips, digging into her wrist so hard that the skin around them went white. It was almost as if she hadn't managed to escape at all. And yet she still felt, obscurely, that his bad behaviour was her fault.

It was growing dark in the stable – she hadn't lit the lamp because she didn't want anyone to know where she was – and she could hear Violet's rough tongue rasping at the bottom of the wooden trough, next to the hay rack, where Father put the hard food: rolled oats, chopped roots, or linseed cake.

Outside the open stable door, a bantam walked past, its crop puffed out. It was talking to itself, as bantams often do, in a hoarse, high-pitched little voice, as if fussily reviewing the events of its day. Turning round to look at it, Florrie wondered what it could have eaten, to feel so contented; perhaps some of the mangolds she'd prepared for the cows, or maybe it had been sipping at the pools of milk in the pigsty.

Life had changed completely since Albie's illness. Mother had devoted herself to nursing him. Night and day she sat beside his bed, coaxing him to sip tiny amounts of beef tea or junket, dosing him with medicines, washing and turning his thin body to stop it developing bedsores. While he slept she dozed and sewed beside the fire that flickered constantly under a kettle. His bedroom had become quite bright and comfortable: Mother was making a big patchwork cover to replace his favourite quilt, which had had to be burnt, and she'd taken the best parlour table lamp up there, the one with the blue leaves painted on the glass shade, which threw strange curved shadows across the ceiling, making the top half of the room as exotic as a tropical jungle. Beneath this, her bright scraps of material were scattered on the floor in front of the fire.

Mother's presence might have made Albie's room prettier, but her absence from the rest of the house was dismal. The kitchen, the stairs, her parents' bedroom, these now belonged wholly to Father, and were subjected to a rough, masculine regime. He no longer bothered to wipe his feet when he came indoors, and the floors were littered with dimpled squares of dried mud which had fallen off the soles of his boots. The kitchen fire was still lit each evening, and the lamp was trimmed, its glass rubbed with Father's handkerchief twice a day, but everything else had become grimy, sticky and damp. Pleased by this general neglect, a brown fungus, shaped like a small shelf, had begun pushing its way out of the wall of the back kitchen, and yesterday Florrie had successfully balanced a pint mug of cider on the top of it.

Father seemed almost to relish the change in the domestic arrangements. He'd bought himself a big box of his favourite food – dried salt cod – and put it on the wooden seat under the kitchen window, and he'd made an arrangement with a local baker to have a sack of stale bread delivered every fortnight. He was quite happy to live off a diet of fat bacon, rock-hard loaves, and the strange things that came out of the salt-cod box: brown and crispy, and smelling strongly of putrefied fish. Perhaps it was the increased volume of cider he drank that made this menu palatable, but Florrie missed the feminine extras that Mother's butter-money had once bought: leaf tea, sugar, currants, soft white flour, and green soap.

Mother had stopped making butter. She no longer had the time and, anyway, the carrier had refused to take it after hearing there was diphtheria in the house. Every week Father would churn some for eating in the house, and take the rest, in crude lumps, to market to sell, but he couldn't get a decent price. So a great quantity of the milk went to the pigs, and they were growing vast, with billows of wobbling fat, on this rich and plentiful diet.

Florrie had tried to take over Mother's role in the kitchen: to cook decent meals, to keep the washing up together, and scrub the floors, but Father kept obstructing her. Whenever she got the copper fired up, and began boiling the great backlog of soiled linen, he'd call her away to help with hedging or ploughing. He couldn't see the point of doing housework when there were more important jobs waiting outside. His appearance had deteriorated, too. His corduroy breeches had grown two black, greasy patches on the inside of the thighs, where the bucket splashed when he sat down to milk. Florrie didn't like to look in their direction any more.

She could have tolerated this discomfort – she loved her little brother, and was prepared to suffer for his sake – if it hadn't been for the fact that lambing had just begun. Each year she became more and more indignant at the way Father conducted this operation.

He didn't like sheep. He kept them because they were an

essential part of the ancient system of farming, as vital to the welfare of his pastures as the rotation of crops. Without sheep how could he clear the remains of his root crops before planting the corn? How could he get his wheat shoots to thicken when they first came through? The animals he really loved were his cows: he spent hours grooming their coats, planning the purchase of pedigree stock, and talking to them in a high, whimsical voice with a slight chuckle in it.

The cows got the best food on the farm; when the sheep needed feeding in winter, he grudged every mouthful. He kept forgetting to give them water, so Florrie had to fetch gallons of it from the river on her own, and when they started lambing he never had their pens ready for them on time. He wasn't cruel, or a bad farmer; he did eventually provide them with whatever they needed. He just always waited until the very last minute. But also, and this was quite obvious, he used them to play a wicked game with Florrie. Each year she'd simmer with impatience, waiting to be allowed to do some job the sheep desperately needed. She'd bite back what she longed to say to Father, until the pressure became quite unbearable, and then she'd venture some innocent comment, perhaps about it being time to give them some oats, and Father would round on her, furious, a look on his face suspiciously like enjoyment, and tell her not to nag, to leave the important decisions to him. (Then, of course, he'd delay giving the oats even longer, just to tease.)

Florrie wasn't as meek and forbearing as Mother, and she didn't respond to Father's charm. His face would mottle with anger, and he'd bang his fist on the table to silence her. (Much, Florrie thought, as a ram stamps its foot to terrify a rival. It might be a comical sight, but you know only too well that, if the stamp doesn't work, the animal will put its head down and charge.) Florrie did stand up to Father, but only so far; when he got too enraged she'd retreat into an aggrieved silence and do what he told her. And without Mother to keep the peace, their differences had been more bitter this year.

Florrie smoothed Smart's coarse mane and made a little plait of one lock, twisting it round her finger. Just as she finished, she heard a pair of boots creak, out in the yard, and slipped off the horse's back, in case it was Father. But when she went out into the cold twilight, the hedges around the farmyard coated in old snow that had gone hard in the January frosts, she saw Samuel. He was walking towards the house, and stopped when she appeared.

He looked exceptionally clean. His fringe was smoothed back with grease, the collar of his shirt spotless, his boots new. Florrie felt ashamed of her own lank, tangled hair.

'I got something to show Albie. I thought it'd please him,' he said. 'It's a bit of a poem. I saw it on the wall of the Blue Boar.' He handed Florrie a piece of paper covered in unfamiliar copperplate, adding hastily, 'I had the barmaid write it out. You know I'm no scholar.'

> 'I dreamt that I died
> And to Heaven did go.
> "Where do you come from?"
> They wanted to know.
> "I come from Furzey Moor."
> Cor! Did they stare!
> Saying, "Come right inside,
> You'm the first one from there!" '

Florrie read it through with a severe look on her face. 'Do you think it's true?' she asked.

Samuel shifted uneasily. He reminded her, all at once, of Smart: he had the same large bones and awkward dignity. 'It's only a bit of nonsense, like.'

'I meant, d'you think our village is wickeder than most?'

'Hell about no! There's plenty of good folk in Furzey Moor.'

'It's only – I were thinking of the still . . .' Somewhere, up in the woods on Silver Hill, where the gypsies lived, there was rumoured to be an illicit still. Whenever the wind was in the north she'd catch its sickly smell. 'And there's the poaching.'

'It's only food and drink after all, ain't it? Seems to me it's not much of a crime to feed yourself if you'm hungry.'

He smiled. Florrie only just noticed the movement in the gathering dark. He waited for her to speak, so at last, wearily and unwillingly, she suggested: 'You'd best come in and see Albie.'

She showed him into the house, disliking the way the kitchen looked. The fire hadn't been lit, the few bits of clothing she'd set to dry had fallen off the clothes-horse and been sat on, hairily, by the dog – and there was a half-eaten dish of bacon and eggs congealed on the table.

She didn't go up with him. Instead she went over to the hearth and began trying to lay the fire. There weren't any firing sticks, so she had to go and chop some with the axe, and when she came back in and arranged them in a neat little tepee, she discovered that the matchbox was empty.

'Flaming heck!' she said. 'Flaming heck!' She crouched in front of the fire, the empty matchbox in her hand, trembling with the pent-up frustrations of the day.

'It's all right,' Samuel said from behind her. 'I'll light it.'

'I don't need anyone to light it,' she said through gritted teeth. 'I's not a baby. I just needs a match.'

There was the sound of a match striking, and he handed her a little flame. It caught at once, and the sticks began to burn.

'What's wrong?' he asked gently.

'It's everything. The sheep's lambing, and the pens ain't ready, and the house is a mess, and Father's a right . . .' she searched for the rudest word she could think of '. . . axwaddler.'

It was curiously appropriate. It conjured up his large nose and rocking, bow-legged gait.

'He's a hard old nut, your dad.'

Samuel lit the lamp, and the room immediately looked cosier and brighter. Feeling more light-hearted, Florrie scraped the egg and bacon into the dog's dish outside the door, and set a pan on the flames to heat.

'The victuals is evil, but you're welcome to them,' she said.

Father was delighted to see Samuel when he came in, and the two of them had a long conversation about crops, and local goings-on, which Florrie found hard to follow. An enormous fatigue was overtaking her. She sat in the hard wood armchair with the padded seat, and after eating a little bread and milk, fell sound asleep at the table.

When she awoke she was in her own bed, and dawn was breaking. She got up in a panic, anxious about the sheep: she didn't trust Father to watch them properly at night, when most of the lambs were born. She found she was fully dressed, except for her boots, which had been placed neatly on the floor, and someone had tucked the poem into one of them.

Out in the farmyard someone – she suspected the same person – had rolled all the old carts out of the long shed that looked out on the orchard, and deep inside made tidy little sheep-pens out of scraps from all over the farm: odd sheets of corrugated iron, an ancient door, pieces of a bed that had lain in the nettles by the river since Florrie could remember. They'd also used up all Father's woven hurdles, lashing them together with rows of unusual knots.

Father was sitting out of the wind beside his storm lantern, half-asleep. He was better-tempered than Florrie had seen him for days.

'He's a good fellow, that Samuel of yours,' he said when he saw her. 'Knows his business.'

Florrie hurried over to look at the lambs that had been born while she was asleep, and Father got slowly to his feet, as if his rheumatism pained him.

'He had a piece of news, quite flabbergasted me, it did. You know Arthur Boucher's farm at Lower Ash? The one that's all swamp and furze? It have been sold, that's what.'

'Who'd want to buy that rotten old place?'

'It's the property of the Bandinellis now, or will be in a month or more.'

'The Bandinellis?'

'Your friend and mine, the fool with the barley-straw hair, Sir Valentine.'

Twelve

A gun fired. It sounded close, but Florrie knew it had to be at least a quarter of a mile away because, when she hopped on to one of the sheep hurdles and looked over the roof, she saw a cloud of pigeons scatter from the spinney at Lower Ash.

The noise startled a farm cat, dozing on the tiles. It raised its head, but its body remained prone. It had an exceedingly stout body at the moment, with a bulging stomach and glossy fur. All the farm cats were looking corpulent. Lambing was paradise for them: the plentiful sheep afterbirths ensured that there was more rich food laid about the farm than they could possibly eat.

Florrie jumped down again, and continued her work of cleaning lambing pens with a dung-fork, and shaking out fresh straw. In the centre of the shed was a larger holding pen where the most imminently expectant mothers were kept. There was a young ewe in there, lying on her side, and since she was a first-timer, she was groaning. The other ewes were clustered round, gazing at her with confusion, as if thinking, 'What's happening to *her*?' Florrie tried to imagine what it must be like to be a pregnant animal and not have the slightest idea what lay in store. To get more stoutly uncomfortable each day, to feel pain, to be at last helpless in the face of an overpowering need – and then to be presented with one or more strange companions, smelling uncannily familiar. She shook her head. It was a wonder animals didn't die of surprise or outrage. She'd leave the ewe half an hour longer; it was always better if they managed to give birth on their own.

A pheasant called out in panic, its throaty voice echoing across the late afternoon landscape, and there was another peppering of gunshot, the sound more ominous because she knew Valentine was causing it.

She'd seen him last Sunday, in church. He'd been sitting in one corner of the high, carved pew belonging to the Lightbush family, his hand on the arm-rest, his expression stern and unforgiving. She hadn't been able to tell if he'd noticed her; she'd been in the choirstall, hemmed in on all sides by other singers, and it was unlikely that he had, but just as a precaution she'd pulled her hair forward, on the side nearest to him, and hidden behind it as if it was a curtain. As she'd sung the hymns she'd tested her own feelings towards him, and all she'd been aware of was a numb uneasiness, like the sensation you get when you touch the scar of a deep cut, long since healed over.

She'd tried to concentrate on the sermon, gazing at the stained-glass window above the altar that showed the Crucifixion, but even that had distracted her. The damp weather had caused algae to grow on the other side of the glass, and Florrie hadn't been able to stop herself from thinking, most irreverently, that it looked as if Our Lord was growing dense black fur on his arms and legs, like a werewolf.

After the service she'd lingered a long while in the vestry, hanging up the surplices, and putting sheet music into neat piles. When there had been, finally, no further excuse for delay, she'd come out into the main body of the church and joined the last stragglers waiting to shake hands with the vicar. Most of these had been ancient, and dressed in stiff black clothes that smelt of boiled dinners, moth repellent, and damp. Old Mrs Turl, in a lace bonnet, had offered her a black peppermint ball to suck, favouring her with a crumbly brown smile, and over her shoulder, through the open door, Florrie had seen

Valentine, standing by the church gate. He'd had his back to her, and she'd noticed how he was clasping and unclasping his hands, clad in neat grey gloves. The next glimpse she'd got she'd realized, with some alarm, that he was with Colonel Lightbush, and they were both talking to her father.

Colonel Lightbush – Father's landlord – had been bending forward as he spoke, as if addressing a child, and compared to him, Father had appeared diminished. Florrie had noticed, as if for the first time, how big Father's shoulders and arms were, how grossly muscular, compared to the slightness of the rest of his body, which dwindled down to two thin legs, in a pair of cracked, much-polished boots. Beside Valentine, he'd appeared all but misshapen. And his attitude had been so humble: head bowed, fingers gripping his trilby hat at waist level. It had been a relief to Florrie when the two men had turned away, and Father had glanced back at the porch, searching for her, his back straightening, his eyes fierce.

There'd been nothing ominous about the meeting. The colonel had only been informing Father, out of courtesy, that he and Valentine intended having a rough shoot across Valentine's new property at Lower Ash the next week, and might end by pursuing some game on to Father's land. Ruffled by the encounter, Father had walked home muttering to himself, and just before they reached the farm he'd told Florrie a long and bitter anecdote about a neighbour of his, whose prize cows had got lead poisoning from being shot at (by mistake) by cack-handed gentry.

The sun was dipping lower in the sky. Florrie crouched down beside the young ewe and stroked her gently. The animal was scarcely aware of her, its panic was so great. It had stopped groaning for the moment, and was just panting deeply and regularly, its eyes clouded.

Florrie looked at her hands. They weren't clean enough. If

she was going to help the ewe she'd have to scrub them. Father never bothered with such niceties, but then the sheep didn't do so well under his care. Many died after complex births, from what Father called 'plain cussedness', but she'd always suspected might have more to do with the state of his fingernails.

She jumped out of the pen and ran round to the front of the house, towards the pump. As she did so she could hear Mother singing upstairs, in Albie's room. It was Mother's favourite, a Hebridean song about a cuckoo. Its appeal lay in the way it had been so carefully structured for a frail voice. Confined to its narrow, easy range, even an inexperienced singer could sound impressive. Florrie had sung it, with added trills, as her audition for the church choir. She guessed Albie was going to sleep now: Mother had always used it as a lullaby when they were babies. It made even Florrie feel secure and drowsy, hearing it out here, in the yard, in the early evening.

Reaching the pump, she worked at its handle, and just as the water began to pour out heard Valentine say, from behind her, 'Might a poor hunter crave a drink?'

She wasn't surprised. She'd been certain, all day, that she was going to see him, becoming more and more so each time she'd heard his gun in the distance. His voice sounded unsure, as if he wasn't convinced she was going to answer him.

She turned round, and was pleased by how different, even ordinary, he looked. His hair was hidden by a cap, his face dirty, and there was a gun over his arm and game birds hanging from his waist. He was dressed almost as her brother Joe might be – except that his brown jacket and dark breeches were far newer under their mud and grass stains than anything Joe had ever owned.

'I'll fetch a cup,' she offered.

'No need to.' He put his gun down and cupped his hands under the pump, looking up at her as he drank from them.

There was a queer intimacy about the gesture – or else it was the expression in his blue eyes, which seemed almost to glow – which half-scared her. But then she remembered that she was safe: outside her own home, with her father near by, and her mother singing upstairs. He couldn't harm her here.

'Has you had a good day, good shooting?' she asked shyly, standing well back from the pump. He wasn't skilful at drinking with his hands. He spilled more than he swallowed, and she couldn't help laughing at the sight. He smiled back.

'Fairish,' he answered. 'I liked walking through the woods. It's a pretty farm, Lower Ash.'

'It's prettier in the spring.'

'I'll look forward to it.'

She spoke carefully, eyes wide, sure that he was going to bring up what had happened last time they'd met – be angry with her for striking him, perhaps. But he didn't and, looking at him, she found it odd how she hadn't missed him one bit since their last meeting, and yet, now he was here, she felt so delighted. She did remember, though, how he'd behaved before, and she was determined to be cautious. It was as if the person who'd once walked with him at Earlshay had been a silly younger sister. She was wiser, now. If he asked her to go anywhere with him, if he even took a step towards her, she'd bolt for the house.

He seemed as determined to observe the proprieties as she was. When he'd drunk his fill, he walked a small distance away, and sat down on the low wall beside the woodshed. He unhooked the birds from his belt, as if they slightly repelled him. There were two pigeons and a woodcock.

'Would you like these?' he asked.

'If they's no good to you.'

He didn't attempt to hand them to her. He put them beside him on the wall, balancing them carefully on the mossy stone. She couldn't help noticing how his hands were only clean on the palms and insides of the fingers, where the water had fallen. The rest of them were still stained brown from the woods.

He must have sensed that she'd begun to relax, feel more at ease, because he said in the mocking voice she remembered so well: 'You can accept a present like that? A lady can accept three small corpses without compromising herself?'

She looked at the ground, confused, and then, realizing that he was watching her with wicked amusement, and wouldn't stop until she answered, she looked him straight in the eye and said firmly, 'If you'm going to talk like that, I won't take them after all.'

'I like the way you're so fierce,' he replied. 'It's a rare quality. I'm not so pleased, of course, when you attack my nose.'

'You didn't ought to have done what you did.'

'I won't again, I promise you.'

'Won't get the chance, more like.'

'Won't you trust me again? Ever?'

Florrie shook her head; but she couldn't help smiling at the same time, which spoilt the effect.

The singing stopped. 'Who's you talking to, Florrie?' Mother called out. 'Is it Samuel?'

'No. It's the new owner of Lower Ash.'

'You fetch Father, then. I won't have you talk to strangers.'

Valentine got up from the wall. 'Can I visit you again?'

Florrie shrugged.

There was a scuffle at the bedroom window above, as Mother struggled to open the catch. It almost sounded as if she was flailing her petticoats against it. 'Do you hear me, Florrie?' she called, her voice hoarse with anxiety.

Valentine paused by the gate. His voice soft, scarcely more than a whisper, he said: 'I do care for you. Truly I do.'

The ewe had given birth by the time Florrie got back to it: a big single lamb with a black head. It had come out so recently that vapour was still rising from its body. Florrie knelt down and wiped its face on her skirt, feeling inside its narrow, bony mouth for any obstruction. It had long ears, and its eyes opened and shone in its dark face like a tiny demon's. She pulled it round to show the ewe, but the poor mother hardly noticed, she was so ruffled and miserable. When pressed to, she gave the lamb a reluctant nudge, and it bleated.

All the while she was doing this: coaxing the mother to rise, testing her teats to see if the beastings – the yellowy first milk that would prevent the lamb from catching infections – was coming freely, Florrie kept hearing Valentine's whisper, over and over. It made her heart beat faster, and her hands shake.

When Valentine got back to the house Sybil was dressing for dinner. The door of her bedroom was open, so he went in and stood behind her while she tried out earrings in the mirror.

'I hope you're going to have a bath,' she said, wrinkling her nose.

'In a minute.' Their eyes met in the glass, and he kissed her on the forehead.

'Did you enjoy it? Did you like shooting?'

'I did.'

'You sound surprised.'

'I didn't expect to, but I find I've rather taken to it. It suits my devious nature. There's a definite trick to it that appeals to me: blending with one's surroundings, trying to look harmless . . . when one's taking the most fiendish aim at some little creature's heart.'

Sybil smiled maliciously, her eyes going triangular at the outer corners, like a cat's. 'Just so long as it's not housemaids you're hunting,' she said.

Thirteen

In late February, early March, Father liked to spread manure. He'd cart it out to the flat, fertile fields beside Lower Ash where he grew his corn and had his best pastures, and leave it in rows and rows of small, neat heaps. Florrie's job was to follow on behind, on foot, and knock each heap down with a fork, spreading the contents evenly over the ground. Usually it was a long, monotonous task she didn't much care for, but this year was different.

Valentine kept appearing at the boundary. He'd only come if she was alone, and he wasn't always there – she saw him perhaps twice a week – but she began to look forward to his appearances, and would go over and talk. She didn't think there was any harm in it, as they were always separated by a thick hedge or a five-barred gate.

This morning she'd plaited her hair with pink ribbon and trimmed the neck of her jersey with a scrap of lace, just in case she saw him, but it wasn't until late afternoon that she noticed a figure leaning on the gate at the bottom of the field. He was scribbling in a little book. She stuck her fork in the ground and ran over to see what he was doing.

As she got closer he shut the book abruptly, but seeming to change his mind opened it again at the beginning and held it out to her. On the first page was a picture of Father driving Smart in the tip-cart. Florrie didn't think much of the drawing of Father, but Valentine had caught Smart exactly. It was almost cruelly comic, the way he'd emphasized the contrast between Smart's haughty, aristocratic expression and worn, sway-backed body. The sketch was done with a fine black pen; Florrie touched the lines wonderingly with a finger.

'Is you an artist?' she asked.

'No.'

'What does you do, then?'

'You mean, what gainful employment do I have?'

She nodded. Valentine took back the book and tucked it in his pocket. Then he folded his arms on the top of the gate. Florrie noticed his blond moustache; it only showed when the sun caught it, or you were very close.

'None.' Valentine continued, 'I'm totally idle. A parasite on society. I just follow you around from field to field.'

Florrie giggled. Then, forcing herself to be more serious, she asked, 'Has you done any drawings of me?'

'Dozens.'

'Can I see them?'

Valentine looked at her consideringly, his eyes narrowed. She'd never noticed before how long his eyelashes were. 'Only on one condition,' he said.

'And what's that?' Florrie stepped back a pace.

'You have to put your hand in mine.' He held it out as he spoke.

Florrie shook her head.

'I won't harm you, I promise.'

'That's what you says.'

'I swear I'll stay this side of the gate.'

'You better!'

Florrie bit her lip, thinking. She wasn't convinced Valentine would be entirely harmless, even if he did keep his side of the gate; but on the other hand, she secretly liked the idea of touching him. She glanced back at the farm, but there was no sign of Father. Valentine was wearing the clothes she'd first seen when he'd gone shooting with Colonel Lightbush. They weren't as pretty as his others, but they reassured her, somehow. They made him look as if he belonged in the landscape; he no longer stood out, like a fashion plate cut from an illustrated magazine. He'd never done any hunting since that day: she hadn't heard him fire a single shot.

He'd changed in other ways, too. These last few weeks, talking to him out in the fields, he'd appeared gentler, kinder. He didn't make sarcastic remarks any more; instead, he paid her compliments. When she wasn't with him she'd remind herself: 'He cares for me. He thinks my dimples are adorable. He says my hair's the colour of spun caramel.' And these thoughts had a special resonance because he was so wealthy, and came from another world. She couldn't help believing that being admired by a baronet carried infinitely more weight than the same sentiments from an ordinary mortal.

So she stepped forward, and with a swift, awkward gesture, slipped her hand into his. His fingers closed over hers very delicately, and nothing terrible happened. He just smiled – although she had to admit that he looked a little too pleased with himself. Also, there was a certain tigerish quality to his expression, gone as soon as she'd glimpsed it.

'What did you do today?' he asked. 'This morning. Describe your whole day to me. I like to imagine what you're doing when I'm not there.'

So she described milking to him, and the way the oldest cow, a Shorthorn called Strawberry, had a faulty teat and could no longer hold all her milk in decently until her time with the bucket came round. She leaked on the floor. And how Father's dog would watch the pool of milk from his place by the door of the cowshed, one eye open a slit, his tail twitching, and not dare approach until Father was safely out of sight.

She wasn't sure that Valentine really listened. He watched her face carefully, his eyes half-closed, his mouth looking as if it was about to curl into a smile, and with one finger he traced a pattern on her wrist – the movement touching her deep inside, near her heart, and sending invisible quivers through her body – but he didn't seem to be attending to the sense of what she said. When she stopped talking he didn't immediately notice.

'What about you?' she asked, the icy wind off the fields stinging her cheeks.

'What about me?' Valentine was almost startled.

'What d'you do in the mornings?'

'Very boring. You wouldn't want to know.'

'I would, too.'

'All right, then.' He raised his eyebrows, looking suddenly older and more serious. 'I usually wake to a particular sound. A harsh rattle. I open my eyes, and do you know the first thing I see? Ruby's rump. Or backside, as you'd say. It's rather a full, heavy one, in a pretty striped dress, and she's lighting the fire in my bedroom. And when she's gone I close my eyes like this, and I imagine that you're there, beside me, and that if I move my face I'll feel your hair on the pillow.'

Florrie stepped back mock-indignantly, trying to pull her hand out of his. 'Don't talk like that. It ain't proper!'

His fingers, which had seemed to touch hers so lightly, held fast, and he pulled her towards him and kissed her on the wrist before releasing her. 'You wanted to know how I spent my mornings, didn't you?' he said.

'And where's these pictures, then, you promised to show me?'

'Oh, I'll have to bring those another day. Unless you'd like to open the gate and come with me? I think they may be in Lower Ash cottage.'

'You don't catch me twice!' Florrie was laughing.

'What makes you so certain of that?'

Back home, remembering this encounter helped keep her spirits up, because the domestic arrangements had worsened. The fat bacon they'd been eating had run out, and though Florrie had often longed to be free of the lardy, salty stuff, she had to admit she missed it strangely once it was gone. All that was left was buttermilk and bread, last year's potatoes gone soft and whiskery, and occasionally one of the slower, more absent-minded cockerels.

The cows still ate well, though. Early evenings, when she was scooping up the feed that had lain steeping for them all day – chopped mangold, molasses and chaff – she'd often find herself bolting back great handfuls of it in a passion of greed, black juice trickling down her chin. She'd have to stop herself, because she already stole some of the food to keep Smart and Violet from losing flesh. If she took too much, Father might begin to notice.

It wasn't quite dark when she got back to the kitchen, but the lamp had been lit in there, and the fire stirred into a blaze and piled with wood. The table was covered in game: mainly large, plump rabbits, but also pigeons, pheasants and snipe. It looked as if someone had laid a furry quilt across the top of it: all russets, blue-greys, and rich, spongy vermilion.

Joe was sitting in front of the fire in the wooden armchair, his hands clasping the rests. Florrie noticed at once how unnatural his attitude was. Samuel leaned uneasily against the dresser. He nodded at her when she came in. Ignoring the peculiar atmosphere, Florrie took off her coat and called out to Joe, 'Back for long?'

'Only as long as it takes.'

'As long as it takes for what?'

'To straighten you out.'

'Me? Why do I need straightening out?' Florrie picked up the nearest rabbit and began skinning it. It was typical of Joe to bring all this food in but not set any of it to cook. What did he expect to eat for his dinner? The rabbit had already been pouched, so Florrie just slipped her fingers into the cut that had been made and began easing the skin away from the flesh.

Joe turned in his chair, his face stiff with anger. 'We was over Lower Ash this afternoon, Samuel and me, reckoning the place fair game now Arthur Boucher don't own it no more.'

'Oh?' Florrie struggled to free the rabbit's legs. When she'd got them out they resembled a little red man's, wearing fluffy boots. She tried to concentrate on the rabbit, although she could sense trouble.

'What's you been playing at?' Joe asked.

She wished he hadn't chosen to talk like this in front of Samuel. She stared back at her brother, trying to ignore Samuel's long dark shape on the periphery of her vision.

'Well, excuse me,' she answered fiercely. 'I forgot that when you has a private conversation with a friend other folk feels free to creep up behind and listen.'

'A friend? That's what you calls him? Kissing and holding his hand, and talking about . . . I won't say what.'

Florrie felt hot with embarrassment at the thought of Joe and Samuel eavesdropping on her conversation with Valentine. 'It's got nothing to do with you,' she said.

'Nothing to do with me, if my sister's ruined?'

Upstairs, in Albie's room, Florrie heard Mother drop a cotton reel. It scuttered across the floor, coming to rest in a corner. Florrie had forgotten how clearly any conversation in the kitchen could be caught from above.

'Now look what you've done,' she said softly. 'And all to no purpose. I ain't done nothing I's ashamed of.'

The rest of the evening was an agony. Mother came downstairs, and Father walked in from bedding down the cows, and she had to answer a long, detailed enquiry into her conduct. She felt herself to be innocent, but all the same, it was queer how many small details she had to conceal in order to establish this truth. She had to pretend, for instance, that she'd returned the dress to Earlshay without ever seeing Valentine, and make his early behaviour sound far more benevolent than it had really been. Even so, her parents were horrified.

'But I can't see what I done that's so wrong,' Florrie wailed at one point in the cross-examination.

Mother gave her a hard look from the edge of the dresser, where she'd been running a finger along the little shelves and glancing at the dust on it, all through Father's questions. Mother was paler and fatter than before Albie's illness, but her green eyes were just as sharp.

'If he means so well,' she said, 'why'd he run off when I opened the window that time, and why do he steal round the back of the farm like a thief? Couldn't he have come up here and spoke to me and Father, asked permission decent? Samuel did.'

Florrie stood, eyes downcast, at the end of the table.

'You're not to see him again,' Father said. 'You bide at home with Albie – go on up there now. I don't care to lay eyes on you for a while.'

Up in Albie's room, Florrie gazed into the fire. Below, she could hear a rumble of conversation, but she didn't listen to it. She didn't want to hear what they were saying. The worst, the very worst bit of the whole evening had been when Joe had re-enacted her flirtatious conversation – to a grim-faced company. It was terrible how such a light, happy interlude could be used to make her feel defiled and humiliated.

Albie moved in the bed. 'How's the pigs?' he asked, in a sleepy voice.

'Fat as ticks,' Florrie murmured, and his hand searched for hers. She touched his fingers. They were so bony and small. She swallowed. 'The biggest one, she were talking yesterday about how lonely she were, in spite of having a friend. And how what she wants, more than anything, is a piglet or two.'

'She'll have that, won't she?' Albie answered.

The door creaked. Florrie didn't look up.

A bowl of bread and milk was slipped into her free hand. She didn't want to eat it. She couldn't imagine ever wanting to eat again. She knew it was Samuel standing beside her, and she felt profoundly irritated by him, by his baggy trousers and his coat with the too-tight sleeves. She hadn't glanced in his direction all evening, yet she knew exactly what he'd look like: the lank hair, the expression of patient concern. She shut her eyes, conjuring up instead a picture of Valentine smiling, his eyelashes dark gold.

There was a rustle as Samuel crouched beside her; she smelt carbolic soap. He spoke hesitantly. 'Whatever you does,' he said, 'whatever it is – and today were nothing, nothing at all – I won't stop . . . I won't ever stop feeling the same.'

She didn't move or respond, and after a while the door creaked again, and he was gone. A hot tear fell on her skirt. It was more a tear of self-pity than anything else. Samuel's words didn't register. They were too like Valentine's, and the words Valentine spoke were the ones she wanted to remember.

Fourteen

Albie only liked good-hearted stories with blissfully happy endings. It made it difficult, keeping him amused, because apart from a few fairytales, the only stories Florrie knew came from the Bible. These didn't suit at all. Albie disliked them all, for differing reasons. He hated the story of Noah's Ark, because of the entirely blameless animals that failed to get on the boat, and were drowned; he loathed hearing about Samson because Samson was blinded; and generally, he took objection to the way small boys were so frequently victimized. Why did God punish the Egyptians by killing their baby sons? Why was Herod allowed to slaughter the innocents? Albie was even incensed by the story of Moses in his little rush basket, which Florrie had always liked, because its sentimentality made her cry.

In desperation, Florrie was driven to thinking up imaginary livestock for characters in the Bible, and describing, in detail, the happy years of farming that went on before each story began, and long after it finished. David's pedigree herd of Friesian cows (which he established after defeating Goliath) was a particular favourite, though a detailed life story of each of the animals present at the birth of Christ ran it a close second. This evening she had just begun telling Albie about Joseph of Arimathea, and the smallholding he ran in the shade of Jesus's tomb.

'And what were on this smallholding?'

'Just two gilts. They was both heavy in pig,' Florrie answered, with a fatal lapse in concentration.

'Ain't you better check ours?'

'Father's doing it,' she answered. She opened the bedroom window and looked out. It had just stopped raining and the wet yard wavered in the light from the kitchen window. She heard a comfortable grunt from the sty, and wondered how Albie's two gilts were managing. She knew Father was in the kitchen because only a short while ago, while leafing through the Bible for a suitable story, she'd heard Mother say to him, in a voice full of anguish, 'Oh, Cecil, I been upstairs too long.'

Florrie couldn't begin to guess what this was about: she'd listened for a reply from Father but heard nothing beyond a gruff murmur. If he'd made a blunder, and was in trouble, she was glad. For the last couple of weeks she'd been in more or less continuous disgrace at home, and she thought it about time somebody else was picked on. The worst of it was that, although her family were treating her differently, they did it in subtle ways that were hard to challenge head-on. Father and Joe had developed an unwillingness to look her in the eye, and were always busy whenever she approached. Mother was more forgiving, but even in her Florrie sensed a core of disappointment which expressed itself in tiny slights: a pinched reluctance to return smiles, a habit of watching Florrie as she worked, as if still weighing her behaviour in the balance.

Florrie wouldn't have minded so much if she'd felt she really had sinned, but she still couldn't understand how a few caresses and a kiss could be so very wrong. It wasn't any good trying to discuss the subject, though. Whenever Florrie even mentioned Valentine, Mother assumed a look of sour distaste, like a tomcat catching wind of its rival.

Albie sat up in bed, anxious. 'Couldn't you just look at them?' he asked.

Florrie crept downstairs. To her surprise the kitchen was

empty, the door to the yard wide open. Two little leather-bound notebooks were set out on the table, their pages moving in the draught. Florrie pulled on her coat and boots and went out.

The sows were separated now; one remaining in the sty while the other was bedded down in the back of the wood-linney. Although they were used to each other, Father had thought it better to part them up for farrowing. Gilts could be unpredictable when they had their first litter: sometimes they savaged their own offspring. Florrie had even heard a grim story, from Ellis, of a gentleman farmer who went out one day to give some hot mash to a farrowing gilt and was never seen again. His leather boots and gaiters were all that remained of him.

'They was good *quality* leather, mind,' Ellis had insisted, adding, as his final comment on the story, a wondering 'Cuh!'

The sow in the sty was rearranging her nest. It was an extraordinarily messy structure, the size of a smallish bonfire. Made of straw and dried bracken, the pig had been jumbling it with her nose and pulling at the edges with her teeth for the last couple of days.

The other sow was lying down. Florrie fetched the lantern and peered into the depths of the wood-linney, and saw that the animal had successfully delivered seven piglets. They were lined up, suckling. She leaned over the piece of corrugated iron sealing off the entrance and looked to see if the sow had cleansed, but there was no sign. Father wasn't anywhere about, either, and she couldn't hear his voice in the distance, only the mournful bang of a door beyond the cowsheds.

Albic opened the bedroom window, his white nightshirt swaying behind the glass. 'What's up?' he called.

'She've had seven young. I'm stopping here. Get in before you catch your death!'

He retreated back into his bedroom, and Florrie wrapped her coat more firmly around herself and sank down, her back against the sheet of corrugated, to wait. She heard the church clock strike seven, its sound clear on the damp air, and the pig grunt every so often, her sides clenching, her back legs shifting uneasily. Nothing further happened.

Florrie's hands were getting cold. She tucked them under her arms for warmth, and at the same time saw the clearest possible image of Valentine in front of her. She could almost feel his breath on her lips. This often happened, nowadays, and she wondered whether it was caused, in any way, by him: whether, at the precise moment she received these visions, he was thinking of her, too. She rather doubted it. If he had really wanted to see her, he would surely have gone to church. She always looked for him in Colonel Lightbush's pew, but he was never there. Had he ever reappeared at the boundary with Lower Ash? – had he wondered what had happened to her?

The sow fidgeted again, her discomfort obvious. Florrie decided she'd better help. She crouched at the back of the animal, talking in a steady, reassuring tone; amiable nonsense about a dear little blossom. The pig seemed to appreciate this flattery. It wheezed with pleasure and shut the one eye that had opened suspiciously when Florrie moved position.

Florrie slipped her hand inside. It was tight in there, strong muscle gripping at her arm, wringing it painfully whenever there was a contraction. Her fingers crept through the narrow cervical opening, and she closed her eyes, the better to visualize the recesses they were exploring. She was using her left hand, too, because since she was right-handed, it was less familiar to her, and so more sensitive.

Just beyond her fingers was a tough, slimy wetness. She felt further and came across a perfect miniature foot, complete with a trotter. The other side of it, folded up tight, was a tiny plump leg and buttock. She explored until she'd found another back leg and a tail like a fleshy spring, then gripped both legs and pulled. Veils of matter wrapped themselves round her

124

fingers, the sow pushed, and a piglet slithered on to the straw. It lay motionless, its head swathed in afterbirth. Florrie cleaned it off, but it wasn't breathing. Father usually swung little creatures like this round his head to get their lungs working, but Florrie had her own, kinder method. She cradled the piglet upside-down, and holding its front legs in one hand and its back legs in the other, pushed it in and out, in and out, as if working up to play a tune on a soft pink accordion. Bubbles gathered at the edges of the piglet's nose and mouth, and it gave a sudden, explosive sneeze. She set it on the ground and it tottered, legs too wide apart, towards the sow.

As she ran across back to the house she saw her parents in the distance, in silhouette beside the cowshed. Father had his arm round Mother's waist, and they were standing motionless. It was an odd, uncharacteristic glimpse of them.

Florrie bent over Albie's bed. He'd fallen asleep waiting for her, and his eyes opened unwillingly.

'The other sow's had eight,' she whispered, feeling a sudden, tense movement against her vest.

Albie propped himself up on his elbow. 'Cor, don't you ever smell of pig?' he said, his voice sleepy. 'It's shocking strong.'

'That's because,' Florrie said, jumping on to the bed beside him, 'I've one up me jumper.' She slipped a piglet into Albie's bed, and he gave a shriek of joy and dived under the covers to get it.

After discovering this piglet asleep in Albie's nightshirt, Mother decided he was well enough to spend part of the day lying on the settle in the kitchen, and maybe an hour, well wrapped up, outdoors. Florrie fetched the old pram from the

125

back of the feed shed, and hammered away at the rusty front of it, until she managed to smash the metal down so Albie could sit inside, his legs dangling, and be pulled about the yard. After a day or two she began dragging him up the little lane that led to the signpost, and taking him on brief trips along the road.

He liked the pram, because now he was allowed up he seemed to feel weak and exhausted most of the time, and didn't enjoy walking. Florrie would pull like a horse, facing forward and tugging the handle behind her. She'd given up wearing her coat – it had fallen to tatters – and instead wrapped a couple of sacks round her shoulders, which wasn't as warm. As she walked, listening to Albie behind her, talking about the shapes of clouds, dreams he'd had, and odd ideas for games that had occurred to him – little disjointed sentences that just floated on the surface of her brain without disturbing deeper thoughts – she kept hoping she'd meet Valentine, and deliberately ended each small journey by passing along the top of the narrow lane that led to Lower Ash.

It was a week before she saw the car parked there. Shiny and green, open-topped, its seats were upholstered in pale brown leather. She didn't think it as fine as the doctor's car; that one had wonderful blinds in the windows with plush bobbles on the ends.

'Bentley Speed-Six,' Albie said, as she trundled him past. Once she was the other side of the car, Florrie could see down the lane to Lower Ash, and she stopped, because Valentine was walking up it, his hands in the pockets of a long leather coat. The lane was so overgrown that it was scarcely possible for one person to walk down the middle without being snatched at by brambles and overhanging twigs, and Valentine was walking very slowly, avoiding these snags, his movements graceful, like a subtle dance. He was lost in thought. Florrie waited for him, and when he looked up and saw her his smile made her heart lift.

'I've missed you,' he said, his expression childishly pleased. 'Who's this?' he continued, looking at Albie.

'Oh – that's my brother. Say hello to the gentleman, Albie.' Albie didn't say hello, just directed a bright, cheeky glance at Valentine, and in order to distract him and prevent him carrying tales to Mother, Florrie wheeled him to the back of the car, where he could peer at his distorted reflection in the polished nickel casing of the rear lamp.

Florrie walked to the front and rejoined Valentine. 'He've been poorly, Albie has,' she went on. 'He can't walk proper. Well, he *can* walk, but not for any distance, not without his breath going pusky.'

'You don't look well either,' Valentine said gravely. 'You're thinner.'

Florrie shrugged. 'Maybe.'

'Is that what you've been doing, looking after your brother?'

'You could say that.'

'What else could you say?' Valentine leaned against the bonnet of his car, arms folded, as if expecting a long story.

The cold wind caught Florrie and she shivered. 'I's not allowed out in the fields by Lower Ash no more.'

'And why's that?'

''Cos my family knows about you. They saw us that time, and they didn't care for it. I ain't supposed to talk to you, not ever again. They says,' she hesitated, feeling her words were going to sound ridiculous, but knowing no other way to put it, 'they says that your intentions ain't honourable.'

'That's very astute of them.'

'What's that mean? It's true what they says?'

Valentine seemed to flinch at the tone of her voice. He was silent for a while before saying, 'I'll be honest with you, Florrie. I'm not an honourable man. I do care for you – that's true – and if you'd let me, I'd look after you. But,' he shook his head almost sadly, 'not marriage.'

She lifted her chin, determined to show no sign of disappointment. Behind her eyes she could feel something horribly like tears begin to gather, but she fought them back.

'Well, what use is that?' she asked fiercely.

He stood up and took off his coat. He put it round her shoulders, his touch tender, like a mother's. The coat felt deliciously warm, lighter than Florrie had expected from such a large quantity of leather, and it smelt faintly of cigars. After making sure her hair wasn't caught inside the fur collar, Valentine took hold of the pram handle and began pulling Albie back towards the lane that led to Fightingcocks. Florrie followed, in a daze. She was totally enveloped in his coat, and hoped the hem wouldn't drag on the ground and get dirty. It reminded her of being a toddler, and dressing up in all the old work-coats with Joe, one day years ago, when Mother had left the two of them shut up in the kitchen and gone milking.

'I suppose it was wrong of me not to be honest with you from the start,' Valentine said, his words getting blown away by the wind, so that sometimes she heard only pieces of them. 'But it was like a game to me, you know. You're so pretty, and you seemed so tough, so well able to look after yourself.'

She didn't answer. She was grieved by what he was saying, but all the same, couldn't help wishing it took longer, getting from Lower Ash to Fightingcocks, pulling a small, converted pram.

'I've liked being with you,' he went on. 'And if you should ever change your mind, if circumstances ever alter, I hope you'll come and see me.'

They'd reached the top of the lane down to the farm. He turned to her and, holding her face gently in his hands, kissed her on the lips. Forgetting that Albie was present, and could tell on her, she shut her eyes, losing herself. She wished it could go on, could be more like the kisses at Earlshay, but it didn't. Valentine stopped. She felt foolish, responding so passionately to a brief, goodbye kiss, and turned away, struggling out of the coat. 'You'd best have this back,' she said.

'Keep it.'

'I can't do that. It don't even fit proper!'

There was a roar from the bottom of the lane, and Florrie turned to see her father standing there, framed by the trees. He stamped up towards them, rocking slightly from side to side, like a wicked dwarf in a fairytale.

'Hoi!' he called. 'You clear off! I've had enough of you creeping round my farm.'

Valentine didn't move. Florrie saw his face assume a familiar sarcastic expression. She was pleased he wasn't frightened by her father, but at the same time alarmed, too.

'Here, Florrie!' Father bellowed, as if she was a dog. 'Here!' He was closer now, his face dark with anger. She pulled the pram towards him. He didn't look at her, he was shouting at Valentine again.

'What's you waiting for? Bugger off!'

'I don't choose to,' Valentine answered coolly. He picked up his coat and dusted it off, taking his time about the job. 'It's entirely my affair whether I walk up and down this lane or not, and if I were you,' he fixed Father with a cold eye, its blueness making it seem more menacing, 'I'd be more careful what I said.'

'And why's that?' Father still sounded belligerent, but there was an edge of doubt in his voice.

'Because it's always a mistake to insult your betters. As you'll find out.'

Fifteen

After letting the cows out to pasture, Florrie went up to the top coppice to fill a bag with greenstuff for the pigs. The warmer weather had made the grass grow again, and everywhere the broken-down, dirty look of late winter was vanishing. This was lucky, because there wasn't much else to feed the pigs on, and with fifteen piglets suckling, the sows were ravenous. All Father's barley had run out a week ago, and Florrie was having to keep them going on cut forage and scraps begged from Aunt Louisa's vicarage. Still, she reckoned the labour worthwhile, because Albie loved the piglets so much.

He'd discovered a silly (and extremely risky) game to play with them. When he was sure that Mother and Father were safely out of sight he'd climb over the wall of the sty where all the pigs now lived in harmony. Finding a dry bit of bedding, he'd lie down on it and carefully lay out, on his arms and legs and torso, little scraps of food: crusts of bread soaked in buttermilk, apple cores, crumbled dog biscuit. Shyly, the piglets would approach him, giving tiny squeals and grunts, but fearful of tackling the upper slopes of his jersey. Then one of them, usually a stocky type Albie had christened Jacob, would recklessly spring on to Albie's stomach, and soon little pigs would be swarming all over him, catching their sharp trotters in his clothes and snuffling at his face. When Florrie asked him why he liked doing this he said it was because when he was covered in piglet he could almost imagine he was one himself. (It was roughly the same impulse that led him to press his head sideways on the ground to examine a captured slug.)

Florrie would sit on the roof of the sty with a pig-board in her hand, ready to head off any mother who suddenly went savage. But she wasn't needed: the sows seemed to regard Albie much as their offspring did – as an over-large honorary piglet – and scarcely bothered to raise their heads when he got in the sty.

As Florrie filled her bag, she saw that the first bluebells were starting to come out, just a few, among the drifts of full-blown daffodils. She loved it when the woods went that unearthly purplish-blue.

She felt cheered by the coming of spring. Everyone at home was bad-tempered or looked ill and tired; even Albie had a semicircle of spots on his forehead. It was always an unhealthy time of year, as if the winter cold and lack of sun had drained the goodness out of people – but in her family the usual symptoms had been aggravated by worry.

Florrie had discovered what Mother had cried out about, that evening back in March. It was the state of the farm account-books. While she'd been preoccupied, nursing Albie, Father had allowed himself to get into debt. It wasn't all his fault, he couldn't help the twenty-one guineas owed the doctor, or the loss of the butter-money; but it was his fondness for buying cattle feed that had run up such a big bill with the corn chandler, and they wouldn't be able to have any seeds for spring planting unless the account was settled. Worse, the quarterly rent had been due on Lady Day.

Father had tried to make light of the problem by explaining that most of these debts could be deferred. The doctor was a decent man, who knew their circumstances; Colonel Lightbush had always been reasonable about rents; and the chandler could probably be won round by a little on account. Mother wouldn't be mollified. She'd felt each penny of debt to be a stain on her integrity, and she'd turned her face away and refused to discuss the subject. Finally, in a cold rage, Father had driven all the ewes to market, along with their lambs. They hadn't made very much money – barely two pounds a couple – too many other farmers had chosen to pay their rent arrears the same way.

'Don't you come asking me how I'm to pay Midsummer's quarter now,' Father had said miserably to Mother afterwards. ''Cos I always paid that with the fat lambs and the wool clip, and now they's all gone. Finished.'

It was sad, with the sheep sold. Florrie missed them. As she left the wood she walked down through the field where they'd last grazed, and its grass was nibbled away to nothing, a litter of wool scraps and black droppings scattered across it. It still smelt of them too, making her feel they might be just around a corner, basking in the April sun.

Below her, Florrie could see the rickyard, its few remaining stacks of hay and straw grey and weatherbeaten. A black hen was hurrying between them, and Florrie stopped where she was, because she wanted to find out where the bird was laying. The light breeze caught its plumage, and it turned sideways to the wind, each ruffled feather shining green-black. The chicken was a particular favourite of the old cockerel – his dollymop – and Florrie had always noticed how the cockerels preferred their wives to be dark. It was the reverse of the human world, where men were supposed to favour fair-haired women.

The thought of courtship made Florrie frown. She hadn't seen Valentine since that last meeting in March, despite numerous small trips into the woods at Lower Ash, under the pretext of gathering pig food. Once, she'd even ventured as far as the cottage there, and found it more or less derelict, a pair of sparrows flying in through the open door and nesting in the chimney-breast. The ground around, and the path up to the road, had shown no sign of human disturbance at all.

The hen had squeezed herself through the hedge round the rickyard, and begun to walk along the edge of the field when Florrie noticed a movement in the farmyard below. A man was standing in the yard. He had a bag slung over his shoulder, and a cap on, and she had to squint into the sun before she was sure that it was Samuel and not Joe. She waved, and he waved back, and began walking up to meet her. The hen crept into the pool of shadow under a hedge and was gone, and when Florrie got closer she saw it sitting under a sweep of bramble perfectly camouflaged. Only its amber eye gave the game away.

'I was hoping I'd catch you,' Samuel said, from behind her. Florrie sat down near the hen and looked up at him. He was very muddy. His clothes were stiff with the stuff, and one leg of his trousers was torn. He dropped his bag and sat down next to her. 'I want to talk to you first, like, before I sees your mother,' he added. 'Joe've been caught poaching.'

Florrie picked a daisy from the grass beside her; the tips of its petals were deep pink. 'I don't reckon Mother'll be too vexed,' she replied calmly. 'He have been summonsed before, you know.'

'This is different altogether.' The seriousness in Samuel's voice made her turn to look at him. His face surprised her – it was much browner than she'd expected, the cheeks rosy. He looked supremely healthy; except, that is, for a fresh bruise on his forehead. 'He were over Earlshay.'

'Oh.' Florrie didn't say more. She'd learned not to have an opinion whenever any topic remotely connected with Valentine cropped up. Father was still simmering from his last encounter with the man.

'I was with Joe. We often goes out together . . .' As Samuel told his story he tried to describe the scene to Florrie. It was difficult to conjure it up on such a breezy, sunny morning: the still woodland at midnight; the house beyond the lake, all its windows mysteriously ablaze.

134

Samuel had seen the silhouette of a deer drink from the water; it had raised its head, fearful, before dipping again. He'd scanned the network of branches against the dark sky, looking for roosting pheasants.

'I favours a catapult,' he said. 'I've an aversion to noise, but Joe's a proper shooting man. He's had five birds with one bullet before now, and he likes to fix a damp lucifer-match to the foresight. It gives off a whisper of a glow, and makes the aiming easier at night. It's an old trick.

'Anyway, we'd fetched ourselves a half-dozen pheasant and a nice doe when I gets this queer feeling – uneasy.' He moved his shoulders as he spoke, and Florrie, too, could sense that itchy, uncomfortable premonition. 'I were all for going home, but Joe, he says I's imagining things, so we walks on, and we was just climbing a bank when these keepers come out of nowhere and jumps us.'

'You didn't put up a fight?' Florrie asked anxiously, looking at the bruise.

'I know better than that! Half the time they's provoking you, pretending to let you go so as they can set their dogs on you. I just do what they says, and acts obliging, but you know Joe. He gets a bit antsy and I has to hold he back something terrible.'

'So what's that, a five-pound fine?'

Samuel rubbed fiercely at his boots with a handful of dried grass, and his reluctance to look at her made Florrie ask nervously, 'Where's Joe to?'

'I were coming to that.' Samuel described how the gamekeepers had insisted on taking them back to Earlshay, saying the master of the house had left special orders. 'So we's shown into this room off the main hall while they goes and fetches him.' Samuel put down his clump of grass and examined his leg instead. The trouser wasn't too badly torn, but there was a deep graze underneath.

'It was a big room, books up the walls, and a desk, with one of they fancy electric lamps on it.' Samuel went on: 'And Joe, seeing as we was left alone, he goes up to this box on the desk and helps hisself to cigarettes, tucks them in his pockets.' Samuel smiled. 'Ain't he ever a heller, your brother? Always been wild, he have, ever since I knowed him. Trouble is, he can't control his temper. Don't want to, I reckon.

'So then the head gamekeeper, he comes back, all respectful, with that Sir Valentine. It was the first time I ever seen him close, face to face. I noticed his eyes, particular . . .'

Samuel stopped, and Florrie didn't respond. She saw she'd rolled the daisy into a tight, damp ball, and dropped it in the grass quickly.

'He looked tired of the whole game – he had this haughty look on his face – and it sounds like there's a party going on, what he's missing, music and laughing and that. And he half sits on this desk and looks at his nails, like being with us is the dullest job he can think of to do of an evening, and we says we're sorry, does a bit of bowing and scraping, what these nobby folk likes, and it's all going the way it usually do, when all of a sudden, he asks us our names. And when Joe gives *his* he brightens up, and this smile come on his face, though it weren't what I'd call a friendly one.'

Florrie could guess exactly what that smile had looked like; she could visualize Valentine, too. He'd probably have been wearing a white tie and tails, a collar at his throat like half a butterfly. She imagined waltz music in the distance, or maybe a lady warbling at a piano. She smiled to herself.

' "Joe Tavender?" he says,' Samuel went on. ' "Would that be from Fightingcocks Farm?" And when Joe says yes, he starts talking about you.'

Florrie felt herself go hot. She was sure she'd blushed. She wanted to know what Valentine had said, but Samuel didn't volunteer the information. Instead he asked, his voice sounding worried, 'What do you reckon to this Sir Valentine?'

She didn't answer at once. She glanced at the chicken instead. It was about to lay: its pupils had swollen up until they almost eclipsed the golden iris. She sensed Samuel was impatient for her answer, and she didn't know quite what to say. If she'd been talking to anyone else she wouldn't have replied at all, but she trusted Samuel not to be unkind or censorious. He was perhaps the only person to whom she could tell the truth.

'I were like you,' she said slowly. 'I didn't care for him at first. I always had this feeling, like he was just biding his time, waiting to get at me, perhaps hurt me. But I reckon I misjudged him. Because he has been good to me, and behaved decent, and he said he weren't an honourable man, but he is.'

She looked down into the rickyard, watching scraps of straw blow about in the wind. She felt she hadn't given the whole case, and she fumbled for other words, ones that wouldn't hurt Samuel's feelings, but would describe the pleasure of studying Valentine's face, the feel of his hand in hers, his tenderness at their last meeting. 'He's master handsome and all,' she added, her voice uneven.

Samuel, watching the same pieces of straw, felt a similar difficulty in framing a description. In his mind he could see the scene in that room at Earlshay. The lamp shining on the honey-coloured desk, Valentine leaning casually beside it, his bow tie at a slight angle. It was his cold expression Samuel had disliked most: you wouldn't trust a horse with eyes like that, you'd shoot it first. Also, his arrogance: Samuel had come across this particular characteristic before, but it had seemed to him, as he'd stared at his boots and mumbled insincere apologies, that Valentine was the kind of petty tyrant to relish submission for its own sake. The type to enjoy provoking people, just for the pleasure of slapping them down hard. And when he'd learned Joe's name, he'd straightened and said in a mocking tone, 'So you're the one whose sister's a bit too free with her affections?'

And, of course, Joe had hit him.

Samuel hadn't. He'd mistrusted Valentine from the start and felt the best response to him was a passive one. More important, he'd known he was lying about Florrie. Joe didn't stop to think, but when did he ever? He'd landed a terrific haymaker on Valentine's chin, knocked him right out – which Samuel couldn't help being pleased about – and he'd smashed the lamp, too, but the rest of the night was best forgotten. Joe was in a shocking state by the time the gamekeepers had finished with him, and not likely to be released on bail, either.

Florrie had looked so much happier when Valentine was mentioned that Samuel didn't like to hurt her feelings by telling her what he'd said. He'd toned down Joe's injuries, too, but he couldn't do the same to the charges.

'Assault and battery, trespass to goods, night poaching with a firearm.' He shook his head. 'There's no way Joe won't go to prison. Trouble is, he've a record, and the magistrate comes down cruel on anyone from Furzey Moor.'

'Has he seen a doctor?' Florrie asked, her face pale, but whether she meant Joe or the other fellow, Samuel couldn't be sure.

Sixteen

Florrie paced the room, restless. Out of the window she could see a corner of a formal garden, hemmed in by tall hedges: a fountain with scroll feet, a stretch of lawn that rippled in the breeze, its tips made silver by the sunlight.

She was so hot. She'd run nearly all the way here – along empty, dusty roads – talking to herself, rehearsing the arguments she was going to have to use with Valentine, to persuade him to have Joe released. She'd imagined him alternately haughty or kind, but she'd never thought he would make her wait so long, in such intimidating surroundings. The room was big, with a high ceiling, and it was dark, because it had only one window, hung with thick curtains. In one corner was a desk, and behind it, bookshelves.

She guessed this was the room that Samuel and Joe had been shown into last night. There was no lamp on the desk, only what looked like a fresh scar on the polished top. The books behind were old, their bindings gone soft and crumbly, so that they resembled, in both colour and texture, the queer little brown toads that lived beside the pump at home.

The door to the passage was open a few inches, and through it came the steady tick of a large clock, its sound severe. The whole house smelt alien: of polish, fresh paint, new fabric, and some delicate refined food – thin, dry toast, perhaps. Florrie dipped to look at herself in the brass surround of the fire. It was a roasting hot coal one, and she couldn't pause in front of it for longer than an instant, but she didn't want to; she was so disconcerted by her reflection. Her clothes looked dusty black, and the darns were far too visible. She did wish that Valentine would come. The longer she had to wait, the more doubtful she became about whether she should be here at all.

When the news of Joe's misfortune had been broken to her parents they hadn't reacted as she'd expected. She'd hoped her father would be fired with energy, would go at once to the prison or the magistrate's to see if he could sort the problem out, but instead he'd appeared totally confounded. They'd all sat in the kitchen discussing the problem, while strong sunlight poured through the open door, and hens clucked out in the yard.

Early on, Mother had fetched her best hat, and fixed it in place with two great pins, meaning to go at once and ask Louisa's advice, but she'd paused to listen to Samuel's account, and her urge to be gone had faded. Instead, she'd cleared a corner of the table, fetched a china basin, and begun baking. She always liked her hands to be occupied. It was certainly soothing to watch her strong, fat fingers form the dough, and then pinch and slap most cruelly at its elastic substance.

Samuel had said he thought Joe might be imprisoned for a year, and that he'd probably go to the Magistrates' Court on Monday, and Father had nodded in agreement, Mother giving him an anxious glance, a smudge of flour trembling on the brim of her hat.

'It wouldn't grieve me so – if it weren't for that Bandinelli fellow at the heart of it,' Father had said fiercely to Samuel. 'I hates to see him get the better of a Tavender.' Florrie had thought this might be the prelude to some daring plan to free Joe – but it hadn't been. Father'd seemed to be expressing his anger only in order to be soothed and calmed by the others.

'Ain't you going to fetch a lawyer, to speak for Joe in court?' Florrie'd asked.

'Where's the money to come from?'

'But ain't you going to fight?'

'It's foolish to fight if you've no chance of winning.'

'But how can you be certain?'

'You quiet down, Florrie, and let the men sort it out.' Mother's voice had been sharp.

All the rest of the morning, as she'd helped Mother do the Saturday clean of the kitchen – scrubbing the chairs, the top and underside of the table, and the flagstones – Florrie had burned with impatience to set things right herself. And when Mother had gone, finally, after a hurried dinner, to see Aunt Louisa, Florrie had set an extra pan of water to heat on the stove, put up the clothes-horse to act as a screen, and washed herself carefully, rinsing her hair in cold rainwater from the butt. Albie had been asleep in his room, and she'd seen Samuel and Father lean over the sty, scratching the pigs and talking, and she'd waited until their backs were turned before running out of the kitchen door and up the lane to the road, the breeze catching her damp hair and lifting it off her shoulders.

It was dry now, of course. She sat down on a strange kind of sofa by the door. It only had one arm, and was extremely tightly covered in fuzzy brown and red fabric, the back studded with darker buttons, so that it resembled the stomach of some female animal with far too many nipples.

'Veronica, darling. Can't you get Vallie to be reasonable?' Sybil enquired.

Veronica glanced across the table at Valentine. He'd eaten nothing, and was leaning back in his chair, a napkin clutched in one fist. His jaw was still a little swollen along the bone and he looked mulish and miserable.

'I don't think anyone could push Vallie into doing what he didn't want,' she said lightly – although in his present mood she thought the opposite. He was like a resentful child, and

Sybil was being more overbearing than usual.

'Oh,' Sybil laughed and patted her hair, 'Mama usually wins in the end, doesn't she, Vallie?'

'I'm not going to London.'

'But why not?' Sybil persisted. 'There's nothing to do here, and we're missing out on the most glorious parties. I've even fiddled an invitation to Miss Whigham's coming-out in Audley Square. It was so clever of me,' she went on, turning to Veronica. 'But then, of course, it's never frightfully difficult to get an invitation for a handsome young baronet with twenty thousand a year.'

'Why the devil do I have to go to these foul parties?' Valentine growled. 'Why can't I be left alone?'

'But why do you want to be? That's far more of a puzzle. I can't understand it, Veronica, he just sits indoors, brooding, day after day. He won't even go on his walks any more. It's madness.'

Anxious to keep the peace, Veronica said gently, 'I do think you'd find it more amusing in London, Vallie.'

'I'm staying here,' he said, speaking through clenched teeth. He dipped his napkin in the bowl of iced water beside him, and pressed it to his jaw, wincing. He'd been doing this all through the meal.

'Is it frightfully uncomfortable?' Sybil's enquiry would have sounded tender if it hadn't been uttered in such a syrupy, insincere tone. Veronica wished she hadn't accepted the invitation to lunch, now. She detested it when Sybil and Vallie had rows; she could never understand why Vallie was so defenceless in the face of his mother's needling.

'I hardly notice it,' Valentine lied.

'I do wish you'd see a specialist. There's the most marvellous little man in Lon—' Sybil began, but stopped, because the butler had entered the room and was standing respectfully beside Valentine's chair. It annoyed her, but the butler never seemed to treat her with the deference she expected. He tended to assume – quite wrongly – that Vallie was the head of the household.

'What is it, Bennet?' she asked, but he didn't hear. He had inclined his head and was speaking quietly to Vallie, so softly that she couldn't catch a word. Vallie nodded approval, and the butler spoke again, and then she heard Vallie say, 'Tell them to wait. I shan't be long,' his tone curt.

He put down his napkin and turned to Sybil. 'It's only some dull matter to do with a tenancy.' He stifled a yawn. 'I shall have to see it through, though.' He made no move to get up from the table.

'Can't I manage it for you, darling? Really, you shouldn't do anything too taxing this afternoon.'

'I hardly think so, Mama.'

It was peculiar, Veronica thought, how fundamentally Vallie's mood had altered. She could have sworn he'd been about to leave the room in a fury a few minutes ago, and yet here he was, smiling warmly across at her, and using a teasing tone of voice to his mother. His eyes sparkled and he pulled his chair up close to the table.

'Do you know,' he said, 'I suddenly find I have an appetite after all.'

The clock out in the passage made a peculiar noise, like someone fumbling with a parcel and dropping it, and shortly afterwards began a series of mechanical chimes, finishing by bonging a small interior gong four times. Then it relapsed back into its slow tick, sounding, this time, a trifle self-satisfied.

Far away, Florrie heard a door open, and the murmur of female voices – perhaps Valentine's mother was one of them. She waited, and was suddenly convinced that he was at last on his way to see her. She couldn't hear anything, but she knew it

Lucy Pinney

in her heart. She sat up straighter on the sofa, hoping to seem composed.

The door shut with a tight click and she looked up. It was him. She made as if to rise, but he forestalled her, sitting quickly beside her. All this while she'd been imagining him dressed in some severe, dark outfit, like the scene conjured up by Samuel this morning – but instead he was wearing loose, pale clothes, and his shirt was open at the neck, the collar crumpled. He appeared distracted, and she noticed that he looked tired – there were faint circles under his eyes.

'Florrie,' he said, his voice caressing. 'If only I'd known it was you, I would have been quicker.'

She noticed that the sharp lemony perfume he wore was stronger than usual, as if he'd just put it on, and the hair near his ear was damp and clung to the skin. Perhaps he'd washed his face before coming to see who his visitor was; she found the idea touching.

'How's you keeping?' she asked 'Only I heard . . .'

He made a grimace. 'I had the misfortune to meet your brother. I think, on balance, that I prefer being punched by you.'

'I'm sorry.' She glanced down at her hands, where they lay in her lap. She'd scrubbed them with oatmeal before coming here, and yet they still looked too brown. 'That's what I come to talk to you about. I wants to ask you about Joe . . .' She faltered, and he didn't make it any easier for her.

'I hoped you'd come to see me about something different,' he said softly. She didn't respond, and he took one of her hands and held it in his. 'Did you think about it, about being with me?' he asked. She wished he wouldn't talk about that – he must know how painful it was to her, how she longed to be with him, but couldn't accept anything less than marriage. She hoped that if she turned her face away and didn't answer, he'd talk about another subject altogether, but it didn't work out

144

that way. He began to play with her hand, running his fingers very lightly over the knuckles, so lightly that they tickled, and turning it over so that he could trace the lines of fortune on her palm with the edge of a fingernail. She wriggled and tried to pull her hand away, and he lifted it to his lips and kissed the plump base of her thumb, not an entirely gentle kiss, either; it had a bite in it.

'Stop it!' she said, unable to keep a note of pleasure out of her voice. She turned to face him. 'I'm here for ever such a serious reason.'

'Tell me what it is, then.'

She tried, solemnly, to talk about Joe, but it was difficult to keep her mind on the task, because Valentine kept distracting her with tiny, affectionate liberties: playing with a lock of her hair, running his fingers a few inches under the wrists of her blouse, kissing her fingers. They were all things he had done, or nearly done, when they were talking out in the fields by Lower Ash – so she was used to them, liked them – they even sent delicious hot shivers up her body – but somehow today they also made her uneasy. She sensed he was overstepping some fixed line of propriety, but she couldn't have said how.

'You ain't listening proper,' she complained. He'd seized both of her hands by now and was gazing at her, a wicked, slightly wolfish smile on his face.

'I don't need to,' he said. 'I already know what you're going to say.'

She looked back at him, fascinated. He was so very handsome in that shadowy, yellowy light. It turned his hair a tawnier gold, made his eyelashes darker against the blue eyes. His mouth, she thought, looked almost like a child's, the upper lip so soft and full.

'What is I going to say?' she asked playfully.

'You're going to ask me to drop the charges against Joe.'

'And what's your answer?' She tested the strength of his

grip on her hands – she reckoned they were pretty well matched – and they swayed to and fro, as she pushed a little against him, and he pushed gently back. It was a bit like the silly fighting games she used to play with Joe – only more enjoyable.

'My answer is . . .' Valentine hesitated. 'Anything.'

'What's that mean?'

'It means anything. You can have anything you want. Just say it, and I'll give it to you.' He spoke in a whisper, and she didn't trust the look in his eyes. He pushed against her hands with sudden force, so that she found herself on her back on the sofa, her hands either side of her head.

'Valentine,' she answered doubtfully, half-pleading. 'I don't . . .'

He shook his head. 'No,' he said. 'I'm not letting you go. Not this time.' He kissed her, fiercely, sliding his hands together above her head. When they were touching he caught both her wrists in one hand, and with the other began undoing her clothes and his. She tried to struggle, but it was almost impossible, since he was lying across her legs. And also, it wasn't just him she was fighting against, it was herself, too. As he kissed her she felt dizzying waves of feeling: she loved his touch against her skin. But she hated it, too, because she disliked the indignity – she was ashamed of her pitiful underpinnings and hadn't wanted him, ever, to know that she fastened her stockings with binder twine. Also, she wished he hadn't felt the need to force her, to grip her wrists so tightly that the skin burned.

She shut her eyes, and stopped even the pretence of a struggle and, except for holding her wrists – which he never ceased doing, never trusting her not to try to escape – he was as gentle as he could be. She was aware that he was trying to give her pleasure, but though she responded with fluttering violence to any caress, somehow the moment he entered her was only painful.

Afterwards he opened one of her eyes with a fingertip.

'It'll be better next time,' he said. 'Do you hate me?'

'No. I couldn't hate you, ever.'

He stroked her hair, and the curve of her cheek. He held her tight against him.

Suddenly shy, she asked, 'Will you really help Joe?'

'Didn't I promise? I do keep promises. I'll look after you, too. I'll buy you a house. Where would you like it to be? Shall I build one at the end of my drive? Then I could visit you every day.'

He propped himself on one elbow, and looked down at her, the skin of his body as creamy white as the skin of his face. She could see faint blue veins near his shoulder blades and at the deep hollow below his neck.

'Likely,' she said, putting a teasing tone into her voice.

'I will. I'll buy you beautiful clothes, too, and jewels and furs.'

She smiled at him a little sadly. 'What use would they be? I can't take anything from you. Might as well wear a big sign around me neck saying "whore".'

'You don't have to live here. I could buy you a house in London. It's wonderful in London, you'll see.'

'I know how that ends and all.' Florrie sat up and turned away from him, doing up her little vest, and bodice, and fastening her stockings. The sun was no longer falling in a deep band across the carpet, and even the fire had burned low. She stood up and pulled on her skirt. She couldn't find her hair-ribbon. It was lost. She glanced back at Valentine. He was still lying on the sofa, one arm behind his head, watching her. He looked so young without his shirt on – it was as if only his clothes had made him appear older and more powerful than her, and now some of them had gone she could see that he wasn't much more than a boy. For all his strength, he wasn't even very muscular – his arms were almost as slender as a lady's, and delicately curved from shoulder to wrist.

She let herself out. There was no one in the hall, or on the drive. Ahead of her, she could see a wide expanse of deep blue sky – a shade lighter than Valentine's eyes, and scattered across with scraps of golden cloud. The walk home was more unsettling than the walk out had been – largely because the countryside was now alive with tramps. They were all making for the workhouse at Poffit, which closed its doors at six in the evening, and each time she heard the jingle of kettles and cans, or saw one of their tall, ragged silhouettes, she'd climb through the hedge and run along the fields instead – but even there she wasn't altogether safe. Once she saw a man in a broken top hat, pushing a rusty pram, come out of a spinney and work his way across a ploughed field. These visions of beggary were the more disturbing because she knew she was ruined, and because she'd learned, from countless songs and cautionary tales, that to be ruined was to come to a bad end. Sure that she looked entirely different, that any passer-by would know at once what she'd been doing, she wondered if any of her life was left intact – if her parents would even let her into the house when she got home.

Seventeen

The church clock was striking the impossibly late hour of eight o'clock as she reached the crossroads. A chaffinch sang in the hedge beside her, and she looked down through the trees at the farm, realizing that milking must be long over: the pails were lined up against the wall of the house, scrubbed and upended to sweeten in the evening air. The hens had started to roost, too; she could hear the panicky flap of their wings as they fought their way up the walnut tree beside the stackyard.

A little smoke drifted off the top of the chimney and, fearful of the angry reception that awaited her, Florrie stopped to plait her hair, fastening the end with a piece of twisted grass. She had no idea what her face looked like: her mouth felt bruised and shapeless, and she could still taste Valentine's lips against it. Her whole body didn't seem to belong to her any more, it was all unfamiliar aches and sore patches, and her mind felt empty and frozen.

All the way home she'd been conducting a conversation with herself, in which she'd felt obliged to defend Valentine, but found that each point she made was received with a hostile and emotional inner silence. 'He didn't truly violate me,' she'd whispered at one point. 'I were willing enough.' But somehow, as soon as she'd said it, she'd known it wasn't entirely true. It was the same when she'd tried to console herself by thinking that, after all, he did care for her. She'd discovered she didn't believe that either.

149

The farmyard was silent. Even the dog didn't jingle his chain when he saw her, and when she opened the kitchen door she found no one inside. The fire roared up the chimney, and by its light she saw that the table had been laid for five people in a bizarre and lunatic fashion. The knives and forks had been placed the wrong way round and upside down, the best china cups from the parlour had been put out – without any saucers – and there was a flower vase filled with milk in the centre. Beside it sat a loaf of bread, balanced precariously on the tin dish the dog usually ate out of.

A pot hissed on the fire, rattling its lid and spitting into the flames, and when she moved it to a cooler spot she saw that it contained a meat pudding. It was a queer shape, and discharging volumes of mysterious grey froth, but didn't smell too bad.

As she tried to replace the lid it slipped out of her hands and spun on the floor, and she heard an answering thump from Albie's room. Then there were footsteps, and Samuel appeared on the stairs. He'd been asleep – one cheek was pinker than the other, where he'd been lying on it – and his eyes were heavy.

He blinked at her and yawned, and she asked, 'Where's Mother and Father?'

'I ain't seen your mother since dinner,' he said. 'But Cecil, he went up Cullerton way round about half-two to fetch a lawyer.'

'I thought he weren't going to bother!'

Samuel came further into the room, walking on stockinged feet, and warmed his hands at the fire. Florrie didn't like the way he acted as if he belonged in the house. He'd taken off his jacket, too, and rolled up his shirt-sleeves. 'He weren't,' he replied. 'I talked him into it, didn't I?'

'Whatever did you do that for?' she asked, appalled that her visit to Earlshay should have been in vain, and Samuel turned to her, his voice level, but with an undercurrent of irritation.

'I reckoned it was what you wanted. You was carrying on enough about it.'

'That was this morning! I been walking – and thinking – since.'

'You took your time,' he said drily. 'Cecil looked all over for you before he left. Made me promise to stay and mind Albie till you come back. Good job I did, too, else the cows wouldn't have been milked, nor the stock fed.'

'I'm sorry.' Florrie smiled at him, attempting to coax him into a better temper. It was an odd sensation, having Samuel annoyed with her; he was usually so sunny and anxious to please.

'Sorry's not good enough,' he answered. 'Where's you been?'

'You wouldn't want to know.'

'What makes you so certain you know what I want?'

The expression on his face was both angry and hurt, and she watched it, mildly interested by how little his emotions affected her. It wasn't right. She ought not to hurt his feelings – he'd always been considerate of hers. Besides, she'd far rather explain herself to him than to Joe or Father.

'All right,' she said. 'I'll tell you. I been over Earlshay, to see if I could get—' she paused, not wanting to say 'Valentine' because that would imply an intimacy she didn't care to admit to. 'To see if I could get him to drop the charges. His mother were there, too,' she added, feeling her face burn at the evasion.

Samuel didn't appear to notice. There was a tightness in his eyes, as if he expected to flinch at whatever she said next. 'And will he?' he asked.

'He says so, yes.'

'And do you trust that?'

'I don't trust him at all.' She was shocked by the emotion in her own voice. She sounded so much angrier than she'd intended; she had to swallow before she felt in control again.

Samuel crouched down and began fiddling with the fire, and when he spoke again, his voice was gentle.

'Has you been crying?'

'No. I never felt less like crying in all me life.' It was true: Florrie was too confused for tears.

'And is you going to see him again?'

'Not if I can help it.'

He turned to look at her, his brown eyes as bright and alert as a robin's. 'I thought you was quite took up with him,' he said.

'Well, I ain't now,' she answered. 'And I don't reckon he'll show his face again here, neither.' She said it with a mixture of triumph and bitterness, relieved at the idea of freeing herself from Valentine. Why should he ever want to see her again, anyway? He'd got what he'd wanted, hadn't he?

She caught the clatter of Violet's hooves, then, as the cart slowed at the crossroads and turned down the lane, and she quickly set the table to rights. Looking out of the kitchen window as she finished, she saw Mother being helped off the cart by a man in a greasy tweed suit. He had the kind of voice she associated with tinkers: loud and threatening. It set the hackles rising on the back of her neck, and she could hear the dog begin a low, singing growl, in sympathy, but Father didn't seem concerned: he was treating the stranger like an honoured guest.

Mother bustled into the kitchen, ignoring Florrie, and said to Samuel, as she pulled out her hatpins, 'I hear my Florrie went missing?'

To Florrie's astonishment, she heard Samuel describing how he'd found her up in the top coppice, checking rabbit snares, not five minutes after Father had left. He told the lie well, looking into Mother's face in the most innocent and artless manner possible. It left Florrie speechless. He didn't spoil the effect, either, as Joe or Albie would have, by winking or smiling: when he'd finished his story he excused himself politely and hurried out into the yard.

Mother looked in at the meat pudding, tutting with disapproval; then she walked over to Florrie and caught hold of her by the chin, tilting her face so that the dim light from the window fell across it. They were roughly the same height, but as Mother scrutinized her, Florrie felt like a guilty little girl.

Finally, Mother said, 'Don't you go kissing that Samuel too frequent, mind, or I'll be after you with a big stick.'

'I never!' Florrie answered hotly, stung by the injustice of the accusation, but Mother just gave her a hard pat on the side of the face with the palm of her hand – and it was difficult, from the feel of it, to tell whether it was intended to be reproving or affectionate.

Mother chuckled. 'He won't wed you for your cooking, that's for sure,' she said, and added, '*peasan beag!*' which Florrie knew to be Gaelic for 'little minx!', before going into the back kitchen to fetch some potatoes.

Remembering all this, Florrie paused in her work and wiped the sweat off her forehead with the edge of her sleeve. It was a hot, sunny May day, and Smart was standing beside her, his body in the shafts of the tip-cart, his head lowered, his eyes shut. If she stood on tiptoe she could see a small scar on his back, just where the neck began. Three weeks ago, when she'd come back from Earlshay, that scar had been a bump the size of a man's knuckle.

The worst part of that evening had happened as Florrie was setting the potatoes to boil. A piglet had squealed outside, the sound slicing through Florrie's skull like a hot knife. It had stopped almost as abruptly as it had begun, to be succeeded by a low, unpleasant laugh. Footsteps had scampered across the floor upstairs, as Albie had bounded out of bed and opened the window.

'What's happening?' she'd asked Mother.

Mother had been slicing a big cabbage at the table. She hadn't looked up. 'He's selling the pigs,' she'd said.

'But he can't do that. They's Albie's!'

'He's your father, he can do as he likes. Besides, if he don't sell the pigs he has to sell the cows, and us might as well pack up straight away and go live in the workhouse if he starts selling the cows.'

'Why's he got to sell anything?'

'Because the solicitor'll cost money, and even if Joe don't go to prison he'll have a big fine to pay.'

'But he might . . .' Florrie had said, and stopped. There'd been no way she could explain that Joe might not need a solicitor or have any fine to pay at all. Albie, dressed only in a nightshirt, had run down the stairs at that point and out of the kitchen door, and she'd run after him, but she was too late. When she'd got outside she'd seen that Samuel was holding him by the arms, fending him off from where the pigs were being loaded into the cart by the man in the greasy suit, while Albie did his best to punch and kick and struggle. Samuel had lifted him high in the air, and carried him over to the wall by the wood-linney, and sat him down, holding him firmly by the hand. Florrie had noticed how the fight had ebbed out of her little brother. He'd turned his face to Samuel, and listened intently to what he had to say, his jaw tightening with resolve. Finally Samuel had left him on the wall, and gone back to helping load the pigs and, though the piglets had shrilled as they were picked up by the back legs, and the sows had snarled in panic, Albie had remained there, watching, his shoulders hunched, his hands clenched into fists, tears streaming silently down his face.

Long after, when the cart had gone, and Florrie had been putting him to bed, he'd asked her: 'Do animals have souls and go to heaven?'

'Course they has,' she'd said. 'I wouldn't like to think of Smart not having a soul. He's a real good sort, he is.'

'Well, ain't they angry with us, when we gets there, 'cos we've ate them?'

'Who says humans is good enough to go to heaven?' Florrie had said fiercely. 'I reckon it's all pigs and horses up there.'

She turned away from Smart and ducked through the narrow door of the calf-shed. The weaned calves had been kept here all winter, and as a result the muck was nearly three feet deep. Cleaning it out was a terrible job, because it was packed so tight: layers and layers of dirty straw, glued together with manure. When she pulled at it with a fork, great pieces, as long and unwieldy as lengths of damp mattress, would unwind themselves, and these had to be hacked smaller before they could be hefted out to the cart. To make matters worse, the inside of the shed was alive with small, jumping flies.

Still, she didn't altogether dislike insects: they could provide unexpected entertainment. The day after the pigs had been sold – the afternoon Joe had been released, and returned home – she'd left everyone else talking in the kitchen and gone out, alone, to the stable, to climb on Smart's back. Lying there sadly, she'd felt a lump against her cheek. At first she'd taken no notice: she'd been repeating to herself, as if that could dull the cruellest edge of it, Valentine's remark about her being too free with her affections. But then she'd put up her hand and realized that she was touching a warble.

A warble on Smart! It was rare for the horses to get warbled: usually she just searched the backs of the cows, and Father invariably got there first, because popping warbles was one of the countryside's special – if slightly ridiculous – treats.

Of course, the animals didn't see them in that light. When they heard the high, penetrating buzz of the warble fly they'd panic and bolt, breaking through fences, smashing down hedges, doing anything to get away. It was as if they sensed the discomfort the fly was going to cause them, and knew how its offspring were going to grow inside their bodies.

Florrie had sat up, and put her thumbs either side of the bump, which resembled a miniature volcano in shape, even having a dark hole at the top. She'd pressed down hard, and a brown segmented maggot, as big as a thumb, had come shooting out of the hole with an audible pop and cracked most satisfyingly on the ceiling of the stable. As it had passed, she'd even had a fleeting glimpse of something like a face – a little round gaping mouth and two smudges for eyes.

But that had been three weeks ago. Now, as she staggered through the door with a load of dirty straw, and hefted it into the tip-cart, she thought she saw a movement beyond, in the little courtyard. A shadow on the hard-packed earth there. She quickly slipped back into the shed, her fork in her hands, trembling. If it was Valentine – and she suspected it was – she didn't wish to see him.

She waited, catching her breath, hearing the pleased cackle of a hen in the distance. Then the light from the doorway was blotted out, and she saw him standing the other side of it. He had a hat tipped over his face, and his clothes were almost too studiedly elegant, as if he'd spent hours rearranging them in a mirror. She backed deeper into the shed, until he became a silhouette with a gold edging. 'Florrie?' he enquired, and she felt a familiar shiver at the sound of his voice.

Making her tone as unfriendly as she could, she called out, 'What do you want, then?'

'What do you *think* I want?' he asked, mockingly. 'I've come to see you since you show very little sign of coming to see me.'

'I thought you'd finished with me.'

'Not in the slightest,' he said. 'I've hardly begun.'

There was a wide soggy patch of muck, just by the door, and each time Florrie had walked across it with a forkful of straw her legs had sunk in to mid-calf – liquid seeping round the edges of her gaiters – and somehow she didn't think that Valentine would care to negotiate it in his fine suit and polished shoes. So she called out rudely, 'What's you going to do if I don't fall in with this plan of yours? Break my ribs, like you did my brother? Give me a black eye?'

When he answered, his voice was low and seductive. 'Why don't you come out here and find out?'

'Not flaming likely,' she muttered, more to herself than to him, because she did feel a terrible longing to go out there into the sunshine. Two things stopped her: the memory of all the hurt he'd caused; and the way she looked now. He'd hardly admire her if he saw how muddy she was.

He took a step into the shed and hesitated, glancing at the floor. 'Why do you always seem to be handling this beastly stuff?' he enquired.

'At least it's honest dirt.'

'That's aimed at me, is it? Tell me – what am I supposed to have done? Didn't I keep my word? Didn't I have your brother released?'

'You kept your word all right, but it weren't no good to me, just like the dress you sent, and the feelings you said you had. I'd have been better off without the lot of them.'

'I can't believe you'd rather stay in a rat-hole like this than come and live with me.'

'At least I ain't tempted to be too free with my affections in here.'

'So that's it!' He laughed softly. 'It's that one remark.'

She waited for him to explain or deny it, but he did neither. Instead he said, 'It's no good hiding. I'm quite prepared to come in and get you.'

Although she wanted to be hard and unforgiving, and had

planned many fierce speeches to upbraid him with, Florrie couldn't, for some strange reason, stop herself from smiling when he said this. She was glad he couldn't see her face.

Another voice broke into the stillness of the little yard. It was cool and polite, with a slight quiver of uncertainty at the heart of it, and it belonged to Samuel.

'I think you'd better leave, sir,' Florrie heard him say.

'And what business is it of yours?' Valentine, who'd been so maliciously delighted by Father's anger, seemed disconcerted by Samuel's deferential tone.

'I'm a friend of the family, sir.'

'Yes – I remember the face.' Valentine's tone was sarcastic. 'Well, since you're such a great friend of the family, you might be interested to know that I purchased this farm yesterday. So you see, I've a perfect right to come here whenever I like.'

'You may have bought the farm,' Samuel answered, 'but you ain't bought Florrie along with it, and if she wants you to leave her alone, you're not a whit better off than the rest of us. You just has to knuckle under and do what she says.'

'All right,' Florrie heard Valentine say, 'if she wants me to leave, I'll go.'

'I want you to leave!' Florrie shouted, from inside the shed, and then clapped her hands over her ears so she couldn't hear his reply; but even so, she caught it.

'Believe me,' he said, his voice intensely angry, 'I won't be back.'

When he'd gone she emerged into the yard, blinking. The sun wasn't as warm, or as yellow, as she'd imagined it would be, and Samuel was looking at her with a wary expression. He didn't answer when she thanked him for helping her, and it made her feel uneasy, as if she'd been caught out in a lie.

The cart was full, so she led Smart into the field to empty it. There was a newly released calf out there, skipping delightedly about in the grass, and butting at the trunk of an oak tree, as if challenging it to a fight. And despite this pretty sight, she couldn't help thinking that the farm looked so much duller, and less colourful, now that she'd made the right decision and sent Valentine away.

Eighteen

Sybil was slightly tipsy on champagne. She cupped her slim waist with her hands and said, 'Isn't this darling?'

Veronica, lying in a soft armchair near her, legs hooked over one arm, back propped against the other, gazed at her friend's reflection in the full-length mirror. Sybil was wearing a pink dress so pale that it was almost white. A tight bodice forced up her breasts, the seams trimmed with pearls, and below it the wide, panniered skirt billowed out, a mass of swags and ribbon. She was wearing a tall white wig, too, trimmed with a pink ribbon and a silk rose, and beneath it her face glowed with pleasure, the skin shimmering like satin.

The whole confection had taken weeks of planning. To begin with, her dress for the Mozart party had been pale gold, but after a series of fittings she'd become convinced that the colour made her skin look grey, and the entire outfit had been scrapped. (It was hanging at the end of her dressing-room, in disgrace.)

This one was far prettier, but looking at it, Veronica felt uneasy. The bodice was so very low-cut, and the bleached-out colour couldn't help reminding her of a wedding dress.

'Does Vallie like his costume?' she asked hastily, to avoid giving an opinion. She and Sybil had been up here since tea-time, and she was beginning to feel sleepy from the wine, and the heat of the bedroom. It was full of plump cushions, and smelt of Chanel No. 5, and even the gilt cupids holding up the

161

bedposts looked on the point of fainting.

'You know Vallie,' Sybil snorted. 'He's being difficult, as usual. He won't try it on, and he keeps insisting he's not coming to the party, but he will.'

'What makes you so sure?'

'Because, although he likes to think he defies me, he never really does, not when it comes to anything I care about.'

Veronica nodded languidly. 'Ah,' she said. 'But he won't go to London, will he?' Sybil took a velvet beauty spot from a box on her dressing-table and leaned forward to place it beside her mouth. 'I don't mind in the least about London,' she said. 'Because everyone I want him to meet will be at this party next week. And besides, in a month or two he'll be begging me to go to London. He'll be down on his knees saying, "Mama! Can't we go? Please, please, please?"'

'Why on earth would he do that?' Even in her present, slightly sozzled state, this scenario sounded deeply improbable to Veronica.

Sybil moved the beauty spot to her left cheekbone, where it emphasized the malicious expression on her face. 'Because he'll have no further reason for staying here. He's having an *affaire* at the moment, and I can tell it's almost over.'

Through the fuzziness induced by drink, Veronica felt a dull pain in her heart. She tried to regain her poise, but she was aware that Sybil had turned to watch her with sharp, glittering eyes – and her own had unaccountably filled with a fine mist. 'An *affaire*!' she said faintly. 'Why haven't I heard about this before?'

'Because it couldn't be less interesting, that's why. It's just some common little servant-girl he's got hold of. I can't even be bothered to find out who she is.'

'It's not serious, then?'

'No. Of course not.' Sybil turned back to the mirror and touched the rose on her wig. Even in the glass, her eyes still studied her friend, and Veronica, who was beginning to feel queasy now, had a sudden, unpalatable insight. Sybil had guessed at her secret fondness for Vallie and was enjoying her distress, even deliberately provoking it. She'd always known Sybil had a wicked side – she'd enjoyed hearing Sybil's incisive, catty remarks about casual acquaintances – but she'd never thought to see it turned against a friend.

'I don't think he's ever been in love,' Sybil went on. 'Not properly. Perhaps he's incapable of it. He's really nothing more than a spoilt little boy.' She picked up the silver patch-box and turned it over in her fingers. 'Perhaps if he was to meet a stronger, more mature woman . . .' Her voice was low, with a suspicion of a laugh in it, and, certain that she was being cruelly teased, Veronica tried to meet Sybil's eyes, but Sybil wouldn't look up. She moved away from the mirror and perched, instead, on the very edge of her dressing-table, studying the tips of her own satin shoes.

'Of course,' Sybil continued, 'these flings Vallie has with his little sluts rather suit me, because the last thing I want is for him to get married. It'd be ghastly. He wouldn't be an eligible bachelor any longer, and we couldn't get invited to the best parties. Also, I'd be the Dowager Lady Bandinelli. Can you see me as a dowager? I can't. It conjures up the most beastly vision of an old hag with a hump on her back.' She looked up and smiled from under her white ringlets and pink ribbon, and her expression was so sweet that Veronica was suddenly convinced she must have imagined the earlier malice.

'Don't you want him to marry, ever?' she asked, unable to keep a wistful tone from her voice.

Sybil kicked out one of her feet so that it touched the mirror and set it rocking dizzily on its axis. Veronica tried to fix her gaze on her friend, but kept being distracted by the disjointed scenes that the mirror was reflecting: the white ceiling with its fine mouldings, the satiny walls, the open door behind them, the deep violet carpet, the door again.

'Not unless he marries a princess,' Sybil laughed. 'But he won't. Do you know why?' She leaned forward confidingly. 'Because the only woman he has ever come close to loving is me.'

The mirror beside Veronica spun downwards, its surface winking like water, and she caught a fleeting glimpse in it of Valentine, standing in the shadows of the passageway beyond the door, his face pale with anger. Then he was gone. She pointed at the glass. 'Vallie!' she said warningly, but Sybil only broke into a peal of cruel laughter.

'I don't mind,' she said. 'He can eavesdrop all he likes. It might even do him good.'

It was late, past ten o'clock, and the others had gone to bed, but Florrie couldn't sleep. She was too excited. She was going to a dance – her first proper one – tomorrow. Samuel had asked her if she'd like to accompany him and Joe to the Kittenhole sixpenny hop, and Mother had given permission. In fact, she'd done more than that. She'd led Florrie into the tiny parlour, and opened the bottom cupboard of the small, part-glass-fronted cabinet that she referred to proudly as 'my buffet'.

The parlour was a strange place, rarely entered, except for Christmas and the visits of Colonel Lightbush, and it contained few pieces of furniture – only two stiffly upholstered chairs and the cabinet – and since it was always shut up, and positioned under the soggiest end of the thatch, it was extremely damp. The air inside it twinkled with moisture, and sitting on either of the chairs was like sinking into an overripe mushroom; whenever she did so, Florrie half expected the cushions to explode and fill the room with inky spores. Even the glass on the cabinet was always misted with a faint green dew, and when they'd entered Mother had rubbed this off crossly with her sleeve, as if its presence was the rudest kind of affront.

She'd crouched down, her knees cracking, and fitted a little key in the cupboard door. Inside had been a yellowing bundle tied with string, and Mother had unwrapped it to reveal a pair of low shoes in black leather, with tarnished gilt buckles, a few letters, a dried rose, and a rolled-up piece of blue cloth.

'Go on,' she'd said, pushing the shoes at Florrie. And Florrie had unlaced one of her boots and gingerly tried on the old-fashioned slipper. It had looked pretty on her foot, making her ankle appear fine and slender – but pinched at the heel. She'd been more interested in the blue fabric, but hadn't dared mention it because she'd guessed Mother was doubtful about giving it to her.

Mother had pulled up one of the chairs and sat down in it, the bottom of her skirt riding up a few inches to reveal her boots and a piece of solid calf, encased in wrinkled fawn wool stocking.

'Your father and I,' she'd said, pressing her hand to her ribs to ward off the indigestion, 'we courted eight years before we was wed. Cor, weren't it ever hard? I were in service then, and he in the Navy, and I didn't spend a penny-piece from one year's end to another – not even on a ribbon or a new pair of stockings. I saved it all. Seventeen I were when I first laid eyes on Cecil, and twenty-five when they read the banns.'

'Eight years!' Florrie had echoed, aghast. She couldn't imagine waiting that long for anyone. The idea of service filled her with dread, too. There'd been a bit of talk about it in the last few days, ever since her mother and father had learned about Valentine buying the farm. She was aware of it hovering, as a distinct possibility, in the minds of all her family – a way of putting her safely out of the reach of a man they distrusted.

'See,' Mother had said, leaning forward to put the rose and the letters carefully back in the cabinet, 'there weren't no choice about it. Us couldn't afford to wed before then, not without the money to start a farm, and that was that.'

165

She weighed the blue cloth in her hands. 'This Samuel of yours,' she went on, 'he's decent enough. He've been master good to Albie, and always behaved respectful. But,' she sighed heavily, 'that house he has with Ellis, it's in a shocking state. Roof half off, and damp as a frog. And the work he does! Well, he's not much better than one of they tramps: walking halfway across the county for a bit of labouring, and sleeping under hedges.'

'I ain't got no plans for marrying him,' Florrie had said firmly. 'Not the way things is at present.' And Mother had handed her the cloth, locked the cabinet, and said no more.

The bundle of cloth had revealed itself to be a blouse. Florrie had tried to wash the fustiness out of it, set it to dry on a bush by the front gate, and at the moment was pressing it with the flat-iron. Along with steam, a powerful smell of damp church pews was rolling out of the fabric, and she couldn't help noticing that some creature, possibly a mouse, had eaten part of one of the sleeves, where it joined the bodice. Luckily it wasn't a large hole; she'd just have to be careful not to raise that arm when she was dancing.

Dancing! The idea of it made her so delighted that she had to put the iron down. She reached up to the mantelpiece and felt behind the tea caddy for the ring Samuel had given her. Slipping it on her finger, she tried to think about him in a sentimental light, but it was impossible. Whenever she imagined him kissing her she just conjured up a polite touch on the cheek. And he'd looked so solemn when he'd invited her to the dance.

Reckoning that the blouse was dry enough to try on now, she was unbuttoning her own black one when she heard a low tap on the front door. She did up her blouse again and opened the door cautiously, and Valentine was so often in her thoughts that it didn't surprise her to see him, not even this late at night. He dipped his head to avoid the lintel, and came in, though she hadn't invited him. He didn't shut the door, either. He just stood in front of it, so that she could see, either side of his body, the still, moonlit yard. He was wearing evening clothes under his leather driving coat, the shirt brilliantly white against the black suit, and his expression and behaviour were odd – uncharacteristic.

He looked unhappy – that was what she noticed most – as if he'd just come from a funeral; a funeral which had made him both sad and furiously angry. His eyes even looked wet.

'What's you here for?' she said, careful to speak quietly. She didn't want to wake her family. 'You know I can't see you no more.'

He frowned, and narrowed his eyes.

'You'd best go,' she continued fiercely. 'I means what I says.'

He seemed so preoccupied that she wondered if he'd heard her at all, but he did answer, in a low voice.

'I've something to tell you. Then I'll go.'

She edged towards the fire, anxious that she should give him no opportunity for approaching her. She knew how weak she became whenever he was close.

'I want to make you an offer. If you come with me – now – this instant – I'll marry you.'

'You must think me a proper fool,' she said, smiling. 'I know I been daft in the past, but this do beat all.'

He didn't smile back. 'I mean it. I promise it – and you know I do keep my promises. I'll get a special licence, or I'll drive you to Gretna Green. Whatever you want. But you have to decide now.'

She lifted her hands. 'How's I supposed to decide?' She gestured at the blouse, close to tears. 'I's going to a dance tomorrow, with Samuel. And besides, you ain't treated me too well in the past. How can I trust you?'

He shrugged, and turned towards the doorway, and the

possibility of him going, of the chance being lost for ever, made her realize, with violent clarity, what she really wanted.

'Can I leave a note for my mother?' she asked.

'If it's a short one.' His expression softened.

She searched on the dresser and found an old envelope and a stub of pencil, and while she was writing, scarcely conscious of the words, her mind was in tumult. What was she doing? Was she really going to go? If Valentine didn't keep his promise what would happen to her?

She put the note on the dresser and, on impulse, weighed it down with Samuel's ring. Then she looked up at Valentine. He held out his hand, and she slipped hers into it, and he walked out of the door and up the lane, so fast that he was almost dragging her. The moonlight was clear, and lay on the ground thick and silver, and the trees either side of the lane were a magical, still, velvet black. A cat streaked across the lane, crying, and Florrie stopped, wishing to have one last glimpse of the farm, but Valentine pulled her on, to where his car waited by the crossroads.

Nineteen

The Bentley drove between the stone gateposts of Earlshay, roared down the drive, and came to a sudden, gravel-crunching stop. The place was crammed with cars. Lights shone from the windows of the house, and a tail-coated silhouette waited in the open front door. Now that the engine had died Florrie was aware of music playing, too.

Valentine made no immediate move to leave the car. He pulled off the strange leather helmet he liked wearing when he drove, and gave her a closed-lips sphinx-like smile. She didn't want to get out of the car, either. It had been one of the few fixed and familiar points in her life since that wild night, a week ago, when he'd taken her from Fightingcocks Farm.

He'd wrapped her in his coat, then, and settled her in the passenger seat, and the Bentley had shot forward with terrifying speed and power. At first she'd been stunned by the noise of the engine and helplessly incapacitated by her own hair, which had developed a sadistic will of its own, beating her about the face and stinging her in the eye. She'd struggled with it unsuccessfully, trying to stuff it down the neck of the coat, until Valentine, without taking his eyes off the road, had passed her a white silk scarf, which she'd bound round her head like a bandage.

After that she'd watched through the two layers of windscreen as the empty roads stretched out mile after mile, the curves ahead gone as quickly as they were glimpsed, distant badgers and foxes frozen for one ghostly instant in the dazzle of the headlights. They were going so fast that she was convinced she was going to die, and she'd almost enjoyed the feeling, as if the decision to go with Valentine had been a pact with the devil. It reminded her of all the other stupid, dangerous things she'd done in her life: dropping off the top of the oak tree, for instance, into the deep pool of water where the sheep were washed. That had given her just the same dizzying rush of exhilaration and terror.

After perhaps half an hour of panic her body just hadn't been able to remain tense any more, and she'd found herself relaxing back into the warmth of the coat, while silent towns and villages flashed by in the moonlight. From time to time she'd turned to look at Valentine, but his face had remained expressionless beneath the hat and goggles, and he hadn't once glanced back at her.

Gradually, she'd fallen into a fitful doze, although she'd thought she never would, and woken, confusedly, to discover that a low canvas roof had appeared above her head, protecting her from the worst of the cold wind. The car had stopped, and she'd been able to smell petrol and hear Valentine talking to someone else, his arrogant, patrician tones comforting in the darkness. Then the car had started again, and she'd slept.

She'd woken again in the morning, and noticed the grey light filtering round the sides of the cover, and lain passively, wondering what her mother had thought when she'd come down into the kitchen to light the fire and seen the note on the dresser.

The car had stopped moving, and after a while she'd heard footsteps and Valentine had rolled back the canvas tonneau above her head. He'd looked tired: his dinner jacket had been streaked with white dust, the skin around his goggles raw from the wind. She'd heard birds singing, and seen a vast bowl of sky emerging from fine mist, and she'd sat up, excited, never having seen so much sky, and such a flat landscape, in all her life.

They were parked beside a few cottages on a village green, and the bonnet of the car was clicking as it cooled.

'It's no good, I'm afraid,' Valentine had said, pulling off his goggles and leaning on the side of the car. 'I've been inside and asked if they'll marry us and they say they can't. If you don't happen to have the misfortune to be Scottish you have to wait three weeks.' He'd sounded almost relieved.

'Is this Gretna?' Florrie'd asked. He'd nodded.

'And where's the Old Forge?' He'd tilted his head, gesturing behind him, and she'd seen a low building, as covered in signs as a fairground stall: 'This is the famous Old Blacksmith Shop and Marriage Room', 'Relics of the Old Priests and other Antiquities'.

'Mother told me of it,' she'd said. 'But I always longed to see it for meself.'

'Look all you like.' Valentine had folded his arms. 'But we can't be married there today.'

'Why ever not?'

'I've just told you, because neither one of us is Scottish.' A note of irritation had crept into his voice.

'But I am,' Florrie had answered proudly. 'I's Hebridean. We only come to Devon when I were a baby. I were born on Islay, like my mother before me. Do you think I'd have let you bring me here, to Gretna, if I weren't?'

Valentine had married her, after all, but he'd been curiously subdued throughout the ceremony. The 'priest', a Mr Rennison, a big, stocky man who'd reminded Florrie of one of her uncles, had kept winking at Florrie, and she'd laughed back, but Valentine had seemed impatient with their frivolous behaviour. Afterwards he'd climbed back in the car and driven south again, and though they'd stopped for a quick meal at an inn by the side of the road, he'd hardly spoken a word to her.

Late in the afternoon they'd reached a market town and he'd stopped outside a hotel whose white stucco façade had shone brilliantly white in the last of the sun, and ordered a room. Florrie had noticed the man at the desk casting a sharp glance at the gold ring Valentine had put on her finger.

When they were finally completely alone, and had closed the bedroom door, Valentine had said to her, 'I'm sorry, but I have to sleep,' in the coldest, most unfriendly tone, as if she were some stranger he'd just met in the passage outside, and lying down on the bed fully dressed, had become unconscious in an instant.

She'd taken off her boots and curled up beside him, wondering what she could have done to offend – and whether he'd forgive her for it in the morning.

But by then he'd gone. She'd woken to find the room empty, except for sunshine pouring through the chintz curtains, and she'd got up and wandered over to the window, and looked down into the street. People with unfamiliar accents were calling to each other out there, driving carts, and unrolling shop awnings with long poles, and she'd felt a sharp stab of homesickness. She'd wondered if she was allowed to go home now she was married – if her family would forgive her. But it had been a little hard to envisage how she was going to get back to Furzey Moor if Valentine had abandoned her here, in this hotel.

When tears had started to well up in her eyes she'd rebuked herself firmly, the way Mother would have done. Mother always said that self-pity was a terrible waste of time. In an attempt to become more cheerful, Florrie had taken a towel from the washstand and gone out into the corridor to find the peculiar mahogany water closet Valentine had introduced her to the night before. Beside it, its door open, breathing out an enticing soapy perfume, she'd discovered a bathroom.

Fascinated, she'd locked herself inside. There had been a strange method of sealing the drain-hole in the tub: a type of hollow metal tube that only fitted in place with difficulty. She hadn't been able to see why the people who owned the bath didn't fit a neat cork bung instead, like you got on a hogshead barrel. It would have been so much simpler. But then the gentry often preferred a complicated solution to an easy problem. (What other explanation was there for the way they hunted foxes, when everyone knew the animals could be killed effortlessly with a bullet or a loop of wire?)

Far more interesting, of course, was the way that water poured from the bath taps. She'd heard of such things, but even so the magic trick was endlessly astonishing at first-hand. She hadn't been so impressed, though, by the taste of the flat, bitter stuff that came out.

When the bath grew cold she'd run another, and this time tried to see if she could do shallow dives off the steep enamel sides, but it hadn't been easy, and she'd kept wishing Albie could have been there too, to try it out. She was sure he would have had some helpful suggestions. Finally her toes had begun to crinkle, and she'd put her knickers and stockings in the water and given them a scrub with the wispy remains of the soap, before going back to her room refreshed and ebullient, the hotel water pipes banging and rattling with outrage behind her.

Valentine had been sitting at the table in the window, his back to her, reading a newspaper, a tray of breakfast in front of him. She'd grinned to herself with delight at seeing him again, then crept silently to a chair by the bed, and hung her wet things off the back of it. When he'd spoken it had made her jump.

'You can throw those away for a start,' he'd said.

'Whatever for? They's perfectly good, with hardly any darns.'

He'd put his paper down and turned round. 'Because I don't like them. And having gone to the immense bother of becoming your husband I was hoping there might be some faint chance of you doing what I wanted. Just for a change.'

The grim, frozen expression had entirely gone from his face, and he'd looked softer and more playful, the way he'd used to when he was flirting with her over the hedge at Lower Ash.

'There's something for you on the bed,' he'd added, raising his paper again, and she'd darted over to look at the bags and boxes piled there, scooping back her hair with one arm, so that it shouldn't drip water on the coloured paper. She'd turned her back on Valentine when she'd opened them, because she knew she was bad at receiving presents: Joe had told her so. She hadn't the trick of looking delighted at once. (At least, not with the things Joe had given her: half-mummified hedgehogs and unusual droppings he'd found in the woods.) She always preferred to examine any gift secretly, on her own.

As she'd undone the bags she'd discovered silk and lace underwear, cream-coloured stockings, a set of ivory brushes, and a deep pink linen dress. There'd been little bottles of perfume and scented powder, too, and a pair of soft kid shoes, and she'd scarcely dared hold them in her hands. They'd seemed far too good for any human to touch, let alone herself.

Valentine had sat down beside her on the bed and asked gently, 'Don't you like them? Shall I take them back?'

'They's beautiful,' Florrie had answered, her voice low. 'It's just that I can't believe I's truly married to you.'

'I should hope not,' he'd said, tipping her back on the bed and undoing her clothes. 'It would take all the pleasure away if you did, wouldn't it?'

This time he hadn't held her down; he'd left her free to escape. More than that, he'd kept stopping whenever she became excited, so that she'd had to plead with him to continue, and his smile had reminded her of a cat's as it plays with a mouse it knows is completely in its power. But she hadn't minded, because she'd no longer wanted to be anything else.

He opened the door of the car and helped her out, slipping his arm around her waist as they began to walk across the drive. It seemed as if, since that moment on the bed, they'd scarcely stopped touching each other, had always been in some sort of contact, even if it had only been his fingers on her wrist as they drove to another hotel.

To her surprise, Valentine didn't go up to the front door, but opened a wooden door in a wall beside the drive, and pulled her through. They ran along formal gardens she'd never seen before – full of smooth lawn, clipped yew, and stone statues, terraces and staircases – all the time aware of the noise and activity in the big house near by, where brightly dressed figures moved behind lit windows.

Finally, Valentine led her to a door at the back of the house, and Florrie smelt food cooking, and saw servants at the end of a passage, bustling round a big kitchen, and he guided her past a series of empty storerooms until they came to a corridor that she recognized: every detail as vivid as a nightmare. Above her a steep staircase twisted upwards, and the walls were painted cream and green.

'Why's we going this way?' she started to ask, but he put his finger to his lips, and she fell silent.

The little rooms at the top of the stairs were almost exactly the same as they had been when she'd first seen them at the age of eight, except that there were now a few pitiful possessions scattered on the iron beds and lopsided chairs. She wanted to linger, but Valentine pushed at the green baize door, and at once she found herself in an altogether different world, where the air was warm from the party down below, and filled with perfume and cigar smoke, and she could hear the murmur of voices floating upwards. Valentine led her across the landing, up another flight of stairs, and into a room crowded with gilt furniture and white cushions.

He released her here, leaving her in front of a big, full-length mirror, and vanished through a further doorway. She waited passively for him, hardly recognizing herself in the glass. Her hair was the same, despite a recent visit to a hairdresser, because Valentine had sat beside her while it was done and insisted that only the ends were trimmed and the fringe straightened – but everything else had altered. Her body, in the light-coloured drop-waisted dresses that Valentine kept buying her, looked grown up, sophisticated, instead of childishly bulky. And her face was unfamiliar, too, since she'd spent so many hours studying Valentine's changing expressions. Her eyes were larger than she remembered, her skin milky from a week spent in hot hotel bedrooms, wrapped in his arms.

He came back holding a bundle of yellow silk. 'Take off your dress,' he said.

'You never stops saying that,' she answered cheekily. 'Just the one idea you've got in your head, haven't you?'

'I mean it, Florrie.' His tone was mock-menacing.

She pulled off her frock, and looked idly round the room. It was so warm that she felt as comfortable in her underthings as fully clothed. 'Who sleeps here?' she asked.

'My mother.'

'Will I meet her?'

'I guarantee it.' Valentine fastened a wide petticoat, stiffened with hoops, round Florrie's waist with cotton tapes, then pushed her arms through two yellow sleeves. As the silk unrolled itself and dropped down over the petticoat she drew in a breath of amazement. It was like a dress in a fairytale, with a low front, a nipped-in waist, and a skirt that parted in ripples of ribbon to reveal a false white lace underskirt. It was tight, too. Once Valentine had fastened the back she could hardly breathe.

He stood back and surveyed her critically in the mirror. 'Unfortunately,' he said, 'I haven't a wig for you.'

'What the blooming heck would I want a wig for?'

'Quite.' Valentine gathered up her hair in his hands and began trying to fasten it with pins at the back, but it kept falling out, and after a minute or two he abandoned the effort. He rummaged in the drawers of a dressing-table, and found a packet of long white gloves, which he carefully rolled on to Florrie's fingers and up her arms, to just above the elbow. Her palms were so plump that the buttons there pinched cruelly when he did them up, and looked about to burst open.

She followed him out of the room, her skirt rustling, and along another landing into a darker, cooler place, decorated in dark greens, which she guessed must be his bedroom, because he began opening cupboards and pulling out clothes in desperate haste. A waltz she recognized as 'The Blue Danube' started playing as he pulled on a curly white wig only a few shades lighter than his own hair. It made him look older and more ruthless, exaggerating the hard lines of his mouth, and she couldn't understand why he was wearing it.

Downstairs, Sybil tried to contain her panic as she received the last few guests.

'What am I going to do if he doesn't come?' she whispered to Veronica, for the twentieth time.

'He will. I'm sure he will,' Veronica answered, in the steadiest, most comforting tone she could manage. Privately, she thought it sinister that Valentine had disappeared so soon after overhearing Sybil's malicious remarks. The last few days she'd been worrying about a car accident, but there had been nothing in the paper.

They were both standing at the foot of the main stairs, and either side of them were massive floral arrangements that continued up the banisters, winding in and out, a profusion of lilies, stephanotis and maidenhair fern. There were more flowers in all of the ground-floor reception rooms, and a huge mahogany bath banked with layer upon layer of lilies beside the front door. In front of it, the butler, Bennet, was standing with a silver tray of dance programmes in his hands. As Sybil watched him, a young footman came in from the garden and murmured in his ear. Bennet turned and advanced to the staircase.

'Your ladyship,' he said, 'Sir Valentine's Bentley has just been discovered in the drive.'

'Thank God.' Sybil fanned herself. The music seemed louder – she could see couples whirling through the big double doors that led to the white drawing-room. She had to admit that it all looked magnificent. 'He's here,' she said to Veronica. 'He didn't let me down. And do you know – I really think this party might be a success after all.'

A movement caught her eye. She turned to look up the stairs and saw Valentine at the top. His clothes had been put on too hurriedly – the lower buttons of his waistcoat weren't fastened, and his wig was slightly askew – but she scarcely noticed these details, because he wasn't alone. There was a girl on his arm. She was casting curious glances at the dancers, and also soft, sideways looks at Valentine. It was obvious that she was entirely bewitched by him. Valentine wasn't returning his partner's attentions: his eyes were only fixed on Sybil's as he walked down towards her. But though she wanted to stare back at him she couldn't help her gaze returning again and again to that stranger, who was very young, scarcely more than a child, with a mass of dark blonde hair and a merry expression. When she turned sideways to look at Valentine her babyish face, its mouth half-open, reminded Sybil irresistibly of a plump little bird's, poised to sing.

Just before they reached her Sybil recognized the dress. With a terrible surge of fury she realized that it was hers, the gold-coloured outfit she'd abandoned two weeks ago.

'Won't you introduce me to your charming companion?' she said sarcastically to Valentine, as he drew level. The waltz stopped and there was an expectant hush.

'I'd be delighted to, Mama.' Valentine bowed, and his voice rang out clearly, audible through the big hall and right to the other end of the white drawing-room. 'Let me present my wife, Florence Cherry May.'

His partner bobbed an awkward curtsy that nearly tipped her off the stairs and said, in the broadest Devonshire accent imaginable, 'Cor, ain't I ever pleased to see you?'

PART TWO

1930

'This is the essence of my culture, society and religion, where a woman is a toy, a plaything. She can be stuck together at will, broken at will . . . The culture where I was born and where I grew up sees the woman as the honour of the house . . . In order to uphold this false "honour" and glory she is taught to endure many kinds of oppression and pain in silence.'

Kiranjit Ahluwalia, quoted in *Eve Was Framed*, Helena Kennedy, 1992.

Twenty

'A lady never sneezes,' Sybil said, a look of intense affront on her face. She half turned away, as if Florrie had done something so revolting that it could scarcely be borne.

'How do she help it?' Florrie enquired cheerfully, from behind her table napkin. 'It ain't as if she has much of a say in the matter. When a sneeze wants to come, he flaming well comes.'

'A lady always has self-control,' Sybil replied. Recovering her poise, she handed Florrie a scrap of lace. 'If she feels a sneeze coming she presses a handkerchief to her face and gives a little cough.'

'I'll remember that, then,' Florrie said, blowing her nose thoroughly into the lace. 'Though I don't reckon on it being half as easy as you makes it sound.'

They were having lunch alone together in the dining-room, as Valentine had gone to London. Florrie had been disconcerted by how different he'd become since returning to Earlshay. He spent hours in his study 'dealing with estate papers' and was apt to disappear with no warning in his car. At first she'd been hurt that he didn't want her with him at these times, but then her natural common sense had asserted itself, and she'd realized that of course he needed time to do his work and enjoy a little solitude. Besides, when they were alone together at night he was attentive enough to make up for any amount of coldness in the day.

What she couldn't understand was his behaviour to his mother. He seemed to want to annoy Sybil as much as possible – even at the cost of insulting his own wife. For instance, on the very first evening, when Sybil had enquired politely where Florrie came from, and who her family were, Valentine had answered: 'She comes from a perfectly delightful little hovel just outside Furzey Moor. And I rather think you may have met her brother. He's the thief who tried to break my jaw a few weeks ago.'

Sybil's face had remained impassive and, a little later, when Valentine had turned away, she'd drawn Florrie's hand through the crook of her gloved elbow, and patted it, saying in a surprisingly soft, girlish voice, 'You mustn't mind Vallie. He does so love to tease.'

Florrie had nothing but admiration for her new mother-in-law. She'd never seen anyone quite like her before. Magically slim and pretty – for an old woman – she had the wonderful quality, when her face was at the right angle, of looking exactly like Valentine. (Except that her nose was more delicate, and her eyes a lighter blue.) This resemblance made Florrie feel secure. She knew her voice and manners were different, rougher, than Sybil's, but she was certain that, deep inside, Sybil appreciated that difference and found it amusing, just as her son had.

For her part, Florrie longed to be as well groomed as Sybil. The most perfect bit of Sybil's appearance was her hair. A flattering colour, midway between pure white and the palest blonde, it was always clean and fluffy and framed her face in a series of deep waves, rippling up and away from both her forehead and a side-parting. Florrie wished she could touch it, because she was puzzled by its seeming softness, and the way that it remained immobile, even in a strong draught, as if it had been carved from stone. But she sensed, despite the fact that Sybil had patted her hand, uninvited, at the party, that her mother-in-law was one of those people who recoiled from physical contact.

They'd finished their soup, and Sybil shifted in her chair, a thoughtful look crossing her face, so that for an instant Florrie was reminded of Smart's expression as he readied himself to break wind. But of course nothing of that nature was happening to Sybil. She was merely pressing her foot on an electric bell-push concealed beneath the dining-room carpet. Florrie knew it was there because she'd got down on her hands and knees to look, this morning. She'd done it when she was alone, in case ladies weren't supposed to be interested in bell pushes.

She did so want to please her elegant new relation. When the footman handed round the mutton cutlets Florrie watched to see how Sybil helped herself from the dish, and then mimicked her exactly, down to the disdainful pout on her mouth. Feeling that she'd been silent too long, and that it would perhaps be more polite to make small talk about the weather, Florrie gestured with her fork at the window, where a breeze rattled the glass, and the clouds had gone grey.

'Smells like rain, don't it?' she said.

'Really? I can't say I'd noticed.'

'Well, I had,' Florrie continued, encouraged. "Cos our father, he always makes his hay early as he can, and I been watching the weather these last few days, and I reckon he'll have started, taken a gamble, like. But, see, the wind's gone round today, and the hay'll have to be carried sharpish, and I's scared it won't be fit.' She steadied a glass, which her gesturing hands had almost knocked over. 'It's terrible when the hay's damp. You gets this bubbly white mould grow on the stack, and he goes all black inside.'

Sybil dropped her knife and fork with a clatter, and pushed her plate away, and Florrie followed suit, not without some regret, because the mutton tasted good, and she'd barely had a mouthful.

'I've been meaning to have a little talk with you, Florence,' Sybil said, leaning forward. 'But I didn't want you to be offended.'

'Oh – I don't offend easy.'

'I do hope so. You see, it's about your clothes.'

'My clothes!' Florrie was astounded. 'But my clothes is new. Valentine give them me.'

'I know he did. And of course we both love Vallie to distraction, but his taste in clothes is really frightfully provincial. I ask you, who wears dropped waists nowadays?'

Florrie looked down at the skirt of her beautiful green linen frock. 'I does,' she said doubtfully. 'I likes them and all.'

Sybil gave a low laugh. 'I know you do, Florence, and you look ducky in them, too. But if you wish to be really well dressed you'll have to wear something altogether different.'

Florrie was wearing the despised dress as she reached the crossroads overlooking Fightingcocks Farm. The colour looked just as pretty against the cow-parsley in the hedgerows as it always had, but the shape of the shoulders and skirt now worried her. She hated to be vexed by such a trivial detail. What did it matter if a dress was a few months out of fashion? As if in answer, a large drop of rain fell out of the sky and splashed warmly on the front of it.

Below her and in the distance, up against the boundary with Lower Ash, she could see a group of figures building a stack while the two horses gathered up the hay, a wooden sweep between them like a giant comb. Even from this distance she could make out her mother's solid figure, her black clothes dusty against the bleached stubble of the field.

This was Florrie's second visit home since her marriage. She hadn't stayed long the first time, because Valentine had been waiting for her in the car at the crossroads – she'd only just been able to run down and reassure her mother. This visit was different. It wasn't simply anxiety about Father's hay that had made her decide to walk here on her own. It was another, more imprecise emotion. After lunch, Sybil had pleaded a migraine and retreated to bed, and Florrie had found herself entirely alone.

The empty spaces of the house had been silent, except for the tick of the grandfather clock as it marked out the seconds until the next meal. Even the continual bustle from the servants' quarters had ceased. The overcast sky had made the rooms cold and uninviting, and she'd found herself standing in the big hall, gazing up at the portraits there.

These were of a collection of remarkably ugly people, each with a subtle disproportion to the shape of their face or hair. One woman had the suspicion of a beard, another bulgy eyes like a frog, and most of the men were unwholesomely fat. They all had unhealthy, grey-white complexions, too, and each stared down at her with an identical expression. It wasn't dislike so much as an insultingly cool appraisal, as if they couldn't give a fig for what she thought of them.

She'd found herself stepping out of the side door into the garden, and walking rapidly towards the drive, and almost before she'd realized what she was doing she was on her way home.

Thunder rumbled across the hill, and Florrie ran up to the group of workers, discovering, to her discomfort, that one of them was Samuel. Luckily he had his back to her, and was working high up on the rick with Joe.

'What's you doing here?' Mother asked, between breaths. She was pulling hay from the bundle that had dropped from the tines of the sweep and throwing it to the men with a pitchfork, but Florrie could tell that the work was too hard for her. As she turned to speak she moved the fork to her left hand and pressed her right against her ribs, in a characteristic gesture of fatigue.

'I come to help. I been fretting about the hay.'

'You'll spoil your good clothes.'

'I don't care.'

'Let her if she wants to, Mother,' Joe called down. 'Us could use an extra pair of hands.'

Florrie pulled a fork from the side of the stack and began pitching as fast as she could, exhilarated to be using her body for proper work again. She was pleased by its strength, but a little dismayed by the aches that gathered almost immediately in her upper arms and stomach.

'Tired of being a fine lady already?' Joe sang out mockingly. 'You can come up here and change places with me if you is.'

'I'm not tired,' Florrie called back. 'It's the men as gets tired and can't cope with heavy work, isn't it, Mother?'

'It's the men as goes to Silver Hill, for certain,' her brother said from the stack, and Mother called out sharply: 'You keep quiet, Joe.'

'Quiet about what?' Florrie asked.

'Nothing. It's just his foolishness.'

A light patter of drops fell across the field. Florrie could hear Father's voice calling out to his horses as he coaxed them towards the stack, and then it began raining in earnest. She didn't dare look at the state of the hay, she just pulled and pitched, dipped and stretched, while her hair grew damp and clung close around her neck, and her skirt, heavy with water, sawed at the backs of her legs. Finally Joe called out to her to stop – they were going to pull a tarpaulin over the top and wait until another day to thatch it – and Mother tugged at her sleeve with some urgency, and the two of them struggled back across the field together, the rain so hard now that it was difficult to see the way.

When they reached the kitchen another clap of thunder sounded overhead and Mother pulled a coat off the back of the door and held it out to Florrie.

'Best put this on,' she said.

Glancing down at herself, Florrie noticed that her dress had gone semi-transparent in the rain, not that it revealed much more than the outline of the brassière Valentine had bought her. She was reluctant to cover it up, it seemed such a badge of maturity and sophistication.

Mother riddled the fire into a blaze and set the kettle to heat. It was odd how after the rooms at Earlshay – which Florrie didn't admire – this kitchen seemed so low and dark, like the lair of an animal.

'So what's it all about, then?' Mother asked, sitting next to her on the settle. Florrie held out her wet hands to the fire.

'I just missed home, wanted to see how you all was. Ain't I allowed to do that?'

'I wouldn't make a habit of it. Your place is with your husband.'

'But he ain't there half the time,' Florrie said, a note of disappointment in her voice that she hadn't thought she felt. 'He's busy, he don't want me with him. And there's nothing to set your hand to in that place. Servants does all the housework, and he don't run a farm. I wants to be up and doing, that's why I come here.'

Mother's eyes were shrewd under her damp cotton bonnet. 'What's this Lady Sybil do all day?' she asked.

Florrie sighed and pulled her hair out in a wet curtain to steam before the flames. 'Gets herself all prettied up, talks on this here telephone, reads and writes at her desk with a pair of them gold eyeglasses on, has migraines on her bed . . .'

'You'll have to do likewise then, won't you? You follow what she does, make yourself like one of them. Else your marriage won't last.' Mother got up to reach for the tea caddy on the mantel, so that her last words were muffled, and Florrie couldn't see her face as she spoke them. 'And there's no place here for you if it don't.'

'Truly?' Florrie asked, her voice trembling.

'It's a hard road you've set your foot to, but there's no turning back.'

Mother wouldn't discuss the subject any further. She sent Joe off to fetch the hire car from the village, saying that it wasn't right for Florrie to walk back to her husband in the rain, and Florrie's last glimpse of the farm, as she sat on the cracked seat of the old hire car, wool stuffing oozing between her fingers, was of Samuel standing awkwardly beside the wood-linney, water streaming off his face, carefully not looking in her direction.

Valentine was home when she reached Earlshay. His Bentley was in the drive, and she hurriedly pulled off Mother's old coat and gave it to the butler, ashamed of how wet and untidy she was. She ran up the stairs, her shoes squeaking with damp, and met Valentine in the passage outside her room.

He was wearing a beautiful tawny-coloured coat that fitted tight around the shoulders, and there was a smile on his face that she hadn't seen there for a week or more: pleased, feline.

'Where the devil have you been?' he asked. 'Swimming in a pond?' He picked a long piece of straw out of her hair, and the way he held it in his fingers made her feel that he didn't like her looking so bedraggled. It didn't appeal to him.

'I been home to see my family.'

He didn't comment, just raised one eyebrow in disapproval. 'Mama's got you a maid,' he said, as he turned to go. 'She seemed to think you needed one to help you dress. Perhaps you do.'

When Florrie opened the door of her room she found a young girl inside, laying out an evening gown on the bed. Her appearance was a shock, because she looked so unlike the other servants in the house. They were as plain as the portraits, most of them well into middle-age, but this girl couldn't be any older than Florrie herself. She had large brown eyes, a triangular, impish face, and glossy brown hair cut in a bob of immaculate smoothness. She curtsied when she saw her new mistress, and Florrie was aware of conflicting feelings: pleasure at having a companion her own age, and a strange stirring of unease.

Twenty-one

'Is it kind? Is it true? Is it necessary? That's what Nanny used to ask me. If it isn't, then you shouldn't speak at all. And no farmyard stories, nobody's interested in that sort of thing.'

These instructions of Sybil's made conversation a problem. Was any polite exchange strictly necessary? Florrie smiled at the man sitting on her left – who was talking about fishing – and hoped that would be sufficient.

Apart from the difficulty of impersonating a lady, Florrie was enjoying her first big dinner party. She loved the flowers and the silver, the beautiful fabrics, the warm air – smelling of lawn clippings – that floated in through the open windows and made the candle flames quiver.

The other end of the table she could see Valentine's blond head as he listened attentively to a lady with black hair. The sight of her husband made Florrie's heart move painfully. This new life of hers was all about distance: spaces between people, carefully and elegantly preserved. Without giving a reason, Valentine had moved out of her bedroom, so that their marriage was now conducted on a more formal basis. It made his company almost agonizingly pleasurable, when he did decide to visit her in the evenings, but it wasn't what Florrie would ever have chosen for herself.

The woman with black hair laughed up at Valentine, her mouth open. She was slim and attractive, resembling a carved Dutch doll, with her dark painted eyes, scarlet lips and shiny hair. Even her legs looked whittled, like a wooden toy's; Florrie had noticed them in the drawing-room before dinner. Florrie was especially interested in this woman since she was Sybil's closest friend. Called Veronica, she'd been writing Sybil letters all summer.

Florrie knew about the letters because, having complained to her mother-in-law about feeling restless and unoccupied, she had been set a number of tasks to do in the afternoons: adding up the account-books in pencil (Dress, Various: £5,762 2s 7d; Presents and Charities: £1 7s 5d); cleaning tennis-balls with a fiddly mechanical gadget, and cutting used stationery into 'spills'. Spills were long strips of paper pleated into a fan-shape and kept in jars on the mantelpieces so that gentlemen could use them to light their cigars from the fire. The construction of these objects gave Florrie a special insight into the private life of the house, since they were made from the contents of Sybil's and Valentine's wastepaper baskets.

There were incomprehensibly dull letters from the bank, all signed 'We remain, Sir, Your most Humble and Obedient Servants'. (Florrie couldn't help wondering whether the format changed if you ran out of money, perhaps to 'We remain, Slave, Your most Insolent and Overbearing Masters'.) There were sheaves of stiff, creamy paper, bearing abandoned sketches by Valentine, and there was Sybil's correspondence.

Florrie liked Valentine's drawings best, and had smoothed out a dozen and kept them for herself. They showed half-completed glimpses of a gypsy encampment: hooped canvas tents, scrawny dogs, two-wheeled spinner-carts, dignified women in long dresses. Every now and then there'd be a particular face in the crowd, caught crouching to light a fire, or spreading washing on a gorse bush. It was a young girl's, and she was scarcely older than Albie, with much the same look: wasted by childhood illness, but full of spirit and mischief. Florrie couldn't help liking her, and wondering if she was real, or if the whole encampment had just sprung from Valentine's imagination.

Veronica's letters described an altogether different world: strawberries and cream in marquees, hats at Ascot, dances in London, picnics on the river. Reading about these delightful-sounding things, Florrie wondered why Sybil had chosen to stay at Earlshay, instead of going off with her friend to do the Season. She could only guess that the answer must be connected with Sybil's gorilla.

Florrie had never seen Sybil with a gorilla, or even heard her mention one, but there were many allusions to it in Veronica's letters. Florrie had spent hours searching the Earlshay outbuildings for this animal, but so far found no trace of it. She'd even swum out to the island on the lake, in case it was kept there. (It wasn't.) The only place she hadn't yet managed to investigate was the big new hothouse beside the kitchen garden, whose key was kept jealously guarded by the irascible head gardener. Sometimes she pressed her face close to the glass of this place, hoping to catch a glimpse of Sybil's gorilla swinging through the grape vines and melons.

'My love to your little gorilla,' Veronica would usually write, just above her signature, and once: 'I do hope you succeed in *house-training* the gorilla soon. The autumn will be so fearfully dull if you don't.'

Florrie's companion at the dinner party had stopped talking and was staring at her hopefully. He had an amiable face, round and slightly damp, with bulging eyes, and was called Mentmore.

'Do you reckon a monkey could live in a greenhouse?' Florrie asked him.

He seemed pleased and interested by her enquiry. 'I don't see why not. Tough little chaps, monkeys. My uncle keeps a whole barrel-load of them in his park.'

'So you knows a bit about them?'

'Only what I've picked up.'

'But if I showed you a place, you could tell me if a gorilla were living there?'

'I could make a decent stab at it.'

'Sybil!' Veronica shrieked from the end of the table, causing other conversations to come to a halt. 'What's the largest thing you've ever killed?'

'A wasp, darling.'

'Nothing bigger?'

'I'm far too squeamish.'

'She means squeamish about outright murder,' Valentine explained pleasantly to the company. 'If there was a subtler, more underhand method of destruction Mama would, of course, be the first to employ it.'

An uneasy silence followed this remark. Sybil's face became smooth and impassive, and to fill the awkwardness the guests began to confess what they themselves had deliberately killed: guinea-pigs, pheasants, foxes, bluebottles, a pet dog with distemper. When it came to Mentmore's turn he said, blushing slightly, 'A triple crown,' and seeing Florrie's puzzlement, explained. 'That's when you have to bag a brace of grouse, a stag – and catch a salmon, all in one day. It's jolly hard, I can tell you.'

'Any advance on Mentmore's stag?' Valentine glanced round the table.

'A stag don't weigh hardly as much as a pig, do he?' Florrie ventured shyly, mindful of Sybil's strictures on farmyard stories. 'Not a good fat porker of thirteen score?'

'You've killed one that big, have you, Florrie?' Valentine asked. His voice had the husky, caressing quality to it that she liked. He sounded almost tender.

Emboldened by his response, and by the friendliness of her dinner-companion, Florrie said, 'Yes, I has. It's terrible sad, really, when the old pig has to go on. You gets so fond of him, see. It's like killing an old friend. It's queer, too, how he guesses what's up, starts squealing before you's halfway to his sty.'

'And what exactly do you do to him?' Valentine prompted.

'Well, you gets a good firm grip on a felling-hammer . . .' Florrie began, but before she could get any further Sybil struck the table hard with the flat of her hand, so that the glasses and cutlery jingled, and said in a high, angry voice: 'Stop it, Vallie! I forbid this conversation! Not at the dinner table!'

Valentine smiled, a wide, childish grin of triumph, before Sybil excused herself and left the room.

Veronica turned to him, shaking her head in mock-disapproval.

'What have you killed, Vallie?' she asked. 'You haven't told us yet.'

Valentine looked straight at Florrie, the smile still on his face, though now it had a sarcastic tinge to it. 'All hope for the future,' he answered.

Later, as Florrie's maid, Coral, was preparing her for bed – brushing her hair and recounting gossip from the servants' hall – Valentine came in and stood by the dressing-table, swaying slightly.

Florrie had had a happy evening, because after Sybil had left the table the party had become far less formal. Someone had wound up the gramophone, and there had been dancing, and after a while she and Mentmore had crept out into the gardens with a candle, and found their way round to the greenhouse in the dark.

'So you're pretty certain there's a largish monkey in here?' Mentmore had said, trying the door and finding it locked.

'It's the only place it could be, I reckon.'

Before she'd realized what he was doing, Mentmore had picked up a brick and shattered a pane of glass. 'Head gardeners always get above themselves,' he'd said, opening the door.

'You need to smash a few hothouses every now and then, just to keep them in order.'

Florrie had lit the candle, and they'd explored the high, leafy expanses of the house in silence. There'd been a dead hedgehog at the bottom of a sunken tank of water, and a strong smell of greenery and warm manure – but nothing else. Mentmore hadn't appeared surprised. He'd picked a couple of bunches of grapes and sat down on the floor, spreading out his handkerchief for Florrie to sit on. 'Here,' he'd said. 'Try these. Fruit always tastes better when it's stolen. So tell me,' he'd continued, 'what made you think there was an animal in here?'

Biting into tepid grapes, juice running down her chin, Florrie had explained about Veronica's letters. To her dismay Mentmore had reached across and stroked her hand with his. 'She doesn't care for you much, your ma-in-law, does she?'

'I don't know why you says that,' Florrie had countered indignantly, struggling up from the floor. She liked Mentmore, he was pleasant company, but it wasn't right for him to touch a married woman. 'She's always been good to me.'

Mentmore had got up, too, and ushered her out of the hothouse, blocking the hole in the glass skilfully with his handkerchief. As he'd closed the door he'd said to her in a serious tone: 'When you find that monkey – as you will – you come and see me. A jolly girl like you shouldn't have to spend her time rummaging through other people's rubbish.'

Valentine didn't speak to begin with, just watched Florrie and Coral as they stared back at him. Despite the difference in hair and skin there was a definite similarity between the two of them, he thought. A kittenish quality – to do with roundness of eye and steady, untroubled, cheeky gaze. He wrenched off his tie and stiff collar, and began slowly unbuttoning his shirt, noticing with pleasure that the maid had coloured up.

Murmuring an apology, she bolted. Valentine kicked the door shut behind her.

'It ain't terrible polite to take your clothes off when she's here,' Florrie remarked gently.

'She's only a servant.'

Florrie sat on the edge of the bed and smiled up at him, enjoying the contrast between his dark, formal clothes and the warm blond skin that was emerging. She liked his expression: the eyes narrowed, very blue.

'What difference do that make?' she asked absently.

'It means I don't care what she thinks.'

'She's still a person, like you and me.'

Valentine seized her by the shoulders. His breath smelt of wine, his skin, too, as if he'd been bathing in it. 'Are you telling me how to behave?' he growled. 'That's a bit of a liberty, coming from you.'

'Is it?' Florrie's eyes sparkled and she rolled back, soft and compliant.

'I know all about your escapade with Mentmore.'

'You don't want to fret about he.'

Valentine ran his hands swiftly down her body, feeling the curves of her breasts and hips. And without any further caress, gritting his teeth as if in pain, he entered her. He was drunk – she knew that now. Not because of any unsteadiness in his speech or gait, but because with him, liquor always had the effect of disconnecting feeling from action, so that although he moved inside her efficiently, showing none of the softness she'd heard about in coarse jokes, there was no passion there. No urge to give her pleasure, and no delight for him, either.

She couldn't feel any progression, as he rocked inside her, from rising to uncontainable excitement: just a barren motion, that gradually became uncomfortable for her, desperate for him. She didn't have enough experience to understand what was happening, but she was aware that as the summer had gone on he had, more and more often – especially when drunk – found it difficult to gain any relief from making love to her. She kissed him, stroked him, moved against him passionately, but every action left him unmoved. Finally he pulled away from her and lay on his back.

'I'm not jealous of Mentmore,' he said, in a small, bitter voice. She heard him swallow in the darkness. 'The man's a pansy. I just don't enjoy seeing you make a fool of yourself.'

Twenty-two

Now that she slept alone, Florrie was always up at first light, if not before. She'd hear the first faint stirrings of the servants – a stove door banging in the far, echoey depths of the kitchen, the rustle of a print frock on the stairs – and unable to stay in bed a moment longer, would slip quietly down to the hall and let herself out into the garden.

She never felt comfortable in the house, it smelt unfriendly, was too big, and she had to behave so unnaturally whenever she was in it, but she loved the garden. It astonished her. Huge plants, studded with flowers, rose up, higher than houses, out of carefully tended beds, and there were trees she'd never seen in her life before: with scarlet leaves, cones like rams' horns, blue-green needles, or black, crinkly pods. What she liked doing best was sitting at the top of a slope beside the house, and marvelling at the layers of landscape that dropped down before her, their colours gradually revealed in the morning light. First lawn and lake, then a band of woodland, then faded sage-green fields and brush, then pink earth and yellow stubble, then pale blue hills, then white sky with threads of cloud.

All around her birds would hop across the grass and challenge each other for possession of the rare shrubs, and she'd hear gardeners raking the paths, pushing wheelbarrows and talking in subdued tones. She always hid when she heard them approach, because she knew how disagreeable it is to labour while others sit idly by, how it destroys all the pleasure of the work. If she could she would have joined in and helped, but she'd tried that already and it wasn't allowed. The head gardener complained.

This morning, though, she forgot all about the garden, because as she was letting herself out of the house she heard a whinny. It was an odd noise to catch at Earlshay, since Valentine disliked horses and kept none. There was a well-equipped stable-yard and tack room beside the house, but it was always empty. The only living creatures she'd ever seen there were a pair of ducks from the lake. On rainy days they showered under the overflow from the stable gutter, and tasted the puddle water with thoughtful greed.

When she reached the yard she ran up the square, looking into the stalls, but didn't find what she wanted until she came to the corner by the tack room. There was a big loose box there, with iron bars set into its walls above shoulder-height, and through these, its eyes open wide enough to show an ill-tempered ring of white, she saw a horse. For an instant its expression, and the way it was standing, made the hairs rise on the back of her neck, then she looked more closely and recognized it. It was the gelding Valentine had been riding when she'd first met him in the woods above Fightingcocks Farm. It had to be: the height and colour were right, and the shape of the head. She thought it must have arrived late last night, while she'd been asleep.

Back when she'd looked after this animal at the farm, she'd considered it sour-natured – it had had a tendency to snap at Smart and Violet, and she'd always been aware that it was sizing her up for a kick – but its character seemed to have darkened since then. As she put her hand up to open the door its ears went back and it bared its teeth with real menace. The door wouldn't give: it was padlocked.

She was still talking to it, trying to coax it into a better mood, as she heard the chapel clock strike nine. She raced back to the house to wash for breakfast, and when she reached the dining-room found Valentine already there, hidden behind his copy of *The Times*. Sybil never ate breakfast. She stayed in her room until midday, so it was the one meal where Florrie could behave much as she liked, without being hedged in by other people's disapproval. There weren't even any footmen present: all the food was left in hot silver dishes on the sideboard.

Valentine didn't look up from his paper when she came in. As usual a place had been laid for her at the opposite end of the table; as usual, too, she moved it so that she could sit closer to her husband. Then she looked to see if he'd already eaten, and since he had, she went over to the sideboard and began emptying the silver dishes on to her plate. A great variety of fare was on offer each morning, and Florrie had enjoyed sampling little bits of it until she'd learned from her maid, Coral, that leftovers were invariably thrown away. Ever since, horrified by such waste, she'd determined to use up every scrap herself. Porridge, kippers, haddock, kedgeree, boiled eggs, scrambled eggs, fried eggs, bacon, sausages, kidneys – she piled it all up on her plate like a large, multicoloured molehill.

She'd eat a little of it and slip the rest surreptitiously into handkerchiefs and pockets, carrying it upstairs and hiding it in the bottom of her wardrobe. Later, she'd attempt to get it to Fightingcocks Farm.

Valentine just didn't share her feelings about food. However passionately she argued, she couldn't convince him it was a crime to throw food away uneaten.

'But that's what money's for,' he'd once said, his tone coaxing and affectionate. 'If it does nothing else it frees you from hoarding scraps and adding up columns in a panic. If you need more gold for your family you can have it – but please, don't let's have all this nonsense with bits of old buttered toast.'

She couldn't accept his attitude. There was no way she could ever learn to stand by unmoved when fine bread or lean bacon was tipped into a dustbin. The very thought of it grieved her, so that getting every particle of waste to Mother came to seem far more important than just sending the usual weekly present of money.

Smuggling the food up and downstairs wasn't easy, though. The servants were affronted by it. She'd hoped, on first coming to live at Earlshay, that the servants would become her allies, but instead they had proved the most implacable, the most stony-faced of enemies. They didn't like her keeping buckets of swill in her bedroom, and objected fiercely to her carrying them down the back stairs, and she'd often failed in her mission, and been forced to tip the food on to a windowsill in order to avoid becoming involved in a violent (and always fruitless) quarrel with the butler.

Valentine disliked talking at breakfast, so Florrie usually kept silent, just admiring the slenderness of his hands as they moved the pages of the paper, and the top of his blond head as he leaned forward to follow a particular story. She liked the sound the paper made, too, and the faint perfume of soap, fresh linen, and warm skin that came off her husband; it made up, a little, for not seeing him at night.

This morning, though, curious about the arrival of the horse, she gave a polite cough to attract his attention. It was the kind of stifled, inoffensive sound that a lady was supposed to make: Florrie felt pleased with the effect.

Valentine put down his paper. It formed a tent over the high, ornate toast rack (which was empty – all twelve slices of toast being already in Florrie's skirt pocket). 'Yes?' he enquired, in a weary voice.

'I were wondering,' Florrie began, 'about that horse in the stable.'

'You were, were you?'

'He's the gelding you had before Christmas, isn't he? Is you going to ride him?'

'No.' Valentine's eyes were cold as he looked at her. She noticed that he'd cut himself shaving: there was a tiny bead of dried blood on his cheek. It made the texture of his skin look unfamiliar. For an instant she wasn't able to recall what it felt like to touch.

'You selling him, then?'

'Despite what you may think, Florrie, I don't happen to be a total cad,' Valentine said, the anger in his voice disconcerting because she couldn't think what she'd done to provoke it. 'That animal's thoroughly dangerous, a bolter. It could kill someone. I'm certainly not going to ride it myself, and selling it is quite out of the question.'

'You'll be knocking it on the head then, will you?' Florrie said, quite reasonably, she thought. That was what her father would do, in a parallel situation. If an animal was an incurable rogue then it was only decent to send it on.

Valentine studied her disdainfully before answering, his gaze lingering on her pile of breakfast. 'Not everyone's a bloodthirsty little peasant like you,' he said. 'Some of us are slightly more civilized.'

His paper rustled as he hid himself behind it again. Florrie didn't think the word 'peasant' was an insult, but he'd certainly spoken it like one. He'd been strange lately: unpredictable, suddenly hostile. Even his tastes seemed to be changing. Yesterday, as they were coming down the stairs to dinner, he'd stopped her, put his hands gently either side of her head (the unexpected caress making her tremble), and pressed her hair flat, as if trying the look of her face with a less exuberant frame. Half-frowning, he'd asked, 'Why don't you ever smooth this down?'

And Florrie, flustered, had answered, 'I never thought to, before now.' The truth was that before they were married he had told her, over and over again, how much he admired her hair – its abundance and waviness – and made her promise never to cut it short or even tie it back. Barely four months had passed since then; it was only September now. Had he stopped liking it so soon?

Florrie wrapped up her breakfast. Even if he had grown tired of her, he still ought to treat her with respect. She was his wife, wasn't she?

She got up, and standing beside him, said with crushing dignity: 'I thought "civilized" meant being polite, not insulting folk for no good reason.'

She turned to sweep out of the room, but the effect was spoiled by Valentine calling her back and pressing something soft into her hand.

'You dropped your haddock,' he said.

As she ran along an upstairs corridor Florrie caught sight of herself reflected in a pane of glass. It was raining outside, and night had fallen, turning the windows into dark mirrors. She'd been feeling light-hearted and dizzy from champagne, and entirely forgotten about her appearance, and it was disheartening to be faced with it so suddenly. She was wearing a curious dress Sybil had given her. It was all orangey-browns – colours Florrie'd never liked – and made out of a slithery, clammy fabric that gripped her waist tight before dropping to her ankles. Wearing it, Florrie felt as if she was encased in another person's skin: perhaps Sybil's, because it smelt so strongly of Chanel No. 5. The general effect, she thought, looking at herself with dislike, was of a ludicrously bad impostor – a coal-heaver pretending to be a duchess – since the thin straps of the dress revealed her powerful shoulders and arms, the muscles bulging from years of heavy labour. She could never manage to get her hands white enough, either.

Even her face looked wrong – too broad and shiny – because,

in a vain attempt to get her hair to look smooth, she'd got Coral to pin it back in a knot. She was just pulling it free when she heard low voices near by, and she crept a little further along the corridor.

Valentine was giving another big party, and after dinner they'd begun playing children's games. At the moment it was 'Sardines', a type of hide-and-seek which involved everyone cramming drunkenly into the same small hiding-place. At least Florrie thought it was supposed to be like that, but it was difficult to be sure, because most of the guests hardly seemed to be playing at all. They roamed the house in sniggering gangs, and she could hear the piano being strummed fitfully downstairs, either 'Why Is The Bacon So Tough?' or 'Falling In Love Again'. She knew those were the titles, because she'd heard them being sung earlier. The party had been more enjoyable back then, perhaps because the champagne had made her feel as if she was floating, the conversation had seemed miraculously funny, and Valentine had smiled at her from the other end of the table.

The voices became more distinct. Recognizing Veronica's, Florrie paused in the doorway of a dark bedroom.

'It was just his rotten luck,' she was saying. 'Vallie's not the horsy type.'

'It bolted with him, didn't it? More than once, too. He shouldn't have sold it on.'

'Nonsense, darling. You've sold dodgy horses before now. What about Viper? Didn't he have a thing about hedges?'

'That's different.'

'No, it isn't, it's exactly the same.'

'Viper didn't kill anyone. And Primula said Vallie didn't even warn them. That's definitely not playing the game. That's *criminal*.'

'I still don't think it's his fault,' Veronica insisted.

'You're so stuck on him, Veronica, I can't see why,' another, thinner voice announced peevishly from near the ceiling. 'He's only a filthy little parvenu, after all. Didn't his pa *buy* the title from Lloyd George? You know what they call this house? "Tainted Meat Towers." Because the family made their money out of tinned beef: "Bandinelli's Bully-Beef".'

'I know, I've heard,' Veronica said in an irritated tone. 'Screamingly funny, isn't it?'

'And as for that wife of his . . .' the thin voice continued, but Florrie, realizing too late the perils of eavesdropping, skipped out of the doorway and made a heavy stepping sound in the passage.

'Has I found a sardine?' she asked, but no one answered, so she switched on the light.

'It's not pukka to do that,' Veronica said from the bed, where she was lying on her front, her slim legs in the air. 'You're supposed to blunder about in the dark.'

'Besides,' the thin voice said – it turned out to belong to a blonde girl with a long neck and floaty blue dress, who was perched on top of a wardrobe – 'we're not sardines, we're just having a private talk, so you can just toddle off.'

Feeling this was reasonable, Florrie switched off the light and retreated. Behind her there were stifled giggles, and she heard Veronica say in mock-reproof: 'Really, Poff, you are a stinker.'

Walking back to the main landing, Florrie began to feel sick of the party. She was growing tired of her dress, too, which itched around her waist. She was going to pull it off and stamp on it, she decided. As she made her way towards her room, she passed Sybil's, and glancing inside saw that two men from the dinner party were sitting on the dressing-table. They'd thrown a pink scarf over a lamp, and in its rosy light were staring into Sybil's mirror and trying on her hats and jewellery. One of them even had a corset on, over his dinner jacket, and was making a kissing face at himself. This sight made Florrie more cheerful. (Possibly because she remembered Sybil telling her how well bred the two young men were, and what delightful manners they had.)

She was about to run up the stairs to her own corridor when she heard the green baize door flap on the landing, and saw a darkness flutter there before vanishing. The piano had stopped, and a silence fallen. For a moment all she could hear was the wind moaning outside the windows, then the baize door creaked gently, as it settled, and thinking that the players might have gone that way, and that she was missing out on the game, Florrie hurried over, and pulled it a little wider. She could see the long servants' corridor ahead, illuminated by a faint light which came up the stairwell, and two people standing by the curve of the banisters, locked in an embrace. One of them pulled away, and she heard her maid say, in a voice like the cooing of a bird: 'You're bad, that's what you are, bad as bad can be. And worse.'

The door slammed behind Florrie, and Coral bolted down the stairs. Curious to see who her suitor might be, Florrie walked along the passage towards the figure that still leaned against the banisters. Before she got there, she knew who it was: Valentine.

He straightened as she got close, and smiled teasingly. 'I suppose you think I ought to apologise,' he said. 'But I'm not going to.'

She couldn't speak. She felt consumed with emotion and fury, and at the same time she was lost, too, unable to make sense of anything.

'I don't see why I shouldn't do what I want,' he went on. 'You knew what kind of person I was when you married me. Didn't I say I wasn't honourable or decent?'

Florrie shook her head. 'Not so I truly understood it.'

He sighed. 'Well, then, let me explain now. It won't make the slightest difference how you behave, how angry you get, what you say to me. I shall still do exactly as I please.'

'Don't you care for me any more?' Florrie asked, her voice barely more than a whisper.

'What's that got to do with it? The trouble with you, Florrie, is that you're such a narrow-minded little puritan.'

She stood in the rain, hearing those words in her head, and then she walked towards the stables, as if in a dream. All she was aware of was an overpowering need to be comforted, to feel safe, to be able to think things through and come to terms with them. The memory of Smart's kindly presence made her go up and look at the horse which slept quietly in its iron-barred prison. She rubbed the tears from her face and twisted a nail in the padlock, wrenching it open. It was curiously consoling to fight an inanimate object – and win. She opened the door and, seeing that the horse was now thoroughly awake, made a sudden run at it, and jumped on its back, grabbing its mane firmly in her hands. It reared and bucked and squealed, trying to fight her off, but she was on too securely for that. It wheeled around, charged out of the open door, clattered on the cobbles, and was out in the wind as she clung fast to its back, feeling a strange triumph as it bolted.

Twenty-three

Florrie's hand felt strange. It trembled, her fingers were sprinkled with damp earth, and a furriness pushed its way past her palm. She opened her eyes and saw a mole sniffing the ground beside her face. It was a small one, its trunk-like nose the colour of a cut strawberry, and when it turned to wander in the opposite direction she couldn't resist reaching out and catching it round the waist. She wished she hadn't, because the movement sent a sharp ache up her arm. The mole expressed a similar regret by writhing in her fingers, its body as solid and hard-packed with muscle as a human knee, and she let it go.

She was lying below a chestnut tree, looking up into its branches, and she felt peaceful – perhaps because it was like being in the old pram at home, under the trees beside the gate. The light glowing through the trees and branches was cold and white and she could hear church bells ringing. They sounded much clearer than they ever had when she was at home.

She squinted down at herself and was puzzled by the dress she was wearing – brown, soaked dark by water – and began to sit up, to get a closer look. Immediately she was struck by a heavy, nauseating pain on the side of the head. This pain seemed to be a part of her – it was unpleasantly familiar, as if it had been there a long time, and knew her well. It brought memories with it, too, fragmented scenes, none of them good.

She remembered a wet branch, its leaves prickly and shiny with rain, swinging towards her with a hiss. She recalled Valentine's face, lit from beneath by the light from the kitchen staircase, and the curious expression on it – like a naughty child's – a mixture of shame and pleasure, as if being caught by Florrie had only made his indiscretion more amusing.

The feeling of helpless misery that she'd felt then returned, and she remembered how, as the horse had bolted out of the stable door, and they'd galloped down the drive, she'd grimaced to herself and thought: So nothing I does'll make the slightest difference, hey? What about this, then?

There was no sign of a horse anywhere under the trees. She looked round for it carefully, keeping her head as steady as possible, so not to disturb the pain, but even so a cold breeze caught at a rawness of her cheek and temple, and something moved up there, shifted, like a curtain. She didn't put her hand up; she didn't want to know what it was. Instead she struggled to her feet, dismayed to discover that she had no shoes, and that it was damp underfoot, so that her silk stockings squelched in the grass. There was a road winding through the trees, and she recognized its curve and the line of the horizon: she was halfway between Kittenhole and Furzey Moor.

It seemed unusually deserted. She guessed, from the church bells, that it had to be Sunday morning, and as she emerged from the spinney and began walking down a narrow slope she saw that there were rabbits everywhere, sitting up in the potholed road and staring impudently at her. They only bounced for the safety of the hedge an instant before she reached them. Seeing a house up ahead she quickened her step, but it was derelict.

The bells were ringing louder now, the joyful peal that signals the end of a service, and she walked along the road in a dream, the landscape swimming in and out of focus. At one point she crouched on a pile of stones beside the road, vomiting convulsively, and when she could finally stand again the light was brighter, and the side of her face stiff. She knew Samuel lived somewhere near here, and she was sure he'd help her to find the horse, if only she could reach him. But it looked so different from the last time she'd been this way. She'd passed three houses so far, and all had looked abandoned, and the hedges, higher and wider than ever before, loomed over the road, throwing out great ropes of bramble, heavy with blackberries.

Even Samuel's house had changed, when she finally came to it. It looked as if it was in the process of burying itself in the ground: corrugated iron had been laid over the rotten thatch, and on one side the walls had collapsed completely, tilting the roof at a crazy angle. As she gazed at it a voice she hardly recognized said, 'Florrie?' doubtfully, and she turned to see Ellis Rawes standing beside her.

He was dressed in what must, she guessed, be his Sunday best: a black coat gone grey and shiny at the edges, a celluloid collar, a red handkerchief that covered the place where his shirt and tie ought to be, and old dark breeches that were ridiculously loose, as if they'd been loaned by a kindly, large-bottomed giant. His boots gleamed with polish but seemed odd. Florrie narrowed her eyes. If only she could concentrate properly. They looked as if they had bits missing from them, the gaps blacked in with soot. A queasy dizziness overcame her, and she felt herself falling, and when she next opened her eyes she was inside the house, seated in an armchair that smelt of dog. Ellis was crouching in front of her, a bowl of water and a rag in his hand.

'I's sent Mrs Turl for the doctor,' he said.

'Has you seen a horse?' she answered. ''Cos I were riding one and fell off.'

'A horse did this to you?' he asked. 'He wants knocking on the head, he do. Cuh!' His special word had a new, bitter edge

213

to it that Florrie hadn't heard before.

'My husband don't want to do that – says it ain't civilized,' Florrie said, and Ellis didn't answer, just tilted his head and curled his mouth, as if he'd thought of saying 'Cuh', but decided to snarl instead.

Now she was sitting down Florrie felt weaker than when she'd been walking. Her voice sounded as if it was coming from a long distance away, too. Even so, she was aware of odd, sharp details. As Ellis leaned forward to clean her face she noticed how wiry he was: his forearms, as they came out of the jacket, were as dark and spare as staves of wood. She'd never realized before how closely he resembled his nephew, Samuel. He had exactly the same dark eyes and stiff way of holding his shoulders.

'You're so like Samuel,' she said, before she'd realized it.

'I didn't know your ladyship ever give him a thought.'

'Yes, I do. I'm fond of him.'

Ellis squeezed out his cloth and dabbed at her cheek, his touch so light that she could barely feel it. 'Yet you never told him straight you was carrying on with this other fellow. You led him on and led him on.'

She opened her eyes wide. 'No, I didn't!' She was sure she blushed as she said it. 'We was just friends.'

'Friends when he give you his ring? Friends when you was courting proper?'

'We weren't courting.'

Ellis, exploring the left side of her face, gave a sharp hiss, as if he'd just burnt his hand on a hot kettle. 'You mayn't have been,' he said levelly. 'But he were. Broke his heart, you has.'

'Where is he now?'

Ellis shook his head and put his cloth away. 'I daresn't touch that cheek,' he said. 'You've tore it something dreadful. Best wait for the doctor. It's beyond me.'

'You haven't said where he is.'

214

He stood up, no longer fiercely angry, just sour. 'I don't know meself. He went off up-country three month ago, looking for work. Not that there's any to be found. There weren't much of a harvest this year, too damp, see, and most of the farms is gone on.' He sighed. 'I'd best go look for this horse of yours, hadn't I? Else your husband won't be best pleased.' He emphasized the word 'husband' in a meaningful way, Florrie didn't know why.

'Please stay,' she said. 'At least till the doctor comes. I promise I'll help Samuel all I can. I didn't mean to hurt his feelings, but I'll make it up to him.'

It was two weeks before she came down to dinner. The hall and the stairs looked brilliantly, richly colourful after the darkness of her bedroom, where she'd had to lie with the curtains drawn, day after day, to recover from the concussion. Sometimes Sybil's elderly personal maid had brought her a meal, or stood grim-faced, a towel in the crook of her elbow, while Florrie bathed, because she wasn't to be left alone while doing anything so risky. (Coral had vanished, without explanation, the evening of Florrie's accident.)

Florrie hadn't felt unwell – the dizziness and headaches had gone after the first few days – she'd just lain there in the dark, her mind humming to itself, and once, very late at night, Valentine had sat on the side of her bed, and touched her hand. She'd known it was him because of his sharp, flowery cologne, but his presence, in the blackness, hadn't felt like Valentine. His fingers in hers had seemed young, insecure; it had been like holding Albie's hands when he'd been ill and they'd slept in the big bed together. The instant he'd spoken, though, the childishness had melted away.

Guessing she was awake, he'd said, 'I'll have the horse destroyed.'

'I don't want that.'

'Why not? Wasn't that what you were trying to prove to me?' He'd lifted her hand and kissed her fingers.

'I didn't do it for no reason. It were an accident.'

'An accident that the padlock was smashed?' His tone had been affectionate.

'I just wanted to get on his back, for comfort, like. I misses having a horse about.'

'I'll buy you another.' His kisses had become soft, teasing bites.

She'd sat up, the bedclothes rustling. 'I don't want another. I wants him.'

'Why?'

''Cos –' she'd gripped his hand tightly in hers, and he'd tried to free himself, as if the fervour in her touch and voice had offended him – 'I don't believe in giving up on anything. So he's vicious? Well, I can tame that, I can make him safe. I knows how to do it. And I want to try. I want to make him gentle as a little lamb, so he trembles and kneels down when he hears my voice.'

Valentine had laughed softly. 'And will you still want him when he does?'

'I'll find out, won't I?'

'Sadistic,' he'd said, his voice warm, amused. 'I always thought that was why women liked horses so much. Gives them a chance to order a great big animal about and hit it with a whip. Evens the score a little.'

'It ain't like that at all, and you knows it,' Florrie had answered, and after a while he'd loosed his hand gently from hers and left.

Now she paused at the door of the dining-room. She'd washed her hair and fluffed it out so that it hid the left-hand side of her face, and she didn't think she looked too bad. You could still

216

see raw red lines where the skin had been sewn back, and bruising, but the rest of her was just as pretty as it had ever been.

She remembered playing with her mother's hands once, and exclaiming at how lined and worn the skin was, and Mother saying stoutly, 'Nothing amiss with that. Shows I've worked hard. Ain't nothing wrong with scars, nor wrinkles neither. Shows you've led your life proper, lived every bit of it with a brave heart.' Florrie had whispered this to herself as she tried out ribbons and combs in her hair and abandoned them. She hoped Valentine wouldn't mind too much about her cheek – he hadn't seen it since the accident. She suspected he might, and she could just imagine how sarcastic he'd be about her mother's words, if she repeated them.

She turned the door handle. The gong had gone a few minutes ago, she'd heard its sound eddying up the stairs like ripples from a stone. It wasn't just Sybil and Valentine in there – she could hear other voices too: Veronica's, and a man who sounded like Veronica's brother.

'In my opinion the working classes should be lined up against a wall and shot,' Sybil was saying, as Florrie entered the room. She stopped, her mouth open in a round, painted O.

'Won't you continue, Mama?' Valentine said. 'I'm sure Florrie would be fascinated by your attitude to the working class. After all, she does have what one might call a personal interest.' He inclined his head to summon the footman standing behind his chair. 'Lay another place for her Ladyship.'

He didn't look directly at Florrie – not then, and not during the meal – and she could tell, from that one omission, that he did mind about her face, very much. Sybil made polite enquiries about Florrie's state of health, and then Florrie sipped at her wine, listening, bright-eyed, to the flow of conversation. She was careful not to put her elbows on the table and to hold her soup spoon at the correct angle. These details, once so apparently trivial, weren't any more. She needed to be like the others, didn't want Valentine to find her grotesque.

The scene was lit by a curious kind of candlelight – an electric variety. Valentine was amused by ingenious inventions, and this was just one of the many he'd installed at Earlshay. They looked exactly like real candles, except that instead of a flame at the top of each wax column there was a filament enclosed in a frail glass bulb. These mock-candles were plugged into a wire tablecloth hidden under the stiff damask one, and a thick cable twisted away to a plug beside the fireplace. In the past, Florrie had found them disturbing. They flickered ominously when any voice was raised, and the light they gave off was dim, but this evening, because of her scars, she was grateful for their subdued glow.

Veronica's brother, a Justice of the Peace, was talking about poaching, and the vast increase in its frequency, and the pressure being put on him – against his will – to be lenient in court. Sybil, casting occasional fascinated glances at Florrie's face, complained about the lapse in moral standards and the irritation of finding trespassers on her land. Veronica's attitude was more Christian. She wanted Valentine to set up a soup kitchen and hand out parcels of food to his tenants, to alleviate the hardship that was driving them to steal – and Valentine, aware that Sybil and Veronica were competing for his attention, sat like a golden lion at the head of the table, a subtle smile on his face.

'What do you think, Florence?' Veronica asked suddenly. 'After all, you know these people best, don't you?' She gave a cool, social smile, and Florrie was grateful for the way Veronica acted as if there was nothing unusual about her appearance at all.

'It might seem kind to give out soup and that, but it isn't, not really,' Florrie answered. 'It's humiliating. What they needs is proper work. Why can't you pay them to plough up all the fallow round Earlshay and farm it? Used to be cornfields round here, could be again.'

'Because I don't happen to like farming,' Valentine said. 'It doesn't interest me. As far as I'm concerned it's just a monumentally dull way of losing money.'

'I reckon I could make it pay.'

He half shut his eyes, as if in acute boredom. 'No, you couldn't. Even the great Cecil Tavender wouldn't last five minutes if you didn't slip him money on the sly. It's very simple. If you can't produce corn, or whatever other foul substance you choose to grow, cheaper than they do abroad you can't sell it, and you go bust.'

'Why's that?' Florrie was enjoying the conversation. If only polite conversation was always this interesting. She sensed the eyes of the other guests on her, felt she was showing herself to be intelligent, worth talking to.

'Haven't you ever heard of Free Trade?' Valentine asked scornfully. 'No? Well, I suggest you read a newspaper tomorrow morning, then, instead of stuffing your pockets with scrambled egg.'

'Stuffing her pockets with what?' Sybil enquired.

'With egg, Mama, and haddock and bits of toast. Florrie's the one who's been decorating your windowsills for you.'

Veronica began laughing, and Florrie had to listen, her hands curling into fists, while her breakfast habits were teasingly described by Valentine. She didn't know why he was being so unkind. All she did understand was that she had to hide the dismay she felt. He didn't like it when she showed weakness, and he was repelled by tears. Her brain working furiously, the conversation a formless hubbub in her ears, she waited for a pause before saying clearly, 'I knows something you could do, that *would* work.'

'Do tell us, I can hardly wait.' Sybil was still smiling from Valentine's stories about the breakfast.

'You could build a wall. A proper high one all round the estate. I've walked round it meself, and most places they's just a bitty scrap of wall barely four foot high, or a strand or two of wire, or a hedge. Now if you was to build a ten-foot wall' – seeing the interest on Sybil's face, Florrie added jokingly, 'with broken glass on top – not a single poacher could get in. And more than that, it'd take hundreds of men to build. Why, everyone round here'd be in work for a couple of years or more.'

She rather spoilt the effect of her speech by knocking her wineglass over as she gestured, because as the liquid hit the tablecloth a fizzing noise began and the fake candles exploded, but during the confusion which followed she did hear Sybil say, in a thoughtful tone, 'Actually, I do think it's rather a ducky idea.'

Twenty-four

Valentine was abroad, motor racing. He'd been gone part of October and all November, and Florrie had grown used to the silence in the house, with only her and Sybil at each meal. After lunch they'd usually sit in the blue drawing-room, and Sybil would work at her embroidery. Just one corner of silk would poke from a flowery bag on her knee, and she'd concentrate on it fiercely, through gold spectacles. Florrie guessed, from the way the rest of the fabric was kept hidden, that it must be underwear, and it tickled her that Sybil should apply the same intent, perfectionist attention to the embellishing of her own knickers as Mother had to the carving of butter, or Father to the ploughing of a neat acre.

'I had such problems bringing Vallie up,' Sybil sighed, this afternoon, as the wind rattled the windows and lifted the carpet by the door with a low hum. Florrie sat quietly on the opposite side of the fireplace, her head in shadow, a book on her knee. Ever since Valentine's sarcastic remark about her never reading the paper she'd begun steadily working through not only *The Times* but every volume in his study, however dull or peculiar.

Lifting her eyes from the pages of *The King of Elfland's Daughter* she heard Sybil say, with unexpected candour, 'His father deserted me – did you know? He ran off with a singer from the music hall. And I had to live in lodgings in London: two rooms off a flight of stairs. I can't tell you how dreadful it was, and how desperate I became.'

As Sybil described her anguish, Florrie tried to sympathize, but Sybil's destitution was harder to believe in than the fantastical descriptions in Lord Dunsany's book. She just couldn't visualize Sybil scrubbing a floor, or eating a pig's head, or even wearing ordinary clothes, and she felt her failure to conjure these images was vindicated when Sybil added, in a sorrowful tone, 'I was so poor I actually had to sell my tiara.'

She put down her sewing and peered at Florrie through her spectacles, like a severe blonde owl. 'This is why I do insist on you learning good manners, because when one's money and prospects have utterly gone, that is what one is judged by.'

In a low, respectful tone, appropriate to the solemn mood, Florrie asked, 'What were Valentine's father like?'

'Beautiful – of course. Those dark Italian looks; but rather brutal and uncultivated. And hopelessly unfaithful. I've always found that hardest to forgive, infidelity. It's so deeply wounding, don't you think?'

In the safe shadow of her chair, Florrie blinked. Did Sybil know about Valentine kissing Coral, then? How could she have found out?

'I wouldn't have an opinion,' she answered in steady tones. 'I hasn't had what you'd call much experience of the matter.'

'No. Silly of me.' Sybil sounded annoyed. 'I keep expecting you to be more sophisticated than you actually are.' She unpicked a line of stitches with a hiss of dissatisfaction, and Florrie watched her for a while, thoughtful, uneasy, before returning to her book.

'Would you like me to find you another maid?' Sybil asked at length, without looking up from her work, leaving Florrie in no doubt that her previous remarks on the subject of infidelity had been very precisely aimed.

'If I has to have one, I'd sooner choose her meself.'

'Very sensible. You know, Florence, I do so *admire* you for the way you coped with Coral. It gave Vallie the most fearful fright when you bolted on that horse. You should have seen his face! It was *ashen*. I daresay he'll be a great deal more discreet next time.'

'Next time what?'

Sybil gave a silvery laugh. 'I can't believe anyone could be so naïve! Surely you know what Vallie's like by now?'

'As you say, I'm as daft as a handcart,' Florrie answered, setting her book down and leaving the room with dignity.

Once free of the drawing-room, she raced up the stairs, changed into her riding-habit, and slipped out of the house by the servants' entrance. Outside she was less aware of the wind than of the bright December sunshine. The park rippled and shook itself, like an animal settling its fur, and somewhere in the distance she could hear the steady thud of an axe. Perhaps they had at last started to clear the foundations of the wall. She'd ride out that way in a minute.

The horse was waiting for her in the stables. He'd grown more biddable, but she still didn't trust him. He no longer tried to bite, but she had the feeling he was biding his time, anticipating the one day when she'd fatally relax her guard.

In a way, coping with the horse was like talking to Sybil: you had to skirt any situation where harm might be done to you. And yet Sybil could be disarmingly kind – it made the times when she was malicious more painful. She'd been sympathetic over Florrie's injuries, had shown Florrie how to draw a lock of hair forward in a long ringlet in front of her ear in order to hide the scars, and lent her some powder to effect a camouflage.

'Remember, Florence,' she'd said gently, as she'd demonstrated these techniques in the big mirror in her room, 'you must always have compassion for yourself, treat your body kindly when no one else will.' Florrie hadn't understood what she was talking about, but even so, as Sybil had held the ringlet in her painted fingers she'd almost, but not quite, felt like Mother.

Florrie rummaged in the tack room, looking for equipment to make a safety harness with: two leather hobbles, a running W-swivel, a surcingle, and a length of rope. Last week, when Sybil had gone to London for a dress fitting, Florrie'd done her best to cure the gelding of his habit of bolting. She'd walked him out to a big fallow pasture beyond the edge of the park, where the hedges were so dense and high that even the most determined animal couldn't jump or break through. Her ruse had worked, because when the horse had bolted, he'd had nowhere to run to. He'd simply circled the field at a gallop, with Florrie gripping tightly to his back, until, dripping with sweat, he'd come to a standstill from sheer exhaustion. Then, as kindly and firmly as she could, Florrie had urged him to a last brief trot, just to prove that she was the one in control. Now she was going to try something riskier.

The horse stood patiently while she fitted the hobbles. As she checked the smooth running of the swivel, Florrie tried not to think about Valentine and the possibility that he was unfaithful. All she had ever seen him do was kiss Coral, but she was uneasily conscious that everyone around her – not just Sybil, but visitors to the house, even her own brother Joe – kept hinting at more. It was only a half-awareness, like her half-awareness of Sybil's hostility, because she didn't want to believe it. She refused to. Faith could move mountains, that was what she had always been taught. She would go on believing in the fundamental goodness of others, and her faith would keep her strong.

As Florrie opened the door of the loose box the horse gave a high whinny of excitement and cocked his head, as if awaiting an answer. She swung on to his back and urged him forward, and he trotted lightly round the side of the house, and down the drive to the woodland beside the front gate. Not once did he show a flicker of disobedience; ears pricked, he listened to whatever Florrie murmured, and followed the urging of her hands with a silken mouth.

There weren't many working on the wall. As she got closer, Florrie heard a bonfire crackle and saw a familiar shape.

Joe was there, leaning on an axe and cupping his hand to light a cigarette. 'There's beautiful game in this wood, and no mistake,' he called out to her. 'I only been here an hour or two, but already I seen a good half-dozen roe deer. Cor, weren't they ever fat? And venison's making a tidy sum in market.

'Yup,' Joe went on, in a slightly quieter voice, 'it's like stepping inside a big pantry here – all the food you could wish for. And those pheasants! Why, they's so tame they almost walk theirselves into your waistcoat!' Saying this, he opened his jacket slightly, acting out the words, and Florrie was shocked to see a warm, feathery mass plumping out his inner pocket.

'Joe!' she whispered. 'You can't do that. Valentine's ever so hard on poachers. He'll go maze if he finds out.'

'No, he won't. You'm his wife. It's just as much your game as his – and seeing as I's your brother it's as near as makes no difference mine too.'

'If it's yours, why's you hiding it in your coat?' Florrie asked cheekily, and Joe turned away, with an air of injured dignity. From behind, the bulge in his coat looked deeply suspicious, and bits of reddish feather floated round his feet.

'Have you seen Samuel? Is he back with Ellis?' she shouted after him.

'Ask him yourself,' Joe replied – and she saw him go up to a figure heaping brushwood on the fire, and the figure break away and start moving towards her. All at once she became uncomfortably conscious of the fact that she was sitting high up on a glossy, fine-bred horse, and that she was dressed in a fashionable habit and wearing a bowler with a curly brim. She

225

didn't want to look and act as if she was superior to Samuel, was providing him with work out of charity. She had no wish to humiliate him. But running alongside this feeling was another, less honourable one: she was curious as to what he'd look like, now she had it on good authority that his heart was broken.

He walked towards her, cap in his hands. He'd altered since she'd last seen him – grown more sinewy – he'd lost the childish quality he used to have. He waited for her to speak, staring at her face as if it hurt him to do so, as if her presence pained him. But not in a tender, romantic fashion: he seemed angry, locked up tight in a fierce, bright resentment.

She put her hand up to shade her eyes, the afternoon sun was surprisingly strong for winter.

'Is everything all right for you?' she asked shyly, as the horse, sensing at once that one of her hands had gone from the bridle, shook his head.

'Perfect,' Samuel said flatly. 'Couldn't be better.'

'Wages good enough?'

He nodded.

'I heard from Ellis how hard things was.'

'He's always been an old woman for gossip, Ellis.' The conversation proceeded in this dead fashion, with her making polite enquiries, and him responding with a brevity that came close to rudeness. All the while she studied him, searching for the person she had once known so well, and finding no trace. The old Samuel would never have spoken like this to her, however upset he was; he would have preserved a quiet dignity, behaved in a well-judged, reasonable manner. And gradually it was borne in on her that Samuel hadn't wanted to work on the wall at all – he had wished to keep as far as possible from her and Earlshay – but had been forced into it by extreme desperation. She saw, too, how deeply she must have hurt him, how her actions had destroyed every bit of their earlier friendship. It wasn't comfortable, being in his company, it made her feel like a villain.

Troubled, she gave him a polite nod of greeting, kicked her horse, and trotted away. She could tell that her earlier lapse of attention had pleased the gelding, given him hope that he could outwit her, and now the stretches of woodland around them, fallen leaves stirring in the wind, filled him with excitement. His stride lengthened, he put his head down, and she saw that he was heading for a low thick branch at the edge of the wood, where it met the curving drive.

She had the ropes of the safety harness in her hands, and as he bolted she tugged, hard as she could. The ropes tightened on the hobbles round his front feet, pulling them up under him, so that he toppled forward on to his knees, but he fought to keep his balance, and he was strong. He plunged ahead, struggled to break her grip and keep moving, and as the ropes burned into her fists she found herself at as steep and perilous an angle as if he were bucking. She knew that if she failed, she would fall to the ground and be crushed – but she wasn't going to fail. All her frustrations at the impossible conversations she'd had that day crystallized into one clear wish: to conquer the horse.

There was a moment when he was almost free, but she kept a firm grip on the ropes, and he was defeated. As he went down for the last time she could smell the panic in his sweat, and when he twisted his head and screamed at her, it was as if he was cursing her with a string of bad names. With any luck, Florrie thought, that would be the end of his bad behaviour. He wouldn't bolt again: he'd be too afraid of the consequences. He fell silent, and she could just hear his heavy breathing, and feel the pounding of his blood beneath her chest.

She could hear another noise, too: the hard tap of studs on stone, and she looked up and saw someone walking along the drive ahead of her. The sight was disconcerting, because for an instant Florrie had the queer feeling that she was looking into the past, and seeing herself as she'd been less than a year ago. A few yards away was a young girl, slim to the point of boniness, and wearing very much the same dark, old-fashioned clothes as Florrie used to possess, complete with cracked, oversized boots. She looked nervous, as if strung up with resolution to tackle a difficult task, and when she saw Florrie her nerve failed completely, and she scampered into the undergrowth the other side of the drive and ducked down out of sight, like a rabbit.

Twenty-five

The girl reappeared on Christmas Eve. Florrie was washing her hands at the time, in the bathroom at the end of her landing. She loved this room. She could never get over the wonder of a lavatory that wasn't invaded by swarms of cockroaches and maggots, or of a polished brass tap that spouted hot water whenever you turned it. She liked the ranks of stiff, ironed towels, too, and the soap. Unlike the soaps of her childhood – hard green Puritan, or nose-wrinkling red carbolic – this was a pure white, and smelt of roses, and you could make piles of froth out of it that stood up by themselves, or blow giant wobbly bubbles between your fingers. She was also interested by the way that if you got the flat edges of the basin sufficiently wet and soapy, and then upended a glass on to them, the glass would slide eerily about on its own, making a faint squeaking, moaning noise.

Some of her happiest moments were spent up here, playing with the basin and glancing sideways out of the window beside it, watching the sun set, in bands of brilliant colour, behind the trees in the park. She still didn't really feel at ease in such a big house, but she was growing fonder of odd details of the place: the fat, worried look on the face of a terrier in one of the family portraits; the smell of new books, and the taste of the figs that grew on the south wall of the garden. She was no longer sure that she'd want to return to live at Fightingcocks Farm, even if she was allowed to.

It was tea-time, the end of a cold, bright day, one in which a storm had threatened – with dark blue clouds – but never materialized. Now the garden below was flooded with a last electric burst of light, and she saw that a ragged, black-clad figure was walking across it. The figure was wearing a white cloth bonnet, and holding a bundle, and for one instant Florrie thought it might be her mother, delivering a Christmas present. But at second glance it was too slender and frail to be her; it drifted closer, paused beside a wide flower-bed that had been newly dug and dressed with manure, and tipped back its head, looking up at the windows of the house.

Despite the fact that it was so far away, reduced by distance to the size of an almond, Florrie recognized the face at once. She had the feeling she must have seen the girl many times before without being aware of it, her features were so familiar. Her eyes looked larger, her expression more tormented, than before, and on seeing Florrie she didn't bolt, but gazed steadily upwards, her face and bonnet grey-white against the dark green shadows on the lawn.

Florrie dropped the soap and struggled to open the window, but it was stuck. While she banged at it with the heel of her palm the girl below turned her head abruptly, as if she'd been called to by someone at a lower level. She walked forward, out of Florrie's line of sight.

Florrie dried her hands and raced downstairs as quickly as she could, stopping by the giant Christmas tree in the hall and listening for the usual sounds of a visitor being admitted to the house, but there was nothing. Just a muffled voice singing carols behind the green baize door that led to the kitchens, and much nearer, and clearer, layers of conversation, relaxed, sleepy-sounding, coming from the open door of the big drawing-room.

'Oh, but frightfully jolly,' a voice was remarking, while simultaneously someone else chanted softly:

'Never, never, let your bum
Pointed be, at anyone . . .

' . . . only I can't think how to finish it.'

She heard Valentine, in the intimate tones he adopted whenever he was half-lying on the sofa, his arms stretched out along the back, say, 'Don't you think manipulative women are at their most lovable when depressed and peaky? The difficulty lies, of course, in keeping them that way.'

Florrie tiptoed along the hall until she reached the front door at the very far end. There was no one outside on the step. All that happened was that the draught made the green baize door creak slightly on its hinges. Defeated by the mystery, she went to join the others at tea.

Valentine smiled at her when she appeared. He'd come back from racing more affectionate, and looking different: his hair blonder and his skin more tanned. She sat down on a stool near his feet and noticed that Mentmore was sitting near by, a bewildered expression on his face.

'We were talking about mothers,' Valentine said to Florrie. 'And I was telling Mentmore about a curious discovery I made in my youth – that I always felt happiest and most alive whenever my Mama lay down in a darkened room and placed a damp sponge on her head.'

Florrie looked round to see what Sybil made of this remark, and was surprised to see that she wasn't present. Veronica was pouring tea near the fireplace, and Florrie rather hoped that she'd be overlooked when the cups were passed round. The tea they drank at Earlshay was a strange watery substance that tasted and smelt of face-powder.

'Do you like your mother?' Mentmore asked. 'I've heard a lot of girls don't.'

'Oh yes, I'm fond of her all right,' Florrie said, adding, because it was him, and she felt at ease in his company, 'but I keeps dreaming about her, like she's the other side of a big window, trying to tell me something, and I can't hear proper.' A cup of tea materialized in her hands and she tucked it neatly under the sofa. 'It must be 'cos I misses talking to her. I never been troubled by dreams much, before.'

'It's my nanny I miss most, I hardly knew my mother.' Mentmore looked so forlorn as he said this that Florrie leaned forward, and almost touched his hand to comfort him.

'Grandmothers *is* good company,' she agreed.

'He means the miserable old servant who looked after him.' Valentine's voice was sarcastic. 'Mine was vile. Beat me with a slipper whenever Mama was out of earshot.'

'You don't seem to have had much luck with women, do you, Vallie?' Veronica remarked sweetly, passing him a cup of tea.

'You're absolutely right.' He was amused. 'I don't know what it is about me – I must bring out the worst in them.'

'What have you brought out in Florrie, then?' Veronica sat down beside the fire again, and leaned forward, one hand cupping her chin, in what Florrie considered to be a parody of intense interest. But it flattered Valentine.

He surveyed Florrie from the sofa cushions. It was like being inspected, she thought, by a Roman god reclining on a pile of clouds, and the outcome was just as uncertain. You never knew whether he was going to tease or be brutally unkind. It bore no relation to how you'd behaved recently or even to his current mood. It was as if the pleasure of talking, and having others listen to his voice, seduced him into forgetting about feelings altogether. When he'd injured you, he'd usually try extra hard to be charming, and win you round again, but it still hurt.

His eyes narrowing, he considered the question.

'Definitely not the best,' he began. 'In appearance she's grown rather too Sybilized, and as for character, she's tamer, more subdued than she used to be. She's starting to get a certain expression – like a cornered mouse – look, you can see it on her face now, frustrated, almost bitter . . .'

Before he could say anything worse Florrie asked quickly, 'And what about Veronica?'

Valentine chuckled to himself. 'You know, I rather love this kind of conversation. I fail to see its appeal to the ladies in the company, though. Still . . .'

A smile on his face, but visibly fading, he continued, 'I think I have to have a very *close* relationship with a woman to have an effect on her, and Veronica and I have never been close. Not physically, and not emotionally, either. Somehow, I doubt we ever shall be. I'm not tempted.'

'I think you have a bad effect because you're a monster,' Veronica snapped back.

Florrie didn't hear Valentine's reply because Mentmore turned to her and asked her about the horse, and they were soon lost in a long, intricate conversation about animal behaviour. They awoke from it, dazed, to find the drawing-room emptying as the other guests began to prepare for charades. Florrie hoped she would be allowed to sit quietly in a corner and be the audience. She disliked acting, especially as whenever she was given a part at Earlshay it was always as a rustic character – like the pig-keeper in the Good Samaritan.

Outside, in the hall, she could hear excited footsteps overhead, as drawers and cupboards were ransacked for costumes. Down the end of a long corridor, in the gunroom, where the telephone was kept, Sybil was yelling, her voice shrill with anger, 'I don't care if I am making a scene.' She always talked into that knobbly black instrument with astonishing vivacity, one leg raised, smiling and frowning and raising her eyebrows as if the person on the other end could see her face. She shouted, too, so that you couldn't avoid hearing her.

'I'm sick to death of it,' she cried out now, from behind the closed door, adding, more outrageously, 'And I couldn't give a tinker's fart about you.'

Florrie had been sent to fetch the big Chinese parasols that were kept in a cupboard the other side of the gunroom, and now slowed her pace as she walked back up the corridor, fascinated. She hadn't thought Sybil would ever use a rude word like that.

'I wish you'd stop them breeding like rabbits, too,' Sybil went on. 'I'm sick of their foul babies. They keep hauling them round here, and pressing them on me, and demanding money, and weeping bucketfuls of tears . . .' She sounded on the point of tears herself. Florrie wondered who these inconvenient visitors could be. They sounded vastly more interesting than any of the guests she'd ever met.

Before she reached the drawing-room door she stopped to look at her favourite family portrait, and caught the eye of the little terrier, with his black nose and apprehensive expression. The gunroom door opened behind her, and she heard Valentine say, his voice light and amused, 'You ought to be grateful. That gypsy could have been your daughter-in-law. It was only the merest chance that I asked Florrie and not her. I don't think you'd have found it so easy to house-train a diddicoy.'

Florrie remained frozen in front of the picture, transfixed by the discovery that what she'd overheard hadn't been a telephone conversation at all, but an argument between Sybil and Valentine. His parting shot took a while to register. As she gripped the parasols in her hand he walked up to and past her, at an easy pace. She thought she heard him begin to whistle a tune as he went by, but she couldn't be sure.

The next thing she was properly aware of was being in the stable, with the lamp lit, and rhythmically brushing the horse down, from the tips of his ears to the base of his tail, over and over, cleaning the brush with a currycomb and beginning again whenever she finished the job. Her dress was covered in grease and hairs, and she was sweating, which she knew a lady wasn't supposed to do, but she didn't care any more. The dinner gong had gone an hour or more ago, too, and she didn't care about that, either. She just worked steadily on the gelding. She didn't want to lie on his back for comfort; he wasn't as sympathetic a character as Smart, and besides, she felt the need to keep her hands occupied.

She tried not to think about Valentine. Instead she relived the conversation with Mentmore. She'd explained to him how she was trying to train the gelding so that he'd respond to the voice, rather than the bit, like a plough-horse, and Mentmore'd asked her if she'd consider breaking some hunters for him?

'I'd like that better than anything,' she'd said at the time. 'But I don't reckon Valentine'll allow it. He says he hates horses and can't see the point of them – I'm to have this one and no more.'

Now, for some queer reason, the words 'no more' kept sticking in her head.

Also an image kept presenting itself to her mind, perhaps triggered by Valentine using the word 'house-train'. Years ago, when she'd been a little girl, she and Joe had attempted to tame one of the feral cats that lived on the farm, and she remembered grabbing it by the scruff of the neck and rubbing its face in its own dirt, to teach it to be clean around the house. She felt that that was what Valentine was doing to her now, over and over again: he was deliberately rubbing her face in things she could never accept, was constitutionally incapable of accepting. But why, she didn't know.

The stable door opened and shut quietly, and she knew that he'd come in. She didn't look in his direction, just half squinted at his shadow out of the corner of her eye. It was a peculiar shape: long-skirted like a woman's, with an uneven outline to the head. He didn't say anything, so after a long while she asked, in a steady voice, as stripped of emotion as she could manage, 'Is it true? Is it true what you said to Sybil? Did you almost marry another girl?'

'In a manner of speaking.'

'What's that mean?'

'It means that looked at from one perspective – yes, it is true. I did nearly ask her to marry me. It was just an accident that you were there that night, willing to come away with me, and she wasn't. But maybe I did prefer you – slightly.'

She cleaned the comb with her fingers. 'So you didn't love me?'

His voice was as low and steady as hers. 'Did I ever say I did?'

'I thought marriage were a way of saying it without words.'

'Not for me.'

She turned round to look at him. She wasn't crying – tears were a long way off. She felt numb, as if he'd just hit her, hard, and she hadn't caught her balance yet.

He was dressed in towels to look like an Arab prince; he even had some of Sybil's make-up on his eyes. The charade costume made it seem that he didn't care what he'd said or done to her: it was all a game to him, a pointless, silly one, that grown-ups played to pass the time.

'What did you do it for, then?' she asked, and the contempt in her voice must have stung him, because he answered angrily,

'Don't tell me you didn't want to get married. I can't believe that. Didn't you want to live in a big house, and have all the clothes you could possibly buy? Didn't you want to be lady of the manor? Wasn't that what it was really all about?'

Florrie was silent, unable to deny it. She felt childish again, confused.

'So just be satisfied with what you've got. There's no need for emotional storms, or suicide attempts, or even for you to miss dinner.'

They stared at each other, Florrie wide-eyed. Valentine

wasn't smiling, but she could tell he was pleased, even perhaps amused by the scene.

'I hates being humiliated in public. I won't stand for that,' she said suddenly.

Taken aback, he agreed: 'All right, I'll be careful.'

'And I want to be allowed to train horses here. Just a few, to keep me cheerful. I needs something to do with me hands, you know? I can't do nothing all day. If you had to choose yourself a wife, why'd you have to choose me, who hates stopping indoors, hates parties, and can't even talk proper?'

Without her wanting it to, her voice was becoming more and more emotional. Valentine walked to the door, his robes swishing on the cobbles.

'I can't imagine,' he said drily.

'And I can't accept it,' Florrie shouted after him. 'I can't never be happy. Never, never, never.' She hit her head against the side of the stable door, and the pain was a relief, so she did it again and again.

PART THREE

1939

He maketh the barren woman to keep
house,
And to be a joyful mother of children.
Psalms 113; 9

Twenty-six

'I want to show you something, darling,' Sybil said. She and Veronica were upstairs, and it was early evening. Lights were on in the great hall, down below, but here, in this narrow corridor with neat doors either side, they were almost in darkness.

Sybil gave a mysterious smile and opened one of the doors, pressing a switch inside, so that a central lamp went on. Veronica found herself looking at a nursery. It was an immaculately pretty one, like a room inside a doll's house. The walls were striped blue and white up to the picture rail, and above that was a frieze of circus animals, dominated by the slightly sinister figure of a black poodle, which most frequently appeared standing upright on its back legs, like a golliwog, and brandishing a whip.

There were white curtains fluttering at the open window, a white cot, and a dapple-grey rocking-horse with the name 'Dobbin' hung on a plaque around its neck.

'Don't you think it's enchanting?' Sybil enquired. 'Isn't it the most adorable room you ever saw?'

'I do rather love the poodle,' Veronica said, reaching up so she could run her fingers over one black leg. It was a paper cut-out, glued on to the white background and varnished. 'Especially his moustache. He reminds me, quite irresistibly, of Herr Hitler.'

Sybil wasn't pleased. 'Do be sensible, darling. I want your

honest opinion. What do you think?'

'Who's it for? Is there a child coming to stay?'

'It's for my grandson.'

'Sybil!' Veronica resisted the impulse to kiss her, knowing that Sybil didn't like to be touched. 'I am pleased! How madly exciting!'

Sybil didn't reply, just looked thoughtful, so Veronica added, 'When's the baby due?'

'How should I know?'

'You mean . . . ?'

'I mean there's no sign yet.' Sybil hesitated. 'Nothing.' Seeing Veronica's expression she added hastily, 'I just did it to please myself, for comfort. I'm allowed to do that, aren't I? Isn't a lonely woman allowed a little pleasure, a little indulgence, in her life?'

Veronica sat down on the window seat. 'Oh, Sybil,' she said sadly.

Over the last few years she and Sybil had grown apart. It was Valentine's fault. If he hadn't got married, or if he hadn't started playing such cruel games with Veronica after his marriage – flattering and flirting with her, keeping her dangling after him, only to pull her up short with a sudden savage remark – then she might never have taken up her cousin's offer of a flat in London. But she had, and though she'd kept in frequent touch with Sybil it hadn't been quite the same. Sybil was really only interested in her house and her family (and the latest fashions), and when they met Veronica would sometimes get the queer feeling that she was lunching with an elderly relative, rather than a close friend: Sybil always refused to discuss the news, and any talk of war was taboo.

Also, Valentine and Florrie had been married for nine years now, and since the second summer Sybil had begun holding forth to Veronica – with increasing bitterness – on the subject of grandchildren. At first, Veronica had found it amusing: each time she'd met Sybil in Claridges, or visited her at Earlshay, she'd made a point of enquiring, mock-solicitously, after Florrie's health, knowing that this would unleash a torrent of invective: on Valentine's numerous illegitimate peasant offspring, or Florrie's obstinate refusal to see a Harley Street specialist. Lately, though, Sybil had become sentimental, and begun talking for hours about her longing for a golden-haired infant, which Veronica found harder to enjoy.

'You think I'm mad, don't you?' Sybil asked suddenly.

She had such a sweet, pathetic expression on her face that Veronica leaned forward and said, as warmly as she could, 'Of course I don't. It just seems . . . a little foolish to anticipate the event. And won't it upset the gorilla?'

'I shan't let her see it,' Sybil said quickly. 'There's only one key, and I always keep that in my pocket. And I swore the decorator to secrecy.'

Downstairs, someone began playing the piano, and the sound floated across the wide space of the hall and up into the nursery. It was a gentle, rolling melody. In the distance Veronica could also hear the murmur of voices: on the few occasions when Valentine was home he preferred to be surrounded by company.

Sybil leaned her elbows on the sill of the open window. 'I know it was loopy to decorate this room,' she said. 'But I have such a strong feeling – I can't tell you how strong it is – that my grandson is just waiting to be born. He's going to come here, one day, and nothing is going to prevent it.'

Veronica leaned out, too. The moon was up, and she could see the lake shining in the distance. It was almost too warm for spring. 'I'm glad you have such optimism,' she said. 'When I look out into the night like this I only feel frightened. The things I see coming aren't nice at all.'

Sybil put her hands over her ears in a theatrical gesture. 'Oh *don't*!' she said. 'Don't spoil the evening. I can't bear it when people talk about war. I can't let myself think about

Vallie getting hurt.' She took her hands away. 'Anyway, I have this superstitious feeling that as long as we remain here, in this house, nothing will change, and we'll survive. Can you imagine the park ceasing to exist, or the drawing-room?'

Downstairs a voice began singing to the piano. Veronica recognized the song. It was 'The Dream' from *The Bohemian Girl*. The singer had a clear, true voice, not especially strong, and the faintest trace of Devon accent, lingering round the 'r's, made Veronica realize that it must be Florrie.

'I dreamt that I dwelt in marble halls
With vassals and serfs at my side
And of all who assembled within those walls
That I was the hope and the pride . . .'

'I've never heard her sing before,' Veronica said.

'Frightful, isn't it? She's been practising for weeks. Said she wanted to surprise Valentine. You can't imagine what the din's been like.'

'So you two aren't getting on any better?'

'Oh,' Sybil sighed, and locked the door of the bedroom behind them, tucking the key into a little frilled pocket at the front of her striped silk organza dress. 'I suppose we rub along. We have to, really, we're alone together so much. Of course she spends most of her time out in the stables, caked in horse manure and surrounded by the most ghastly little wizened men.'

As they crossed the hall, the song reached its final chorus:

'But I also dreamt, which charmed me most
That you loved me, you loved me
Still the same.'

The door of the music room was open, warmth and cigar smoke spilling out into the hall, and as the last echoes of the song faded away Veronica heard Valentine start laughing. He had a very distinctive laugh, a harsh, barking 'ha! ha! ha!' which gradually subsided into a low chuckle. Sometimes, when Veronica heard it, she could almost imagine that it was forced – that he wasn't really amused – he wasn't the type, she didn't think, to lose himself in anything as overwhelming as laughter.

But as she went through the door Veronica saw at once that he was genuinely overcome. There were tears on his cheeks and he was shaking with mirth.

'So marvellously silly, those maudlin Victorian songs,' he said, getting up from his chair to greet her. 'And Florrie's expression – did you see it? So soulful . . .' He bent over and howled with laughter, and Veronica glanced across at Florrie, curious to see if she minded.

She didn't seem to. She was sitting at the piano, her fingers still on the keys, a dreamy expression on her face.

When Valentine called out, 'Have you another song for me?' she answered in a light, good-humoured tone, 'I do not. I've had enough of your teasing.'

Veronica thought that Sybil's superstitious belief about Earlshay – that nothing would ever change there – might have some basis in fact. Sybil and Valentine had been almost magically untouched by time in the ten years or so that they'd lived in the house. Sybil didn't seem to have grown any older: her carriage was just as straight, her hair as blonde and her skin as carefully painted as when Veronica had first come calling. And as for Valentine, well, maybe he had become a fraction stouter – he now had a small but perceptible stomach beneath his well-cut dinner jacket – but otherwise he was no different. He still looked at Veronica the same way, too: standing close, a knowing expression in his eyes and a faint smile on his lips, as if he could see right into her heart and tell at once that she still had a weakness for him.

It sometimes puzzled Veronica that his marriage to Florrie

should have lasted so long, but when she'd voiced this, Sybil had been dismissive. 'Pooh!' she'd said. 'Why should Vallie end it, when it suits him so well? It means no other woman can take him seriously.'

Florrie was the only one of the three who showed any real sign of alteration. The difference was subtle, but Veronica always noticed it whenever she returned to Earlshay after a long absence – as now. Perhaps this was because her mental image of Florrie was always of the girl she'd first seen at the costume ball. She still remembered the painful envy she'd felt then, as she'd seen Florrie walk down the stairs towards her. Florrie had brimmed with happiness and vitality, a creature of peachy skin and rippling dark-gold hair.

She was thinner now. You noticed this particularly when she was in evening clothes, because her collar bones stood out like wings above the expensive and exquisite dresses she always wore. Above them her calm face remained unpainted, and her hair – nearer mouse than gold now – was always pulled back in a severe twist. Her eyes were still as bright and green as ever, but when she looked at you, or anyone else in the company, it was always as if a shutter had come down, as if she wasn't really seeing what she was looking at, just enduring it patiently.

Over the years, Veronica had occasionally tried to engage Florrie in conversation, moved – to be honest – more by curiosity than sympathy, and had noticed how much more careful Florrie was, each time, to reveal less and less of her feelings and opinions. Her voice had changed too, the country accent gradually fading as the content of her conversation became more formal and clipped.

Watching her tonight, Veronica felt, for the first time, a certain fellowship. She'd just got married herself, and the joy that this had brought her had entirely vanquished the last fragments of envy she'd felt for Florrie, and even made her wonder, a little fearfully, what it might be like to be married to a man like Valentine.

'Marriage suits you, Veronica,' he said, as they took their places at the table. He leaned back slightly, so that the footman might shake out the napkin and place it on his knee.

Veronica glanced down at her rings, pleased. The stones weren't valuable; Hugo had only recently started in practice as a doctor, and they weren't well off. She wished he could have come with her this Saturday to Monday, but he was working. She'd grown so used to his presence already that she felt strange, almost naked, attending a party without him.

'I hope you're not being too sanctimonious about it,' Valentine continued.

'You wouldn't like me to?' Unintentionally, Veronica had slipped back into her old habit of flirting with Valentine. It was hard to avoid: she'd often noticed how the women at a dinner party would end up bridling and competing for his attention, like little girls trying to please a capricious father.

'Certainly not. Haven't you realized yet that fidelity is nothing but the most abject kind of cowardice?'

'What makes you think that?'

'Because most people would cheat on their partners if they weren't so frightened of getting caught.'

'I think you're too cynical for your own good,' Veronica said sharply, and Valentine smiled, delighted by her response.

'So you are being faithful! I shall have to devote the rest of this evening to encouraging a more frivolous attitude.'

Veronica couldn't help turning to Florrie to gauge her reaction, but Florrie wasn't listening. She was reading a piece of paper that the butler had just handed her, and a few seconds later she got up from the table, and after pausing to whisper an excuse to Valentine, left the room. She had a huge bow on the rump of her tight Schiaparelli gown, and the satiny creases in it winked in the candlelight as she slipped through the door.

Twenty-seven

The stable-yard looked deserted. Florrie, rustling into it in her tight dress, knew that it wasn't, that there were six horses hidden away among the many stalls, and that her younger brother Albie was here, too: the note she'd received at dinner had been from him.

He lived in a converted loose box beside the tack room. She went there first. Inside there was a smell of freshly snuffed-out candles, and by the light of the embers in the little stove she could see Albie's terrier lying asleep on the rug, its stout, greyish-pink stomach bulging out over one small, hairy leg. It whined, and smacked its lips as it dreamed: if it was here, then Albie couldn't be far away.

She began walking down the lines of stalls in the yard, opening and closing the wooden doors. In some, there was just scrubbed, slightly damp emptiness, in others a horse would look round sleepily, its legs bedded deeply in straw. She wished she could keep more horses, but she'd tried that, and it hadn't been allowed.

Once, about a year after her marriage, she'd had the beginnings of a thriving business here. Every stall had been full, she'd spent from dawn until dusk out in the rough fields and woodland beyond the park, training other people's hunters, and she'd even persuaded a few of the younger gardeners to work for her as grooms. Then Valentine had come back from motor racing in Monaco, and been furious with her.

She remembered the occasion so clearly. She'd been away from Earlshay all afternoon, buying a load of hay from a farm beyond Poffit, and she'd let herself into the house very late, too late for dinner – but then she'd begun to miss most of the meals anyway, since they took so long, and kept her away from her work.

Valentine had been waiting for her at the entrance to his study. She'd run to him, to kiss him, but he'd recoiled.

'Where have you been?' he'd asked, and when she'd explained about buying the hay he'd said with dangerous calm: 'Listen, because I'm only going to say this once. I agreed to you having some horses, as an amusement, while I was away. I did not agree to my park becoming a horse-breaker's yard.'

'I'm making money,' Florrie had answered cheerfully.

'I don't need money. What I need, what I demand – is a wife who is here when I come back, who is decently dressed, and who doesn't spend her time playing around with all the young men on the estate.'

She'd gazed at him open-mouthed, a smile still on her face, unable to believe that he could really mean what he was saying – be so strait-laced and humourless about her behaviour when he demanded such licence for himself. Besides, she wasn't playing around with young men, she was employing them. And then it had occurred to her: perhaps he was jealous. Perhaps he'd been distressed to come home and find her missing.

'I didn't mean to hurt your feelings . . .' she'd begun, but he'd cut in harshly, 'You haven't hurt my feelings, you couldn't. You've annoyed me. Don't do it again.'

He'd shut himself in his study, and she'd run upstairs, troubled, and spent the rest of the night planning how to make her business less intrusive. But in the morning those plans had proved unnecessary: when she'd gone out at dawn to the stables she'd found them utterly deserted.

All the horses had been sent back to their owners; even

Valentine's mean-spirited gelding had gone (she never found out where), and all that had remained had been lines of dirty stalls and a mass of wheel- and hoof-marks in the gravel.

It had been a long fight back to where she was now. Valentine had finally been persuaded to let her keep a few horses, as long as she looked after them on her own, without grooms, and was always in the house when he wanted her.

After Mother's death, Florrie had coaxed Albie to come and live at Earlshay. She'd done this because he'd been more or less an invalid ever since his childhood diphtheria – constantly short of breath, his heart so weak that he could hardly manage to do anything without feeling faint – and she hadn't trusted Joe and Father to look after him properly. He'd refused, after one look at Sybil's disapproving face, to move into the house, choosing to live in the stables instead, and this arrangement suited Florrie well: it meant that Albie could watch over the horses for her whenever Valentine was home.

Nowadays she took nothing for granted. Each day that she was allowed to keep horses, and visit the stables, was precious. She was well aware that at any moment, on a whim, Valentine could sweep it all away again.

It was odd, distressing, how her relationship with him had slipped through her fingers like water. Once she'd had such influence over him, had been able to amuse him, please him, just because of the way she was, the way she acted naturally – and then it had all gone.

Thinking about this as she walked through the yard, Florrie found herself involuntarily touching the place beside her cheekbone where the scar was. She could hardly feel it at all now, and in the mirror the marks on her skin were so faint as to be scarcely visible at all, but that didn't matter. Valentine had ceased to find her attractive round about the time that she'd hurt her face; if he still found the scar disfiguring, then it must be.

Harder to understand was the way that he had grown tired of her character, too, although she supposed that for men the two things – finding a woman pretty, and liking her – were closely bound up together. He wanted her to be in the house, present at all his parties, but she wasn't sure why, because he hardly ever looked in her direction, and never spoke to her if he could help it. Sometimes she thought that when she was with him she was lonelier than when she was by herself: it was like endlessly trudging through an icy landscape, with no warmth or comfort in sight.

But she didn't want to avoid him, or leave. It wasn't just the fear of the unknown, of being destitute, that kept her at Earlshay. It was a sense of loyalty, a conviction that marriage was for ever, and that if it went wrong you had to stick with it and endure whatever came. Also, she was always hoping that things would improve. She couldn't help believing that if only she kept trying to make contact with Valentine, kept herself affectionate, and free of bitterness or despair, then one day she would succeed in touching his heart, and he would turn to her, and be kind again.

That was why she had sung 'The Dream' to him this evening. It had been the only way she could think of to communicate her feelings. And for a moment he had listened. She'd been watching him out of the corner of her eye as he'd sat on the sofa with a whippet-thin, very fashionable woman called Laetitia Pitt – whom he always referred to, mockingly, as 'the bottomless pit' – and for quite a while he had stopped talking and closed his eyes, and a smile that she remembered from their courtship had crossed his lips. But he hadn't been touched. Recalling that song now, Florrie winced. How childish, how ridiculous she'd been to sing it to him.

Albie was in the furthest stall, with a small black mare that had arrived the previous day, from Mentmore's

Northumberland estate. He wasn't alone, because as Florrie opened the door she heard voices. He was standing beside the horse, combing her mane with his fingers, while Samuel sat on an upturned bucket in the corner. Albie hadn't grown much since childhood. He was small and bent, and despite a weatherbeaten face and thinning hair, had somehow managed to retain the expression – and temperament – of a cheeky twelve-year-old. The stable was dark and cosy, being only fitfully lit by a lantern, and there was a sombre but companionable atmosphere, as if Albie and Samuel were at the sickbed of some distant acquaintance.

Samuel stood up awkwardly on seeing Florrie, and Albie called out, 'Florrie! I didn't mean for you to leave your friends. It's only a touch of colic that she has.'

'I wasn't too sure what you meant when I got your note,' Florrie answered, laughing. 'You know what your spelling's like. Far as I could tell that butler handed me a bit of paper with gibberish on it.'

'Well, I weren't too sure how many "k"s there was in colic, that's why I put stomach trouble. Only stomach's a bit of a puzzler, too. Ain't that right, Samuel?'

Florrie wasn't surprised to see Samuel: she knew he often dropped in to talk to Albie, it was just that he usually chose a time when Florrie was unlikely to be there. Whenever the two of them met their conversation, though perfectly polite, was always strained and uneasy.

Now he leaned forward and muttered to Albie, who answered, 'No, you mustn't think of going. I can't manage on me own if the mare do get worse, and Florrie won't stop long. Her husband gets antsy if they's parted more than a minute.'

Florrie could tell Albie was nervous – he was talking too fast – and wishing to put him at ease, and smooth over any awkwardness, she said warmly, 'I would appreciate it if you'd stay, Samuel. It'd be a help to both of us.'

He bowed in reply, and she immediately felt uncomfortable. Somehow, whenever she saw him he made a point of exaggerating the social distance between them, touching his cap in the most servile manner, or referring to her in the third person, as in: 'Would Lady Florence care to sit herself down?' Although it was always done straight-faced, she was sure that he meant to annoy.

Turning away from him, she walked over to the mare. She tried to do this with dignity, but it was difficult, because her high heels got clogged with straw, and her skirt was so tight that it felt as if her legs were roped together. She stumbled, and had to catch at the mare to avoid toppling over, but the animal didn't react. Her fingers closed on a hot, damp coat – the mare had sweated up terribly since she last saw her – and Florrie noticed that she was standing with her head low, a look of thoughtful anxiety on her face, as if she was trying to trace, and come to terms with, some complex inner map of pain. As Florrie watched, the discomfort became too great to bear, and the mare kicked at her own stomach with a back leg. Then she shifted position, groaned, and began to sag. Anxious that she shouldn't get down and roll, Florrie seized her by the head-collar, and pulled her forward.

'I reckon she needs a gripe draught,' she called out to Albie. 'Can you fetch one? There's dill water and laudanum in the tack room, I know.'

It was a strain, keeping the mare up, not just on Florrie, but on her beautiful outfit. As she stood there she felt the heel of her left shoe slip sideways and collapse, and somewhere deep inside her décolletage a piece of wire sprang free and began to jab insistently at a nipple. She closed her eyes. Why did her clothes always revenge themselves on her if she did anything useful or exciting? It was like being wrapped in the most stringent and unforgiving conscience.

As Albie came hurrying back with an old beer bottle full of

liquid for the mare, and Samuel handed it to her with the faintest of smiles, she did have one moment when she thought seriously about the consequences for her eau-de-Nil dress. Then a wild fit of rebellion took hold of her, and she decided that just this once she didn't care a damn if she wrecked her clothes or was late returning to the dinner table.

'Don't you ever worry about the house and park, and what will happen if there's a war?'

'You sound like my accountant: horrifyingly dull.' Valentine's voice was dreamy, entirely free of its usual sarcasm.

In the distance the chapel clock struck eleven times, the sound very clear across the water. Veronica, half-wrapped in one of Sybil's fur coats, was sitting on the lakeside diving-board, while Valentine floated on his back a few yards away, drifting in and out of a great raft of water-lilies. Veronica didn't much enjoy bathing naked in the Earlshay lake: she had too-vivid childhood memories of swimming there with the Holdens and coming out to find her legs covered in leeches. Also she hated the sensation of pushing through mats of waterweed, so while she had splashed about, just briefly, to demonstrate that she wasn't a prude or a coward, she'd got out as quickly as she could.

She'd put on the fur, too, with some relief. Although she considered her body perfectly adequate, she was self-conscious about the tops of her thighs, and knew only too well what a perfectionist Valentine was. The most damning remark he could make about a woman was that she was fat. This was applied to females who were scarcely over standard weight, and was always said with a look of intense distaste, as if the very word contaminated his mouth.

Even though she wasn't comfortable, Veronica didn't wish to return to the house. The others were slowly drifting that way: she could hear a few of them shrieking and mock-fighting on the wide slope of parkland above the lake, and their distant shouts made her conversation with Valentine seem especially intimate.

There was a silver candelabra beside her, its flames scarcely stirring in the still night air; she touched the tip of one candle with her fingers and picked off a little ball of molten wax. She threw it at Valentine, but it missed and plopped gently in the water.

'My brother says they're drawing up plans for requisitioning all the decent-sized houses in the county. Won't you mind if soldiers are billeted on the place and start firing off salvoes at the portraits and chopping down the trees?'

'I doubt it.' Valentine raised one foot out of the weeds, his skin ghostly in the moonlight. 'After all, if there's a war I shan't be here, shall I?'

'What about Sybil – and Florrie?'

'Whatever happens, Sybil will complain, and Florrie will put up with it.' His foot disappeared without a ripple, and a slight edge of bitterness crept into his voice. 'She won't enjoy herself, but she'll make a nauseatingly good job of seeming to. I wouldn't be surprised if she got a medal for it: "For Martyrdom Above and Beyond the Call of Duty".'

He began to swim for the bank, and as she watched Veronica realized that she had already decided to let him seduce her. Maybe it was because she'd wanted him for so many years, or because she had always been curious as to whether a woman-izer, a cast-iron Casanova, would be better at it than anyone else. Would Valentine be the one, elusive man to finally set her on fire? Her marriage seemed remote, unreal, its only effect to make her confident enough not to be frightened of what Valentine might do.

So when he touched her, his hands so cold and wet that she couldn't help shuddering, she didn't draw back or protest, just whispered in his ear, 'And I thought you only fucked the lower classes!'

'That was in my salad days. My tastes are far more catholic now. Besides, as Sybil is always saying, good servants are getting frightfully hard to find.'

The mare was no better. She'd managed to get down in her stall and roll, in a delirium of agony, before Samuel and Florrie had succeeded in hauling her up again, and in the struggle her head had got injured. The skin below one ear was now swollen and crusted with dried blood, and it gave her black face an even more bewildered air.

After the gripe draught, Albie had mixed up some chloral balls to dull the pain; the remains of this sticky concoction were still clinging to the sides of a mortar abandoned on the floor. The mare had resisted the idea of swallowing a ball with astonishing vigour. When the first one – wrapped in a screw of newspaper – was slipped into her mouth she'd spat it out contemptuously into the manger. They'd finally got one down, but it had been a hard battle, and there were now little bits of spit-covered paper all over the stall (and its occupants).

In between attempts to give her medicine, Samuel and Florrie took it in turns to walk the mare outside, feeling that if only they kept her moving, the constriction in her gut might ease of its own accord.

They'd been working for nearly four hours now, and Florrie did feel a bit tired, but it was the best kind of fatigue: it only affected her body, not her mind. Her dress had long since got ripped up one side, and she'd taken off her shoes and stockings and put on an old pair of Albie's boots. The feel of the air on her bare legs, and of the worn leather against her toes reminded her, deliciously, of the freest moments of her childhood.

While Albie sat on the floor and dozed, his back against the wall, and Samuel walked the mare somewhere out in the moonlight, she busied herself mixing up a solution of liquid paraffin and soft soap in a big jug. The door was open, and she could hear faint shouts and shrieks of laughter from the lake; she couldn't help hoping that Valentine was safely preoccupied by some game or conversation, so that, just once, he wouldn't notice she was missing. She'd meant to leave the stable hours ago, but had somehow never got round to it.

Samuel took longer than she expected, and when he returned was in a queer mood. Earlier, while they'd been dosing the mare, and Albie had been fooling about and teasing Samuel, he'd relaxed enough to be almost friendly to Florrie, but now he'd obviously frozen up again.

'Is it colder out?' she asked, just for the sake of making conversation.

'Mild enough,' he said shortly.

'And the mare, is she better in herself?'

He didn't answer, just shook his head and turned away.

Florrie poured the liquid paraffin into the beer bottle, annoyed. She couldn't see why Samuel had to go on being hostile; surely the past was dead and buried by now? Also, she saw the stable-yard as a haven, quite separate from the rest of her troubled life. She loved the continual banter that went on there, between her and Albie, and felt there was enough grimness in the world without Samuel deliberately spoiling a merry atmosphere. She had intended to administer the liquid paraffin herself, but since Samuel was being difficult she passed him the bottle and stood back, holding the jug.

As he eased the bottle into the mare's mouth she asked, 'Where'd you go, then?'

The bottle slipped, and liquid paraffin flowed down the front of his jacket, where it glistened, jelly-like. 'Along the lake,' he answered, holding out the bottle to be refilled.

'And were they swimming? They often do that when they get fired up with champagne. It makes them do the maddest things. One time they squirted each other with hoses off the fire engine. Had themselves a proper duel, they did.'

Samuel didn't reply to this attempt to amuse him. He just looked at Florrie, a searching, severe gaze. The bottle in his hand slipped again and liquid paraffin spilled on to his shirt, dripping down towards his belt.

'Do you want her to have any of it?' Florrie asked innocently. 'Or are you just going to pour it down your trousers?'

'Do Lady Florence want to change places, then?' he answered crossly.

'No, she flaming well doesn't. And if I were you I wouldn't call her Lady Florence again, not when she's got a full jug of liquid paraffin in her hand.'

They glared at each other, and calm wasn't restored until Albie got up and dosed the mare himself. He gave the halter to Florrie, but Samuel stopped him.

'No,' he said. 'I'd rather you took the horse, Albie, if it ain't too much to ask. I wants to talk to Florrie.'

She waited, arms folded, leaning against the hay rack, until the mare had left the yard. Then she said, 'So?'

Samuel seemed unaccountably ill at ease. He glanced all round the stable, and when he spoke Florrie sensed that he was forcing himself, as if what he had to impart was painful.

'Who's that lady?' he began. 'The one with the short black hair and face like a doll? Talks to old Lady Bandinelli frequent; I seen her before when we was building the wall.'

Florrie was careful not to smile. Was Samuel attracted to Sybil's friend? 'Veronica?'

He nodded. 'Could be.' He hesitated. 'Is you and her friendly, like?'

'No.' The reply slipped out before Florrie had a chance to think about it. 'She acts like she's a friend, but talking to her's like gliding on treacle: all sugar on top, and malice underneath.

Most of them are like that up there. You can't trust them.' She stopped, annoyed with herself. She hadn't meant to tell the truth; she was usually so careful to present only the rosiest picture of life at the big house. Once, when Joe had begun to refer to the mistresses Valentine kept at Cullerton and Poffit, she'd silenced him by saying in a confident tone, 'My husband's got all the corn he can mow at home – all the corn he can mow.' Now she added hurriedly, in case she'd dashed Samuel's romantic hopes: 'Of course, Veronica might be different with a fellow.'

He smiled so sadly when she said this that something prompted her to add, 'I want to ask you a favour, Samuel, although I know I don't have the right. If I had the chance to farm the land round here, on account of the war coming – would you work for me?'

Twenty-eight

Father was sitting in the farm kitchen, eating his tea, when Florrie arrived. The front door was wide open and he was watching the setting sun. A few yards away, by the hedge, a bantam hen was balancing on tiptoe and jumping up, clumsily pecking at ripe blackberries.

Father didn't seem surprised to see Florrie. She guessed he must be feeling as numb as she was, as stunned by this morning's news. She felt as if a great bell had just stopped tolling, and her ears and body hadn't yet begun to recover. It was incredible, past belief, that the world could suddenly be at war today, and stranger still that the countryside should remain as calm and beautiful as ever.

She sat down beside him. Father was applying himself to pigeon stew, working the little bones out between his teeth and laying them in neat lines round the edge of his plate.

He pointed at the dish with his fork. 'You grubbish?'

She shook her head. There were four children at the table, too, bibs tied round their necks, watching her with grave curiosity. Three of them had beaky noses and curly hair like Joe, but the eldest, a girl of nine called Belle, was completely different, with white-blonde plaits and blue eyes. Florrie smiled at them all, trying not to let her gaze linger too long on Belle.

'Where's Joe and Dorelia?' she asked.

'Up the village.' Father spoke shortly, unwilling to stop his dissection of the pigeon. He ate as if the meal was a tiresome

261

duty, rather than a pleasure, but then his whole attitude to life had altered since Mother's death. He looked far older now: frail and bent and grey, like a dog that's been savagely beaten.

One of the children giggled, and Father frowned and stopped eating. He wiped his mouth on his thumb and said in a gruff voice that could equally well have been fierce or affectionate, 'If you chickens is finished you can run along and leave us be.'

The three smallest scrambled down and bolted outside, but Belle stayed to clear the table. Florrie found her presence unsettling, even painful. While she talked to Father she couldn't help being tinglingly aware of the little girl moving quietly round the room – pouring water from a kettle, scrubbing the dishes with a rag, climbing on a chair to replace them on the dresser – because Belle was Valentine's child.

She looked so like him. Her hands were exactly the same shape as his, her hair the same texture and colour. She even had identical mannerisms: playing with a curl beside her ear while thinking; smiling with her lips closed; sitting still as a statue, eyes narrowed to a line of ice, when seriously annoyed.

Florrie was never sure why Joe had married Belle's mother. Had he been genuinely in love? She doubted it. They'd married barely a month after first meeting, and they showed no special fondness, now, when they were together. Had Joe married Dorelia in order to wound Florrie? Sometimes Florrie considered this painful idea, turning it over and over in her mind like a sharp stone, testing its possibilities. Joe had certainly never liked her relationship with Valentine, and he'd been hostile to her from the moment it first began – but no, she didn't think he was capable of deliberately setting out to hurt her so cruelly. Or had he married his gypsy wife to gain some kind of power over Valentine? This motive seemed the most likely, because at the time when Joe met Dorelia – the Christmas she'd arrived at Earlshay with her bastard child –

he'd been in trouble for poaching, and after the first banns were read Valentine had dropped all charges against him. He'd done more: he'd issued instructions to his gamekeepers to ignore whatever Joe did, so that Joe's depredations became a tax Valentine was prepared to pay, just for the privilege of never seeing or communicating with him again.

Belle carried two perilously full cups of tea to the table. Father's she placed in front of him; Florrie's she was more cautious with: she set it down six inches to the side of her aunt, as if she was well aware of Florrie's ambivalent feelings towards her.

'Them girls come yet?' Father asked, grasping his cup in big, heavily knuckled hands.

'No. There's no sign – not a whisker. Old Lady Bandinelli's fretting something terrible.'

'I'll bet her is.' Father sounded tickled. He always liked hearing about Sybil. She was a curiosity: he could both marvel at the oddness of her behaviour and find it charmingly silly, too.

'They were due to come this morning,' Florrie went on. 'And she started fussing that they might throw ink and toothpaste around? So she's got the footmen nailing Essex board to the upstairs walls. It's all silk paper there, see.'

The girls Florrie was referring to were Sybil's evacuees. Back in the spring, Sybil had been persuaded by Veronica that the only way to avoid the ultimate horror – of soldiers – was to offer her house freely to more congenial lodgers. And who better than the pupils of her former school, St Hilda's? Florrie had since endured many lectures from Sybil on how nicely behaved these girls of good family were going to be. But it was a trifle hard to believe in Sybil's enthusiasm after she'd covered the hall parquet in linoleum (lest it should get scuffed by tiny, well-bred feet), and had the best furniture packed up and sent to Exeter for storage. Almost daily Sybil would imagine a fresh outrage that the girls might possibly commit, and tax the ingenuity of the estate carpenter to render it impossible.

'What's they like, these nobby chiels?' Father asked. '*Is* they saucy?'

'I wouldn't know. I've never seen them. But I don't reckon any child could be as wicked as Sybil thinks. It's queer, really, because she's always talking about . . . well . . .' Here Florrie paused. She nearly said 'grandchildren', but couldn't bring herself to. She didn't want to raise the subject of her infertility with Father. He never raised it himself, but that wasn't surprising. After all, it was from him that she'd first learned how mysterious conception could be: how an animal might fail to conceive because it was too fat or too lean, or hadn't been put out to graze at the right moment. Even if the magic ingredients were there, they could lose their potency. Hadn't Mother wanted more children after Albie and been denied them?

So it didn't puzzle Florrie that Valentine should be fertile, and she herself – according to the village doctor – perfectly fit, and yet no pregnancy result. It was a sign, physical proof (as if she needed it) of the wrongness of their relationship. If only she could make things better, then perhaps . . . Meanwhile the desperation of her longing seemed to wither her inside, turning her soul black and rotten. It was almost impossible to remain Christian; to make herself congratulate Dorelia on each new addition to her family. It seemed so unfair. But then, Florrie would remind herself, life was unjust. The trick of living decently lay in accustoming yourself to that injustice, making the best of whatever you'd been given.

' . . . how pretty and sweet Valentine was, when he was small,' she finished.

Father sucked at his teeth sourly, as if he had grave doubts about the truth of that.

Florrie pulled an envelope out of her pocket and slipped it under his hand. She was always uncomfortable about giving Father money, and he seemed to feel the same, because he never thanked her. He quickly laid his palm flat over the envelope, so it was hidden, but Florrie could sense Belle's sharp eyes upon it.

'It's not the evacuees that trouble me,' she continued, to smooth over the awkward moment. 'It's what's going to happen when the servants go. They're starting to drift away already – the gardeners have all taken the King's shilling. And sometimes I catch her ladyship looking at me, thoughtful-like, and I can almost hear her thinking, "Well, maybe it isn't such a wicked shame after all, that we've a good strong peasant girl in the family!" '

An indefinable expression flickered across Father's face.

'Oh, don't get me wrong,' Florrie said hastily. 'I don't mind helping with the housework, it's only right I should. It's just that I want to do more – to do a useful, permanent job.'

'And what would that be?'

'I want to borrow your plough – the one you never use? And I want to start farming.'

'I hasn't got he any more. I sold him back along. Ploughs is like gold dust now. Besides,' he turned to look at her, and she noticed how white and bristly his eyebrows had grown, 'I thought your husband was set against you touching his land.'

Since Florrie had married she'd occasionally got the impression that Father perceived her as trivial, frivolous, obsessed with clothes; a powerless adjunct to a man he disliked intensely. She sensed him thinking this now, as she leaned forward, the dark stuff of her riding-habit slipping against her silk shirt.

'He is,' she said firmly. 'He wants his land to remain wild, covered in rabbits and deer. But you know, as I was listening to Mr Chamberlain on the wireless this morning it came to me

265

like a lightning-bolt: it's all different now. It doesn't matter if Valentine'd prefer not to have his land farmed – it has to be. It's like her ladyship wanting four different drawing-rooms to sit herself down in – she doesn't have that choice any more. None of us has.'

'So Sir Valentine's left, has he?' Father said, and Florrie nodded, feeling guilty, like a child plotting rebellion.

'He's been gone a fortnight. He's pulling strings – he wants to join the Air Force.'

Father's eyes crinkled up, and he looked thoughtful. 'Well,' he said, 'if you wants that land ploughed up fast – the whole lot cleared and worked down and seeded before winter – you'll have to go to Samuel. He's got one of they tractors; he's making a good bit of money from it, too.'

'He won't help. I asked him once if he'd work for me and he said no.'

Father put his hand out and touched Florrie's cheek. It was a delicate, loving gesture, but she pulled away; she didn't like anyone to go near the scar.

'You'll have to change his mind for him then, won't you?' Father sounded amused, but Florrie couldn't be sure, because he got up from the table and turned away, so that she couldn't catch his expression.

When Florrie got outside it was twilight. She began walking up the lane to the chestnut tree, where she'd tied her horse, and as she did so heard footsteps. She turned and saw Belle. She felt in her pocket for a coin but the little girl wouldn't take it, backing out of range instead.

She looked a creature of indeterminate sex, halfway between male and female – flat-chested and round-stomached, with a fiery, intelligent little face under the tight plaits – and she pursued Florrie up to the crossing silently, like a revengeful ghost.

As Florrie swung herself into the saddle, Belle finally spoke. Her voice was strange: hoarse, as if she hardly ever got to use it.

'Mother and Joe's fetching some boys,' she said.

'Some boys?'

'Big growthy ones, as'll help with the farming. Joe says girls is no flaming use.'

Hearing the bitterness in her words, Florrie answered gently, 'I'm sure he doesn't really think that. When we were small he never said I was no use.'

Belle didn't reply, just gazed up at Florrie with eyes as fierce as a wild bird's, and it came to Florrie with a sudden shock, because she'd never really thought about Belle's feelings before, that maybe the child was desperately unhappy – and Joe wasn't kind to her.

'Where's Joe getting these boys?' she asked.

'They's giving them away for nothing, up the village hall.' Belle's voice was shrill. 'And it ain't fair, it ain't fair at all, 'cos Joe says they'll have my bed and I'm to sleep in the tallet.'

'No one's giving them away,' Florrie said soothingly. 'They're evacuees. And you mustn't be jealous of them . . .'

But Belle had vanished; and an instant later Florrie heard the rumble of cartwheels on the road ahead. She guided her horse into the shadow of an overhanging tree, feeling as unwilling to face Joe as Belle was. After he'd turned down to the farm she didn't turn left to go to Earlshay; instead, on impulse, she urged her horse to a gallop and made for the village.

Furzey Moor parish hall was almost deserted when Florrie reached it. There were only four people inside, but you could tell it had recently been crammed full, because the air was hot and close, and smelled of damp overcoat and exhaled breath, and there were pieces of rubbish scattered across the floor. An orange had rolled under one of the benches and been stamped on, and there was a small dark puddle by the entrance. A man Florrie didn't recognize was sitting on a chair by the door, writing in a notebook, and she saw the pear-shaped body of the vicar's wife, clad in misshapen, porridgy tweeds, walking away from her towards the little kitchen at the rear of the hall, her leather brogues making an echoey sound on the board floor.

Florrie had the disconcerting feeling that she was seeing the whole scene through the eyes of a scared child; the squashed orange, the polished brogues, the man's notebook with its cramped writing, each separate image swollen and distorted like a sequence from a nightmare. Maybe this was because, ever since talking to Belle, she had been thinking and worrying about the little girl. She remembered moments in her own childhood when she'd felt trapped and friendless, but she'd always been able to go to Mother and have those painful emotions soothed away. How isolated must Belle be, if she was driven to approach Florrie, whom she hardly knew?

There were two boys in the hall, Florrie saw them the instant she walked in, and perhaps because she was still affected by her encounter with Belle, she could sense their fear and misery spreading out into the warm fuggy air as clearly as if it was blue smoke from a bonfire. They were crouched on a bench against the wall, and though they were too dissimilar, physically, to be brothers, they were holding hands tightly, their knuckles white with effort. The smaller of the two had spectacles on – smeary ones, roughly mended with sticky brown paper – and the front of his jacket was stained, as if he'd recently been sick. The other had a misshapen nose and the wary, belligerent expression of a natural pugilist. They were both extremely dirty. Florrie couldn't remember ever having seen such ingrained filth before; even Samuel, after his long journey to Furzey Moor in the coal-cart, hadn't looked as bad. She guessed at once that no one in the village had been prepared

268

to take these children home with them, and she walked quickly up to their bench.

'Hello, my birds,' she said. 'Would you like to come and live in my house? There's plenty of room, and I've a horse you can ride, too.'

Twenty-nine

The two boys had chatted happily through the lanes, riding on the horse while Florrie walked alongside, but they fell silent once they emerged from the long Earlshay drive and saw the house. It looked so forbidding. All its windows were blacked out, so that it resembled a vast and sinister mausoleum, the moon drifting in curd-like clouds behind it. For the first time since leaving the village hall, Florrie felt a twinge of doubt. Had she been wise to take the boys? If living at Earlshay had taught her anything, it was that impulsive feelings weren't allowed; they were best stifled or hidden.

She rang the doorbell.

'Ain't you got a key to your own place?' Sid asked. He was the most talkative of the two, seven years old, and fond of reading and drawing. During the journey Florrie had begun to picture him as a large, thick-set, sunny creature. His companion, Gilbert, was more reserved. Although only eight, he gave an impression of bitter maturity, so it was disconcerting, when the butler opened the door and she found herself under the strong light of the chandelier, to see how very small and babyish the boys were, after all.

At the far end of the hall the grandfather clock chimed nine times in a solemn tone, and this, together with the tantalizing odour of roast lamb and potatoes that hung in the air, reminded Florrie that she'd missed dinner. Sybil and Valentine were strict about mealtimes: if you were more than a few minutes late you had to go without.

There was no question of raiding the kitchen for a snack, either. The cook resented any intrusion on her territory, and had to be humoured, in case she was tempted to give notice. Florrie, who didn't mind going hungry on occasion, had grown used to these rules, but tonight, with two children to look after, they suddenly seemed absurd.

So she nodded at the butler and marched across the new lino to the dining-room, hearing the boys patter shyly along behind her.

Sybil was alone, dressed in black and silver, her dress as shinily tight around the arms and torso as a snakeskin. Sitting up very straight at the end of the long dining-table, she had just finished eating a King William pear with a razor-sharp knife and fork. Florrie couldn't help thinking it was rather a pity. The boys would have enjoyed the spectacle: Sybil showed the most astonishing skill when eating fruit with cutlery. Her fig was the best; Florrie loved the contrast between the flashing silver and the bored, disdainful expression on Sybil's face.

'I'm afraid you're far too late,' Sybil said now, pushing her plate away. Her social smile wavered. Florrie guessed that the boys must have strayed into her line of vision.

'Can I introduce Sid and Gilbert?' Florrie said. 'I've asked them to come and live with us.'

'To live with us? Really, Florence, I hardly think that's practical. We shall be up to our ears in little girls tomorrow.'

'I'm sure we can find . . . an extra corner for them,' Florrie said, pleased to have found a use for one of Sybil's favourite expressions. She often talked about 'finding an extra corner' when one of Cook's puddings was especially delicious.

'And I'm equally certain we can't. We simply don't have the space. Besides,' and here Sybil smiled at the two boys so widely that her sharp incisors became visible, 'I'm sure they'd be far happier elsewhere.'

'And where would that be, then?' Florrie asked quietly, an unfamiliar emotion creeping up on her. It was a prickling of anger. Somehow, she'd always found it impossible to defend herself properly against either Sybil or Valentine. She tended to feel that they must have good reason for criticizing her, that she ought to change, accept whatever strictures they laid down. Hadn't Mother told her to? But this was different. Obviously the two boys should be offered a home at Earlshay – and Florrie could tell, from Sybil's evasive smile, that her mother-in-law knew herself to be in the wrong, but was determined to get away with it.

'Oh, there's bound to be some village woman who'll take them in,' Sybil said carelessly.

'There is,' Florrie answered. 'Me. I'm a village woman, and I'm doing it.'

Sybil shook her head. She paused, half-smiling, before delivering her next remark. 'I'm sure Valentine wouldn't approve.'

Normally, any mention of Valentine's wishes was enough to make Florrie capitulate. Crossing him was too painful. But today, strengthened by that unfamiliar feeling of righteousness, she answered firmly, 'It isn't a matter of what anyone wants. It's a matter of doing what's right.'

Sybil made an angry little huffing sound: the kind of noise she produced when the Lagonda wouldn't start, or she noticed a run in her silk stockings. 'I am not going to stand here and argue with you, Florence,' she said. 'But I do assure you of one thing; I am not going to have those two little ragamuffins in my house.'

'It's my house, too. I've as much right as you to say who lives in it.'

'There are some people one hesitates to invite into one's

home, whatever the circumstances,' Sybil remarked in a fastidious tone. 'I'd have thought you'd have learnt that by now.'

'Oh,' Florrie answered, becoming aware of a strange sensation. It was as if something ferociously enraged had suddenly leapt into her skin and taken possession: a sow deprived of her piglets, perhaps, or a giant wasp. She could almost feel herself swell with indignation. 'You mean people like me? Common, working people?'

'Yes,' Sybil said, moving to the door. 'I wouldn't have put it like that myself, but – yes.' She sounded almost surprised to hear it expressed so clearly.

Florrie searched her brain for the rudest possible rejoinder, and a snatch of conversation came back to her, that she'd once overheard. 'What makes you so certain,' she called out, 'that selling tainted bully-beef makes you a finer person than any other in God's creation?'

Sybil stared at her with distaste, before saying coolly, 'That remark is exactly what I'd expect from someone like you,' and rustled out into the hall.

When she'd gone, Florrie took a deep breath and glanced round the dining-room. Despite the profusion of flowers, napery, silver and glass, there was nothing edible in sight, except for the beautifully curled skin of Sybil's pear, and four brown pips. Even the cheese had been removed. Florrie couldn't help wondering if Sybil had deliberately hurried over her meal, getting the servants to clear the dishes extra quickly, so there should be no scrap left for any late-comer.

She turned to the children. 'Sit yourselves down. I'll fetch us some dinner.'

'Is there going to be more shouting?' Sid asked anxiously.

In the distance, Florrie could hear Sybil yelling into the telephone. The cook wasn't going to be pleased, either, when her sanctum was invaded. However, Florrie felt curiously exhilarated; she even looked forward to the coming confrontation with Mrs Gatehouse – or, as Valentine always called her, with his fondness for absurdifying everyday names, 'Mrs Grape Nuts'.

'Yes. There's going to be a great deal more shouting, but it won't signify. You're staying here, and that's definite.'

Gilbert spoke up. 'Can we come along and watch, then?'

Florrie couldn't sleep, so after a while she got up and stole out to the stables. She didn't know why she felt so restless, why her mind seemed to fizz with ideas; after all, she hadn't exactly won her confrontation with Sybil. The boys might still be in the house, but she knew, from long experience, that Sybil always triumphed. You might face up to her, seem to win an argument, but Sybil would inevitably plot some complex and subtle retaliation that slipped through your defences and defeated you in the end.

That didn't matter: at least the truth was out in the open now. Florrie had found out that her struggle and self-denial had been in vain – that however hard she tried to dress and behave correctly, and speak with the right accent, Sybil was never going to forgive her for the one thing she couldn't change: her background. It was curiously liberating to discover this. It made Florrie think that the frustration and unhappiness she felt might not be her own fault, after all.

As she walked a horse out of the stable-yard she heard Albie and his little dog snore in unison, Albie's noise marginally deeper and growlier in tone. She didn't want to wake them, so she waited until she was halfway up the drive before swinging into the saddle.

The cold night air slid into the front of her blouse and made her shiver; she pulled her jacket closed with one hand. Maybe it had been foolish to put on her favourite green blouse – a crêpe de Chine one – but she couldn't help loving the deep colour and, besides, she wanted to look nice for Samuel, because this ride had a purpose. Halfway between getting out of bed and beginning to search for clothes she'd discovered where she wanted to go: she would catch Samuel before he left for work, and persuade him to do the ploughing for her. Surely she could accomplish a little task like that when she was in such a determined, optimistic mood?

She wasn't surprised to see a light when she finally reached the lane where he lived. It was just after four in the morning, and she knew he had to bicycle a long way – the other side of Withy Hollow – before he reached the farm where he was contract ploughing.

It made her feel a queer blend of nostalgia and unease to see that light in his kitchen window. It didn't flicker, like firelight, and she guessed that he had just lit a lamp to dress and eat by, not having the time to revive embers and heat a kettle. She remembered so many mornings long ago when she'd done the same herself: come downstairs half-asleep and stumbled round an icy kitchen, getting ready for work. The light was greasy-looking behind the wet windowpane, a shadow moved; she could almost feel rough, damp wool against her skin, taste stale bread and fat bacon. She shivered with distaste.

After tying her horse to the gate, beside Samuel's rusty bicycle, she knocked at the door. No one answered, so she let herself in. The first thing she saw, and it was incongruous enough to make her blink, was a sheep standing stiffly beside the table. It was a Dorset Horn ram, with magnificently curly horns, and its head was dipped low to the ground, giving an impression of frowning concentration. Its pose was so rigid that she guessed at once it must be dead; she touched it all the same, and found it cold.

At that moment the clumsy wooden door opposite, which she knew led to the back garden, opened, and Samuel came in. He'd obviously been washing at the pump outside: the skin of his face was a brilliant browny-pink. He didn't see Florrie at once, and this was probably because she was in shadow, and he was dazzled by the lamp balanced on a shelf beside him. He didn't look tired, despite the earliness of the hour; his dark eyes were wide open, and Florrie felt puzzled, without knowing why. Then she realized what she found so odd about his appearance: he was all sharp contrasts – black hair, vivid skin, white shirt – and he was half-smiling to himself. Whenever she'd seen him at Earlshay he'd appeared colourless; you could almost say he'd been in hiding, muffled in a coat, hat pulled low, turning away from her. It was a shock to see him look happy.

But as she was thinking this, he saw her, and the liveliness went from his expression. He dipped his head, shut the door behind him, and snatched up a jacket that lay folded on the table.

'Florrie,' he said, appalled. 'What's you doing here?'

She stepped forward, feeling her riding-habit rustle around her. She loved the severe cut, the rich, dark blue fabric. The skirt was so full, the jacket so stiff with silk lining, that when she was enclosed in them she felt larger and more splendid, like a hen in full feather. She wasn't so sure about her green hat, though. An hour ago, in the mirror, it had appeared elegant, typically French; now, with Samuel looking at her, it just felt silly. She snatched it off and stuffed it in her pocket.

'I wanted to talk to you,' she said shyly.

'You mustn't come in here, at this hour!' He hustled her out of the door in a flurry of brotherly disapproval. 'Us can talk as easy outside.' He was taller than Joe, and much stronger; she noticed this as he gave her arm a gentle push to ease her out into the garden.

'I don't know why you're in such a pucker,' she protested, indignant.

'Ellis ain't home, and you don't know what gossips they is

277

in this village.' He hesitated on the step. 'Here,' he added, 'I has to go to Fightingcocks, you can keep me company on the way.'

He dipped back into the house, and she untied her horse and waited. The light went out, and he came sideways through the door, carrying some bulky, awkwardly shaped object. She was amazed to see, when he reached the road, that it was the sheep. He carried it under one arm, like an enormous stuffed toy, and wheeled his bike with the other.

He didn't refer to it, and she didn't like to seem nosy, so for a few minutes they both kept silent. Once they were out of sight of any other houses, and on the lonely, winding lane that led to Fightingcocks Farm, he walked slower. It was still dark, although she heard a distant cockerel crow hopefully. The narrow lane, with its high hedges cutting off the wind, was almost cosy, and the horse's hooves beside her made a companionable clatter, while Samuel's bike gave off a soft spinning sound as its wheels idled on the road.

'So what was you wanting to ask me about?' he said finally.

'It's difficult,' Florrie began, thinking that it was, in reality, much easier talking to him, like this, in the darkness, when she couldn't see his face. She felt very safe; she always did, she realized, when she was with Samuel. It was like being with a member of her own family. 'You know, I do understand why you wouldn't want to work for me, but can't that be put in the past? Can't it be forgot? I am truly grieved that I ever hurt you, and I have tried to set it right.'

She waited for him to reply, and when he didn't, glanced across at him. He was gazing straight ahead; she could see the ram's snout sticking out below his profile, and it seemed to wear – although she couldn't be sure in the darkness – roughly the same grim, noncommittal expression.

'You see, there isn't anyone else I can go to for help,' she went on. 'And I reckon that if I don't manage to plough up the farm before Christmas I'll have lost my chance. The way things are going the government'll take it over – if they're requisitioning houses now, it'll be land next.' She hesitated. 'It probably doesn't seem important to you, whether I get control of the farm, but it means the world to me. I've felt so terrible useless these past few years. I've achieved nothing . . . I feel I'm just wasting my life.'

Samuel cleared his throat. 'You ain't the only one that's ever felt that way.'

She stopped and turned to look at him, astonished. 'It's the same for you?'

'Course it is,' he said mildly. 'I often feel there's no point to anything – and if it comes to that, there's plenty of things I want and can't never have. I's just grown used to doing without, that's all. I's learned to be thankful for what I has and not go howling after the moon.'

This was exactly Florrie's philosophy, and yet, coming from Samuel, it sounded too dismal – a dingy, depressing way to live. She was surprised by how violently she disagreed with it.

'That's wrong,' she frowned. 'You musn't put up with second-best. You have to keep struggling for what you really want. You might get . . .' she searched for the right words, 'crushed, pulled back, stopped at every turn.' Her voice grew louder, more passionate. 'But you have to keep on trying, else you might as well be dead.'

'And supposing there ain't one chance – not one chance in a thousand million, that you can have what you want. What then?'

'There always is a chance,' Florrie said firmly, finding a conviction deep inside herself that she hadn't known was there. 'Always. You just have to keep on looking for it, and fighting for it.'

She couldn't see Samuel's face clearly, although he was quite close. It was getting lighter, and the greyness played

279

tricks with her eyes, so that she wasn't sure of his expression. 'I suppose that means I got to plough for you,' he said at last, in a light, teasing tone. ''Cos you won't give me any peace until I does.'

They walked on a little further, and feeling at last able to satisfy her curiosity, Florrie asked: 'Will you tell me what the ram's for?'

'Oh – it's only a bit of foolishness.' She could hear in his voice that he was embarrassed. It was disconcerting how well she knew him, from all those times she'd spent in his company as a child. She could visualize the look on his face: the edges of his eyes crinkled, his teeth clenched. He'd made that grimace whenever the teacher called him out in front of the class at school.

'Go on,' she said coaxingly, 'tell me.'

'Well,' he stopped in the road, and she saw that they'd reached the big chestnut tree that marked the turning down to Fightingcocks, 'you know I's working over Withy Hollow? It's a master big farm, and they keeps half a dozen rams, and this one, he were dead in the orchard. They's an old chain harrow there, what the grass is growing up through, and he got his head stuck in the chains, grazing. He died standing up, see, and by the time they found him it were too late, and he weren't no good for eating. So, I asked if I could have him, thought I could play a trick on Joe. He's always fooling about with me, teasing, like. I fancied evening up the score.'

'What are you going to do with it, then?'

'I don't know. Maybe I'll put the ram in the wood-linney. Have him looking out the little window, so Joe don't see him straight off.'

Florrie laughed. 'Marvellous!' She reached into her pocket and pulled out the green hat. 'Here. Put this on his head, it'll give Joe more of a fright.'

Thirty

Florrie had spent the afternoon in a haze of happiness. Perhaps it was due to the crisp autumn air, or maybe to a daydream she'd had that morning. Lying in bed, having overslept and woken in a shaft of sunlight, she'd remembered a story her father had once told her, about his time in the Navy.

How one summer he'd walked home from Plymouth with his cousin, and how, twenty miles from home, as the night was waning, they'd come across a line of sharpened scythes, propped against a hedge. There'd been a gate beside the scythes, leading to a meadow of deep grass, and on impulse Father and his cousin had stepped inside and begun to mow, working steadily, using up the scythes as they grew blunt. When the whole pasture was cut they'd fastened the gate and walked on, chuckling to themselves at the thought of how perplexed the mowing gang would be, when they arrived to start work.

As a child, this tale had infuriated Florrie. She hadn't been able to see why Father thought it so delightful, so infinitely worth retelling whenever he got tiddly on cider. Listening indignantly, she'd felt far more responsible and adult than he was; *she'd* never scythe a meadow to tease and astonish folk she'd never met.

But this morning, waking in a bed as warm as a midsummer haystack, Florrie had finally understood. Emerging from sleep, she'd sensed the magic of the scene: the line of shining scythes, the dewy grass. It was the very pointlessness of Father's gesture that made it so endearing.

Maybe her attitude was changing because her life had become so simple. She slept more deeply now, and it was an effort to stay awake after nightfall, because she was doing so much hard physical labour.

Each day, she'd harness two of her stockiest hunters to a makeshift sledge and drive them out to the overgrown fields beyond the wood. The horses hardly conformed to Father's ideal for a working animal – 'a face like an angel, a body like a barrel, and an arse on it like a farmer's daughter' – but they were reasonably strong. She'd chop down saplings, hack at swathes of bramble, and dig up roots: all the preparatory work that had to be done before the land could be ploughed. The air was frosty despite the sunlight, and as she worked in a blaze of autumn colour, plump pheasants would creep out of the undergrowth beside her, their tail feathers trailing in the fallen leaves.

Perhaps she found her father's story more amusing because of her experience with Samuel's sheep. The morning after helping him deliver it to Fightingcocks, she'd been wandering round Earlshay, calling her evacuees in for breakfast and, walking through the low, cavernous garage, had seen a dark presence in the front of Sybil's Lagonda. When she'd got closer she'd realized, with a jolt, that it was the dead ram. On one horn of its moodily down-turned head it had worn, at a sophisticated angle, Florrie's green Paris hat.

She would have liked to have ferried it back to Joe's farm and continued the macabre joke, but the animal was wedged so tightly into the front seat of Sybil's car that, after a long and discouraging tussle with it, Florrie had just removed the hat. This had been a mistake, because Sybil had assumed (in defiance of all logic, since the nearest sheep farm was a dozen miles away), that the boys must be responsible.

Although they had now been staying at Earlshay for a month, Sybil wasn't any fonder of Gilbert and Sid. All her attempts to have them removed had failed. The billeting officer had been unsympathetic, and his refusal to bow to Sybil's money and influence had made Florrie realize more than any other incident – giving blood at the village hall, or having to carry her gas mask, in its elegant velvet container, at all times – how much the war was altering their lives.

Nearly a month ago, too, a party of girls from St Hilda's had arrived. They hadn't liked the boys either. Unfortunately Florrie had discovered, while giving them their first bath, that the boys had lice, and having no other immediate or effective remedy to hand, had simply shaved their heads. This baldness had been remarked on, most rudely, by the girls from St Hilda's, and as a result the boys tended to spend all their spare time patrolling the attics of the house or exploring the more distant reaches of the park. This made them the most unobtrusive of guests.

Occasionally they would seek Florrie out, wherever she was working in the fields, and ask for some puzzling detail of the estate to be explained. They had been horribly fascinated, for instance, by the vermin board in the wood, where the gamekeepers hung up magpies, buzzards and hawks – and confused by the bells.

This last interest of theirs troubled Florrie. Explaining the function of the bells had involved a long tour of the house, and the boys had been so very captivated by the enamelled plaques in the servants' corridor, with their mysterious legends – Lady Blackstone's Boudoir, Green Powder Room – and so thrilled by the electric buttons hidden under the carpets. Florrie couldn't help feeling that it was, to some extent, her fault that afterwards the bells' behaviour had become erratic. Some had begun to shrill in the early hours of the morning, especially those in the gunroom and the old pantry – all the more mystifying, since no one lived in either of those rooms. Occasionally, too, all the bells in the house would ring at once, in a subdued tinkly cadenza that was strangely irritating to the nerves.

It was growing late. A mist was rolling up from the ground, but Florrie was reluctant to stop working and go back to the house, even though she was hungry, because she was hoping that Samuel would arrive soon with his tractor. He'd told her he'd try to come this afternoon, and ever since lunch-time she'd imagined she heard the engine approaching. Once it had been an aeroplane, another time a car roaring up the drive.

She left the mat of brambles she was working on, and scrambled up the hedge to look down at the swathe of land she'd cleared. The house at Earlshay was on a hill, so that all the land around it sloped, but beyond the wood it did so very gently – it wouldn't be difficult to farm. She liked the crisp new outlines of the hedges, and felt a sense of achievement when she saw the bald, dark patches where long-neglected pasture had once been swamped by undergrowth.

There was a crackle of sticks behind her, and she caught a whinny from one of the two horses waiting patiently beside the sledge. Someone was approaching. Brushing off the worst of the leaf-mould on her jacket, she turned round. It wasn't Samuel, as she'd expected, but Valentine and Veronica. They were walking along a path between the trees, Veronica leaning gracefully on Valentine's arm, and there was some quality in his secretive smile that made Florrie's heart falter.

Veronica's clothes were much finer than usual. She was wearing a silvery frock, and a grey fur stole that looked as if it had been dusted with sugar, and because Valentine was dressed in a blue uniform the two of them appeared out of place, as if they belonged in a nightclub, rather than a wood. This effect was made more eerie by the mist, which hid their feet and swirled in soft layers round their ankles.

Florrie, who had been working in a pair of Albie's breeches and an old tweed jacket, wished she could run indoors and tidy herself before meeting Valentine, but it was too late. He glanced up and saw her, and she noticed how his expression changed as he registered who she was; the smile being replaced by a look of weary annoyance.

He seemed to wake abruptly, as if up until that moment he had scarcely been aware of his surroundings at all. He surveyed the charred remains of the bonfire, the pile of cut wood Florrie had made, the deeply scored ground.

'What the devil are you doing?' he asked.

'I'm readying some fields for the plough.' Florrie tried to sound confident. All this time, working out in the fields, she'd known that Valentine wouldn't approve, but she'd tried not to think about it. She'd just followed her strong intuition that what she was doing was right. Now, seeing him in front of her, she realized the enormity of her problem.

'And who said you could do that?' he enquired. She could tell, from his too-controlled tone of voice, that he was beginning to get angry.

'No one. It was my decision.'

'Really? And when you made this decision, did you take into account the fact that I would dislike it immensely?'

Florrie watched him with care, alert to any alteration in his expression, every nuance in his voice. She stood very straight, her hands by her sides – as always when she was near him she had to resist a powerful urge to open her eyes wider, to assume a flirtatious, childish innocence. Once he had been attracted by that kind of behaviour, and even now, when other women did it, he would respond warmly, but it no longer worked for her. It repulsed him.

'I knew you wouldn't be best pleased, yes,' she answered.

'But I thought it the decent thing to do, seeing as how everything has changed.'

'Nothing has changed.' Valentine half smiled, and although he didn't turn to Veronica, she caught the expression from him. On her face it looked spiteful. 'I still own this land, and I still decide what happens to it.'

'But it has to be ploughed whatever happens, doesn't it?' Florrie answered. Sometimes it was possible to win Valentine round by appealing to his intellect, and presenting some course of action as being a matter of common sense, backing it up with arguments culled from newspapers and books. Sometimes – but only if he was in an exceptionally good mood; she sensed that today, with Veronica there, she was unlikely to succeed, however carefully she put her case. She continued nonetheless: 'They were saying in *The Times* that . . .' but Valentine cut in.

'I don't want to listen. You've disobeyed me. You've spoiled my land.'

'I haven't – I've improved it.' Florrie knew it would be safer to look contrite, but her enthusiasm got the better of her. 'The hedges haven't been laid properly for years,' she went on, her voice nearly reverting to Devon as she got caught up in her subject. 'And it's so fertile! Why, the docks were six foot high, and the horse-dashels like fuzz-bushes. And the worms! You've never seen the like.' She stooped down and picked up a handful of earth, holding it out eagerly to Valentine. 'Isn't it beautiful?' she asked. 'It'll grow a master crop of corn.'

He didn't take the earth. His eyes narrowed fractionally – a warning she registered far too late – before he hit her hard across the face. The sound of his slap echoed through the wood, and Florrie staggered and nearly fell. She clutched at her cheek, her hand icy against the hot skin.

'I'm not interested,' Valentine said. 'Do you understand? Now go indoors and clean yourself up. You haven't heard the last of this.'

Florrie wasn't aware of the pain, only of the humiliation, of the shock of him striking her in front of another woman. It seemed that some final pass had been reached, some moment at which she could go on no further, but had to make a stand. Her vision became funnelled: all she was aware of was Valentine's face: beyond that Veronica's olive skin framed by silver fox, the trees, the sky – all were a greyish-white blur. It was sad, looking at his face; even the cold look on it was dear to her.

She shook her head slightly. 'No,' she said. 'I don't care what you do, I'm not stopping my work. I know it's right, you see. I know it has to be done.'

'You stupid bitch,' he shouted. 'Don't you understand? There's no point in defying me, because you can't win. How much corn can you plant without any money? Without any horses?'

His threats had a silky quality, as if he enjoyed making them. At his mention of the horses Florrie felt dizzy. She had forgotten that they were always the first casualty of any disagreement between her and Valentine.

'You'd be surprised,' she answered stoutly.

'I wouldn't.' He turned to go. 'Nothing you could do would ever surprise me.'

When they'd gone Florrie walked back to the hedge and climbed up into it again. She didn't look down on the fields; instead she pressed her face against the foliage. Its prickliness was soothing. After a long time she was aware of the hedge shaking as another creature climbed into it, and heard Samuel ask, 'You all right?'

She found she couldn't speak at once. She wondered if Samuel had witnessed her argument with Valentine. His voice was too concerned for someone who hadn't. For an uneasy moment she felt herself on the brink of a wild hysteria. How many others had been present? Would Father emerge soon from the undergrowth, or Joe, or Sybil? She swallowed.

'I'm fine,' she said after a pause, trying to keep her voice light, but aware that it had gone wavery. 'Don't you know that ladies have no feelings?'

'What's that?'

Samuel's tone of voice had a polite distance to it, as if they were discussing the weather. Maybe he hadn't heard or seen anything, after all.

'Oh,' she went on, her voice more level now, 'it's what I've discovered. Sybil's spent years telling me what a lady does and doesn't do, all stuff about saying "what?" instead of "pardon?", but she's never said what a lady *is*. I've had to work that out for myself. And I reckon I know now. A lady is someone who never has hurt feelings, who never gives way to self-pity. She isn't demeaned by anything she has to do, either – and if she finds herself in hell, why, she studies to see what she can learn from the experience.'

The hedge crackled and swayed, and after a while Samuel spoke from behind her. 'It don't sound terrible pleasant, being a lady,' he remarked mildly.

She turned and climbed down too. 'I wouldn't wish myself anything else.'

He was standing near the horses, his normally sensitive, mobile face strangely still. He didn't seem to notice anything odd in her appearance – so the slap couldn't have been that hard – he just nodded at her before crouching down to examine the sledge. 'I never reckoned you would,' he said. 'You always was very firm in your opinions. A real stayer.' He chuckled. 'Who made this, then? Albie? Ain't he ever cack-handed?' She didn't answer, so he stood up again and rubbed his hands on his trousers. 'About this ploughing. Do you still want me to do it?' He hesitated. 'Or has you gone and changed your mind?'

Florrie gave him a sharp look. There was concern, even

pity, in his bright, dark eyes. It made her revise what she'd intended to say. 'Of course I still want you to do it. Only – only maybe next week instead of this.'

His expression altered most subtly. 'Tell you what,' he offered. 'If you's interested in farming proper, and wants livestock, I knows where I can get my hands on a couple of good piglets.'

It was like a challenge, and Florrie never had been able to resist a dare.

'Sounds decent enough,' she said carelessly. 'What have I got to lose?'

Thirty-one

There was still a little patch of snow on the roof of Earlshay, a relic of the long, hard winter. It shrank each day in the spring sunshine, and froze again at night. Approaching the back way, through the woodland below the lake, Florrie was aware of the setting sun – yellowy in a leaden sky.

It had been cold for so long that the park looked broken-down and dirty. At the edge of the water someone small had collected dead birds; the ones that had frozen and fallen out of trees in the winter. They'd been put in neat rows, awaiting burial.

Florrie was driving a dozen yearling calves ahead of her. All breeds and colours, they were the cheapest she'd been able to find in market, but even so, she'd only just been able to afford them, using some money she'd got from selling a pearl necklace. The animals hesitated as they approached the bridge, doubtful about crossing it, and in the clear, cold air she heard a child call out, 'You're never going to do it – never, never, never.' The voice belonged to Gilbert, and held a familiar note of gloating triumph.

'Shut up, will ya?' Despite the fact that he was some distance away, and out of sight, Florrie could tell that Sid was feeling cornered and desperate. The voices had come from the walled garden far up ahead, and Florrie listened anxiously, but there were no further words, just a sound of sticks being broken.

She worried about the boys. The girl evacuees had at least

got teachers to look after them, and went home in the holidays – Gilbert and Sid didn't appear to have anyone. They'd remained at Earlshay over Christmas, and no letters or parcels had come for them. It wouldn't, perhaps, have been so bad if the two boys had got on well, but though they were always together their relationship wasn't easy. They constantly provoked and fought each other.

Yesterday afternoon, while Florrie had been cooking in the kitchen – a necessity, since Mrs Gatehouse had given in her notice – she'd overheard Gilbert jeering at Sid underneath the big, scrubbed table.

'Everyone at school thinks you're a dirty, stinking pansy,' he'd said, his voice a menacing singsong. 'They hate your clothes, and the way you walk. They think everything you say is garbage – gar-bage – and no one wants to be your friend. No one. They all hate you. They laugh when you walk past, with your stupid, pansy walk . . .'

Florrie had paused in her baking, wondering whether to intervene, but Sid hadn't retaliated until Gilbert ran out of insults. Then he'd said quietly, 'At least I'm not soft on that Fiona with the fat legs.'

Gilbert's reaction had been explosive. He'd shot out from under the table and bolted upstairs, and only after hours of searching had Florrie found him curled up miserably behind the hot-water tank in the attic. He'd been beyond speech, so she'd never discovered whether Sid's remark had wounded so deeply because it was true, and Gilbert was secretly in thrall to one of the girls from St Hilda's; or whether it was that to be accused, unjustly, of being so, was simply too great an insult to be borne.

Florrie turned back to her calves and caught Samuel watching her, a slight frown on his face.

'What's they boys up to?' he asked, tilting his head with a graceful, cat-like gesture that he'd caught from Ellis.

He'd happened to be at Cullerton market when she'd bought

the calves, and offered to help her drive them home. It was odd, really: she'd heard from Albie that Samuel was working long hours as a contractor, yet on their occasional meetings he always had plenty of time to spare.

'I reckon they're fiddling with that lock on the greenhouse door,' she answered. 'When I left early this morning they were having a go at the big brass keyhole on the kitchen cupboard. You see, Sid has this fancy in his head that he's going to be a burglar when he grows up. So he's trying to teach himself to pick locks.'

'He got the hang of it yet?'

'No. He's useless. I was hoping to get someone to show him. Do you reckon Joe would know how to do it?'

Samuel didn't answer. Instead he clicked his tongue at the calves and urged them forward, and they ran clumsily on to the bridge, their hooves banging on the wooden timbers. Florrie flinched at the sound. She didn't want anyone at the house to know about these calves – that was why she was bringing them in the back way. They were a secret, part of the little livestock farm she was gradually building up in the stables. Only she couldn't really tell Samuel that. She didn't want him to think she was a coward.

'Easy!' she said, in a light, teasing tone that was an effort to assume. 'You don't want to stir them up, or they'll misbehave and wreck the place.'

'No chance,' he answered, turning back to look at her. 'Them calves is proper respectful. Just the sort for a fancical little farm like yours.' He smiled, showing clenched teeth. It was as if he was aware of her unease, and enjoying it, and this, along with some quality in the dimming light – or maybe just the contrast between his white teeth and dark skin – made him look unfamiliar, piratical, dangerous. It was so unlike the way she usually thought of Samuel that she dismissed it as an illusion.

'What are you implying?' she asked. 'That my farm isn't up to much?'

'Now would I say a thing like that?'

While they'd been talking one of the calves, a bony creature with a coat the colour of stale milk chocolate, had wandered off ahead of the others. By the time Florrie realized what was happening it was about ten yards up the slope of grassland that led to the back of the house. She ran after it, and seeing her give chase, it leapt into the air with excitement and made a noise halfway between a moo and a growl. Then it broke into a fast trot and ran easily up the rest of the slope. Reaching the top, where the garden wall began, it turned to give her an insolent stare before dodging through an open gate.

Following as closely as she could, Florrie found herself in a wide corridor of muddy grass between the wall and a box hedge. Like the house itself, the garden at Earlshay had become a completely different place since the outbreak of war and the disappearance of the staff. Florrie thought it far prettier now it was starting to go wild. Yesterday she'd even seen a deer grazing outside the dining-room window.

The run up the hill had taken more out of her than she'd expected, and she paused to rub her waist, where she had a stitch. She hoped the calf wouldn't have gone far – hopefully just into the vegetable garden, where she could corner it easily.

She knew Valentine would strongly disapprove of her calves, and in fact she would never have thought of buying them if Samuel hadn't somehow enticed her into doing it – just as, before Christmas, he'd provoked her into accepting a couple of pigs. She wasn't a baby; if she really hadn't wanted the animals she wouldn't have allowed herself to be persuaded. It was more that her feelings were fatally divided. She hadn't seen or heard from Valentine since October, and back then, one part of her had been tempted, when he'd sent away all the horses and cut off her allowance, to just give in, and renounce all idea of farming. She did still want to please him. But when Samuel told her there were cheap calves going in the market, or suggested she took on an old milk-cow that a neighbour didn't need, he appealed to an older instinct of hers, long-buried: the desire to take risks, to experiment – and seek happiness.

It was like, she thought, one of those dialogues the vicar used to describe, between conscience and evil impulse. Except, in this case, that Florrie was no longer sure which voice was right, and which wrong. She'd begun to feel that making friendly overtures to Valentine, keeping herself open and loving, might be as wicked as defying him; that by making herself vulnerable she only encouraged him to be more sadistic.

The calf wasn't in the vegetable garden. She didn't find it until she went round the side of the house and stepped on to the drive. It was growing darker now, and someone had left the front door open an inch, so that an illegal line of light spilled out across the drive. There was a car parked there, its bonnet cooling, and Florrie was aware of a horrifyingly strong feeling of dread at the thought that her husband might have returned home. All these months she'd been telling herself that she'd be able to face up to him easily; she realized now that it wouldn't be like that at all.

There was a movement beside the car: an angular shape bent over. It was the calf, licking at the windscreen in a thoughtful, appreciative manner. It looked up at her, a long string of spittle hanging from its mouth and sparkling in the light from the door, and she saw with relief that the car was unfamiliar – an Alvis tourer – and that it appeared to belong to a woman: a pair of pale grey gloves and a hat lay on the driver's seat.

Sybil stood up and opened her arms in greeting. 'Veronica, darling!'

Her cheek felt old for the first time: soft and powdery. The room was hot – a surprise after the iciness of the hall and corridor. The windows out there had had thick condensation running down the glass, and this had made Veronica feel as if she was walking through the inside of a river. A very grimy river, too: the lino had been streaked with mud, the staircase scuffed, and the walls scribbled on – mainly with the one word 'Fiona' reiterated over and over about four feet up from the floor, as if put there by a love-sick midget. Veronica had felt sad that the Earlshay she'd so enjoyed, full of elegant furniture and bright colour, should so quickly have been destroyed. But of course she realized now that it hadn't. It had simply been crammed into this one room with Sybil.

Pictures and plates covered the raspberry-coloured walls up to the ceiling, and there were so many delicate tables and plump brocade chairs, each weighed down by silk cushions, silver frames, snuffboxes and Chinese porcelain, that it was almost impossible to manoeuvre across the floor. In the midst of this, dressed in a flowered gown by Mainbocher, stood Sybil. There was a blazing fire beside her, and just across from it a barley-twist table bearing a lavish, if eccentric, tea. Fruit cake, scones, and clotted cream with a golden crust were flanked by cold roast pheasants and joints of fried rabbit.

'I hope you don't mind being all hugger-mugger,' she said. 'Only I daren't sit anywhere else in the house. One is simply shrammed with the cold.'

'It's divine in here.'

'I've been writing a list,' Sybil continued, sitting down and feeling among the cushions of her chair. After a longish search she drew out a pair of spectacles, a pen, and a notebook. 'Of all the ghastly things I loathe about the war. I find it so comforting to make lists, don't you? Of course, first of all there's the rationing. That's impossible. I mean – how *is* one to manage? And then there's having to share one's home with second-rate minds.'

'Well, I'm madly jealous,' Veronica said. 'I haven't seen cream like that for months.'

'That's Florence's doing. She makes bucketfuls of the stuff. It's no wonder country girls have such foul complexions – all they seem to eat is fat. Slabs and slabs of it . . .'

There was a discreet tap on the door and a girl about eleven years old, with red plaits and a grey school uniform, came in carrying a teapot and cream jug.

'There's a telephone call for you, Lady Sybil,' she said in a loud, but cultivated voice. 'It's the same funny man as before.'

As Sybil hissed with irritation and rustled out into the corridor, Veronica examined a photograph standing on the grand piano. It was of Valentine in his uniform, an imperious look on his face. Veronica knew it well: she'd taken it herself. There was a letter from him, too, tucked into the frame. In some trepidation, in case Sybil returned too soon and caught her, Veronica unfolded it and skimmed through the contents. It was at least a month old, dated March 1940, and it didn't mention her once. She'd just put it back when Sybil returned, angry.

'I simply can't understand it,' she said, settling herself back in her chair.

'What, darling?'

'I keep getting these mysterious calls. It's always a man – at least, that's what the girls tell me – and he has a gruff, continental voice – French or perhaps Belgian. And I go to the frightful bother of walking all the way to the gunroom, and when I get there he's rung off. It's too vexing for words.'

'Could it be a joke of some kind?'

'A joke?' Sybil peered at her doubtfully. 'How on earth could it be? It's not the least bit amusing.'

'A child might find it funny.'

'A child? Are you saying one of my girls is playing a trick on me? A nice girl from St Hilda's?'

Reluctant to start an argument, Veronica said hastily, 'Perhaps not.'

'I should think so, too.' Sybil gave a mollified sniff, and poured out tea, and they had a polite, inconsequential discussion, all about what Veronica was doing in London, and how her husband was coping in the Army. She answered Sybil's questions with difficulty, wishing to have a proper conversation, and be truthful, but uncertain how to begin.

'I haven't actually been seeing an awful lot of him,' she said finally. 'In fact – to be honest – we've more or less separated.'

'I *am* sorry.'

'I'm not. I'm in love with someone else.'

'How blissful! I do adore intrigue! Is it anyone I know?'

'It is, actually.' Veronica paused, watching Sybil's face. There was a greedy expression in the pale blue eyes. 'It's Vallie.'

At the mention of his name, Sybil blinked. When she opened her eyes again the rapacious look had gone. 'I think that's rather a mistake,' she said coolly.

'Why?'

'Because he has the morals of a jack-rabbit.'

'He isn't like that any more.'

Sybil leaned forward. 'Oh, Veronica,' she sighed. 'I never thought I'd have this conversation with you. Over the years I've had it with so many women. I'm sick to death of it. And do you know what they all had in common? They all thought, they were all absolutely *convinced*, that Vallie really cared about them; that no matter how he'd acted in the past, this time it was different.' Sybil didn't look at Veronica; she kept both her eyes shut while delivering this speech, as if too wearied by the subject matter to bother combining it with a facial expression. Meanwhile, one of her fingers absentmindedly sketched a letter. It looked like an F for Florence, an F for Faithful-little-wife. Veronica found herself growing annoyed. Sybil opened her eyes again, and this time her voice had a syrupy, pitying tone. 'My dear innocent,' she remarked, 'it never was different, and never will be.'

'He's changed,' Veronica insisted. 'He's grown up. You'd hardly recognize him.'

'I recognize this conversation.'

Sybil's disdainful expression angered Veronica so much that she couldn't resist saying, 'He wants to marry me.'

'What?'

'He's going to divorce the gorilla.'

'He's said nothing to me.' Sybil's voice had an edge of panic in it. Veronica almost felt sorry for her – almost, but not quite.

'I've told you, Sybil – he's changed. He wouldn't necessarily tell you, anyway. You're hardly close any more, are you?' Veronica was surprised by how intensely pleasurable it was, saying this. She discovered at once, without any sense of shock, that she disliked almost everything about Sybil now: her snobbishness, her senility, her blindness to any truth about her son.

Veronica got up, unable to sit still. She felt so triumphant, so stimulated, that she needed to pace up and down, but it was difficult in that crowded room. She kept tripping over bound volumes of *Vogue* and cannoning into embroidered pouffes. 'I think it's the war, rather than me, that's altered him,' she said reflectively, aware that her self-indulgent tone of voice was making Sybil flinch, and relishing the fact. 'He's so happy now. He enjoyed flying before – and now he's doing it for the RAF he's in heaven. It has all the danger and excitement he craves – and it's useful, too. I know people say that the rich have it easy, but they don't, you know. It can be fearfully disheartening, being able to do exactly as you wish, day after day. I think the poor lamb's finally found his feet, after all these years.'

Sybil gave a muffled snort. 'I'd hardly describe Vallie as a *lamb*.' She rose to her feet, and Veronica thought, disconcerted, that she didn't look so old after all. She held herself very straight and her voice was cool and steady. 'I can see you're impatient to be gone, Veronica,' she said. 'So I shan't keep you. But I do assure you – there has never been a divorce in our family, and there never shall be, either.'

When Veronica had gone Sybil bit her knuckle, lost in thought, for nearly an hour. At the end of that time the little red-head knocked on the door to say that another mysterious Belgian was on the telephone, and received an unexpectedly violent – and foul-mouthed – response.

'I don't like being afraid, and not being able to solve the problem at once,' Florrie said. 'Nowadays I seem to live in dread all the time – there's this feeling that life is about to get infinitely worse, and there's nothing I can do about it.'

She was talking about the war, but the topic was almost pleasurable discussed in such vague terms, because it was a way of approaching her feelings about Valentine, too. Just as one day soon, poisonous gas might start raining from the skies, so, inevitably, he would return.

'I'd like to go out now,' she continued. 'Go out, and just fight the things I'm scared of. Sort them once and for all, not have them hanging over me any more.' As she spoke she made sharp gestures with her hands. It was a habit she'd thought she'd broken herself of – Valentine used to mock it – but whenever she was sitting in the kitchen like this, talking to Samuel, it would drift back. He didn't reply, so she added, 'Don't you feel the same?'

She regretted it almost at once. They were sitting in the

flickering glow of the firebox on the kitchen range, and his face reflected his feelings with such clarity that she could tell at once she'd touched a nerve. He seemed to withdraw into himself briefly; then a hardness settled round his jaw.

'I reckon I'll join up soon,' he said. 'Whenever you talks like this it makes me feel a right axwaddler, stopping back home and farming.'

'I didn't mean it that way. What you're doing is just as useful. The country needs food as much as it needs soldiers – more, even. They probably wouldn't let you join up anyway.'

'Oh – if I set my mind to it they'd let me go, right enough. You can be sure of that.' Samuel's tone was grim.

There was the sound of running feet, and Sid skidded round the corner. 'I done it!' he shrieked. 'I got in the room at the top of the passage! You've got to come, quick!'

As he tugged at her hands, trying to drag her out of the kitchen, Florrie turned back to Samuel. In his dark clothes, still muddy from the chase after the calf, he looked quietly anachronistic, as if he belonged in another, earlier century. He held his cap in his hands, his elbows propped on his spread knees, light reflecting off the clean bits of his leather gaiters, and watched Sid with a bright-eyed, humorous expression. She had a sudden fearful premonition.

'If you ever decide to go,' she said, 'promise you'll come and see me first. Swear it now.'

Sid was jumping with impatience. He could hardly bear to wait while she walked up the stairs behind him; he kept circling, like a little dog, and urging her forward.

'Samuel showed me,' he said, as she reached the landing. 'He give me a bit of wire and told me how to twist it.'

He ran towards the door and waited expectantly. It was a room which Sybil referred to as 'my dear little boxroom', and despite the invasion of children into the house, and the desperate need for places to put beds, had obstinately refused to open; saying first that it was full of suitcases and in bad repair, and then that she'd lost the key.

The door now stood open, and there was a bright light on inside. As she walked along the landing towards it, Florrie saw a section of wall striped blue and white, and above it a drawing of an amazed-looking poodle. It was so perfect, so pristine in appearance compared to the passageway that the contrast was spooky. She was almost reluctant to push the door wider and discover what lay within.

Thirty-two

'Florence – love,' Sybil called out, the last word a little uncertain. Florrie didn't reply, or turn round, but out of the corner of her eye saw her mother-in-law appear just outside the stable-yard. It was early for Sybil to be up – only nine o'clock in the morning – and she was dressed untypically: in a flared tweed coat with gold thread in the weave, and a hat like an upturned flowerpot, balanced at a jaunty angle on her smooth blonde head.

It occurred to Florrie, and she was amused by the thought, that Sybil might have put on those clothes because she imagined they were appropriate for visiting a stable.

Sybil came closer, stepping daintily round a bucket. Florrie had been feeding her pigs, and as she finished she shut the door of the loose box where they were kept, careful to keep her back still turned to Sybil. It was childish, she knew, to ignore her mother-in-law so pointedly, but that didn't stop it being enjoyable. Ever since finding the baby's room at the top of the house she'd felt so angry that civilized behaviour just hadn't seemed appropriate any more.

For days she'd avoided Sybil altogether, but as they didn't normally spend much time together, this had been a coward's response to the insult of that room. Sybil's approach, now, gave her wry pleasure; her heart beat faster in anticipation of a fight.

'Dear me,' Sybil said in a surprised, but social, tone, 'what hordes of animals we have nowadays, to be sure!' She leaned forward, whalebone creaking, to peer into the loose box Florrie had just left. There was a bang as one of the pigs propped itself up against the other side of the half-door, and a nose whiffled at the brim of Sybil's hat. Sybil jerked back out of range.

'Well!' she continued, determined to be pleasant. 'This *is* nice!'

'What do you reckon's so blooming nice about it?' Florrie asked, leaning against the tack room wall, arms folded. 'The smell of the pigs, or the way they look?'

'Their usefulness,' Sybil said firmly, sidestepping a confrontation. 'They are tremendously useful, pigs. Or so I've heard.' She paused. 'From people who know about these things.' She paused again, and when Florrie still didn't respond, gave a secretive, closed-mouth grin that made her look, for one disconcerting instant, almost exactly like Valentine. 'And that includes you, of course, my dear Florence. I can't tell you how impressed I am that you can cope with this sort of thing.' Sybil gestured vaguely at the pigs.

'Queer,' Florrie said, 'seeing as how you never stop implying I was raised in a pigsty. If I'm not much more than a pig myself I should know how to feed them, shouldn't I?'

'Florence.' Sybil tut-tutted and shook her head slightly. 'I can see it's time we had a little talk together, you and I.'

'What about? That room you've made upstairs, for a child that doesn't exist?' Despite herself, Florrie couldn't prevent her voice from shaking as she said the word 'child'. Of course, Sybil picked up on it at once.

She spoke with unconvincing sweetness. 'Dearest Florence, I am so sorry. The last thing I meant to do was hurt your feelings.'

'I don't want your sympathy,' Florrie answered fiercely. 'I just want you to leave me alone. My personal life is private, and has nothing to do with you.'

'Ah – but there you are quite wrong,' Sybil said. Now that Florrie had become passionately involved in the conversation and was no longer leaning back, arms folded, Sybil held herself straighter, her head tilted slightly forward, looking as self-contained as a queen on a chessboard. 'It has a great deal to do with me. I like the way things are now. For all our disagreements in the past, I don't want to lose you.'

'Whatever are you on about?'

'My son. According to Veronica he's thinking of divorce.' Sybil clasped her gloved hands together as she said this. They were tiny, with long, slender fingers. Looking at them, Florrie remembered trying to squeeze her own plump palms into Sybil's evening gloves all those years ago, on the night of the costume ball.

She raised her eyes, wondering whether this was a cruel tease, but Sybil's expression was level and troubled.

Florrie pushed past her and walked out of the yard, breaking into a run as soon as she was certain she was unobserved. The only place she could think of seeking an answer was Valentine's study.

It smelt of soot; quantities of the stuff had fallen down the chimney and spilled over on to the carpet, and there was fine black dust on the papers of his desk. Most were letters from his bank – all unopened. Florrie pulled out the drawers of the desk, not sure what she was looking for, but searching frantically all the same. Maybe there'd be love letters.

In the bottom drawer she found a stack of sketch books, bound in stiff blue card. She turned the pages, seeing at once that they were old. She recognized scenes from the summer and autumn of 1936: figures in the garden, chins propped languidly on hands, playing the endless games of Monopoly that Valentine had demanded.

All the talk then had been about Mrs Simpson: Valentine

had read of the scandal abroad, and propounded a theory that the reason for the Prince's obsession lay in Mrs Simpson's astonishing muscle power in a certain intimate part of her anatomy. Florrie remembered wondering a little wistfully, at the time, why Valentine thought this so much more likely an explanation than true love.

At the very bottom of the stack was a small sketch book that looked familiar. Florrie opened it, and was at once confronted by a picture of Father, driving Smart in a tip-cart at Fightingcocks. She turned another page and saw a young girl, with a great sweep of curly hair, sitting under a bramble-bush, one boot off and held in her hand. The pose was angled so that you saw a length of white thigh above a woollen stocking.

It was so peculiar – it made Florrie breathless – to find these drawings Valentine had made of her all those years ago. Each one was queasily pornographic, some worked from memory – or fantasy – and Florrie examined them in a daze, wondering what it was about her that he'd once liked. She thought, from the evidence, that it must have been a rounded, dimpled babyishness, along with a certain bold, cheeky gaze. Or maybe it had been something altogether simpler. She shut the book. Whatever it had been, she sensed she no longer possessed it.

She looked up, aware of a shadow in the room.

It was Sybil. Her hat was gone, and her hair looked untidy, as if she'd wrenched it off.

'Do you think it's true?' she whispered.

Florrie raised her shoulders slightly.

'I don't know. I never truly understood why he did anything. Often I thought I did, but it turned out afterwards I was deceived.' She picked up one of the sealed envelopes and began to open it.

'Do you think you should go and see him?' Sybil prompted.

'Change his mind – persuade him?'

'Whatever I do,' Florrie said firmly, 'it'll be of my own choosing. I'll not discuss it with you.'

The field looked more like a playground than a workplace. For at least half an hour the two boys had laboured quite creditably, but now they were having an earth and potato fight. The clods of earth were harder than the seed potatoes, it was so dry.

Further away, the girls were drooping over their rows, most in attitudes of extreme exhaustion and martyrdom. Perhaps it was the warm weather, or the dust, but even Father was sitting down in the shade of the hedge. He was talking to one of the prettier schoolteachers, and as Florrie walked past she heard him say, 'There's a barnacle goose on Islay wearing a pair of my spectacles.' It was the opening phrase of his favourite speech, one he launched into whenever he'd been drinking too much cider. 'Snatched them off my face, he did, the beggar, while I were sleeping.'

Reaching the headland, Florrie turned Smart round. Father had given her the old horse just after Christmas. He was well past twenty, and couldn't work long hours, but he had such a steady, patient character that his company made even the dullest job a pleasure. Florrie thought Samuel must have told Father about her financial difficulties, because as well as presenting her with the horse, Father had taken to calling at Earlshay to offer tips on planting or livestock management, and he always tucked a bit of folding money into her coat pocket before he left, showing as much delicacy as she used to, in the palmy days before Valentine had cut off her allowance. The money had clearly been kept in a secret store near Father's cows: the notes were of antique design and smelled strongly of cow-cake and manure.

As she started down another row, splitting the ridges and

covering the potatoes, she saw Samuel over by the gate, talking to Colonel Lightbush. He didn't talk to the colonel the way that Father did – with an attitude of cringing deference – his stance was easy, relaxed, one hand resting on the top bar of the open gate. He didn't have his cap on, which she supposed was a concession to the colonel's status, but he was behaving as if he considered himself an equal. Colonel Lightbush didn't appear to mind.

She watched them thoughtfully, freed from the need to guide Smart along the ridges. He'd used a balking plough so often that he could do the work half-asleep.

Florrie wished she could have been the one to discuss details with Colonel Lightbush, but she knew that that wasn't how it was done, that though she was the one farming and making all the decisions at Earlshay, when it came to ratifying her position with the War Agricultural Committee she needed to be backed up – and spoken for – by her father and Samuel.

She had talked to the colonel earlier, but he'd immediately assumed a twinkly, mock-respectful manner, as if he saw her as a brainless little moppet to be humoured and indulged. She knew, from long experience, that any attempt to change this attitude would only annoy the colonel, and she wanted him on her side. She hated to sacrifice principle to expediency, but it seemed to her, more and more, that to get what you wanted as a woman, to survive, you had to become as devious as Sybil.

Still, at least now there was a strategy, a clear path she could see to follow. She'd lost that confused and helpless sensation she'd so often had in Valentine's company. For one instant she wondered how she'd feel if he did desert her, and was appalled to discover, mixed in with other, less clear emotions, some guilty relief. She wasn't sure if finding the sketches had made her feel like that. Of course she was pleased that he'd once found her attractive (although putting it like that made her sound disapproving and old-maidish). She still remembered the overwhelming excitement she'd once felt in his company. It had just been strangely dispiriting to discover, to begin to realize, that his perception of her had always been limited to just that one, fleeting quality – a plaything.

An aeroplane roared across the golden sky, leaving a white trail, like a knife-cut in a crust of cream. The boys shouted and waved, recognizing the British markings, but Smart faltered at the sound, and before he could step forward again Samuel had caught hold of his bridle.

'Is it all set, then?' Florrie asked.

'Far as it can be. They's hard old nuts if you ain't doing it right, mind. They turned old Astridge off his land 'cos he wouldn't give up his sheep and plough the pasture.'

As he spoke Samuel glanced round at the field. The boys had begun pelting the girls with potatoes, and the girls, particularly a lively red-head Florrie recognized as Fiona, were retaliating with surprising vigour, considering their exhaustion only a few minutes ago.

'Hoi!' Father shouted, rising menacingly from the hedgerow and advancing, bow-legged, towards the children. One or two fled through the gate, the rest shrank back into their rows.

'You want to get he to stop here,' Samuel laughed, 'keep them kids in order.'

'Aren't I frightening enough?' Florrie asked teasingly.

'No one's frightened of you,' Samuel said, emphasizing the first two words.

'Don't you be too sure of that!' She stopped smiling. 'Samuel,' she said, 'when you look at me, what do you see? I really want to know – truthful, now.'

He leaned against Smart's flank. 'I's not so certain I can tell you.'

'Yes, you can.'

He seemed to come to a conclusion. She wasn't sure what it would be – he'd assumed that self-contained, slightly piratical expression that she found so disconcerting.

'Beautiful,' he said softly. 'Ruthless with horses. Smarter than me. I can tell you – I's terrified.'

Sybil was upstairs, on the landing, feeling restless. Maybe it was the spring weather, or the fact that there was no one left to call on – all her friends being tiresomely caught up in the war effort. She'd spent yesterday dieting, lying on the chaise-longue in her sitting-room, drinking hot water and Glauber's Salts, but today even that seemed curiously pointless. Who was there to notice whether she was a pound or two overweight?

She walked slowly into the Chinese room, admiring the way her lizard-skin shoes looked: like a fine pen drawing against the pale linoleum. This room was occupied by the girls now. They used it as a gym: sweaty mats were piled in one corner. Blackout curtains billowed at the open window, and someone had placed a jar of withered daffodils on the sill. On impulse, Sybil went over and stood beside it, gazing out at the park.

Beyond the wood, she could see one of the newly cleared fields. There seemed to be a party going on in it. Children were running about, shrieking, and Florence was standing beside a horse, talking to a man. Sybil took a pair of opera-glasses out of her bag.

She was rather disappointed in Florence. As far as Sybil could tell she'd done nothing at all since hearing the news about Valentine. It seemed uncharacteristically spineless of the girl. Florence was dressed in the untidy, masculine clothes she always wore nowadays, a riding-jacket and breeches, but there was a black ribbon in her hair, and some quality about her pose was coquettish. She was half-turning, and her smile was arch; she seemed more alive than Sybil had seen her for years. Her ribbon fluttered, and the skirt of her dark jacket moved in the breeze.

Interested, Sybil focused on her companion, and was at once conscious of a feeling of disappointment. It was only that little man who came round with the tractor. Florence often talked to him; Sybil found their worthy, platonic relationship inexpressibly dull. She'd even eavesdropped on it once, but been unable to glean anything of interest.

A thought struck her. The opening paragraph of a letter to Valentine seemed to form itself unaided in her mind.

Darling Vallie,

I haven't heard from you for such a long time, and so much has happened while you've been away. I thought you'd be amused to hear that Florence has developed rather a *tendresse* for one of the hired help. They're practically inseparable, and it's *such* a ducky sight . . .

Sybil smiled to herself with pleasure. Perhaps, on balance, it would be better to put: 'one of the hired-help *digging up your woods*' – Vallie had always had rather a thing about his trees.

Thirty-three

As Florrie reached the hayfield she saw Samuel in the distance. He had his back to her, and was walking slowly, stooping every few paces to test the quality of the grass. Florrie was touched by his concern for her meagre hay crop. It wasn't worth much, she didn't think: there was too much weed in it. She wondered whether to call out a greeting, but feeling shy, turned left, instead, to find the old horse, Smart.

Smart was in the deep meadow beside the wood, still fast asleep, even though the sun had risen an hour ago. His huge bulk was visible as a dark mound, rising and falling evenly, half-hidden by the long grass. Florrie dropped over the gate and crept as stealthily as possible towards him. One of his ears twitched to repel a fly, but he didn't sense her approach. She was able to slip on to his back and put her arms around his neck. He gave a sudden snort of dismay, then, and lifted his head, but he knew it was her; he showed no further unease as he lumbered to his feet.

'I reckon you'll need me today,' Samuel called from the gate. 'That grass is over-fit, as I see it.' He looked browner than when she'd last seen him, and his cheeks were rosy with sunburn: he'd obviously been making other people's hay all week. There was even hay in his hair, making it look drier and curlier. He opened the gate for her.

'I don't care to gamble,' she said. 'Father always kept a bit of damp in his, but I've seen enough black hay to last me a lifetime.' She leaned down absentmindedly and picked a piece of grass out of Samuel's hair. 'Besides, no two farmers'll ever agree on the best time to do anything.'

'They do this week. I've to make hay over at Marshalls' this afternoon, but I can help you till then.'

Florrie slid off Smart. She couldn't talk to Samuel properly with such a difference in their heights. The path back to the house, once they'd crossed the corner of the hayfield, was narrow, and Florrie and Samuel walked in front, the horse following slowly behind, his head drooping, his eyes half-shut. Florrie turned to look at him anxiously.

'I'm worried about him,' she said. 'I had to rest him up all yesterday, he got so tired from the turning. I don't know how long he'll be able to work today.'

'You want to use one of they cars instead,' Samuel suggested. 'Fix a hay-sweep to the front. Proper job.'

'You mean Sybil's Lagonda?' Florrie laughed. 'Nail a wooden hay-sweep to the front of that? Likely!'

'Her don't hardly use it, do her?'

'She still wouldn't like the idea. You don't know how that lot think. Even if they don't want a thing themselves they hate to let it go.'

She was aware of sounding bitter, and shook her head to try and free herself of the feeling. A dandelion had seeded near by. A piece of the fluffy head drifted across the warm, sunny air in front of Florrie, and she caught it in her hands. Crushed, it lay in her palm as lightly as a snowflake, and reminded her of the last time she'd seen Mentmore. She began to tell Samuel about it.

It had been back in February, and they'd gone for a walk together, far beyond the confines of the Earlshay estate. They'd stopped when they'd reached a barbed-wire fence, and seen beyond it a line of chilled-looking ewes, their fleeces yellow against the snow.

Mentmore had confided to Florrie his difficulties in adjusting to life in the Army: complaining about how he couldn't get his men to follow orders or respect him. He'd described how, one day, desperate to give them a truly inspiring talk, he'd practised on a flock of sheep the other side of the training camp.

'Pleasant little chaps, sheep,' he'd said. 'Respond to a good talking-to. One of them got a trifle restless, kept shifting from hoof to hoof, as if he was thinking of doing a bunk, but when I waved my finger at him and shouted he looked – well, sheepish, actually – and stayed put. It was jolly useful practice, I can tell you.'

Somehow, Florrie hadn't been sympathetic. She'd felt Mentmore was too weak; she'd been dismayed by his refusal to stand up to Valentine. She knew he'd always disapproved of Valentine's behaviour to her, and couldn't understand why he did nothing to help. When she'd mentioned the horses that had been sent back, he'd made no offer to return them, just gazed at her sadly and apologetically, as if some gentlemanly scruple, too complex to explain, prevented him from doing more.

'You know,' she said, stopping and turning to Samuel, 'Valentine's always despised goodness so much that I'd got into the habit of thinking of it as a sickly, passive thing. But it's not like that at all. It's like farming. It's easy to be a bad farmer: all you do is nothing. Stop feeding the animals, forget about the harvest, let the milk turn sour. Being a good one, the same as being a decent person, is a hard fight: you have to struggle, and plan. You daren't take your eye off what you're doing for an instant.

'And I can't condemn Mentmore, because when it mattered I didn't try hard enough for him, either.' That afternoon, and it must have been on the walk, because Florrie remembered seeing it when they'd set out, Mentmore had lost the silver-

315

tipped swagger-stick that went with his uniform. It had been a very long walk, and part of the way they'd been accompanied by a flock of little girls from St Hilda's, who'd cheekily flung snowballs at Mentmore, knowing he was too chivalrous to retaliate. At some point, he must have put his stick down. Perhaps he'd propped it against the fence or stuck it in the snow when he'd talked about the sheep.

'He went *wild* about it once we got home. He was almost in tears. Kept ranting on about how it was special, it brought him good luck, and he couldn't go on without it. I didn't take him seriously. I couldn't see why he didn't just go out and buy another. It was only a stick, and he had plenty of money. But now I'm haunted by it . . . I didn't even bother to go and look for it, although I said I had. Now I keep thinking . . .' Florrie could hardly bear to say the rest. She spoke in a whisper . . . 'I keep thinking maybe . . . maybe that's why he never came back from Dunkirk.'

She looked at Samuel half-fearfully. She couldn't have told the story to anyone else: she wouldn't have been able to be honest enough. If she'd been telling it to Father or Albie, for instance, she'd have made herself sound nobler, pretended that she had searched for the stick.

Samuel had listened to her attentively, his face reflecting her words: smiling when she talked about the sheep and the little girls, grave when she mentioned the stick. Now he clicked his tongue at Smart, and the old cart-horse looked up from mumbling at a clump of grass and began to walk forward again. They were just entering the narrow strip of wood that divided the fields from the lake, and Smart's hooves made hardly any sound on the black leaf-mould underfoot.

'What do you think?' Florrie asked.

'There ain't much comfort, is there, nowadays?' Samuel remarked mildly. 'I fills my mind with work, and haytime, getting things done, and it's all like humming to meself as I goes through a graveyard, done to keep the spirits up, and not much else.'

Florrie shivered. 'It is, isn't it? I keep wishing there was someone I could go to and ask, "Will it be all right in the end?" and they'd say, "Yes, of course," and then I'd feel better. But that's for children.'

'It will be all right,' Samuel said gently. 'At least for you.'

'No, Samuel.' She smiled. 'That's what I mean – it doesn't work, hearing you say that.'

While they'd been talking, Florrie had gradually become aware of a piercing cry in the distance. It became more insistent now, startling a pigeon, which beat its way up the branches of a tree, escaping into the sunlight with a creaking of wings. Albie was calling her from the house, 'Flor-rie, Flor-rie.'

There was no sign of him when she reached the stables. The pigs were asleep, the chickens sunbathing flat on the cobbles, wings raised and legs outstretched. Tying Smart in his stall, she ran for the house. In the kitchen she found a kettle boiling dry on the stove, and a spilled jug of milk, the contents still dripping slowly from table to floor. She raced into the old servants' dining-room and out again, past the silver cupboard, until she came to the green baize door. The instant she pushed against it she was aware of a difference in the atmosphere. The house smelled of cigar smoke, and she didn't know if she was imagining it, but the very air seemed turbulent, like a glass of champagne. Beyond the baize she could see a stretch of passageway leading to the front door, and a long rectangle of sunlight falling from a window. There was a suitcase there, and laid on top of it a familiar leather driving-coat. She ducked back through the door. Valentine had returned.

In her room, she searched for the right clothes. Everything she had was too tight, too loose, or too elaborate. She kept holding dresses up against herself and flinging them on the bed, finally deciding on a simple linen drop-waist she'd worn on her honeymoon. At least she was sure that Valentine had once liked it. Did it still suit her? She tried to smooth her hair into a neat roll, but it kept springing free of the pins. Besides, it looked wrong with the dress. She gazed into the mirror, overcome by a sudden wave of misery. She looked frumpy; worse, she looked the type of woman Valentine most despised: coarse, weather-beaten, old-maidish and lacklustre. She could see her scar too clearly, showing silver against the sunburnt skin. She'd grown plumper, too: the dress was tight on the hips. In a fury of self-disgust, all the more puzzling because it was so different from how she'd felt a short time ago – out in the fields, talking to Samuel, she hadn't been conscious of her appearance at all, let alone tormented by it – she struggled out of the shift and replaced it with a silvery frock she'd never liked. She bolted from the room before she could change her mind again.

Downstairs, she listened for voices. The sunlight in the hall was thick with dust; she heard Sybil laugh, and she walked towards the little raspberry-coloured drawing-room, rubbing her hands on her hips to make sure they were dry.

'Here she is at last!' Sybil exclaimed, her voice warm and approving, as Florrie opened the door. Her attitude was peculiar. She was like a teacher displaying her star pupil. 'Doesn't she look well, Vallie?'

Valentine was standing by the fire, one elbow on the mantel-piece. He looked fatigued. It was a shock seeing his face after all this time: it seemed unfamiliar, far too pale and lined.

Florrie stepped awkwardly into the room, moving to a relatively empty patch of floor near the window. It was like being introduced to a stranger at a party, and the presence of Sybil, glancing beadily from one to the other, made the meeting stiffer still.

'How long are you staying?'

'I'm on forty-eight-hour leave.' He frowned slightly, and didn't look at her. Florrie wondered if he'd found out, yet, about her farming. It was hard to avoid seeing evidence of it, even on the approach to the house.

Sybil gathered up a pile of magazines. 'I'll leave you two alone,' she said. 'I'm sure you have simply masses to discuss.'

Florrie didn't know what to say once she'd gone. After a while the silence became oppressive. Her throat went dry, too.

'Have you been in many air-battles?' she asked shyly, aware that she was probably using the wrong words, and that that in itself was likely to annoy him.

'I'd rather talk about what you've been doing.'

'What I've been doing?'

'I don't expect you've just been sitting indoors like Mama, keeping the home fires burning, have you?' There was life in his voice again; it sounded amused. Behind him, as if in echo of his words, a log shifted in the grate.

'No.'

'And I don't expect, either, that you've been doing what I wanted.'

Florrie, who had been staring at a patch of sunny parquet, raised her eyes at this, anxious to see the expression on his face. His eyes looked cold, but there was what might be the beginning of a smile on his lips. Hoping it was, she said lightly, 'You did once say that nothing I did would ever surprise you.'

'When did I say that?'

'Near on six months ago.' Feeling braver, she added, 'It was when you said I wouldn't be able to farm without horses or money.'

'I suppose you're feeling pretty pleased with yourself, then?'

'Not exactly.'

'Not exactly? What does that mean? What venial sin does Saint Florrie have on her conscience?' He moved from the fireplace, coming closer, looking down on her. 'Or is it not so venial after all?'

'I don't know what you're talking about.'

He moved so swiftly that she hadn't time to dodge. He caught hold of her wrists, very tightly. 'You know perfectly well what I'm talking about. Adultery.'

Florrie was astonished. His expression was so angry, the word he used so uncharacteristically biblical, that she began to laugh. 'Adultery! I wouldn't have thought you'd have wanted to bring that subject up – you of all people! Adultery – me? Why, whoever would I have done it with?'

He let go of her. 'There's no truth in it, then? No truth in what Mama says?' He sounded almost childishly unsure.

'You may have broken your vows,' Florrie said, 'but I never have.' She willed him to listen to her properly this time. 'You're my husband. I'd do nothing to harm you.'

He stepped back. It couldn't be, but for a moment she thought he seemed disappointed. 'I should have guessed,' he said bitterly, 'you're incapable of anything so impulsive, so life-enhancing. You're consumed by those fusty Victorian values: honour, duty, decency.' He turned to the window and pressed his face against the glass. His voice sounded muffled. 'Besides, who would want you?'

'Aren't you pleased, then?'

'Go away. I'm tired of talking to you.' He sighed, and then, seeming to notice for the first time what was beyond the glass, straightened. 'What the devil are those?'

Florrie stood on tiptoe to share his view. 'Vegetables,' she said. 'Swede and cabbage mostly.'

'And what's happened to my croquet lawn?'

She shrugged. 'It had to go.'

'Had to? What makes you think you can get away with that?'

'I just can.' She was still dazed by his cruel remarks, but

this was different. She felt on secure ground where her farming was concerned.

'No, you can't. Not if I don't want you to.'

'I don't know how you're going to stop me,' she said. She clung to this one, solid truth, as to a rock. 'You can't take the farm away from me, not now. The government, the Agricultural Committee, has given me permission to work it. Me, not you.' She gazed up at him, clear-eyed. 'You could turn me from the house, I suppose, if you wanted. But then . . .' She hesitated, and the chill dislike she saw in his face made her want to continue, to twist the knife, to pay him back for what he'd said. 'But then, judging by those letters on your desk – the ones you never opened? – the house doesn't rightly belong to you, either. It's the bank's, more like.' He hit her, then, dazzlingly hard. 'And as for the love you owe me as a husband,' she went on, her voice blurred, 'you can't take that away, either, because you haven't given it to me for years and years and years.'

Afterwards she didn't have the stomach to go back out to the fields again. She sat on her bed, on the pile of discarded dresses, and trembled and wept, all the feelings she'd hidden during that terrible meeting pouring out of her at last. When there was nothing left inside but emptiness she went over to the washstand and bathed her face with cold water. It stung.

After a long time she heard Valentine's car roar into life, and the sound gave her the energy to go downstairs – by the back way again, so that no one should see her. Her ribs ached where she'd been punched. She'd done her best to fight back, but he was far stronger than her, he always had been, and life in the RAF had toughened him up still more.

Outside she hesitated, puzzled. Surely that wasn't cigars she could smell? He had left, hadn't he? A sound broke the calm of the morning – in the far distance she could hear the steady purr of Samuel's tractor, but this was different, nearer at hand. She began to run. As she pounded along the gravel paths she saw smoke spiral up into the still, hot air.

Thirty-four

There were other sounds, but the one Florrie could hear most insistently, the one she couldn't bear, was Smart screaming, and the thunder of hooves.

A great chimney of flame roared upwards from where the tack room and hay store had once been. It didn't go directly upwards, but tilted, like a whirlwind, releasing a shower of sparks, and fragments of burning grass. Distracted by her anxiety for Smart, Florrie nevertheless ran first to the tack room and stared through the open door, where a red inferno boiled, dark shapes rippling in the flame. If Albie was in there she was too late. Her hair frizzled and she backed away.

Further into the yard, she tried to open the first stable door she came to. Perhaps it was the heat, perhaps panic making her fingers too slippery, but the catch wouldn't shift. She picked up a heavy stone and struck it open. There were two week-old calves inside. They didn't move, didn't flee out of the open door. Hearing the roof tiles beginning to pop in the heat she ran inside, into thick black smoke, and caught hold of one milky little calf. Picking it up in her arms she staggered through the door. She left it outside the yard gate, and ran back for the other. It had hidden itself in a corner, and she wasted precious seconds trying to find it; as she carried it through the door the latch caught her in the ribs. The pain nearly made her faint, but she clenched her teeth and put the calf with its companion. They stayed where she'd set them down, lowing mournfully.

The next stall held poultry: capons she was trying to fatten. They fluttered in panic, and she rushed in, trying to drive them out, but they wouldn't go, just whirled in the smoky stall like pigeons in a loft. One bounced out by accident, and screeched across the yard, taking off like a pheasant as it gained the gate, but she was too conscious of Smart's cries to care about the rest of the birds. He was further away from the flames than the other animals, but it was his terror that she couldn't stand. She ran down the line of stalls, opening every door and flinging it wide: she didn't have time to coax everything out, to save every creature there – not if she wanted to help Smart. Behind her the roar intensified as the fire took greater hold; she could hear Smart less distinctly.

When she opened the door of his stall she found him black with sweat. The cramped space reeked of it: bitter and masculine. He seemed utterly crazed, too, beyond recognizing her, beyond responding to a soothing tone in her voice. He reared up, head back, tugging hopelessly on the rope which kept him fixed to the wall. His eyes bulged in his head, and every sinew in his old, sway-backed body was stretched tight.

Leaving the door open, shielding her face from the heat, she ran across the yard to the water trough and, ripping off her jacket, pushed it in. Then she was running back with it, slipping on the cobbles, to Smart's stall. Even in that brief time the smoke had got thicker. It prickled the back of her throat and blurred every outline. She edged towards the other end of the stall, shrinking back as Smart's hooves smashed down, and when she reached the rope, cut it free from the wall with her clasp-knife.

'Easy,' she said, grasping the rope as near to his halter as she could manage. 'Easy now.' She pitched her voice higher, so he could hear it above the crackle of the flames, and she tried hard to infuse it with calm, to make him feel the situation was rendered safe and ordinary by her presence. He shuddered from her pressure on the rope, wheeling round, recoiling from the open door. She wasn't dismayed, she'd known he wouldn't go out easily. Father had described stable fires to her, and told her what she had to do. So now she acted automatically, trying to blank out her surroundings and concentrate only on soothing the horse. Distantly, she could hear the pigs: they screeched like steam-whistles. She was conscious of a darkness closing in around her, too, but she ignored it all.

She talked to Smart, gentle nonsense, and gradually coaxed his head lower, until it was possible to ease the wet coat over it, blind him to the smoke. Then she walked him round in a tight circle, disorienting him so he wouldn't know where he was, and would be forced just to trust and follow her. The smoke was so thick now that each breath was torment. She couldn't speak any more. She aimed for the oblong of light that was the door.

Coming out was like breaking through the surface of a pool after dangerous long minutes under water. Her throat was raw, the light dazzled her, and she doubled up, coughing and retching. She staggered forward, though, out of the gate, to safety.

When she pulled the coat and halter off Smart's head he trotted off into the garden. She turned back to the yard but there was no further sound from any of the animals, just the busy roar of flame. The tack room and roof above it had collapsed into a heap of black timbers, and even Smart's stall was now alight.

She coaxed the two little calves further away, into a dusty corridor of yew hedge, and then she sat down on the grass beside them and put her head in her hands, one image, above all, filling her with despair. It was of the yard when she'd first run to it, and of something she'd seen squashed on the cobbles: a half-smoked cigar.

Conscious of shouting, and then of movement near by, she

took her hands away and saw Samuel crouching in front of her. He looked different, maybe because his expression was so grim, or because his lip was split on one side. This cut had swollen, revealing the tips of three sharp white teeth, and the effect was almost alarmingly fierce.

'I couldn't find Albie,' she said to him, her voice sounding peculiar, halfway between a croak and a whisper.

'It's all right.' He pushed back her hair with one hand, a gentle, concerned gesture, less a caress than the kind of action a doctor might make. 'Albie's safe. He were with me.' He frowned. 'And your eye?' His voice sounded tender. 'Did a timber strike you?'

She hesitated; but what was the point of telling lies now? There seemed no reason for it. 'That was Valentine.'

A little way away she could hear Albie calling out, and a distinctive jingle which she recognized as the rusty bell on the old fire engine. She knew it was that because the boys had made rather a habit of playing with it of late. She knew, too, that she ought to get up and help, but the will to do so had left her. What did it matter if the whole garden caught fire now, if the house, even the fields did?

In all her conversations with Samuel she had never discussed Valentine in any but the vaguest terms, but now – and she wasn't sure why – she wanted to be direct. 'He set fire to the stables,' she said.

Samuel didn't answer, just tilted his head.

'I'm never going to get anywhere,' she went on. 'I made the mistake of telling him he couldn't take the farm away from me, but it wasn't true.' She rubbed at her face with her hands, aware that it must be dirty. 'People like him . . .' She blinked, aware of the stiffness in her left eyelid, where a crust of blood had formed. She was grateful for it. It made it more difficult to cry, and she didn't want to do that. 'They just rule everything. They have all the power, all the influence, and they only want to use it to hurt others. How could he kill my animals? How could he?' She looked at Samuel. 'It's best not to mind, isn't it? That's all one can do.'

'I wouldn't say that. No, I wouldn't say that.' His tone of voice caught her attention. It was amused, ironic.

'Why wouldn't you?'

'I had what you might call a little talk with him just now.'

'A talk?'

'Yes. He come out across the fields. I were rowing up the hay, and he come striding across, shouting, like.'

'What was he shouting about?'

'Oh—' Samuel half closed his eyes, as if wondering whether to filter the truth for her. He sat down more comfortably in the grass, too, beside her instead of facing. 'He were telling me to keep me hands off his property and his wife.' Watching his profile, Florrie couldn't determine his expression.

'He hit you, didn't he?' she said suddenly.

He turned to her, laughing. 'First fair fight he ever started in his life. I reckon that's why he lost.'

'He lost?'

'Reckon so.'

'What happened? Is he hurt?'

There was a warning in Samuel's dark eyes, mixed with weary understanding. 'I didn't kill him, if that's what you want to know. I'd have liked to, all right.' He spoke more softly. 'I will if he's ever cruel to you again – told him as much, too.'

'As if that would make any difference!'

'I's never figured,' Samuel remarked, 'why you stick with him, not truly.' The other side of the hedge a terrific hissing began, and steam billowed into the air. Florrie could hear excited screams. It sounded as if all the little girls were helping.

'You can't stop loving someone just because they no longer care for you or want you. Besides, it's not as simple as black and white. You haven't been married.' She saw him wince.

'It's never all one person's fault. I'm bad to live with, too – bad for him. Anyway, where would I go if I left? What would I do?'

'You could live at my house. Not with me and Ellis of course,' Samuel added hastily. 'We'd go elsewhere.'

'If I came to live with you I wouldn't make you leave. I wouldn't be that much of a coward.'

'You're never that.'

'Yes, I am. That's what Valentine says. He says cowardice is all that's stopped me going with anyone else. He's right, too. The values I pride myself on, they're just so much . . . so much ash. Even persistence and hard work: what stupid, stupid things to be proud of! Might as well be proud of being a slave.'

She expected Samuel to come up with the usual soothing response: words to heal the pain and make her capable of carrying on as before. That had become his role, and she'd grown to depend on it. But he didn't speak at all. Instead he kissed her. It was a gentle kiss on the lips, and he didn't touch her with his hands while he gave it, so perhaps he only meant it as a fleeting gesture, a response one shade more affectionate than a kind word, but the moment it was done, everything changed. She didn't want him to stop. She kissed him back: small, hesitant kisses that became stronger, flowed into each other. She wasn't sure how it happened, whether she reached for him or he for her, but when she found herself in his arms she responded as fiercely as if she was drowning and he her only chance of life.

They had eaten their evening meal at Earlshay, so when they reached Samuel's cottage there was no reason to linger downstairs. The early afternoon and evening had been spent bringing in the hay, and when all the ricks were thatched, the two calves safely bedded down in the old greenhouse, and Smart put out to graze in the hay field, Florrie had just put her hand in Samuel's and walked down the drive and out of the gates. It seemed cleaner that way. She'd even taken off her wedding ring and left it on the desk in Valentine's study. It had been a way of telling him that he'd been wrong about her all along: she didn't want wealth or privilege, she didn't even care for conventional morality any more.

It had been a beautiful walk, through quiet, dusty roads. As Florrie pulled off her shoes she saw the hayseeds on the soles glitter in the candlelight. Samuel's bedroom was cramped, with a sloping ceiling and a window that wouldn't close properly. Through the curtain came noises that reminded her of her childhood: owls calling; the comfortable rustle of a pig turning in its sty; the thump and wail of a rabbit caught in a snare.

His bed was narrow, but it had a deep feather bed, and the sheets were fresh. She undressed and crept inside, waiting for him. She didn't blow out the candle.

When he came in, he looked the wrong scale for the little room. He stooped to get under the lintel, and his head touched the ceiling. He sat on the bed and began to unbutton his shirt, and his diffidence made her feel bolder. She knelt on the bed and undressed him, surprised by how different he was from Valentine. Naked, he looked far stronger, more muscular than dressed. He trembled when she touched him, too, and she felt herself shake with longing. He was more passionate, more eager, than she had expected – but most of all, when he held her in his arms she felt that everything was at last perfectly right. She didn't know what she had been looking for, all this long time, but she was sure that she had found it.

It was strange, and delicious, to be equal to another person. With Samuel there was no force, she was as much in control as he was. She fought with him playfully, trying to discover, from his reactions, whether he was a virgin or not. And as she teased him with more sophisticated ways of showing passion, she felt released from the self-consciousness that had always been a part of sex before. In the past she had either felt too closely observed, like an insect under the microscope of a scientist, or anxious as to whether Valentine was sufficiently pleased.

She was in a different world now, a safe one, where there was plenty of time, where her partner was both almost overwhelmed by excitement and seemingly inexhaustible. For the first time she became conscious of her own response. She felt herself open, like a flower, felt a slow, rising warmth, and at last the sense of tipping into agonizing pleasure; trembling, rippling with it.

She opened her eyes. He lay above her. His skin shone in the candlelight, and a lock of black hair had fallen across one eye. He smiled at her, his expression delighted, cocky. She realized, with anguish, that it couldn't be the first time for him, then, that he must have had another woman. Must have, to know what to do, how to give her so much joy. He suddenly clasped her tight in his arms. 'I love you,' he said, his voice muffled by her hair. 'Always have, always will.'

In her dreams she was conscious of an aching sense of loss. The emotion was so violent that it woke her and she sat up, suddenly terrified. There was a faint haze of moonlight. She heard an owl call, and Samuel stirred and put his arms around her.

'What is it?'

'I dreamt I was back in the stable and couldn't save Smart. It was so strong – I could smell the smoke, and the burning skin.' She trembled, strange how impossible it was to convey the full horror of a nightmare.

Samuel stroked her hip, but the feeling wouldn't go, she didn't even feel secure with him beside her. She got out of bed and pulled on her clothes, returning to give him a kiss.

'Where's you going?'

'I don't know. I'll come back, I promise.'

Outside, in the garden, she heard footsteps, distant ones, running hard. The sound was so faint that at first she thought it only the beating of her heart, but it grew stronger. She was almost certain it came from the road that led to Fightingcocks Farm, and now, every so often, she could hear a cry. It was almost like the coo-yip of a tawny owl, but different. Sharper, more agitated. A slight breeze ruffled the trees around her. The running footsteps came closer. She opened the gate, and stood in the road.

The figure ahead was familiar. Small, clad in flowing white, with very pale, long hair. It was Belle. At almost the same moment Belle recognized Florrie, too. She stopped. There was a muddy stain down the front of her nightdress, and her feet were bare.

'There's been a accident,' she sobbed. 'You has to come. Someone has to come.' She turned and ran back along the road, her hair streaming out behind her.

The car was half off the road, the front crushed up against the huge chestnut tree that marked the turning down to Fightingcocks. Steam hissed from the half-open bonnet. Belle stopped a few yards from it, her hand up to her mouth in a gesture of exaggerated surprise.

'It were my fault,' she said. 'All my fault. I run out in front – I wanted to talk.'

Florrie stepped forward. She moved as in a dream, aware of the chill, the dampness of the night air. She opened the car door. Valentine was lying across the wheel. He'd been drinking: she could smell it on his clothes and skin, mingled with his cologne. Such a familiar, such a personal perfume. She pulled him back, so that his head rested against the seat, and he moved oddly. There wasn't enough resistance, stiffness, in his neck.

She reached forward, touching his face, and saw a strange quality in his expression. He was staring at her, and yet he wasn't. As she watched the light seemed to die out of his eyes, as if he was thoroughly sickened by this life, and travelling away from it, receding to some distant, colder place where no one could touch him, least of all her.

She began to wail. 'Oh God. I never wanted this to happen. Oh God, believe me, I never wanted this to happen.'

May 1945

There were rooks beside the chapel. They'd only come since the outbreak of war, but even in that time they'd built a substantial colony. They made huge, untidy nests in the branches of the exotic trees, and fought each other, the losers hopping through the undergrowth: inky-black, long-beaked, evil-looking.

Kingdom spent hours trying to catch them, but then he wanted to play with every living thing he saw. Seeing a furtive movement in the bushes at the end of the chapel garden, he ran over towards it, stumbling and almost falling on the rough grass.

Although he'd been walking for a few years he still wasn't entirely confident, perhaps because he was a trifle stout. From behind he looked ridiculous, especially in the sailor suit Sybil had insisted on buying him for VE day. His face always made Florrie smile, too: he had plump cheeks, a wide mouth, and shiny dark eyes, the whole framed by a mass of black ringlets that reached to his shoulders.

The hair, like his name, was a source of slight friction between Sybil and Florrie. Florrie was sure that whenever Kingdom went to play with Sybil his grandmother damped and rolled his locks. He always looked suspiciously like Shirley Temple afterwards.

'But, darling,' Sybil would say, 'his hair is so ducky. Can't we keep it long? He's the perfect image of his grandpapa: so Italian!'

Florrie had decided to cut the hair when Kingdom went to school, but for now, Sybil was right: it was pretty.

Sybil had been affronted by his name, of course. Florrie had chosen it because it was the name of one of her uncles: solid and religious. She wasn't calling a son of hers anything so fancy as Valentine. But Sybil had corrupted it almost at once to 'Kingy'.

'Dearest little Kingy!' she'd say. 'And haven't you got a clever Grandmama? Why, just think,' and here she'd turn to Florrie with an arch expression on her painted face, 'if she hadn't sent your father that letter you never would have been born. Never, never, never. And wouldn't we all have been sad?'

And Florrie would smilingly agree.

In the far corner of the chapel garden, up against the wall, was a new tombstone: white marble, carved with 'Valentine: 1907–1940' and the words 'Never Was So Much Owed By So Many To So Few'. Sybil had insisted on the words, and Florrie hadn't had the heart to deny her. If she wanted to weave a fantasy around her son, pretend he'd been in the Battle of Britain, why shouldn't she? Florrie privately felt that his death had been just as noble: choosing, in one swift, drunken instant, to sacrifice himself instead of his daughter. Sometimes she wondered whether he'd been driving along that particular stretch of road because he'd been looking for her, but Sybil would never discuss the events of that night. She preferred to live in a haze of unreality, where Kingdom was the rightful inheritor of Valentine's land and title, and Samuel an inconvenient detail – whose only benefit had been to give Florrie the more suitable name of Mrs Rawes.

Florrie could never bear to look at the stone for long. She preferred, instead, to gaze at the willow trees she'd planted round it, their branches pink at the tips. When she'd changed the flowers in the vase, she leaned on the fence. From here she could see the neat fields she and Samuel had tended and sown: the barns, the new milking-parlour – and just on her left, so near she could have thrown a stone to hit it, the remains of an old brick path, where one summer, years ago, Valentine had played Grandmother's Footsteps and other childish games with his dissipated friends. Florrie remembered how he'd cheated: holding a starched tablecloth in front of his legs and feet so they couldn't be seen moving. She could almost hear his laugh now, smoky, expensive-sounding, mischievous.

That was what was good about the passing of time, she thought, the way it enabled you to recall only the nicest bits of people you had cared for. Nowadays she found it easy to remember the look on Valentine's face when he'd been courting her; the sight of him in white tie and tails presiding over a party; the blue of his eyes. All the rest had faded, ceased to hurt. It was like the broken tombstones round the chapel, their inscriptions worn away by the wind and rain. Somehow the effect was comforting, even charming. One over by the chapel door read 'moth' instead of 'mother', and the words were sweeter, more feminine that way. Even, strangely, more accurate. What else had she been but a moth to Valentine's candle? Maybe some people were better as a tender memory than they had ever been in real life.

There was a terrific flapping from the wood, and Kingdom came stumbling back, a rook in his outstretched hands.

'I catched he all right!' he exclaimed, his voice a queer mixture of Sybil's cut glass and Samuel's broad Devon. Florrie picked him up and propped him on her hip, and he cuddled in there, avoiding the bump of her pregnancy. As she put her arm round his waist, to hold him safe, he began sucking his right thumb, holding the rook firmly, like a toy, so that only its angry head could swivel from side to side.

Florrie quickened her step as she reached the gate. She could see her husband waiting for her a few yards off, his back turned, his hands in his pockets, and she wanted to steal up behind him and surprise him with a kiss.

Glossary of Devon Words

antsy, auncy	restless, anxious
axwaddler	idiot
beastings	first milk, colostrum
beaufet	glass-fronted display-cupboard
my bird	my dear
chiel	girl child
daft as a handcart	stupid
fancical	tasteful, particular
fit	ready
flibbert	small object
fuzz	furze
growthy	a good doer, likely to put on weight

grubbish	hungry
Hell about No!	Not likely!
heller	wild person
horse-dashel	large thistle
linney	lean-to shed
master	very
maze	mad
moundery	mildewed
nissletripe	runt of a sow's litter
nobby	upper-class
to plim	to plump up, swell
pucker	fuss
pusky	short of breath
saucy	lively, high-spirited
snooky	odd-shaped
tallet, taller	loft
winnicky	weak, small

Many of these words and definitions come from
John Downes, *A Dictionary of Devon Dialect*, Tabb,
1986.